Betwixt

and

Between

Betwixt
and
Between

a novel

JESSICA STILLING

PUBLISHING

BROOKLYN, NEW YORK

Printed in the United States of America
10 9 8 7 6 5 4 3 2 1

Ig Publishing
392 Clinton Avenue
Brooklyn, NY 11238
www.igpub.com

Library of Congress Cataloging-in-Publication Data

Stilling, Jessica.
  Betwixt and between / Jessica Stilling.
      page cm
  ISBN 978-1-935439-84-4 (pbk.)
  1. Children--Death--Fiction. 2. Future life--Fiction. 3. Liminality-
-Fiction. 4. Domestic fiction. I. Title.
  PS3619.T5475B48 2013
  813'.6--dc23

                              2013015757

For
Addison and Jacqueline

PROLOGUE

"I WON'T GO INSIDE, I won't, I won't," Preston called across the lawn at Peyton and Eva as he ran one way and they the other. Mrs. List, his best friend Peyton's mother, had called them in three times and Peyton and Eva had run one way, gliding toward the Newburgh's house on the balls of their feet, as Preston headed toward the cul-de-sac.

The trees hid the houses, so they didn't have to run far. The trees hid everything. They grew between Preston's yard and Peyton's, between the Hoffstra's and Eva's. There were lines of them, two, sometimes three across, but they did the trick and even though Preston's house wasn't that far from the neighbor's it felt like its own world.

Preston ran past the stone statue of a man on a horse at the edge of the road, turning into the cul-de-sac at Pinetree. When he was younger his father had taken him out in the neighborhood and read every street sign to him, telling him to memorize each word just in case he got lost. Preston could see his father, a towering figure now, though he'd been even bigger to him then, pointing up at a sign and saying, "see, see, P and P means pretzels and Preston and Pinetree."

There were three houses in the cul-de-sac, all surrounded by trees. He looked toward the back where a small stream bubbled, gurgling and galumphing through the backyards toward the heavier woods that touched the neighborhood. The first house was peach colored, and no children lived there, only two adults and three dogs that barked just after dinnertime every night. A couple and their two teenage boys lived in the blue house next to it, one of the boys drove a rusted car and the other was always playing basketball in the driveway.

The yellow house in the corner sat empty most of the time. It was a fairly large house with a bright white front door and neatly painted shutters, like you'd find on certain types of family TV shows. There was a garden at the side, made up of all white flowers planted in symmetrical solid lines, a circle of them going around the white and gold mailbox. The grass was always mowed in neat rows and there were never any clippings left behind. The blacktop up to the white garage door shone a perfect black, the sun settling there like a mirage of water when Preston ran to it. Off to the side stood a basketball hoop hanging from a concrete post. It wasn't like the teenagers' basketball hoop, the regulation red and white; this one, painted in neon colors, hung over a lopsided court that had been drawn with bright pink and green chalk lines.

Preston hardly ever came this way, he'd only been here once before with Peyton and they'd darted away quickly when Mr. Hawthorne came out of his house. Now with Eva and Peyton playing in the Newburgh's yard, Preston wanted to explore this place on his own and so he stepped closer, crossing first the street and then the sidewalk toward the house.

He cringed as one sneakered foot hit the black driveway, worried it might open up a hole he'd sink into. Mr. Hawthorne lived alone, though his house had two floors, and he drove what his father called a "trying-to-compensate-for-something" car really fast down the short, empty streets of the neighborhood.

Preston slowly approached the bright yellow house, each step a new island to Mr. Hawthorne's front door. He could see the tree branches above him, separating Mr. Hawthorne's yard from his neighbor's. There were two cars parked in the driveway, one looked brand new while the other was bright purple with lines of rust clinging to the sides. Preston stepped toward the sidewalk leading to the house. Flowers lined the walkway and he stopped to look down at them. They were not colorful like the flowers in the books at school, but all white, like a snow garden. Preston leaned in, his nose grazing the petals as the front door opened. He could hear the way the knob turned, the sound of the screen door sliding, and when he craned his neck, Mr. Hawthorne was standing on the stoop just outside his house.

He was tall, his face a blank stare, his dark hair cut close to his head like an army sergeant. He gazed out at his yard as if he hadn't seen anything, but right away he caught Preston, who shot up straight when his eyes met Mr. Hawthorne's. He might have run from his neighbor, but he was ten years old, old enough to know he was caught, but not old enough to do anything about it like think up a clever excuse for what he might be doing there. He closed his eyes, expecting Mr. Hawthorne to yell at him, to stick his arm in the air and demand that he leave his property. Maybe he'd take him by the hand and haul him back to his house as Mrs. Cooper had done after he and Peyton had tried to feed berries to the fish in her pond.

"You like the flowers?" Mr. Hawthorne asked, chuckling. "They're called bellflowers, I planted them earlier this spring. Do you like them? Are they pretty?"

Preston watched his neighbor, relief flooding the inside of his stomach. "I like them," he said cautiously, hoping that his liking Mr. Hawthorne's flowers meant he wouldn't tell his mother he'd been trespassing.

"Why thank you," he replied with false importance, coming closer to Preston he knelt next to the flowers, touching one of the soft petals and bending to sniff. "They smell like a garden all by themselves. You know, I have a really nice garden in back if you ever want to take a look. A gardener comes every week, he planted that one, but this little garden up here I did myself."

"That's okay, I should go," Preston replied, aware that it was not all right to just go into the backyard of a stranger, even if the front was a no-man's land it would be hard to punish him for entering.

"I'm Mr. Hawthorne, by the way, Gregory Hawthorne," his neighbor properly introduced himself, holding out his hand in a way that might have been professional if it weren't so forced.

"I'm Preston," he replied cautiously. He took the man's hand, it was cold and thin, swallowing Preston's palm whole.

"You know my housekeeper just made some cookies, they're chocolate chip. She made a whole batch, even though I told her to just make a few, a man like myself can't be eating all those cookies. Would you like to come in for one? It would really help me out, you know, they're not good for my figure and all."

"That's okay," Preston replied, remembering Peyton and Eva, who were probably looking for him. "I need to find my friends."

"Are you sure?" Mr. Hawthorne asked. "They're just cookies. I won't tell your mother you were here," he went on, winking.

Preston considered for a second. He'd heard stories of child abductions, his mother had told him not to talk to strangers, but a stranger was a man in a black coat, a gruff voice in the dark and this was just a guy who liked flowers. Sharing a few cookies with his neighbor did not seem like a part of a sinister plan. "Okay," he said, taking one whiff of the air, hoping he'd catch the scent of the flowers as Mr. Hawthorne stood to let him inside.

"You know my mother used to make cookies for me when I was a little boy. I guess I never got over it. When you grow up you're supposed to outgrow stuff like sweets, but why would you ever want to do that? Why forget things you love just because you get old?" Mr. Hawthorne laughed at himself, though Preston hadn't found him particularly funny.

It smelled a sugary pink in the living room, like a gingerbread house in a fairy tale. There was a big TV in the front room and a video game system lying on an end table next to a bunch of game cartridges. A framed poster of Larry Bird was hung up next to the system, and as Preston walked further into the house he noted that there were taped up pictures of people from television, of basketball and football players, all over the house, which reminded him of a larger version of his own bedroom.

"Here, the cookies are in the kitchen, we don't have to eat in the dining room, too formal," Mr. Hawthorne said and Preston did not understand how a dining room with posters of sports stars hung up in it could be too formal for anything. "I'll get you some milk. Do you want milk, kiddo?" He said the last part, calling him kiddo, a little falsely.

"Sure," Preston replied, holding his hands in front of him, sticky, sweaty fingers knotting together. "Thank you," he added as he entered Mr. Hawthorne's kitchen. It was a heightened version of his own kitchen, almost the same, but more like it had come out of one of those magazines his mother sometimes left out on the counter. No taped up posters here, just the cooking necessities or niceties. It was painted white with an island in the middle; there was a large, silver refrigerator with a water dispenser that had a bunch of blue lit-up buttons around it. Silver pots dangled from a rack hanging from the ceiling and there were a bunch of metal appliances on the granite counter. Despite the kitchen's neatness, someone had been working in there, spoons and measuring cups littered a flour-covered cutting board and the sink was filled with dishes, just the way he left the kitchen half the time after his mother asked him to help her clean it.

The stairs from the basement started creaking and Preston almost jumped when he saw a woman come up them. She looked like the kind of person who might live in a basement with a raw-looking face and ratty too-red hair that was obviously dyed. A large wart was stuck to her cheek as if it came from a Halloween costume, and there were lines near her eyes and mouth. She smiled when she saw Preston, though it seemed that her face almost cracked. "Hello," she said with an accent he could not place. She sounded like the villains in his father's old James Bond movies. "How are you today young man?" she looked down at Preston as if she were scrutinizing him. "I just made cookies, please, you should have some. A growing boy like you, you will not spoil your dinner." Preston found it funny that she knew what time his dinner was, about an hour from now, as long as his father got home on time.

"All right," was all Preston could say, stepping backwards and nearly walking into a life-size cut out of The Cage King, the villain in a video game Preston used to play with Peyton a few years ago.

"Sorry about that," Mr. Hawthorne said, righting the cutout as Preston stepped away from it. "I'm a collector. I should put it upstairs."

"I am going to head home," the lady said, turning around on her heels. "I just wanted to make sure someone was home. Gregory, I will see you tomorrow, OK? Feed the child my cookies, you will make sure, please?"

"Sure, see you," Mr. Hawthorne replied casually, waving as she turned down the steps, leaving through the basement. "That was Mary Clark," he explained. "She made the cookies, she cooks for me. A very nice lady that one. She reminds me of Hilda Handblast, I watch that show all the time," he went on, laughing at himself. Hilda Handblast, Preston knew, was a character in Autowarriors, a cartoon about toy cars that save their owner's house from the evil band of toy trucks that live next door. He'd watched that cartoon when he was eight, but now that he was ten he had outgrown it.

"OK," was all Preston could say as he followed Mr. Hawthorne into the kitchen.

"This place is not kid proofed," he explained as he glanced toward the knife-set sitting a few feet from the stools lining one side of the counter. "I don't get many visitors. It's almost five o'clock; I don't want to spoil your dinner so why don't I just give you a couple cookies? They just came out of the oven, that's when they're the best," Mr. Hawthorne offered, picking a cookie up off a metal cooling rack.

Mr. Hawthorne set the cookie on a blue porcelain plate with delicate white etchings. It did not look like it belonged in a house with cutouts of video game villains in it. This kitchen seemed to be an island of adulthood in this house that had never grown up. The plate was almost too nice to eat off of and Preston nearly said so, but Mr. Hawthorne was being so kind, he didn't want to offend him. "You can't have cookies without milk," he said, taking a quart from his fridge. "Unless you have any allergies?" he asked last second.

"No I don't, thank you," Preston replied, taking a sip of the milk once it had been set before him. Mr. Hawthorne took a cookie off the rack as well, eating it from his hand and not bothering with a plate. This was how Preston ate cookies at home. Even if his mother put a plate out for him he was always carrying his food around, "constantly dragging crumbs from one corner of the house to another," his mother always said.

"Do you like them?" Mr. Hawthorne asked, taking another bite.

"I do," Preston replied, not wanting to make a face as he chewed. The cookies tasted off, not bad, just off. He finished one cookie and took another out of politeness.

"Tastes kinda funny," he commented after a second, looking as if he might spit the cookie out. "No, I don't think I like these," he concluded, finishing the last of his bite and taking the rest to the garbage bin near the backdoor. "But you should finish."

"It's okay," Preston said, gulping down his final bite. "I'm sorry."

"It's all right. I guess Mary must have forgotten the vanilla or something," Mr. Hawthorne speculated. "Oh well, they're not good for my figure anyway," he commented, politely chipper. "But hopefully the milk is all right."

The milk, Preston had forgotten the milk. He wanted to go, he was sure by now Eva and Peyton had gone to his house looking for him, and his mother would start to worry. Once he got home she'd be in the front yard with a frown on her face as she lectured him on how anxious she'd been. He could just picture it as he swallowed the milk, wanting to take every last drop in one final swig. The milk was cold in his mouth, yet felt as if it was burning his teeth, but he dutifully gulped until it was finished. "There," Preston announced.

"You were thirsty, do you want some more?"

"No, that's all right, I really have to go," Preston replied, getting up. "Thank you."

"You're welcome, any time," Mr. Hawthorne offered. "Are you sure you don't want to stay? I have a game system upstairs, we could play something. Four Corners Seven just came out, I have an advanced copy. I know a guy who owns a video game shop. We could play that? Or Fantasy Basketball, I have that as well. Or just old fashioned Monopoly?" He looked so desperate for Preston to want to play just one game. But video games took forever to play, they were the game that never ended, and so Preston shook his head no, deciding to consider the time of day it was, and his mother, and that dinner would probably be on the table soon.

"That's all right, my friends don't know where I am, my Mom'll be worried," Preston explained. Mr. Hawthorne had been nice to him, it might not even be wrong to say he liked him, but at that moment Preston really wanted to be out of his house. He didn't know why but his stomach was starting to hurt and he just needed get back to his own yard, his own room, where things didn't feel so off and unfamiliar.

"Well, if your Mom will be looking for you, please, you can go out the back, take the path near the stream, it'll get you home more quickly," Mr. Hawthorne explained and Preston wondered how this man knew exactly where he lived.

"All right, thank you. I like your garden," he offered as an olive branch.

"Next time you come over we'll look at the garden again, maybe check out that new Four Corners," Mr. Hawthorne suggested and Preston shook his head yes, the waning sun in his eyes as he walked through the back screen door and across the yard full of grass and flowers, by a pristine, empty white bird bath and a couple of trees. It felt like the grown up world out here, wholly different from the video games and posters of sports stars in the bulk of the house. Preston felt bad for going, for leaving Mr. Hawthorne to sit alone all night, but his stomach was really bothering him and had to be home for dinner.

"Bye," Preston called as he walked away.

Mr. Hawthorne remained in his house, one foot on the concrete stoop and another in his kitchen as he watched Preston cross his lawn. Preston started to feel sleepy and a more sick as he walked away. Something churned inside his stomach, something purple and red like a bruise. He felt sick, but not sick as he had ever been before, not the flu or a cold, not even the 104-degree fever he'd had last year that sent his mother racing with him to the doctor. He gulped hard to try and keep himself from throwing up, tasting the sour bile at the four corners of his mouth. He looked back at Mr. Hawthorne, who was still watching him as he marched past another flower garden and toward the stream. He knew the way across it, he knew that if he crossed the water and took the path he'd be nearer to Eva's and once he was there he could make his way through the trees toward Peyton's house and then his own.

His stomach was burning as he hit the trees that separated the cul-de-sac from the rest of the neighborhood and Preston stopped, doubling over as he tried to breathe deeply. "Owww," he said, clutching his insides. He sat down, leaning against the side of a tree, right in the dirt. "If I can just walk a few more feet," he thought, but it felt like a few feet could only be measured in miles. He knew his house was close by, but the trees blocked everything. His father had said that this was what made the neighborhood so nice, the illusion of privacy without actually being in the middle of nowhere. But now he wished someone could see him through these trees as he sat in the dirt, a twig digging into the thin skin of his palm. "Ow, ow, ow," he cried as if his stomach were on fire.

Preston lay down for a second. It felt better when he lay down. He closed his eyes; he was tired now and the pain, it wasn't just uncomfortable anymore, it was a bright, stabbing pain and even when he cried no one could hear him. He hadn't ever felt this sleepy before, it wasn't a going-to-bed kind of sleepy, this kind of tired settled in his bones, he sensed it under his skin as he lay down on the cold, damp ground. He could feel the dirt pulsing under him, as if he could hear bugs moving beneath the earth, the way the trees' roots grew, flowers sunning themselves. Peyton and Eva called out a few feet away, Preston could see them playing in his mind, the sun on their faces. He pictured his mother looking for him, one hand on the front door as she called his name. It was all there, just a few feet away; he'd be there in a second, he thought, just a second and he'd get up. A bird cawed, it got darker and Preston closed his eyes.

cLaiRe

There was something about the silence in the house at nine o'clock, something heavy and final. It wasn't like most days, when nine o'clock was a time to wind down, letting the house rest as if it too were about to head off to bed after the dishes had been put away, the final clutter shuffled into closets or onto shelves, the sturdy pockets of the house. Preston went to bed at eight fifteen, and Matthew, home from work a couple of hours earlier, would already have eaten dinner—on a weekday something simple, maybe a slice of glazed chicken, spiced rice and green beans— and gone to the study to get some work done. The dishes would have been washed and dried, or Claire might have had her hands in the sink, just finishing up. Nine o'clock was an hour before ten, when she would sit down with a recorded sitcom she hadn't had time to watch during the day, a cup of tea resting on the coffee table, maybe a low-calorie cookie wedged in the saucer. She'd rest her head against the cushions of the couch as she unwound her- self from the knots she'd been tied up in all day.

But tonight wasn't that kind of quiet; tonight's quiet raged in Claire's head like her ears were stuffed up and she could see the mouths moving though they did not make a sound. Matthew had been in and out of the house since returning from work. He'd canvassed the neighborhood and come back with his shoulders hunched as he shook his head "no," barely meeting Claire's eyes. That had been at seven and again at eight, after Claire had man- aged, because her mother on the phone from Chicago had in- sisted that she eat something, to choke down two slices of flimsy Wonderbread. She'd felt the food in her mouth, squashed between her teeth and never before had it felt so naked, so bare, as if the truth about food had finally come out and it really was only fuel so that she might pace the kitchen for another hour, so she could place phone calls and rush to a ringing receiver or check out the windows to see if anything had moved in the wooded lot they called a yard.

The house was dark; Claire had only remembered to keep a lamp on in the living room and the cooking light above the stove lit as she paced between the rooms. Everything was strange, as if nine o'clock had come at the wrong time, as if this wasn't the real world, this house with blue curtains and lacey throw pillows, this house that smelled of thin, country dish soap and juniper hand lotion, where all the knickknacks came from antique stores, consignment shops and specialty outlets in West Stockbridge.

She'd just started to allow Preston to play unsupervised around the neighborhood with his friends. It hadn't been her idea. Cara List had started it with her son Peyton. When Preston had come up to her last March, tugging at her sleeve as she was putting the groceries away, and asked her if he could ride his bike over to Townsend Street, she'd wanted to say no, she might have said no, if he hadn't have added, "Mrs. List lets Peyton do it." Peyton had been Preston's best friend since they were babies. Claire and Cara had had play dates together starting from the time their children, only two months apart, had met at the park as seven and nine month olds. If Cara was allowing Peyton to ride his bike to the playground two streets away, did Claire really have the right to say no to Preston? Did she want to be that mother? And hadn't she been around Preston's age, ten years old, when she'd been given her own first tiny taste of freedom? It wasn't as if this neighborhood was unsafe, very little traffic ever drove down these streets, when there was traffic at all, and she and Matthew had done a good job instilling the rules of the road in their son when it came to bicycle safety. She hadn't wanted to say yes, but she had, and Preston and Peyton and Eva, a little girl who lived a few doors down, had been riding their bikes around a three to five block radius by themselves for the past three months. And they had done it unscathed. Claire had been proud of herself for giving in to the maternal peer pressure, for not being a helicopter parent. And now it was nine o'clock; Peyton was at home, safe in bed, Eva had been in the bath when Claire had called the Murphy house for the third time, and Preston was nowhere to be found.

Claire paced the length of the kitchen, clearing the space once, twice, three, four times before she realized what she was doing. The blue and white tiles blended, she saw the granite counter, the silver appliances that looked exactly like the ones in her friend Cara's kitchen. She studied the salmon-colored beams of the house but didn't see them as the growing pit lodged deep in her stomach caused her arms to shake. A shrill shriek cut through the air and Claire turned around. The sound came from nowhere, a spot she could not place and she thought briefly that aliens had landed before she realized the sound was only the telephone.

She'd been willing it to ring all night. First at five when Preston hadn't come home, then again at six, seven, eight and now nine. First she'd wanted Preston to call, or maybe the parent of a friend of his might phone to say that he was over at their house, they'd been having so much fun and lost track of time. Then she'd wanted the hospital to call, even the police. They had all been notified. At six o'clock after her son had been missing for an hour Claire had called Massachusetts General and the Brigham Hospital along with Beverly Hospital and the Emergency Care Center two towns over. She'd notified the police that her ten-year-old was missing. No, she was not being crazy, officer. Yes, he hadn't called; yes, she'd contacted his friends; no, this was not normal, her little boy is ten years old, not a teenaged troublemaker out to scare his parents.

This was the plight of a mother, what all hoped never happened, though as a mother, Claire knew, she was supposed to be prepared for it. The literal waiting by the phone, the hoping it's not a broken arm, a lost limb—or worse. Claire had heard of this, this pacing the floors, this anxiety, of actually having to be responsible, wholly and completely responsible for another human being, but she'd never thought it would be like this, that the worry would feel like a bright red fire threatening to burn her in the night.

The phone kept ringing, splitting her sinuses as Claire answered it, shaking, though a wash of relief flooded her skin that had been covered in goose bumps since 5:15 exactly. Finally something was happening. Something had to be happening, who called people at 9:07 on a Friday night unless something were happening? "Hello?" Claire asked hopefully into the receiver as if she could already feel Preston in her arms.

"Hello, Mrs. Tumber, this is Katrina Patrick calling from The Boston Animal Search and Rescue Society. We noticed that last year you made a donation to our cause and we were wondering if we could interest you—"a mechanical, though human sounding, voice began on the other end.

"You what?" Claire asked, stomach sinking. "It's after nine at night and you're calling for *what*?"

"This is the Boston Animal Search and Rescue Society," the woman started again, not seeming to notice the acid dripping from Claire's voice.

"How dare you call this late?" Claire asked, nearly shouting, though trying to keep her voice down. Claire had been the kind of person, ever since she was a little girl, who tried at all costs to keep her voice down. "Who do you think you are, just because you're a charity, you're just as bad as those telemarketers, there should be a law against you, bothering people at night. Children go to bed before nine, don't you know that?"

"I'm sorry, if you'd like for us to call back," the woman said still mechanically.

"I do not want you to call back. I want you to take me off your list, if you call again I'll consider it harassment," Claire yelled into the receiver. "How dare you call after nine o'clock?" Breathing deeply she hung up before the mechanical voice could say any more.

It sounded like boots traipsing across the wooden floor as the bare night of after nine came in through the large picture windows and Claire turned, having hung up the cordless phone, to see Matthew standing in front of her. He looked wet though he wasn't, soggy and dripping as his blond hair ran across his forehead, shoulders slumped, eyes at the floor as if someone had just scolded him. Matthew was a big man, muscular without being overly so and to see him sagging like that seemed not so much sad, not so much worrisome, as grotesque.

"I called the police again," he offered. "I don't know, they said they're out looking. I think maybe we should be out there too."

"They told us to stay put, in case he comes home."

"I know," Matthew replied. "But I don't like just sitting here. I think it would be better if I got into my car, you'd still be here for him."

"You already got into your car, you looked all the places you can look."

"I know," Matthew sighed as Claire went back to pacing. She hadn't even known she'd been moving, or that she'd stopped, but suddenly she was acutely aware of every tremble of her hands, each turn of her head. She watched her husband's face as she turned back and forth, back and forth. One, two, three, she counted to herself, believing whole heartedly that each time she hit three Preston would walk through the door. Three was the magic number, it had to be. Something had to be. It was the waiting, the not knowing, everyone said that, but it wasn't just that, it was the way it was all different now.

"I knew I should have gotten him a cell phone," Claire cried. "I knew it. At least we'd have something to call, a way to locate him."

"He's too young," Matthew argued. "What if he's out in the

woods where there isn't any service? That's probably what happened, he wandered into the woods and got lost. The police will find him huddled next to a tree."

"It still gets cold at night," Claire countered. "And what if an animal finds him?" she asked and now it seemed as if that was the only possibility. Of course they'd find him in the woods, where else would a little boy be in a neighborhood like this?

"There aren't any bears or cougars or whatever in the woods here, only raccoons and chipmunks," Matthew offered and a net of safety, false or not, was cast around them. Though their son wasn't home, both of them knew where he was now, he'd be safe soon, he'd be back once they got him out of those woods. She did not consider that a child could come out of the woods in any state other than fine, a little frightened, but fine.

"Raccoons can be very aggressive in their natural habitat," Claire commented, pacing once again, now because she saw her little boy being mauled by a man-eating masked rodent. "I can't believe," Claire fired back, facing Matthew, though both of them knew she was not shouting at anyone in particular. "I can't believe this! What is wrong with us? And I told myself he was too young to go out with those kids. And they're fine. They got home safely, they didn't even notice Preston left, they just went right on playing, didn't even think to see if he was okay and now…and now…" Claire shook her head, shrugging Matthew off when he approached.

The soft tan carpet seemed to glow, the lamplight was like that of the moon on a barren field as Claire walked toward the plush white couch, past an antique wooden rocking chair and to the mantel by the fireplace. There was her little boy, an array of snapshots on display like wares at an antique shop. There was Preston at his fifth birthday party when Peyton had dropped his slice of cake and tried to scoop it up with his fork as if nothing had happened; Preston on his first two-wheel bike, it had been red with painted gashes on the side that he'd insisted were "fire marks;" Preston at a beach in Florida the year before, excited to see the ocean down south, though he was disappointed when he saw that it was not as bright as he'd thought it'd be, the pictures in magazines, he'd said, made it look "bluer." The shrieking started once again and Claire closed her eyes as Matthew answered the phone. "If it's that animal charity again call the police," Claire shouted as Matthew answered with a fuddled "Hel-hello?" She could just picture her husband, tall and graceful, but somehow still fumbling, barely holding onto the receiver.

"What are you talking about? I don't understand," she heard Matthew say. "No, I just…why can't you just tell me?" Matthew begged into the receiver and Claire closed her eyes. She'd never believed, not for five seconds, that anything so bad as those things she could not consider, could ever happen. It had been fear, only fear, nothing beyond it and she could not imagine five minutes from now, no less five hours, five days, five years. No, at the very worst Preston had broken a leg, he'd fallen and cut a finger, he needed stitches, she'd even go so far as to believe, to concede that perhaps her precious little boy needed an overnight stay at the hospital. But that was all, really that was all and they would get over it, they would work through it. Nothing else could happen to him.

"The police are coming," Matthew offered as he entered the living room. "A detective is on his way. They have to talk to us, that's all they said, they wouldn't say anything else," he went on, speaking as if he'd stuffed a loaf of bread in his mouth.

When Claire had met Matthew in college he was just a guy, the kind of average that stands out it's so middle of the road. He played poker and watched sports but never once begrudged his wife a trip to the ballet or a conversation about a book she'd read. He had guy friends; he got along with her girlfriends, though never too well. But here, seeing him with tears in his eyes it was as if this wasn't happening. Matthew didn't cry. He'd gotten misty eyed the day Preston was born, he'd broken down at his father's funeral, but this, these prolonged tears were different, unreal, wrong.

The knock on the door came quickly, too quickly, as if a half hour had become three minutes. There was the first knock, polite and kindly, a knock that seemed to understand that it was after nine o'clock and even if this was official police business there were common codes of decency to follow. When neither Claire nor Matthew answered, both of them standing in the front hall waiting for the other to move the seven steps to the door, the knock grew harsher, so much so that the doorbell was dangerously close to being rung. Claire flinched at the thought of such a wildly intrusive bell at a time like this and marched toward the front door, turning the knob carefully as she was met with a heavyset detective in a brown and beige suit. He was an older man with small eyes and a ring of thin hair around the sides of his head. Behind him stood a tall, slim man, more like a boy, with big eyes and a smooth, clear complexion. His short brown hair was cropped close to his head and he nodded politely as he looked Claire in the eye. They both flashed their badges and the older, heavier one did the talking.

"Hello Ma'am, Mrs. Tumber, I'm Detective Jameson and this is my partner Detective Toby, can we come in?"

"Yes, thank you," Claire replied. She'd been standing at the door with her hand on the frame, but she moved to the side, indicating that the detectives should enter.

"I'm sorry to have to come see you under these circumstances," Detective Jameson went on, professionally, though uncomfortably.

"Yes, my husband and I, you can imagine," Claire started just as uncomfortably, her hands visibly shaking as she led the detectives through the foyer and into the living room. "It's just that our son hasn't come home. He went out to play today and wasn't back at five, when he's supposed to be, and he's still…I mean, I called his friends and he's still not home…" Claire started to shake slightly, fighting back tears as Matthew, who'd bucked up since she'd gone to the door, put his arm protectively around her. Claire wanted to shrug him off, but didn't have the strength.

"Is there anyone else in the house?" the detective asked. "Any adults, any other children?" he inquired shaking his discomfort as his voice moved toward pure professionalism.

"No, why?" Claire asked. "Why would you ask that, why would you care?"

"We like to have everyone in the house present when we talk to them...especially when things are as sensitive as this," the detective explained. "Mr. and Mrs. Tumber, we got your call at six oh three and we've been searching for your son since then," the older detective went on. "Are you sure you don't want to sit down?" he asked, pointing to the stuffed white couch in the corner. Claire shook her head no. "It's hard to find a boy that age, or at least to ID him because he doesn't have any form of identification. He doesn't usually carry a wallet or obviously a driver's license or sometimes not even a school ID."

"I understand," Claire said, wondering why all these technical explanations. "Where is my son?"

The detective blinked for an extra long moment before facing Claire and Matthew. "It's that we found a boy in the woods about a half hour ago. He was lying near a tree, not breathing. It looked like he'd been dead about two hours, maybe three. We have to get a coroner's report to find out and to figure out what caused his death."

"His death? His what?" Claire asked and the word felt cold, like floating in outer space. It was as if she were dangling above her body, as if none of it, absolutely none of it were real. She'd heard the words the detective had said as if she'd been listening to a garbled version, as if the truth of it all had been held under water, the words struggling, flailing, drowning. "No? What?"

"We haven't been able to ID the boy yet, but we haven't had any other missing ten year olds and this boy we found matches your description. If you come down to the morgue with us to ID him...."

"What? Come with you?" Claire asked, shaking her head as she backed away. The living room was spinning, salmons and pinks, the soft blue of the curtains, the pictures on the mantle, the way Preston had looked just a few months ago in his school picture. It was all there, it was all real and she couldn't imagine another reality, as if time and space could alter and there could be no Preston. How was that possible? "What? Are you kidding me? He just went out to play, this doesn't make any sense, how could he be...no...I just don't....ID the body? That's something they say on TV. This isn't a crime drama, Matthew, what is he talking about?"

The senior detective stood straight and tall while the younger one looked at the floor. Claire kept pacing until Matthew grasped her arm, looking her in the eye. "Claire, we have to go," he said. "It might not be him, you never know. But we have to go to the hospital. We have to see," her husband's words were slow and sure but very kind.

"No, Matthew, what are you talking about? We can't go. We have to wait for Preston, Preston will be home." Claire smiled and all of a sudden it made sense, it made perfect sense and if they just waited Preston would come back.

"Take your time," the detective interjected considerately as he paced in the direction opposite Claire and Matthew.

"Why aren't they telling us to stay home? What if Preston comes back? One of us has to wait until Preston comes back. Our little boy...we have to wait for our little boy," Claire cried, picturing him walking through the door, tousled brown hair, maybe some dirt on his face.

"I think we both have to see him, we both have to ID him," Matthew explained calmly, "just in case."

"In case what? What's going on, I'm not going," Claire cried, wresting herself from her husband, she marched back toward the kitchen and then out to the dining room where no one had had an appetite tonight.

"Claire," Matthew said one more time and she could sense the moon outside, the woods only a few feet away. She could feel the blue-black of the night, the way the light cascaded onto the yard with its swing set and under-sized basketball hoop, the bike and roller blades, a bat and ball left over from when Preston and Peyton had played in the yard earlier that morning. That morning...and now it was night and it didn't make any sense, none of it made any sense and how could it all have changed?

"Claire, come on," Matthew called and she left the dining room, returning to the front hall as the detectives walked toward the door. "We have to go, no matter what, we have to do this."

"You can ride with us if you like," Detective Jameson suggested, looking as if he was about to reach out to grasp Claire and her floundering husband, who shook his head at his offer.

"No, that's all right, we'll drive ourselves," Matthew said and Claire nodded as they walked with the detectives toward the door.

It was a short ride to the hospital across town. Claire had been there once before, when Preston had fallen out of a tree and they'd thought he'd broken his arm. It had turned out to only be a hairline fracture and Claire had thought at the time, "We dodged a bullet there, we really dodged a bullet." They did not park in the front, in the sprawling hospital lot that went a half mile or so back to the road, but hung a right at the entrance and followed the detectives as they drove around back near a large garbage bin and out of the way picnic table, to a smaller, less well lit lot that had a back alley feel to it.

The hospital morgue was no place for a decent person to be, especially so late at night. It was clean, a woman in scrubs sat at a desk near its entrance and a doctor who wore a mask and ID badge was very polite to Claire and Matthew when they came in, but there was something tired, something dingy and subterranean about the basement room. The place was cold, all the furniture matched, identical muted brown chairs and loveseats that looked as if they'd been hijacked from the nineteen eighties, as if only the lowly, only the dregs came down here.

The moment Claire and Matthew stepped in they were met with clipboards containing forms and requests for insurance cards, not that Claire understood what a morgue would need with insurance. She was starting to think that soon you'd need to show your insurance card to grab a coffee at a hospital cafeteria. No one asked them how they were, not even the secretary, no one told them anything about the body they were there to see. They'd been calling it "The Body," not John Doe, or Child Doe, just The Body, as if to give it a name, any name, would be too callous and might send Claire and Matthew spiraling.

After the paperwork, the secretary very calmly explained that the doctor would be out soon, he had another body in the morgue that needed to be handled. "I'm sorry for the wait," the girl said kindly but professionally, "this isn't what usually happens." The girl at the front desk was young, with fresh green eyes and red hair that accented her royal blue scrubs. "Are you going to be all right?" she'd asked at one point. "Can I get you some water, coffee, a soda from down the hall?"

Claire and Matthew both sat forward, staring at the wall as if to will themselves away, as if to concentrate so hard so as to disappear completely, to make it so none of this was happening. Even a dull formless void would have been better than this.

"Well if you need anything," the girl said into the void, smiling when they did not respond, "just ask."

"Thank you," Claire replied as they waited for the doctor to call them back.

After a wait that could have been five minutes or could have been an hour, Claire could not remember experiencing it she was so distracted, they were finally allowed into the morgue. Detective Jameson, who still seemed even after all this like a total stranger, followed them back. It was cold in the morgue proper and the doctor, a tall, thin man with long arms and skinny fingers came out with a white coat on.

"I'm Dr. Palmer, and if you have any questions, any concerns, please let me know." He was kind, but Claire could tell he was staying as removed and professional as possible. "We have to keep it cold in here for obvious reasons, but there are jackets in the closet if you want them," he offered after shaking their hands (his fingers were freezing).

"That's all right," Matthew declined the coat and Claire nodded that her husband's answer came from the both of them. Detective Jameson, who had, one could assume, done this before, though usually the bodies were not those of young children found in the woods, took a jacket, which, although he was a big man, proved to be far too large for him. Nothing fit right here, nothing worked, nothing connected, not here inside nor to the outside world.

"Just follow me," the doctor said, glancing back at them through his thick-framed glasses. "The Body is on the table. All I ask is that you please not touch anything. Nothing there is going to hurt you, but there's going to be a police investigation and you shouldn't touch anything, even the Body."

"A police investigation?" Claire asked, still staring down at the white tiled floor. She'd been looking at it so hard and for so long that she could see the minute swirls of black and brown, intentional misdirection as she walked with her husband through a pair of double doors into a cold, sterile room, smelling of disinfectant. Most of the room was metal and glass, the epitome of modern medicine, and a humming came from the left side, where a wall of what looked like steel refrigeration units stood.

"I think you should be aware that—" the doctor started.

"Everything is fine," Matthew interjected and a piece of the old college tennis player came out in the force behind his voice as they arrived at a table covered by a sheet about the size of Claire's kitchen counter. It was long and rectangular, though there was something cold, something metal and alien (as if it had come from the mother-ship) about it.

"Let me pull this over so you can see the face," the doctor went on. He pulled the sheet off with gloved hands and Claire thought, literally, Claire thought, figuratively, Claire thought actually and completely that time had stopped, that she had ceased to be, as the red pit, the one that had been building up since six o'clock when it had become painfully obvious that Preston wasn't merely late coming home, burst inside her and she nearly toppled over.

He was there. She saw him. Claire had thought for sure that even if it were Preston she wouldn't recognize him, since he was not himself anymore, but had now been transformed into The Body. She was sure that something about his dead form, his lifeless body would be so much less of him that she wouldn't be able to tell, but there he was and she could see his face. It wasn't the same face, there was something over it, a translucent film no one else seemed aware of, like his blood had turned to ice. His lips were blue, and the rings around his eyes were dark like swamp water, and yet it was the same face, the same hair, the same eyes, which were open, presumably so that he'd be easier to identify, as if a pair of parents didn't know what their own child looked like dead or alive.

"Oh my God," she said, and it had been him. She tried to get to him, to tell them that Preston was okay, that she'd seen him like this before (had she?), he was her little boy and there was no way he was gone, she would have felt it, she would have known. She would have died too. "Oh my God, oh my God, oh my God," Claire screamed and she couldn't remember anything afterward. She would recall his face, she would forever remember that instant whenever she closed her eyes but after that horrific moment it all went black. She could not recall rushing to the body as Detective Jameson held her back, she did not remember running in the opposite direction, tripping over a second table and spilling a bottle of green liquid all over the slippery floor. She could not recall rushing into the wall and the cut down the side of her wrist that it left or Matthew moving off into a corner, crying quietly to himself as he let the doctor and detective deal with his thrashing wife. She wouldn't remember the doctor or Detective Jameson talking to her, the bandage tied around her wrist, the papers she signed or the permission she gave so they could do an autopsy, sew Preston up and send him to a funeral home of her choosing —as if she had the wherewithal just then to chose a funeral home.

Matthew left and did not return right away but Claire couldn't recall trying to find him either. She didn't ask where he was; she didn't even want him there. After they ID-ed the body, everyone was very careful around her, the detectives, the doctor, the secretary, acting as if she might crack in half, right down the middle, if they looked at her funny (or at all). Back in the waiting room the phone rang and the secretary rushed to answer it, not wanting the sound to bother Claire. She whispered into the receiver, saying to whoever was there that she couldn't talk just then. No one asked Claire if she was okay. Of course she was not okay, they knew that.

A psychiatrist came in, a short, thin woman with pronounced laugh lines around her mouth and eyes. She had chin length black hair and wore a professional black skirt and blouse; she looked almost Goth, though she was obviously a professional.

"Hello, I'm Doctor Harper, I work in the Psychiatric Department upstairs, the hospital sent me down," she started sounding friendly and calm, but also very professional, as if she were seven steps removed from the situation. "I want you to know that everyone understands what you're going through, and no one here is going to tell you that there is a right way or a wrong way to act or feel, but they are concerned and it's protocol when something like this happens to send us in. Don't think my coming down is because you reacted to this in the wrong way," she explained, taking the tan seat next to Claire. She looked as if she wanted to make contact, to touch Claire's arm or rest a neat hand briefly on her knee, but she just looked at Claire, not daring to crack a smile. "Is there anything you'd like to talk about?" she asked, her voice incredibly understanding, as if even with these questions she expected nothing from Claire. When Claire just stared at her, shaking her head "no," she went on. "That's okay. But in a few weeks it might be a good idea to see someone, and if you still feel this bad in a few months, I'd definitely suggest getting help. Not that it wouldn't be completely fair for you to feel this way even in a few months, still, you shouldn't have to feel this bad if there's anything anyone can do even just to help a little bit."

"I don't feel bad," Claire said, because she wouldn't have put it that way. Bad was what happened when she invited a friend for coffee and they said they couldn't make it, bad was when the dog ran off for a few hours, bad was when Preston hadn't been home at five-twenty, but they'd passed bad at six o'clock that night and this right here, whatever she was feeling, this wished it were bad, this feeling was to bad what a slum was to a penthouse apartment.

"I understand," the psychiatrist said. "Look, I'm going to go get you a prescription for something to help you sleep. You need your rest right now and I understand that you're not going to get it without help. I'm not even going to make you fill it tonight. I'm going to give you a Valium to calm you down for now and pre-scribe some sleeping pills for when you go to bed tomorrow. You don't have a history of allergies to medications, do you?"

"No," Claire answered.

"Any history of dependency?"

"No."

"Okay, good, then I can prescribe you a couple of pills for the next two days."

"Why can't you give me a week's worth?" Claire asked. "I'm not going to want to come back."

"I know, but it's best this way," the doctor replied, with a sympathetic half-smile. Claire knew the doctor was worried she'd take all the pills at once, that this was not the time to be hand-ing her the keys to an easy and painless suicide. "I'll be back. I'll give you the pill and you can stay here and relax. Your husband will be out shortly," she said and this was the first time Claire had really thought of Matthew since the sheet had been lifted from Preston's face.

"Where's my husband?" she demanded of the girl at the desk.

"I'll call back," the girl said as the psychiatrist wrote her prescription and silently left. The girl nodded at Claire as she listened to the phone she'd just picked up. "He's in back talking with Doctor Palmer. Matthew told me to tell you he called his sister and she'll be picking you up soon to go home."

"Go home?" Claire asked. She hadn't even considered that. What was there at home? The prospect of that big house in such a child-friendly neighborhood, the yard with Preston's toys, the game of Stratego he and Matthew had left out last night for the following day, the one they would have been playing today, it all felt like a gaping wound. If only she stayed here, if she lay down on this cold floor and slept on these tiles, if she never moved from this spot, maybe none of it would be real. "I don't think I want to go home."

"Well, not just yet," the girl said, misunderstanding. "The doctor is going to do his autopsy tomorrow. He needs you to sign one more form."

"Autopsy?" Claire asked.

"The doctor already talked to you about it, you signed a form," the girl replied. "It's only for your son. . .to find whoever. . . ."

"I signed a form?" Claire asked. She shook her head and stared vacantly at the floor, finding it fascinating how the brown and black swirls moved and bent with the light. "I guess I signed a form while I was so. . . upset."

It took a few minutes for anything more to happen and this time Claire felt the time. She watched the clock, noting that it was almost midnight. Maybe the pumpkin would burst, the clock would strike and she'd hear it, waking up with Preston alive and well, with everything as it had been this morning. She'd go check on her son and he'd be huddled under his Spiderman comforter, one arm hanging over the bed as the sun came through the windows, shining on his exposed left foot and reaching up to his face.

The doctor came out first, followed by Matthew, and it seemed as if they'd been cavorting in there. "Where were you?" Claire demanded of her husband, hugging herself as she shivered, pushing the tears from under her eyes with clenched fists. It wasn't even that cold in the waiting room, not like inside the morgue, but she had been perpetually shivering since she arrived.

"I was with Doctor Harper," Matthew explained. "She told me it was best if we both had some time alone and so I took a walk. I called my sister," he went on, shaking his head as he looked at Doctor Palmer. "That's where I saw the doctor." Matthew put his arm around Claire, standing tall next to his wife and she melted into him, feeling weak.

"I want you to know I did a thorough investigation of the body, though of course we won't know anything for sure until the official autopsy tomorrow," Doctor Palmer started, and Claire and Matthew turned to look at him. "I did…" He went on citing medical jargon about tests done on the blood, the hair, the skin, information neither Claire nor Matthew could understand. Claire nodded, looking directly at the doctor before glancing up at Matthew, who also didn't appear to comprehend. "We don't know anything for sure yet, but you should be aware that there will be an investigation."

"What for?" Claire asked, her mind blank.

"It's protocol after a child is found like this to assume— " the doctor started.

"Someone did this to him?" Claire interrupted. And it only made sense, children who were not sick or the victims of horrible accidents did not just die. It was only logical, someone had caused this, she knew it, and yet it wasn't until the doctor suggested it that she fully realized the truth. The feelings she was experiencing, what she had just gone through and what was to come (though she couldn't even begin to think about that), had been done by someone and if that someone had never existed, if that someone had never encountered Preston. . . . If only she had not let him go out with his friend today her son really would be sleeping in his bed, and so would Claire and Matthew and they'd have had dinner with the Smithson's on Thursday evening and Eva would have come knocking on their door at eleven twenty-two like clockwork the next morning. But instead that person had existed, instead they'd found Preston and nothing, not her life or Matthew's, not the house, not the world as they knew it, would ever be the same.

"What?" Claire cried, and turning around she sauntered toward the secretary's desk, grasped the clipboard attached to the sign-in sheet, the first and only object she saw lying out, and threw it onto the floor. It bounced once and Claire stepped on it as if she were extinguishing a fire, as if once it was smashed she'd go on to something else and then something else and something else until the entire world had been trampled.

"Claire," Matthew called, tears in his voice. "Claire, we have to talk to the doctor."

She stopped, the tone of her husband's voice wrapped around her skin and she couldn't think straight. Matthew stood in front of her; he grasped her shoulders and looking at his face, at his blue eyes, the eyes Preston had inherited, she stopped, took a deep breath and calmed down, turning back to the doctor, who had ignored her fit.

"There's going to have to be a police investigation after the official autopsy. They're going to have to look at the body again, are you okay with that?" Doctor Palmer asked.

"Of course, do whatever you need to," Claire informed the doctor.

"Thank you," he retorted, turning around to find the psychiatrist walking toward them. She was carrying a paper cup of water in one hand as the other remained in a closed fist.

"Here, I stopped by the pharmacy," she said, handing something small to both Claire and Matthew. "Since you have a ride coming, I thought I'd give these to you now. They're Valium, they'll help you calm down tonight."

Claire felt the hard, blue pill in her palm and wondered if she should take it. She felt herself sliding down the rabbit hole, the desk was too big, the chair too small, she was ten feet tall, she was the size of a mouse. The world didn't make sense anymore and if she took this blue pill would it make it worse? Would she lose herself forever? Maybe that was what she wanted and Claire downed the pill, taking a gulp of water before handing the cup to Matthew, who cautiously and carefully swallowed his own.

"You'll start to feel drowsy in a little while, but you're not driving so it's okay," the psychiatrist offered. "Here's a prescription for two days' worth, but only take them as you really need them," she informed the couple. She smiled kindly then and Claire nodded at her as she took a seat. She was already starting to feel dizzy and sleepy. Matthew took the chair next to her, he draped an arm around her and Claire hoped she'd fall asleep right there. She didn't want to be here, she didn't want to move or think and the very act of being awake was too much for her.

Footsteps came from down the hall a few minutes later and when Claire looked up the doctor was there again, along with a familiar face Claire didn't recognize right away, she only knew it was familiar. "Your ride is here," the doctor calmly informed them and Keilly, Matthew's sister, ran up to her brother frantically embracing him. Claire watched her with Matthew; she was tall like him, thin and blond.

"I'm so sorry, I just can't believe," Keilly said, holding tight to her brother, letting go, looking at him, and holding tight once more. "I just…and it's just that…. I came as soon as I could," she went on. Keilly had never been the type to speak in full sentences. "And Claire, Claire, are you okay?" she asked, reaching for Claire, who shrugged her away. She liked Keilly, she really did, but she just could not be touched, she could barely be talked to right now.

"We should get going," Matthew suggested, grasping his sister's hand as they headed out. "Unless you need us for anything else?" he asked, eyeing the doctor.

"No, not at all. I'll get you the results of the autopsy. I'm truly sorry for your loss and if I have any more information I'll get it to you."

"Thank you," Matthew replied, seeming to have stiffened up.

"Ohmygosh, little brother, I just can't believe, I mean I just can't...." Keilly said, teary-eyed as she walked with Matthew down the long hall toward the morgue's exit. Claire could see the parking lot through the window. It was after midnight and still the coach was a coach and not a pumpkin; the driver, a driver, the glass slipper, a glass slipper. This was the real world and nothing was going to change.

"I just can't," Claire said as they reached the door. "I just....I can't leave him," she cried, rushing back toward the morgue and at the secretary's desk. She could tell Matthew was running after her, she could hear his footsteps on the tile, the way his shadow covered the florescent light. She felt his arm around her, nearly tackling her to the ground as she thrashed to get away. And why did she have to go, why did she have to leave him? Preston was there, no matter what, Preston was there and it didn't seem right that a mother should abandon her little boy in a place like this.

PRESTON

It seemed as if he were somewhere else. Preston opened his eyes in the woods and the light shifted as if it were climbing down like careful, deliberate raindrops on a spider's web. The forest floor felt like his bed at home, no twigs dug into his palms, no dirt collected between his fingers and when he kicked his leg, a reflex upon waking, it didn't feel stiff or asleep. His stomach did not burn and the pain was gone. Preston opened his eyes wider and sat up. The forest floor was covered in an array of leaves colored for fall in purple, red and gold, not the crisp green of summer. He reached out and touched one and it felt like a leaf, any normal leaf, and yet it did not. It was somehow sturdier, crunchier, like it was made of fine paper.

The sun came through the trees; little specks of dust in the yellow light shimmering, first inside the air and then off the forest floor, wading like tiny pools of translucent film. Preston rubbed his eyes, sitting up straighter he ran a hand through his shaggy light brown hair and looked up through the blanket of branches toward the source of the light.

Rustling came from within the woods and Preston quickly turned his head. He knew someone was there, that someone should be there, but he only had a vague memory of who, as if the face and the name, the voice could be anyone—one person—or another—as if he were playing on the school grounds and then— and there had been a school grounds at one time, Preston remembered that, but not much more, as if all his thoughts were fuzzy.

"He's here," Preston heard the voice of a boy. "He's here, he's in here, I found him," the boy called and the rustling grew louder as Preston looked through the trees. "Hi," a boy with short brown hair gelled back said. He was wearing worn red pants and no shirt, only a jacket that looked like a blazer with holes in it. Preston looked at his own clothes, his brown and white striped shirt and blue jeans, they were nicer and newer, the style entirely different from what this other boy was wearing. "Hi," the boy said again.

"Hi," Preston responded slowly.

"I'm Starky," the boy introduced himself importantly, pointing at his own chest. Preston watched the boy's sagging brown eyes and wondered what it was about him that was so different.

"And I'm Clover," "And I'm Dilweed," "And I'm Oregano," three boys cheered, stumbling out of the woods and talking simultaneously. There was a short, fat blond boy, a tall, lean black boy and a medium built kid with brown hair and glasses. The kid with the glasses swept his hair from his face in a way that reminded Preston of something he'd seen before.

"Hi," Preston said, putting his hand to his head as he stood up, dizzy. "I don't know. . .where am I?" He knew enough to question where, to ask why, he knew that there had been something before and that this was the something after, but as to whether this was actual. . .as to what was going on, he had no clue.

"You're Here," the boy named Dilweed explained as if Preston should have known better. "Come on," he invited Preston as the four of them started walking away. Preston, having stood up, started to follow the boys as they trudged across the crispy leaves through the forest. "We're Here too, but we don't live so deep in the woods."

"Hardly anyone goes this far," Clover elaborated.

"Usually when new kids come, they come all at once, like they're all waiting for something together," Oregano added.

"Kids come Here a lot?" Preston asked as they stepped in time together. He tried to fall out of step, but couldn't. "Where are they, the other kids?"

"Oh, all around, mostly at the tree house, but we go all around, we have the run of the place, not like back home," Starky explained.

"Where am I?" Preston asked again. The words "back home," made more sense to him, he'd heard those words before and he had an incredible urge to be there. "Back home, where is that? Can we go there?"

"No," Starky said simply, shaking his head. "No, not ever again, we don't go back. Only one of us has ever done that, and come to think of it, that one they found in the woods too, but that was even before my time and I've been here almost the longest."

"Shut up, Starky," Dilweed cried, playfully socking him on the arm.

"So maybe I can," Preston thought out loud. "What is it, back home?"

"Don't worry about that," Oregano explained. "He'll tell you everything, he really will. He's good at explaining stuff, that's why he's the leader."

"Who?" Preston asked as they kept walking. The forest had looked the same for a while, trees with dark blackish bark, the way the leaves crackled under them as the sun filtered through, but Preston could see an end, as the light got brighter, seeming to envelop the scene before them, there were other colors and lights flashing and it reminded him of something he'd known before.

"Our leader," Starky replied as if Preston should have known. "You didn't think we were in charge, did you? Do we look like a bunch of leaders? We were just out in the woods hunting Indians and wildcats when we heard something moving. Oregano thought it was an Indian and Dilweed thought it was a wildcat but I've been Here a long time and I thought maybe you were one of those that came from the woods, like the other one did."

"The other one?" Preston asked and Dilweed quickly socked Starky's arm again.

"For someone who's been Here a long time, you sure are stupid," Dilweed complained.

"Anyway, so we decided to give up Indian hunting and go on

an Explore and that's when we found you. I don't know how you'd find him if we hadn't shown up."

"Him? Him who?" Preston asked and something about all this made him remember. Not a real memory, not a picture or words, only a feeling, a bright, an excited feeling that swelled in his stomach before he realized he didn't know what it was.

"The leader," Clover replied as if it really were a very simple concept.

"What's he like?" Preston asked.

"He's a married man," Starky stated as if he'd memorized a list of facts about him.

"He likes to draw and play the flute," Dilweed explained.

"And he can't read," Starky went on. "He's always trying though. Some of the boys brought books with them Here and he's always trying to read them, in any language he can, but it never works."

"He can't tell time either," Clover went on. "He's always forgetting the time."

"But he's the best leader in the world. He can fight better than any of the Indians or the cowboys, he can shoot a gun and slash a sword and he crows and flies better, he can run faster and slay a tiger for dinner.... Besides," Starky went on. "Only pirates need to know how to read."

"Pirates?" Preston asked, intrigued.

"Shhhh," Dilweed, Clover and Oregano hissed together as they wandered out of the forest. "We don't talk about pirates." Preston was about to ask why when the blanket of branches lifted and he saw more light.

The light was not the same as through the trees, there was something flashy, something artificial about it and it took him a second to realize that he hadn't been seeing the sun; it was dark out and for all he knew it could have been the middle of the night here. What he saw were light bulbs, bright flashing orbs, neon lights, colorful bulbs like on a Christmas tree. And there were in fact Christmas trees all around, large, never-ending pines that crashed into the sky flashing with neon and ornaments, and inside a clearing a gigantic multi-colored Ferris wheel stood going around and around. Near that was a bright red and silver merry-go-round, also going forever. Preston walked up to the gate, watching the white horses with golden manes, the pink flamingos and tigers with bared teeth flashing their claws, each brightly painted animal turning to the beat of circus music. Off to the side there were red neon lights flashing the words "Toy Store" over a heap of toys that boys played with—new toys in bright boxes, motorized cars and intricate action figures, and old wooden toys with creaking wheels and pull strings on the ends. Each boy brought a new toy to the pile and picked up an old one as if it didn't matter. There were movies playing on screens, pictures he'd never seen before about racecars and animals, submarines and giant trucks.

It was all the lights really, all the lights that made Preston forget. Maybe it was Mr. Hawthorne's, or that last time playing with Peyton, or his family or school or before, but whatever it was it made it so that he didn't even consider how many other boys there were. Behind the Ferris wheel and the merry-go-round stood a large tree, not like one of the trees in the forest, this one towered above the carnival equipment, its limbs reaching out on all sides, and Preston could see the outline of a roof in the middle, with little roofs scattered all around the branches.

"That's where we live," Clover said, pointing up. "I live in the house on the end, on the sixth branch up."

"Is it like before?" Preston asked and Starky shook his head no.

"You don't know about Before yet, but he'll tell you. He'll tell you everything. It's not our job to show you around, we just found you in the woods. Usually he does all the talking and we meet you later."

"Okay," Preston replied, this seeming to make perfect sense.

He watched the other boys still playing; they didn't seem to know he was there, they didn't notice Clover or Dilweed, Starky or Oregano either, they were off in their own worlds playing, some even playing together, but not in the same game.

They walked closer to the bottom of the tree house; its roots were as tall as Preston, reaching from the ground with their tough, wooden arms. Preston touched the tree and it was warm, he could feel it like a beating heart, it reminded him of his own body, his own self and he pulled his hand away, worried it might burn him.

"The tree's not going to hurt you," Dilweed explained. "Nothing is going to hurt you."

"Not unless you meet a pirate. . ." Starky started and Dilweed hit him again.

"Shut up," he cried and Oregano gave Starky an annoyed look.

More lights started flashing, flickering over and around in circles. They weren't like the Christmas lights, or the flashing bulbs of the Ferris wheel, these lights were alive, a beating heart like the tree. One of the lights came closer to Preston, so close he had to close his eyes as something landed on his nose. It was cool and fresh like diving into a swimming pool, but blinding and it wasn't until he felt a hand on his face swiping the light off him that he could open his eyes again. "Go on, shoo," Dilweed cried, put out as if he were flicking a bug. "Leave him alone, he's new. If you want to help go find him and tell him he's here."

"What was that?" Preston asked.

"Fairies," Starky explained as if Preston should have naturally known. "There's a ton of them, they wander around all the time causing trouble, bothering the boys when they're trying to play. They do some good though; they help the kids who don't have happy thoughts. And our leader is friends with them. But he's friends with everyone except the pirates."

"What about these pirates?" Preston inquired since they had been mentioned so many times. He could feel something, a flash of an instant appeared and he saw a room with light blue carpeting and a window that looked out to a sea green yard; he saw a sandy colored coffee table and a television set, a bowl of fluffy white food that he knew was called popcorn, and a man and a woman. "Wait, I know that. . .I. . . ."

"I hope he finds you quick, you're starting to remember," Oregano warned.

"Do you all remember?" Preston asked the boys as he leaned back on the tree, something about its heartbeat feeling safe and natural now.

"You don't come to forget, you come to remember," Starky explained. "And I've been Here the second longest so I remember the second most. It was in the middle of a great big war and they took me and my family from our home, they put us on a crowded train and threw us in a camp. They took my Mom and sent me off with my Dad. They lined us up and then there were a bunch of showers, they turned on the showers, someone said something about gas and I came Here. A bunch of kids from the showers came Here with me, but I'm the only one that's left of them."

"Why? Where else do you go?" Preston asked.

"We don't know," Starky explained. "He knows, but he doesn't ever tell us."

"But it's great Here," Clover interjected. "And you get to play all the games and with all the toys you want. No one tells you to go to sleep, no one makes you eat your vegetables and you can have dinner whenever you want, you just have to think about it, and you can play with whoever you want and no one complains."

"Really?" Preston asked, and though this was all very strange, it excited him.

The fairies returned. Preston saw them, lights blinking, as he turned his head and looked up. The other boys didn't seem to notice as they went on talking; it seemed to Preston that they were still explaining things, and he thought it might be a good idea to listen, but he couldn't with the lights flashing right in front of him and he wondered how long it took to get used to these fairies that buzzed around like bugs.

"And there are a whole bunch of other people Here, they're not even all kids and most of them play with us, or we play with them—" Starky was saying as Preston turned from them, shifting all the way around to see what the fairies were so excited about.

A boy was standing behind them, his hands playfully on his hips, a smile spread across an impish face. It was as if he had always been there, as if they'd walked up to him, not the other way around. Preston watched him and the boy, who had shaggy, messy, dark blond hair came closer, still smiling. There was something about his face, it was the same as every other face and yet it wasn't. He had a small, pointy nose and dimples, his chin jutted out just a little bit and his ears were shaped funny, not so much abnormal as a little bit pointy. He wore green, dark green shorts with leaves and twigs jutting out of them and a green shirt cut in a long, low V at his collar. He had tied around his neck with a thin braided rope a kind of flute, crudely made of wood with large, jagged holes chiseled into it. The boy, who stood a few inches taller than all the others, seemed to walk on tiptoes, as if he were dancing, though his feet were planted firmly on the ground. The other boys, sensing Preston's suddenly waning interest, turned around as well.

"Hi," the boy said and the way his voice hit the air it seemed to crack the molecules in it and the four others got very quiet. He didn't stop the fun, most of the boys playing on the Ferris wheel and merry-go-round were still doing just that, but there was a certain something in the air, as if it had all changed. "Hi," the boy said again, holding out his hand for Preston to take. "Nice to meet you."

"Hi," Preston replied. There was something about him that made Preston ask, "You're the leader?" He looked like a boy, an older boy, maybe fourteen or fifteen, but a boy and not a married man like they'd said.

"I'm the leader," the boy announced and the others rushed to him.

"We found him in the woods, just like you said you found the other one. . ." Starky started and Dilweed hit his arm once more. "And we brought him here. I don't think he's a cowboy, he's too young, or an Indian, I don't think he's a pirate either."

"Well of course he's not a pirate," the boy said, laughing a belly laugh as if genuine happiness were a part of his physical makeup. "He's not a mermaid or a cowboy   or an Indian. He's a little boy like all of you. A little lost boy."

"Am I lost?" Preston asked, hoping that wasn't the case, since being lost, he knew not from where, meant that he was to be found and brought somewhere else.

"That you are my friend, that you are," the boy replied. "You're lost and Starky is lost and Dilweed and Clover and Oregano. They're all lost. And they're all going to stay Here for a little while, just until certain things happen in certain other places and then they're going to go somewhere else. But for now, you're Here and I'm going to take care of you, the fairies are going to take care of you and the other boys, we're all going to take care of ourselves. Even this place is going to take care of you."   "How long do I stay?" Preston asked as the leader moved seamlessly with him, draping a wiry arm around his shoulders as the others ran off. Preston turned to look for them and they were playing; Starky with a pair of jacks while Dilweed and Clover ran toward the Ferris wheel and Oregano picked up a toy gun and started firing at trees.

"You stay Here until things are better where you came from," the boy explained as they walked up to an opening in the trunk of the giant tree house. Once inside they shot up as if on air and Preston grabbed the leader's arm, holding tight. "It's all right, that's just how we get up to the house. It all happens when we want it to happen, like the Ferris wheel and the merry-go-round, no one takes care of them, they just are. Nothing goes wrong

Here, nothing stops working. Even when things change, even when the boys bring video games and magic moving carpets with them, even then it's all the same."

"Okay," Preston replied cautiously once they reached the inside of the tree. There was a large room with a red carpet where pictures flashed on movie screens and boys handled video game controllers or jumped on mechanical pads.

"This is where we live. Some of the boys like to play inside. It's only been a little while since the inside boys have been Here, the ones who only want to play with TV sets and video games. But you can do whatever you want Here, bring whatever you want. It all just comes," the boy explained. "But you'll remember more later. Your first day you forget, the second day more starts to come and by the time you've been Here a week. . .but I am always forgetting the time, but by about a week you understand everything but it doesn't matter because you're so busy playing."

"Is that it, is that what I do, I play?" Preston asked. The boy walked him through the large room and out a small wooden door that led back outside. They weren't on the ground anymore, but several feet up on one of the branches. Preston could see the forest before a blue-mooned night, the music from the Ferris wheel and merry-go-round rang in his ears as they watched the boys playing below.

"Let me take you to your room, it's on this floor," the boy offered as they kept walking across the long, wide branch. "You can do whatever you want," he went on as they walked down the sturdy wooden limb of the tree. "I just want to say that you've been cheated out of something, you've been cheated out of something good and so have the others who knew you, especially your Mom and Dad. That's why you're Here, so they can grieve. You see, the people who loved you, they need to mourn, and it's different, I mean, whenever someone goes away, whenever that happens obviously the loved ones need to grieve, but when a child goes away and doesn't come back there's a certain intensity to the grief, especially for the Mom and Dad, and you have to stay Here, in Neverland, for a while so they can get used to your being gone. It's not the Before, you're not with them, but you're still in the Universe, they can still feel your presence Here at least in the backs of their minds, and they need that for a little while. If a child's presence simply disappeared right away from the Universe, which is what happens when you go from Here, without giving the parents time to mourn, it would be very bad, the parents would be too sad, they'd do crazy things with their grief, which is why you come Here first, to give them time."

"Why?" Preston asked and the boy laughed as they kept walking, past other doors, some painted red or white or green, some with posters hung up, others with music blasting from them. "Go away from where? Not coming back from where?"

"It's all right, I'll explain later," the boy said. "But this is where you live now. And you can go out with Starky and Dilweed and Clover and Oregano all you want and you can play on the swings or hunt Indians and cowboys and—"

"Pirates!" Preston cried, excited since somewhere, somehow he had heard of pirates.

"No," the boy cautioned. "No, we do not associate with pirates, we do not hunt pirates or provoke pirates or play with pirates. They keep to themselves and we do not go and find them." He raised his voice slightly and, seeing the terror in Preston's eyes, the boy reached out and rustled his hair, calming down. "It's all right. Just stay away from pirates is all. But don't worry, they won't come after you and you're not going to accidentally run into them, okay?"

"Okay," Preston replied still a little shaken by how upset the leader had gotten.

"It's all right," the boy said. "You're okay now. You're one of the special ones, the ones that just appeared, you didn't have to come the normal way and that has to mean something. You'll remember and when you remember I'll tell you everything. That's my job and I do my job, that's why I'm the leader. I don't know what it means, but the last one who came out of the woods was special too."

They walked on a little further and Preston watched the boy. "Well, here's your room," he said, grabbing the handle and opening it for him. The room looked like something from Before, the very room he used to sleep in.

"I remember this," Preston said, walking in and taking a seat on the bed, his bed, he bounced on it a couple of times and the mattress felt like home, whatever home was, a certain smell, snowy shoes on a welcome mat against the wall, cereal in milk on a school morning. "It's all the same," Preston observed, "except that," he said, pointing to a TV set and video game system. "My Mom would never let me have that in my room."

"But you always wanted it," the boy replied. "One of the perks of Neverland. Anyway, I'll let you settle in, I'll see you tomorrow." The boy turned to go, but then he stopped, like a dog he seemed to smell something, as if the air had changed and he faced Preston.

Preston's stomach started to hurt a little and he couldn't remember why. It seemed as if there was a light around the boy, the same light he'd seen coming down through the forest when he'd first woken up and he wondered if the boy had been with him the entire time he'd been Here. Then he saw a woman; she was pretty and familiar with long light brown hair and soft brown eyes. He saw her smiling at him, he heard her laugh and knew he loved her very much and that made him sad because he also knew, though he knew not from where, that he'd never see her again.

Then he saw it, as if time had stopped it was both the blink of an eye and a hundred years. He could see his mother handing him a bowl of cereal that last morning. He heard Peyton knocking on his door asking him to go outside, he saw his friend and Eva running one way and he the other. He remembered the lady with the wart on her face and Mr. Hawthorne and those cookies.

He'd seemed awfully persistent, why else would he so insist that he take cookies? He tried to put it all together, but the images just hung there. He saw other things; getting off a plane and going to meet Grandma in Florida, Christmas when he was seven years old and the way the brightly lit tree towered over even his father; he saw school when he was very small and learning to ride a bike. It wasn't so much that his whole life flashed before his eyes, he could feel it quivering inside his body, a movie projected on auto-pilot. Preston turned to the leader, who seemed to know what he was seeing, though he was a bit disturbed by it.

"It doesn't usually happen this quickly, you don't usually remember so soon," the boy said seriously.

"But I think I see it," Preston replied.

"Well, if you see it, you see it. Now I can answer your questions."

"Will I ever see her again?" Preston asked, referring to the woman with the brown hair, his mother.

"No," the leader said sadly. "I'm sorry, no."

"Can I ever go back?"

"No."

"What comes next?"

"I can't tell you now. It's not time," the boy replied very seriously, more seriously than a boy in ragged clothes, with messy hair should naturally act.

"Who are you?" Preston inquired wondering if he was only called The Leader.

"I'm Peter," the boy replied. "They call me Peter."

London, England 1901

A nurse, the kind with a large bottom and bushy hair tied in a tight bun at the nape of her neck, who looked as if she should have been pushing a gigantic pram, what with her long black skirt, tattered at the ends, and white dress shirt that showed off her heavy arms and chest, moved through Regents Park in London followed by (although sometimes it looked as if she were following) three rambunctious children. It was a spring day, the kind of day that anyone, from the flower seller on the street to the businessman out for a stroll, would call "fine." The weather was not too hot, not the sticky summer that would come in a few weeks, nor were there any inconvenient chills in the air. The flowers had been blooming in Kew Gardens and along the Strand and near the house in Bloomsbury where the children lived. The grass was green and neatly clipped, the trees reached out, some branches scattered with white flowers while others had the fresh green leaves that Netty had grown to admire about London parks in the spring when the children could go out.

"Winifred, Winifred, calm down," Netty called as the children ran on ahead of her. They were racing over a path, the raised dirt blowing on Netty's black shoes, the ones she had just had shined on her way to the butchers. Their play was too much for her, but it was better, Netty knew, to get these children out of the house. The yard was so small, and not only that, there were the Missus' flowers in the back and that dog they were always playing with. And she couldn't very well keep them inside and so after they'd had their lunch Netty had dressed the children and taken them out, though now, seeing how they were behaving, she was beginning to wonder about the logic behind her decision. "Winifred, don't run so much, you simply mustn't . . ." Netty called, raising her skirts and rushing after the three of them.

There was Winifred, a girl of fifteen, who for all intents and purposes should have been sitting politely making gentle conversation with other girls her age. She should have been learning to sew—sew better than she could, not just those buttons she could barely keep in place—she needed to study her times tables and her spelling, to go over the history books her father left her. But instead she was still playing around in the nursery, still off in fairyland with those brothers of hers. There was John, he was nine, a studious enough young man who listened to his father and his tutor, who would be going away to school soon, to Eton like his father before him and his father before him. There was also Paul, better known as Michael to the children because the Missus, though she liked the name well enough, had said there was something too serious about calling a child Paul. "We'll see if he grows into it," is what the Missus had said after little Paul, or was it little Michael, was born. Netty had felt sorry for the Missus, that name had obviously not been her idea and yet she'd carried the child for nine months, she'd gone through the pain of childbirth—and Netty could just picture the screaming— while her husband had sat in the den reading the paper, and still she couldn't name him.

"Winifred, stay back, stay back, don't run so far ahead," Netty called, stumbling to keep up with them as she ran up a hill. The children had just sprung over the top and Netty struggled, though the sun was in her eyes, to see them, sweat accumulating rapidly on her brow.

"On guard," John called, his arm pointing out as if it were in and of itself a very sharp and pointy sword. "On guard," he called again and Winifred stood in front of him.

"It is not 'on guard,' John, it's 'en garde', it's French, you have to pronounce it right," the girl corrected, her long light brown hair tied back in a flimsy blue ribbon. It had looked much nicer before; she knew that, when Netty had done it for her. And her dress had looked much nicer then as well, as had her leather shoes. But then she'd gotten to see the light of day and she never kept anything nice and she didn't really understand why that had to bother anybody.

"Oh, what do you know about French? I'm going to Eton," John called and Winifred pushed her brother until he stumbled. He might have lost his balance and fallen over, smack onto the dirty ground, but at the last second he started flailing his arms like a madman and that seemed to do the trick. "You silly girl, hook it, you, hook it," he called, holding an arm-sword out again as Michael appeared. "On guard," he called once more and Winifred stepped back, laughing. "I'm Captain Redhanded Jack, you dirty old. . .you dirty old pirate," the boy cried at Michael, who also held out his arm as a weapon. "On guard you yellow-livered son of a. . . ."

"John!" Netty called, hustling over the hill, her skirts gathered in her hands.

"And I'll get you, you slimy little snake," the little one cried, his tiny arm "slicing" into John's chest. "There you see, I got you. No one can get away from Captain Ghosthanded Bill you. . .you. . . ."

"Michael!" Netty called and both boys finally turned to her.

"But none of you can have me," the girl called, flopping dreamily every which-way, her hand on her head as if she were a suffering damsel. "I'm Tiger Lily, Princess of the Indian Chiefs."

"You can't be the Princess of an Indian Chief," Michael cried. "They don't have Princesses."

"Well I'm an Indian Princess," the girl argued. "And my Indian Prince is going to come and get rid of all you silly pirates."

"They are not," both boys cried in unison.

"They can't do that, that's not allowed, Indians can't even cross the sea. There are no Indians in England," John countered.

"Who said we were in England?" the girl asked and both her brothers began chasing her. She ran in her delicate white shoes, and Netty closed her eyes, she couldn't look, she just couldn't look at them.

"Children," she called once they'd run ahead of her. "Children behave!" she cried out. And it wasn't fair. Her friend Katy was a nurse to four children over in Little Britain and they were perfect dears, Katy said, they barely gave her a lick of trouble and here she was with these three, and one of them was old enough to be a grown woman, still running around pretending to be an Indian Princess. And didn't they have princesses in England, weren't English Princesses good enough for that one? "Children, come back, be good now, d'you hear? Act your age," Netty cried as she stumbled after them.

She could see them running; they didn't even bother to stay on the path. The boys with their arms out, "swords" displayed. John had the correct posture at least, one hand behind his back, forward knee pointed out. That one at least knew how to pose, but the other young lad, he was flailing all over the place.

"On guard," John called, eyes tense as he rushed toward his brother.

"And I'm Tiger Lily," Winifred said, standing between them. "You have to rescue me, Captain Redhanded Jack, rescue me from that one," she declared.

"What makes you think we're going to do that?" John asked, stopping the game to glare at her. "Go on and shoo, *girl*," he called, sticking his tongue out at her as Michael moved in. The boys ran sideways down the path between the trees like little chipmunks scuffling over a fallen nut. "Children, children, calm down!" Netty called, though she had no chance of catching up with them, not going so slowly, her skirts nearly tripping her.

Winifred watched Netty try to reach them. She had never understood the way women dressed as if they needed to remain still all day. What was the fun in that?

She watched her brothers run down the path. Two men were coming, decked out in black; they seemed as if they were dressed for one of those parties Papa attended sometimes, when he took Mother and she wore her nicest dress, the pink one that went with her pearl earrings. One of the men was wearing a tall top hat that shone in the sun, and he carried a cane, swinging it from side to side as if it had no other purpose. The other man, when he got closer, looked younger; he did not wear a hat, but had on the same nice black suit, as if the two of them were in some kind of uniform. Winifred, as she watched them, could just hear their conversation, "And then my good man, we must go to the club, and after that maybe we'll look again at those numbers. Stocks and bonds and cricket and tea and biscuits and then the office, yes, of course, the office, we mustn't forget the office."

Winifred ran up to her brothers while they were playing, just as Michael crashed into the man with the cane. The older gentleman stumbled for a moment, arm shooting into the air as he nearly tumbled, and he would have if his younger companion hadn't grasped his arm and helped him keep his balance. Michael tumbled at the man's feet, but neither of them bothered to help him up.

"Look out, little brats," the man with the top hat cried, and John rushed to Michael, helping him up. "Hasn't anyone taught you manners?" the man seethed and John looked at the ground. Winifred, witnessing the scene, ran to her brother's aide.

"Don't you yell at my brother," she cried at them, looking the offending man right in the eye. He had a completely shaven face and his big, blackish pupils were round like a cow's. "You have no right to scold children."

"Winifred!" Netty called and the girl turned her head. "Winifred, stop that," the nurse cried, having just caught up to them. Her face was bright red and sweating, her hair damp as she breathed deep and heavily. "I'm very sorry gentleman," Netty went on, embarrassed.

"As you should be," the man with the top hat declared, straightening himself as if he were doing a little dance.

"You should not be," Winifred interjected.

"Winifred, quiet," Netty hissed. "I'm truly sorry, gentlemen, the children are in a state today."

"Well perhaps you should make sure that the children are not in a state before you take them out in public. That's your job, isn't it?" the man asked, turning around and not bothering with the scene anymore. They walked away, in the opposite direction, and though John and Michael hung their heads and walked slowly toward the bridge in the middle of the park, Winifred stuck her tongue out at their backs.

"Why I never...," Winifred started and Netty gave her own "humph."

"You children need to learn to behave, do you want people to think your parents don't take good care of you? Do you want to get me fired, the way you go carrying on like that, it's as if..." Netty shook her head, but it was too late, the incident was forgotten, the children had learned nothing and all three of them were running toward the stone bridge.

"On guard," John called, sword arm out as he and Michael fought each other. Michael, who had discovered a long stick sitting near the edge of the path, held that out, whacking John's arm with it as the older brother cried "ah-ouch" and ran after him.

Winifred, meanwhile, stood at the very edge of the bridge, looking down from it and into the water. It was clear, as clear as could be and she could see the sun shining off of it, shimmering in a twinkling light like little fairies dancing about a bed of rocks and long grasses. "Look down there," Winifred cried as her brothers leaned over the edge. They all gazed down as Netty, still holding up her skirts, tried to catch up to them.

"On guard," John called and Michael, still holding that stick, whacked his brother, this time over the head.

"I'll get you, Captain, no Pirate makes a fool out of me," John cried as Winifred still stood looking over the edge of the bridge.

"And I'm Princess Tiger Lily, soon to be Queen of all the Indians, and look, look," she said, pointing down, "there's my kingdom."

"On guard," both boys cried to each other at once, just as Netty called out, "Be careful you three. Get off that bridge before someone gets hurt!"

Then John pushed Michael, who bumped into Winifred, whose feet were just at the very edge of the slippery stone bridge. She fell face down, tumbling off the bridge. There wasn't much of a splash—not when she fell in, nor when she hit the stream. London had gone without rain for a week and so there wasn't much water, just a slight trickle over the rocks. Netty came running, nearly tripping over the skirts that she'd forgotten to pick up. "What's this! What's going on?" she cried. "Winifred, oh, Winifred!" Netty screamed, stopping at the edge of the stream.

All three of them looked down. Winifred was there, face in the water. Blood trickled down the side of her head and she wasn't moving, she didn't get up, not even when Netty screamed, "Winifred, oh Winifred, wake up, wake up Winifred!" The little girl in her blue cloth dress simply lay there, face in the water. John climbed from the bridge, moving to wade into the stream to retrieve his sister, but before he could, and he wasn't sure just what he would have done once he'd gotten her, a man appeared as if from nowhere.

"I'm a doctor," he said. "Let me help her." John stepped to the side and let the man go in.

"Winifred, Winifred!" Netty continued to cry, her face as red as rare roast beef as she paced next to the stream.

The man waded in and carefully pulled Winifred from the water, holding her draped across his arms. More people had come, nine or ten of them, women in long skirts holding umbrellas, men in top hats with canes, a few more children with nurses who were lucky enough not to be made hysterical that day. The man placed Winifred carefully on the ground; he examined her head, touching the spot that was bleeding. He touched her lips and put his face to hers before lifting her head to check her neck.

"I don't know," he said, sounding very sorry. "I don't know if she's breathing."

"What do you mean you don't know?" Netty cried, pacing back and forth, arms in the air as if she herself were fighting off pirates. John and Michael watched Winifred, looking down at the soft, sad face of their sister. They'd never looked at her before, not like this, not when she'd been so still. Winifred was always playing with them, always running around and now she wasn't. They saw her as if she were a grownup, lying on the grass, her hair wet, her dress stained, blood on her face as if this is how it was once you grew up.

"Police!" Netty cried, running frantically back and forth in front of all these people. Two men ran away from the crowd, which had gotten bigger with Netty's screaming. "Police, police, help, help," Netty cried and the boys watched the crowd grow. They saw the man who'd said he was a doctor lean over Winifred, trying, they assumed as he examined her head, to save her.

cLaiRe

The house didn't feel the same, it didn't look the same, blue was not blue, red not red, as if every aspect of life from the very big to the very small had been slightly slanted left or right. From the moment Claire stepped through the door that night after the morgue it had all been permanently altered. As if she were in some kind of nether-house, the light fixtures shone at odd angles, the furniture sat tilted, she couldn't see the sun through the windows and yet it was the same house, the only place she'd been able to stomach since the news.

It had been poison, that's what the doctor had said after a thorough autopsy. Cyanide and Wisteria, the fruit of a poisonous plant had been ingested; they'd found enough of it in Preston's body to kill a child, though, the doctor had explained, "an adult could have survived such a dose." The doctor had also said the police were looking into it, they'd launched a thorough investigation and soon they hoped they'd be able to move on to an arrest. A neighbor of Claire's was apparently what the police called "a person of interest."

The police might be able to move on, they could stop obsessing about Preston's death and focus on the investigation, but Claire could not. There had been times in her life when bad things had happened. She didn't get into graduate school, her father had died of cancer when she was twenty-three years old, but through all that someone had always been there to say, "You'll move on, you'll get through it, this is not the end of the world." This—is—not—the—end—of—the—world. But this, this was different, this was the end of everything. And how do you move on from that, how do you pick up the pieces once the oceans have frozen over and the land gone fallow, once the asteroid has hit and the sun is no longer shining? It was as if her life had been split down the middle, her time with Preston and her time without him. Claire was thirty-six years old, Preston had encompassed but ten years of her life, and yet looking back he had been all of it, as if her entire childhood and young adult life had been waiting for him and now the rest of her life would only be wanting to see him again. All of it was now gone, all of it was in that powder blue coffin they had just buried in the cemetery across from the church.

It had been a ceremony, that's all Claire could say about the wake, the funeral, the burial and though she'd sat in front, looking up at Father O'Shay and Father Sherman, though she'd been there while Matthew and his mother and sister, while Claire's sister Emily and her own mother had planned the entire affair, still it was as if she were sleeping through it. Those pills the psychiatrist had given her, she'd taken more of them, more every day, and other pills to go to sleep at night. Soon, Matthew said, she'd have to stop taking those pills, she'd have to go back to living her life, to being the woman she'd been. How could he expect that of her? That woman was gone. That woman had been buried in a powder blue box.

After the funeral, there had been food, people moved about the house carrying plate after plate of it. Claire wandered through her dining room and into the kitchen watching the food as if this were not about the people but about the casseroles, salads and plates of brownies everyone had so kindly brought, offering food because their words, their thoughts were not enough. At least a casserole was a tangible expression of their sympathy. It had started the day after she found out. She hadn't told anyone but they knew. Kerry O'Conner had brought over a creamed chicken casserole, Tom and Frieda Spellman a tin of turkey potpie, Kathy

Hannigan chocolate chip brownies, which had seemed particularly insensitive seeing that the only person living in the Tumber house who would have appreciated such a treat was gone. It had all been food, food in trays, in plastic containers, in oversized bowls. And the plastic ware, there had been so much plastic ware, oversized utensils, tiny spoons, even plastic toothpicks dressed up to look like swords, all of it accumulating in her house, taking up counter and refrigerator space. If Claire had been the kind of woman who hated to cook this food might have been welcomed, but she liked stirring stew, roasting potatoes, basting a ham and while she hadn't been in the mood to cook all week, she missed her own food, the things she and Matthew and Preston ate at her table, in a normal world that did not feel as if it were swimming underwater.

Today the food had gotten worse. Jillian Donners had brought a lasagna and Halle Coleman a batch of fried chicken. People were over, it was just after the funeral and of course there had to be a get-together. Like following a wedding or a christening it's not enough to simply go to the church, to listen to the priest, sprinkle some water, sing a hymn—more had to be done, fellowship had to be experienced no matter how macabre and so there was now this party. Claire had been expecting it. When her friend Linda lost her mother last year everyone had piled into their cars after the body was laid to rest, expecting to dish out plates of potato salad and summer squash as if it were a very solemn, very somber barbeque.

Cara List stood near the counter tossing a salad, two forks working away, shaking the lettuce and tomatoes as she turned and glanced at Megan, Preston's friend, Tom Craig's mother, who lived three streets away. They looked like regular women (and it had been so long since Clare had felt like a regular woman), heads tilted toward each other, eyes focused but willing to wander, hands animated. They seemed lost in conversation, as the salad was absentmindedly manhandled and Claire watched them, arms wrapped around herself, feeling weak, as if she might just tumble to the floor. But there was something about it, she couldn't look away, it was so normal, so natural and all she wanted was to be the kind of woman who could just do that again. Cara List nodded knowingly as Claire turned around, walking back through the dining room to look out the windows of the double French doors. They hadn't yet taken the swing set down, though Matthew had put Preston's bike and the little playhouse away in the garage. Taking a screwdriver to the wooden poles and hauling the big aluminum slide up to the attic above the garage felt like too much of an undertaking, too much of a sign that it was over, really over. Not that the yard didn't look as if it had aged a hundred years.

The clamor went on at her back and Claire tried not to notice it. It had been three days of preparation, none of which she'd wanted to do. Her mother had come out from Chicago, as had her sister; they were now sitting on the couch in the family room, sniffling as they went through an old photo album. Her mother had called the funeral home and most of the arrangements had been made through Claire, around and over Claire, though not by her. They thought he should have a powder blue casket with fine, white lining–go ahead; they wanted to read an excerpt from the Velveteen Rabbit–good idea; serve coffee at the wake–great. Everything suggested was fine with her; Claire had no complaints, no needs. There was nothing she wanted and there was no way for the wake, the funeral, even the burial in Matthew's family plot across from the church, to make anything seem better or worse. The priest had wanted Matthew to say a few words, knowing full well Claire wasn't up to it. Her husband had bravely gotten up and spoken about a time he and Preston had gone bowling without bumpers, how he'd always hoped to be able to kindle in his son a love for the Red Sox.

"I took my son to a bar once," Matthew had said. "It was a bar at a pizza place, nothing too wild, and he ordered one of those root beers that come in a glass bottle, that look, you know, like the real deal. I remember watching him and thinking that we had our whole lives together, I remember thinking 'You know, some day I'm going to be able to have a beer with my son.' I just wish I could have been able to have a beer with my son." Matthew teared up, he patted his eyes as he spoke, but did not break down; he simply stood, letting everyone know that he'd had a son, he'd loved him and now he was gone.

Claire looked away from the window and back at this gathering that had transpired against her will. She wanted to watch it all, letting the waves wash against her, to fall to the floor in tears, to grab hold of the carpet to anchor herself before she was tossed out to sea. She just wanted to feel this grief, to let it permeate, to be an all-consuming physical specimen of it, but she had to put on the hostess's face. She was an adult and adults held their tongues; they nodded politely and did not scream in the faces of well-wishers, no matter how old the "I'm sorry"'s got. Adults did not throw a fit because their son was dead while others had been spared. No matter how badly she just wanted to scream right now, societal conventions, the pull of the real world, which was enlightened and civilized, was too strong. She'd given that up for a little while, she'd turned into a bleeding animal at the morgue, and every night alone in her bed, she thrashed and cried and screamed. But to let her connection, even her small connection, to the world go completely would be to lose so much more.

"Claire, there you are," Cara List said, having just set the salad she'd been tossing on the table near an aluminum tray of lasagna and a pitcher of iced tea. "I thought I saw you earlier," she went on, grasping Claire's arm, which was clenched tight. "It was a lovely service, really a lovely service and it just makes me feel so…" Cara didn't finish, instead she shook her head, and Claire could see that she was fighting off tears.

"Hey! Hey!" Peyton cried, running energetically at his mother and grabbing onto her legs as Eva followed. "Over here, I'm over here," he shouted and his mother looked down at him, horrified, as Eva stayed still, staring up at Claire as if she were afraid of her.

"Peyton Andrew List," Cara hissed, visibly embarrassed. "You know better, you calm down and go sit by your father," she instructed with that Mom voice, the kind of tone only certain women could pull off, a tone Claire was sure she did not possess anymore. "I'm so sorry, I don't know what's gotten into him. I've tried to explain to him what happened to Preston, but he doesn't really understand yet and he won't stop acting up. I always thought he'd be a little older before we'd have to start talking about this."

"I know," Claire replied, still hugging herself. She could feel the warmth of her own body, as if the rest of the world were freezing.

"And I just want you to know how sorry I am...how I didn't know and if I had, I wish I had known to call the police when Preston didn't come back to our house. Maybe if I'd done that they would have found him sooner." Cara shook her head and Claire watched her neighbor. She didn't want to blame her, not for neglecting to contact Claire about Preston's leaving her house or for being the mother to initiate the newfound freedom the children had been allowed this year. She couldn't blame her, and though part of Claire really wanted to accuse this woman she knew it would do nothing, it would mean nothing and what was the point—Cara List hadn't poisoned him.

Claire gave Cara the tiniest, tightest smile as she gently touched her arm and walked away, saying a slow, quiet "thank you." Claire knew in another world she'd never have been so impolite to her friend, but she couldn't concentrate now, the pills had wrapped a blanket around her mind and she could barely focus on the people here. Cara stayed behind, turning once Claire left and tending to the salad that a few neighbors had started to dig into. "No, no, no, make sure you take the avocado," Claire could hear her neighbor instruct as she left.

She turned into the living room to find Eva's parents standing there. Claire had never known Gloria and Derrick Murphy very well. Sometimes they chatted at school functions, a paper cup of weak coffee in their hands as they discussed the PTA, the latest class play, what the school was planning to do about the cricket problem. They were doctors and didn't have a lot of time; Eva's last nanny, who'd left a year ago to start a family of her own, had basically raised her.

"I'm so sorry," Gloria Murphy said, grasping Claire's arm as the grieving mother looked at her. She was a pediatric oncologist and Claire was sure this woman had said these exact same words many times to other mothers before. "I can still hear your voice on the phone when Preston went missing, I shudder each time."

"We're really sorry, Claire," Eva's father added stiffly. He was, Claire had heard, the brilliant surgeon the hospital called in when all was lost. He had an entire team of doctors behind him and had probably rarely had to leave an operating room to tell a family they'd lost a patient. He had a staff for that.

"Thank you," Claire replied, nodding kindly, not knowing what else she could do. She pursed her lips and stared at the floor until Gloria Murphy grasped her husband's arm and, sensing Claire's discomfort, moved to walk away.

"Well if you need anything…"

"Thank you, I know," Claire said, moving further into the living room.

She turned and there was Matthew standing with a plastic cup resting at his lips. He sipped from it as he watched Kyle Clinter, his golf buddy, who seemed to be explaining something. Todd Snider and Terrell Jacobs were also standing around as if they were in the driveway after a mid-afternoon basketball game, the kind she'd seen her husband partake in on many a Saturday afternoon. Matthew casually shuffled two steps away from the conversation, but remained with his friends as they surely commented on how "awful" this all was.

The front door opened; Claire turned her head just as it began to creak. No one else noticed it; people had been moving in and out of the house all day. This was the kind of gathering where people came and went, opening the door as if this house had become, at least for the time being, communal property. Only this time it wasn't any old neighbor who entered, or Father Sherman who'd said the Mass, or one of Matthew's mother's friends from Andover. It was the neighbor from two streets down, the one from the cul-de-sac near where Preston had been found, Gregory Hawthorne.

He was a youngish man, his features played up by a pouty baby-face. Gregory was probably about thirty-two, thirty-three, with prematurely thinning dark hair, a pale face and watery blue eyes, the kind of eyes that belonged not to a grown man, but to an old person. He was hunched when he walked and looked too skinny yet a little chunky at the same time. He was the kind of man who would have been made fun of on the playground, the kind who might never have gotten over it. He worked with computers, that was the generic job description the people in the neighborhood gave, he'd made a lot of money that way and he'd never been spotted with a woman, or a man for that matter. Sometimes he could be seen outside shooting baskets in his driveway, only he didn't do it like the teenagers did, he didn't play with anyone else and was always attempting long, elaborate shots and then celebrating excessively, and a bit too loudly, whenever one went in. He stayed alone in his house and ordered his food in; sometimes he had a housekeeper cook for him. It was rumored that he never kept one for longer than a couple of months because, as Shannon Forrester's old nanny had said, "He is too picky, too picky for everyone, they all quit."

He came in wearing a dark blue T-shirt and black jeans. He walked on two steady legs and still it seemed as if he were stumbling. His wide eyes seemed terrified of something, like a kid who knows he's done something wrong and can't make eye contact, and yet he kept on walking, right until he was nearly in the middle of the living room, facing Claire.

"I just want to say," he fumbled and Matthew moved away from his friends, to stand between Gregory Hawthorne and his wife. "Mrs. Tumber, I am so incredibly sorry," the man said, sniffling. "And I didn't know...I mean..." He kept talking despite the tremor in his voice, and the way his hands had started shaking.

"Who the hell do you think you are, coming in here?" Matthew called. "What is wrong with you?"

"Matthew, stop it," Claire shouted and she could hear her own voice pierce the room. She sounded like a wife, a wife trying to keep her husband from getting out of control.

"I didn't know....I swear to God," the man mumbled. "Mary and Mary Clark..." Gregory kept stammering.

The police had been to his house twice to talk to him, they'd come with a warrant once and searched the place, trashing the inside, or so the Huxburries, who lived next door to him, had said. They couldn't find anything, and there was no proof that Gregory was the culprit, only the fact that Preston had been found so close to the Hawthorne house, that Gregory Hawthorne had gone to the hospital with a stomach ache that same night that Preston had been poisoned, that they'd found he'd been poisoned with traces of the same chemical... But Claire, as the grieving mother, only could know so much, and still the police did nothing, because a stomachache, they said, was not enough in the way of proof.

"I want you to go," Matthew said, calmly but forcefully through clenched teeth, and the man still stood there. He looked shriveled, as if a giant monster had taken his entire body in its fist and crushed him.

"I'm so sorry. And he was such a nice boy," Mr. Hawthorne groveled, looking at Claire, he reached out, taking a step toward her. Matthew moved in, grabbed Gregory Hawthorne's arm and pushed him back.

"Get out of here!" he cried. "Didn't you hear me, I said get out!" he was shouting and though no one else could see it, Claire could tell, because she knew her husband, that he was ten, maybe twelve seconds from crying. "I said get out!" Matthew yelled, and though the get-together had stopped, though this solemn gathering had already fallen to its knees, it seemed to break and shatter like glass as Matthew, the father, lost his cool.

"Hey," Terrell said to Gregory, "I think it's time you get going."

"I don't think they want you here," Kyle elaborated, and Gregory Hawthorne stumbled back.

"I just wanted to say," he went on, looking at Claire like a little boy who is truly sorry for something. "I mean, I just wanted you to know, just you, as his mother, that…" He took two more steps toward Claire and she wondered, even with all these people here, should she be afraid?

"Get out!" Matthew cried, and lunged at the man; he had him on the floor in three seconds, holding him down. He swung once, swung twice and Claire couldn't tell if her husband had hit him, but one of the women cried out and Terrell and Kyle ran toward Matthew, picking him up and setting him right. Another one of his friends stood Gregory Hawthorne up, looked him over and grabbed his arm, half dragging, half walking him through the front door and tossing him into the yard.

"I'm sorry," Matthew apologized to the entire gathering, which had stopped to watch. "I'm sorry," he said, sauntering away toward their bedroom. One of his friends looked to Claire and she followed her husband—she knew it was her job even in all this to follow him. That's what adults do, that's what the wife of a grieving husband is for, to follow, to sacrifice, to not break down even when all she wants is to fall to her knees.

As she turned toward the stairs to their bedroom, she passed the window in the foyer. Claire looked out of it for a second, half expecting to see her son's shiny red bike. Instead Gregory Hawthorne was standing there, about to walk away. He shook his head, he turned around, but not before their eyes met and Claire wasn't sure if it was pity she felt for him.

PRESTON

Preston did not remember going to sleep and he did not recall waking up the next day, but after a certain amount of time (as if time were another thing here) he opened his eyes and found that he was in bed. He heard the other kids playing down below, and when he glanced out his window he saw them tumbling off the Ferris wheel, nearly crashing to their deaths before picking themselves up and flying away.

Just after he awoke, as if on cue, a knock sounded on his door and Preston answered it. He didn't call out, like he would have at home when his mother knocked and then barged right in, usually with a laundry hamper full of clothes. Preston could see that the leader and his Lost Boys had a certain respect for a person's space. He opened the door, rubbing his eyes, to find the boy called Peter. He looked exactly the same as he had the night before in his green shorts and T-shirt; his scraggly hair appeared to have leaves in it and that impish grin was plastered across his rugged, though delicate, face.

"Hi," he said. "I wanted to see how you were doing. I was wondering if you were ready."

"Ready for what?"

"For the tour. Usually kids come all together and I give them the tour, or one of the Lost Boys does it, or a couple of them, or I get the fairies to do it, but you came on your own and so you get a private tour."

"I'm different?" Preston asked and all of a sudden he felt sad as he remembered once more. "I can't go back there? Home, I can't go back?"

"You can't go back," the leader reiterated as they walked along the wide branch of the tree Preston's room sat on. The sounds of TV shows, some Preston recognized, or video games with their "pow, pow, peeeew, peeeew," filtered through the doors.

"I remember people, Peyton, Eva," Preston started recalling the memories that had come flooding in last night. "I remember what the house looked like and the trees. There were always a lot of trees."

"Trees are good, there are a lot of trees here," the boy replied.

"I used to hide in them," Preston elaborated. "Where are we exactly?"

"We're Here," the boy said simply, scratching his head. "They call it Neverland because it's a place where children never grow up. I mean, that was the simple way to describe it when she woke up and they ran with it."

"I know Neverland," Preston stopped, remembering further back, to a television and a cartoon of a little boy on a windowsill. "Are you him, are you the. . .you said your name was Peter…are you the Peter?"

"That's what they started calling me, Peter Pan," the boy said as if he didn't know what to do with that kind of question. "This place has been here forever, well before the stories, and one of them came back and she told everyone else about it and some man wrote a play and they were all telling stories and writing books and making movies and now the boys who come Here think they know everything. And it's good, it's good that she told them because now no one is afraid, they think they've been Here before, they think they know it. But I guess to give it a name misses the point and it's just Here and you'll be Here for a while until you're somewhere else. But then again I like calling it Neverland. . .I don't make up my mind easily. But this isn't the end. You can't spend all the time in the universe running around a Ferris wheel and hunting Indians." The boy's words came out of him in a single breath and it was as if his mind were going a mile a minute.

"There are Indians?" Preston asked as they reached the edge of the branch.

"There are," Peter answered. "Now, what do you remember of Before?"

"I remember trees," Preston replied. "And Mr. Hawthorne gave me cookies."

"He did," Peter said as if he knew.

"Then I felt really, really sick, and I went to sleep in the trees and woke up Here."

"I know," Peter went on, hands behind his back as if he were thinking long and hard about something.

"So it was Mr. Hawthorne's fault and he poisoned me," Preston reasoned, speaking as the words came. "He must have done this to me, but he was so nice."

"You shouldn't jump to conclusions," Peter interrupted. "It's okay," he then said. "It's okay," he looked at him as Preston felt tears coming and Peter wiped them before they reached the middle of his cheeks. "We're all going to take care of you," he said and then he walked right off the edge of the branch.

"Peter!" Preston cried, too frightened to care or wonder or miss his Mom just then. The boy came back up, he didn't look like he was swimming as the other boys had, he was just standing there, right on the air, as if he could simply walk on it.

"It's okay," he said. "Come here, I'll show you, you can do it too."

"With fairy dust and happy thoughts?" Preston asked remembering these instructions from Before.

"No," Peter shook his head. "Just walk off the branch and if you know you'll be okay, if you know you can fly, you'll be fine. All children think happy thoughts, they don't have problems, they don't have worries, we're all a bundle of happy thoughts and so we don't have to start thinking them, and as for fairy dust, it's all around, it's in the air, it's a part of the makeup of this place, you don't need a special dose of it."

"Really?" Preston asked and Peter shook his head Yes.

"Step off and see; I want to show you around," Peter called and with that he flew away, doing a double loop and coming right at Preston, who tumbled off the branch, his eyes closed as he nearly hit the ground. Peter was there with him, ready to catch him, and with the sense of the leader's presence, he felt safe, and it lifted him, he felt light and airy, moving through the sky as Peter followed.

They cascaded over the tree house and Preston nearly got caught up in the red bars of the Ferris wheel, but he turned at the last second, as another boy fell off and flew with them for a while. Preston closed his eyes as they dashed above the trees, soaring so he could see this entire place. It was land and it went on for miles, then there was a curve toward the water and he could see a misty lagoon, and on the other side there was a forest where a bunch of tepees stood across from a group of log cabins. Most of it was forest, all those trees separating each world from another, but one group of trees was so lit up it looked as if it was on fire, burning uncontrollably. Preston turned around, and he could see a ship in the water, a big black one that, even from far away, looked as if it was enveloped in smoke.

"Don't look there," Peter gasped, grabbing Preston and bringing him back to the ground. "You don't want to see it and they can't know we're watching them."

"Who?" Preston asked and though he was starting to recall everything else, things from Before, he still couldn't heed the pirate warnings.

"We don't look at pirates," Peter said forcefully. "That's all, just stay away from them; you can fly anywhere you want, just not by them. And you'll know where they are—you'll start to lose your happy thoughts, you won't be able to fly."

"So what're we up to today?" Preston heard a voice call from behind and turned to see Starky followed by Dilweed coming out of the trees. Starky was still wearing his blazer and shorts, but

Dilweed had changed and now wore nicer jeans and a black T-shirt with an emblem Preston couldn't recognize on it.

"He's Remembering," Peter said, descending to the ground as everyone followed him. "I'm going to show him around."

"You're not going to wait for the other kids to come?" Dilweed inquired.

"Can we show him around with you?" Starky asked, eyes wide, mouth gaping open like a happy puppy.

"Of course you can," Peter replied as if to even ask the question didn't make sense.

"What're you going to show him first?" Dilweed asked, seeming to consider whether he'd participate.

"I was going to show him Mermaid Lagoon first and then the cowboys and Indians and then the fairies and maybe we'd go over to the caves and the Neverbird..."

"I want to go," Dilweed announced and Peter chuckled, holding his hands over his stomach as if to keep the joy inside.

"Is that all right with you? Do you want to see the mermaids and the cowboys and Indians?" Peter asked Preston.

"You have cowboys *and* Indians?"

"We have both," Peter explained. "Sometimes they're not cowboys and Indians, sometimes they're policemen and firefighters, or they're teachers and students or they're soldiers on two sides of an army, recently they've been elves and hobbits—it doesn't matter, as long as there are two groups of them."

"Okay," Preston responded and they moved along. Preston might have preferred to fly, he was starting to like the idea, but he didn't mind walking.

At the edge of the forest, where the trees got thicker, so thick Preston thought it might be time to lift himself off the ground so as not to trudge through the bramble, he heard a soft, low rumbling, like the branches of trees shaking. "Holy Cow, no!" Dilweed hissed, grasping Starky, who stood bravely in front, but visibly afraid.

"What is it?" Preston asked, wondering if he had real cause for worry, since there didn't appear to be any actual threats in Neverland when the pirates weren't around.

"Boxwood's here. I hope he doesn't know about you, I hope he didn't find us," Dilweed replied, taking a few steps back as the rumbling grew louder and Peter stood between the boys and the woods.

A boy appeared from the trees like a wounded animal, screaming and hissing before he stopped and stared at them. At first Preston didn't think he was seeing anything, it was as if he were watching make-believe, the child was so unchild-like. He was a little taller than Preston, though not as tall as Peter, and he slumped when he walked, back arched, feet dragging as if he, not just his feet, were broken. He was pale white, like in a horror movie, and there was blood caked on his lips and under his nose like he'd been out eating raw animals. His clothes looked very old, he had a wide gray collared shirt and a black overcoat with holes in the pockets and when he opened his mouth, Preston saw that two teeth were missing and the rest were visibly black. The boy hissed at them, first like a snake and then like a disturbed cat, he looked at the Lost Boys, but also past them, as if he knew there was something there, but couldn't tell what it was.

"Who...what is that?" Preston asked, looking away. He wanted to fly with Peter, but none of them moved.

"It's Boxwood," Peter explained. "He's been here too long. He's starting to grow up."

"What?" Preston asked, looking back at the boy, who did not seem a day past eleven, maybe twelve. "How old was he when he came?"

They all looked at Preston, distraught, and in that instant Boxwood, who appeared to be biding his time, ran at them, grasping Dilweed's arm and biting right into it. "Ouch!" Dilweed cried, pulling away. The raving boy stepped back and Peter started to yell at him as if he were a dog.

"Go on! Go! Shoo, shoo! Go away, go away!" he cried and the boy shivered for an instant, looking like he might attack he was so confused, but instead he ran the other way, back into the woods.

"What happened?" Preston asked, still perturbed. He had been under the impression that if a boy could fall from a tree and be perfectly fine, then he should not bleed after another has bitten him. Before his question could be answered Preston saw a white light coming out of the forest. A few fairies danced on Dilweed's arm until the bleeding stopped and he was healed.

"It's like he's a pirate," Peter explained. "He's been Here too long and I don't know why the Island keeps holding on to him. Every time I think about taking him to the After, first when he was a nice little boy, a boy who had been around for a while, but still a nice boy, the Island told me not to. Then he started to go bad. First he was just cranky, but then he started doing these weird things, pulling the heads off animals, and taking knives from dinner and stabbing other boys with them. Again I wanted to take him, but the Island still said no. Then he left, he ran into the forest and now he just sort of haunts it. He's not a pirate, and the pirates won't have him, he's not one of them. So he lives in the woods and whenever we see him he attacks us. But don't worry, even if he hurts you, the fairies can heal you, that's their job, and he won't follow for long. He's really afraid of loud noises."

"He was a boy like us?" Preston asked. "What happens if you stay Here too long?"

"You grow up," Peter replied. "But not the good kind of grow up like where you fall in love and get married and have kids, or the kind where you learn a lot of new things. Nope, you get cruel, you get mean, you turn into that. . .like a pirate." Peter shook his head and looked over at Starky, who was checking Dilweed's arm, which was fine now, not even a mark. "There are all different signs of growing up, cruelty is one of them; children are not cruel like grownups are and when children are cruel, it's because they learned it from grownups."

"Oh," Preston replied, wanting to know more, but wondering if he should ask.

"Come on," Peter called, perking up, "let's fly over to Mermaid Lagoon."

"Yes!" Starky cried coming off the ground and twirling into the sky as if they'd all forgotten that fiasco. He was over their heads, above the trees, before Peter could catch up. Peter was the next to rocket away, Dilweed following close behind. Preston waited a second until the boys were over his head. He shook the mean, scary boy out of his thoughts and once they were gone, once the memory of the Ferris wheel and video games, of Starky and Dilweed returned, Preston soared over the forest.

He could feel the wind, it had been calm down in the trees, but once he took flight he could sense the air around him, and the shimmering sheet of gold and silver dust that sparkled in an incredible light. It felt like swimming, as if there was nothing to hold onto as Peter led them across the Island.

Peter hovered over a pond-like body of water as Dilweed and Starky followed. "There they are," he cried, pointing down as he nosedived into the lagoon. Preston and the two boys followed, watching as Peter did not back down, cascading through the plane of water and coming up a few seconds later, after Preston, Starky and Dilweed had landed safely on a rock. "That was fun!" he cried, coming up soaking wet, his blond locks dripping as he shook them free like a dog. Peter flew high into the air, careening back down and landing delicately on the surface of the lagoon, directly on top of the water. "Hello down there," he called. "Are you there, is anyone there?"

The mermaids came up, there could have been fifty or a hundred, their silky, wet heads emerging from the bright blue water. Three of them stayed longer than a moment, heads bobbing, placidly smiling as their fish tails splashed the surface.

"What's down there?" Preston asked leaning over his rock.

"Stay back, only Peter can go near them," Dilweed warned.

"They'll pull you in and drown you if you get too close," Peter explained.

The mermaids continued bobbing, smiling and politely laughing, as they pointed past Peter at Preston. Preston could see their forms under the water, some of them had large bellies, others were bleeding from their stomachs, though they didn't appear to be in pain. "That's where the mermaids live," Starky explained. "They have a whole underwater kingdom with houses and Ferris wheels, there are even castles down there."

"Can we go?" Preston asked, excited by the prospect of underwater castles.

"We can't go to the mermaid kingdom, not even I can hold my breath that long," Peter explained. "They'll pull us in, they'll make us stay until we drown if we let them. Not that downing matters Here, you'd wake right up again, but it's still unpleasant."

"Why are they bleeding?" Preston asked. "Why are their stomachs so big?"

"The mermaids came Here like the rest of you. They come from Before and they're all going After, but they're grownups. Everyone else is a grownup."

"I thought this place was for kids?" Preston asked feeling a little lost.

"It is for kids," Peter explained. "Everyone Here is somehow tied to children. The mermaids are mothers who came Here because they died during childbirth. That's why they're all girls and they're the only girls Here, except the fairies of course, they're girls as well, but they didn't come Here like the mermaids."

"They're mothers who died in childbirth?" Preston inquired.

"They come Here for a while. But they're not all happy, they want a child of their own and most of the time their babies survived, besides, babies don't come Here, you have to be over a certain age. That's why they'll pull you under, they'll drown you if you're not careful," Peter explained. "They don't talk to us. There used to be a lot more of them, now we only get a few a day and they're usually gone within an hour."

"Why do they come?" Preston asked and Peter scratched his head.

"I don't know, they're just Here."

The mermaids, who had been watching, flitted their tails and swam away. Preston could see the large belly of one as her bright blue tail flashed through the sequenced water, parting the sun as it shone off the miniscule waves.

"D'you want to see the cowboys and Indians?" Starky asked, jumping up and down.

"Okay," Preston replied, eyes still on the glistening water. Peter rose into the air and the two boys followed. They were off on their way before Preston noticed and, not wanting to get lost, he trailed them into the air and over the forest.

They flew swiftly across the trees to a place where smoke rose through the branches. The island looked so large when Preston took it in all at once, but it didn't take long to fly anywhere, Mermaid Lagoon had only been a few seconds away and as soon as he glided over the forest Preston landed next to Peter at a clear spot in the trees.

He could hear the sounds of drums and tambourines as the wild cries of a man's melodic wailing rang out nearby. "That's the Indians," Dilweed explained, whispering importantly into Preston's ear. "They're always singing and dancing and having parties when they're not hunting cowboys or us kids. Even when they are hunting us they're having a party."

"What do the cowboys do?" Preston asked, looking to Peter, though it appeared all the boys had the answers to his questions.

"The cowboys stay in the saloon when they're not trying to get the Lost Boys or the Indians," Peter explained. "They pour over books and strategize. The Indians don't like strategy, they just do what they do and sometimes they win and sometimes they lose, but they just have fun. But the cowboys are always trying to make a plan."

"Can we start a war with them?" Preston asked, jumping excitedly at the prospect. He could remember a game like this, only not with real cowboys and Indians, with Eva and Peyton where Peyton had been the bad guy and Eva was the princess and Preston had had to save her, but in the end Eva had had to run home for her flute lesson and the game wasn't much fun without her. But Preston knew enough about this place to know that there were no flute lessons and no one had to go home for dinner.

"They're at our disposal," Peter explained as if he could read Preston's thoughts as he watched through the trees as three grown men wearing rawhide pants and brown jackets with fringe on the sleeves danced around a fire singing. A man walked bravely into the camp; he wasn't one of the Indians, who stopped abruptly at his arrival. He had a large white cowboy hat on and wore leather pants and big boots. Once he appeared more cowboys emerged. Preston couldn't hear what they were saying, but after a second they seemed as if they were drawing invisible weapons, the cowboys using their hands as guns, the thumbs as triggers as the Indians reached their arms behind their heads to start shooting with invisible bows and arrows.

"What're they doing?" Preston asked as all four boys stood in the woods, their eyes glued to the battle about to be waged.

"They're fighting a war," Peter explained as the Indians began to cry louder, sounding the alarm as the cowboys ran fast at them, making "bang-bang" sounds with their "guns." They watched for a while, a few cowboys fell over and the Indians dragged them away as one Indian was grabbed by two cowboys and pulled into the forest. They ran around like this, shooting and crying out until finally out of nowhere they stopped, the cowboys who had fallen to the ground got up and walked back to the other side of the clearing to their own kind, and the Indian who'd been captured walked away from the cowboys and back to the Tepees.

"Why are they Here?" Preston asked. "They look like grownups," he went on, remembering that grownups had never acted that way in the Before.

"They're like the mermaids, they're tied to kids in some way," Dilweed explained.

"The cowboys are more the bad guys than the Indians, though neither of them are really bad," Peter elaborated. "The cowboys came Here because they unintentionally harmed a child. This is sort of a waiting place for them to learn to understand children better. Some of them weren't paying attention and ran over a kid with their car, a few of them were told by a child that something bad was happening and ignored it. They come Here when it's their time, but they go to the After like everyone else, they're not that bad, they didn't do anything bad on purpose. The Indians are more the good guys, they're Here because they helped children in some special way. They're Here to be with us, to understand the goodness, the happiness of children, before going to the After. They win more wars than the cowboys."

Preston turned and watched an Indian. This one didn't look like the Indians he'd seen in books and movies, he had short brown hair and pale skin, but he was dressed like the Indians in the old Westerns his father sometimes watched with him. As this Indian stuck a twig into the fire Preston saw a flash of that man inside his head like he was watching from behind a video screen. He was wearing jeans and a flannel shirt and he was in a driveway like the one at Preston's house. He saw the Indian run across the driveway and pick up a little boy just before a car crashed into the side of a house.

"Why do they have to come Here at all?" Preston asked, scratching his head as he watched an Indian, who didn't really look like an Indian, talking to a cowboy. Preston watched the cowboy closely and could see everything that needed to be seen. He saw a flash of white and there was the cowboy driving a car, talking on his phone and not looking at the road. Preston heard a car screech, the driver (the cowboy, though he looked like a man in a business suit) turned the wheel and felt a thud that caused his heart to sink. He saw the cowboy waiting at a hospital, shaking his head as a doctor told him something. He saw the cowboy in a black suit at a funeral, looking down at a tiny coffin, then there was the cowboy with a yellowish drink in his hand, downing it with a bunch of pills, over and over again until he fell to the ground and woke up Here.

"I can see them, what was that?" Preston asked and Peter, who'd been watching him very closely, nodded.

"Only the kids can do that. You know where everyone has been, who everyone is. It's for the best that you know. You don't have to see it, you can look away, but this is another reason why you shouldn't visit the pirates," Peter explained. "You see," he went on as Starky and Dilweed ran off to play, "There are certain things about growing up that we as children should understand. Growing up is about five things. Number one is emotions, having and understanding feelings; number two is intellectual, it's about getting smart and understanding the world around you; number three is about something called society, like your friends and the people around you, and how you act around them; number four is physical; and number five is about cruelty, like Boxwood, like the pirates. It's so much more than that, but that's basically what it means to grow up and we have it Here, and we can watch it even if we won't ever be it. Though some of the grownups in the Before, although they are adults, have never grown up. And for them it's very hard, they never really fit in with the child world, nor do they fit with adults. A lot of them end up Here."

Preston nodded at Peter, who seemed to make sense, though the explanation had been so long winded, he wasn't sure where the speech had started or ended. There was something about Peter, even with his childish manner, that seemed not grown up, but almost, like he was trying very hard to understand growing up, it was on the tip of his tongue, but he just wasn't there. And what was worse, it seemed as if he knew he'd never get there.

"It looks like the fight is over," Starky said a little disappointedly. "Let's show him the fairies."

"Can we see the fairies?" Preston asked and the leader shook his head yes.

"We can look over their part of the forest, but we can't go into the fairy world."

"Why?" Preston asked. "I thought this place was for us."

"There are kids there and we're not allowed to meet those kids yet. Some kids have to go to the fairies first, before they can play with us, so we can't bother the fairies; they come to us whenever they're ready."

"What about when there aren't any kids for the fairies?" Preston asked.

"I wish there was a time when there weren't any kids for the fairies, it would be much better," Peter said sadly. "Let's go," he went on, that impish smile returning as he lifted off the ground and started flying, Starky and Dilweed following closely behind.

They flew over the trees, hovering just above where they started flowering. The new green leaves looked as if they were stoking a great fire and Peter whistled as he glanced down, bobbing like a mermaid in water as he hovered. A few white lights flew up to them, twirling around Peter, and the boy laughed hysterically as if they were tickling him. When Peter caught his breath, he pointed to Preston and one of the lights landed on his arm. Preston could feel it, it was bright, but soft and silky; he tried to look into it, but the light was too intense and all he could see was yellow-white glowing so brightly as if he were looking into the sun.

Peter whistled again and all the fairies dispersed except one, who hovered on his shoulder as if it were about to touch his face. "This is my friend Tinkerbelle. I found her when the fairies came and she's been Here ever since," Peter explained and the light flickered on and off as if it were speaking. "Oh stop that, you," he said at the ball of light before turning to Preston and explaining. "She gets terribly jealous."

"What did she say?" Preston asked.

"Oh, you wouldn't want to know," Peter replied.

"The new boys are almost ready, Peter, they're almost cured," Starky said, lifting himself further into the air.

"Shh…hush you," Dilweed cried, clocking Starky on the arm as Peter stood listening to the Tinkerbelle fairy buzz in his ear.

"Do they live here?" Preston asked and Peter shook his head no.

"This is an outpost, they live in the Fairy Forest, but we don't go there," Peter explained as Tinkerbelle hovered around him.

"So what are the fairies?" Preston asked. "The cowboys are people and the mermaids and Indians are too, but what are the fairies? Are they people?"

"Do they look like people?" Dilweed remarked as if Preston had just asked a very silly question.

"They're not human," Peter elaborated more patiently. "They came after me. There was me and then there were the fairies and I spent a lot of time playing with them before the cowboys and Indians, before the children showed up."

"What are they?" Preston asked again.

"The story is true I assure you. 'When the first baby laughed for the first time, the laugh broke into a thousand pieces and they became fairies,'" Peter explained as if he were reciting. "That's from the book. And after the first baby laughed the fairies came Here. And they do a little more than keep us company," Peter explained, looking down at the trees that twinkled as if they were touched by tiny shards of the sun and moon. "They help kids who come to us, or if the pirates come. . .but they've kept their distance for a while."

"I thought kids fought pirates?" Preston asked. He'd been so good about not mentioning pirates, but now that Peter had brought them up they seemed like fair game.

"I don't know how he got out that time, or why she told them that. He wasn't very nice to her," Peter thought out loud. Preston glanced over at Dilweed, who was looking right through Peter as if he wanted to slug him like he slugged Starky whenever he said something he shouldn't have, but Peter was Peter and didn't get slugged. "I'm sorry," he went on, shaking his head as if freeing himself from a trance. "It's just that you're here and you came the same way and it has me thinking."

"It's dangerous to think too much, Peter," Dilweed warned.

"You're right Dil, yes you are, you are right," Peter said enthusiastically.

"So why aren't there any girls?" Preston asked, remembering Eva. "Other than fairies or mermaids. Do girl children come Here?"

"They do not," Peter answered. "This is for boys. There's another one for girls. I don't know anything about it, I've never been There."

"It's probably filled with princesses and unicorns and rainbows and junk," Starky complained, sticking his tongue out as if to dispel a bad taste.

"That's probably right. Children, girls and boys, they get their own place, they're not grownups," Peter explained, flying just a tad higher than everyone else. The fairies flew with him, quietly trailing, but all of a sudden Peter slammed back down, tunneling toward the trees as Dilweed and Starky followed. Preston remained where he was, unsure of what to do. After a second he felt a hand pull him down, careening with him until he was smack on the forest floor.

"What was that?" Preston asked and Starky looked at him, out of breath. "Where's Peter?"

"He's back up there, scouting," Starky whispered. "He's gotta make sure the pirates didn't see us."

"Why?" Preston asked. "I didn't see anything. I thought they left us alone."

"They leave us alone because they can't see us. They move outside the Cove sometimes, looking for us. If they found out where we lived they might go after us. Peter says it's bad, it's really bad."

"Shut up, Starky," Dilweed hissed, his voice not above a whisper. "Don't be scaring him like that. The pirates aren't going to get us, and they can't see Peter, not with the fairies around, the pirates aren't like us, they can't see beyond the fairies' brightness, it's like we're invisible."

"Peter has to check," Starky elaborated as Peter flew back down, slip-streaming through the air and landing on his feet.

"I didn't see anything," he announced. "That is to say that they didn't see anything. We're okay, but we should know better, we're not supposed to fly that high, not like that, not even with the fairies, but Tinkerbelle was there and she helped us, she made sure they didn't have a chance."

"What're they doing outside the Cove?" Dilweed asked.

"I don't know," Peter said, shaking his head and looking over at Preston. "Strange things are happening."

"I hope it's not like that other time," Starky pondered.

"Shut up," Dilweed warned very seriously and Preston put his hands behind his back, wondering if he should be scared. He had a strange urge to go back. He hadn't wanted to leave until now, he knew this was all very odd, he knew things were off, he missed his mother and father, whom he'd never see again, but something about those pirates. . . .

"Ah, it's okay. Nothing is going to go wrong and it wasn't that bad that time they came, and if it happens again we'll fight them. You forget, you always forget that I'm Peter and nothing bad is going to happen to you while I'm around. And I'm around forever. Nothing can end me, it says so right there at the edge of the world, where eternity was made."

"That's right," Starky called loudly.

"Here, here," Dilweed added and all three boys put their hands together in a high five as they flew toward the tree house.

Just then, as they were flying away, they all closed their eyes as a bright and powerful light slid by them, cascading across their bodies as they remained still in the air. This was not like the other times the fairies had come, something was happening and Preston placed his hands to his ears so as not to hear the humming of the wind.

"What's that?" he asked when the wind died down and the bright lights had moved from the front of the tree house to the back as the boys followed. They weren't the only ones out, all the boys, even the inside boys and the ones who played far into the forest, were huddled near the tree house, looking up at the sky.

"Come on," Dilweed called, running in the direction of the light, pushing past more boys as they ran after it. Some of the boys reached out, trying to grab the fairies flying overhead, but none of them could hold on as they ran, a great stampede to the back of the trees.

It was a giant party and though this entire place was like a celebration, this was different, this moved so fast Preston felt as if he couldn't catch up. He'd never seen all the boys together. There were hundreds of them. They looked different, different races, different heights, some of them looked too old to be boys, towering over the rest and, seeming to know they were right on the cusp of being too old to come here as children, they stood in back, watching over the others.

It was Peter who wasn't there when the fairies stopped, resting in a clearing at the edge of the forest. A great whirling wind followed the bright lights of the fairies, one Preston might have been afraid of if he hadn't seen that none of the other boys were scared. "They've all been through this," Dilweed explained. "I remember when this happened to me, they all remember," he went on as if he understood Preston's confusion. "You just woke up in the woods so you don't know."

The winds picked up and there was Peter, hovering over the storm that accumulated like a contained tornado as if he were conducting it. Peter watched attentively, unafraid as the wind changed from a physical presence to something beyond that. It turned to light; a white light like the fairies and Preston could make out a dense fog streaming down. He watched as children appeared in it. They came one after another, but landed together as if the time difference, the space did not matter.

Preston saw them as he could see the cowboys and Indians. One boy came down in a bed, IVs hooked up to his arms. He was bald and Preston could see twelve seconds before, as a mother and father looked down at his hospital bed, a little sister watching the boy spit up. He watched the little boy close his eyes and he was Here. When he reached the forest floor the bed was gone, shattered and shed—it could not keep him any longer. The boy's hair returned, shaggy and light brown, his limbs fattened, there was color in his cheeks and he ran to the other children.

He saw another boy standing out in the middle of a street, a car came racing at him, he closed his eyes, frightened—fear, he felt so much fear and then he was Here and okay. The child laughed as he ran to a group of Lost Boys as if he knew them.

Preston watched them and as they left the streaming light their stories disappeared, he could only see them for a split second and then they were gone and he would have to get the rest of their stories the old fashioned way.

Most of the children had finished coming down, or so it seemed, no more were appearing and yet the white-lit stream remained. Most of the other boys were busy with their new companions. Groups of Lost Boys huddled around a single new boy and Preston wondered if it was his job now to join one of the welcoming committees, even though he'd only just come himself. Dilweed and Oregano had gone over to the little boy who'd been sick and Starky playfully joined them, hopping up to the group like a curious rabbit. But the stream did not stop; it only became quieter as other lights fell to the forest floor. These lights were dimmer and Preston could see children, children encased in darkness, float to the ground. Preston tried to look at them, but after the first one he couldn't watch anymore. He started to see things he didn't want to see. They weren't stories, moving pictures like what the other Lost Boys had projected, just flickering moments, a man's face, dark and mean, a chair and it was dark.

There were other boys like the first, less brightly lit boys that came down and did not get up. They lay unable to move, unable to speak, and the Lost Boys did nothing to help them. Preston inched closer, stopping just at the edge of the streaming light. "What's wrong with them?" he asked no one in particular, since no one in particular seemed to be paying attention. "What happened?" He looked down at the new dimly lit children and wondered why this disturbed no one else.

Then the fairies came. Their bright lights, brighter than anything Preston had seen yet, engulfed the dimly lit children, standing them up and whisking them away. The dimly lit children remained quiet; they stayed motionless as they were flown through the air, carried by the gigantic horde of fairies over the woods and back toward the trees that looked as if they were perpetually burning.

"What happened?" Preston asked turning to Peter, who had just appeared, hovering behind him with his hands curiously behind his back. The stream had vanished and everything was back to normal. "What happened to those kids? Are they okay? Why did the fairies take them?" he asked desperately, watching after the light from the fairies, which grew smaller and smaller the further away it got.

"Those are the children who need the most help," Peter explained. "They did not live as children should. They came Here from a Before where they were beaten and abused; they come frightened, they come without voices, without thoughts and it's the fairies' job to take care of them. It's the fairies' job to heal them so they can speak again, so they can come and play with us."

"Why can't they speak? What happens when they're with the fairies?" Preston asked, wringing his hands nervously. This had been such a good place but even Here, even Here it seemed the horrors of the adult world could get through. "Why do they let this happen? Why doesn't someone stop this?"

"Someone? Who?" Peter asked. "There's nothing we can do. We don't come from Before, we don't control the Before and believe me if we did it would be a much better place...but we don't and there is a natural order, an order that I cannot interrupt."

"Did Starky come like that? He was sent to the gas chambers, did he go to the fairies? And me, I was poisoned, why didn't I go there?" All of a sudden Preston realized even Here the adult world could get through. "Why do they let this happen? Why doesn't someone stop this?"

"There's a difference between dying violently by someone you don't know and being abused regularly by someone you're supposed to trust," Peter replied gravely, his voice sounding almost like a grownup's. "You and Starky were loved in the Before."

"Who did this to them?" Preston demanded, angry.

"The pirates," Peter replied.

"The pirates?" Preston asked, nervous. "There are pirates in the Before?"

"That's where they come from. Except one, he says he was always Here, but he wasn't, I saw him come, he's lying."

"The pirates," Preston repeated. "So what're you going to do with the other kids, the ones who came Here fine?" he asked. He'd had Peter to himself since he'd appeared in the woods and wondered how things would change. "Will the quiet kids ever get to play with us?"

Peter smiled, he tousled Preston's hair, laughing, and it felt for a brief moment as if it were Before, when his Dad tucked him into bed, when his Mom picked him up from school. "I'll show the new kids around just like I showed you around, I'll talk to each and every one of them, they'll all make friends. And when they're ready, and for each one of them it's different, but when they're ready, the quiet kids will slip into our world, one by one, the fairies will drop them off once they've started to talk, and they'll join in with the games as if none of that bad old stuff ever happened. That's what happens to the quiet kids, it's all okay in the end." Peter nodded, hovering over Preston until he was just about at treetop level.

"All right," he announced to all the new kids, who stopped their play to look up at him. "My name's Peter and this is my tree house and we're all going to live together. Now, if any of you would like a tour of the place, follow me." Peter hovered closer to them. "Just think you can fly and you can, no strings attached, I promise," he explained and several kids shot up after him. A few more took their time, but after only a minute a great line of children were flying after Peter, who'd gone a great distance in the air.

Some of the new kids stayed playing whatever games they'd been playing with the Lost Boys, though most of them followed their leader. Peter could be seen flying backwards, his hands behind his head as if he were simply lounging there, explaining the trees and the lights and Mermaid Lagoon.

Preston approached Starky, who was standing near the Ferris wheel, pointing up at it for the benefit of two new kids. "Hi," he said, hands in his pockets as the other kids turned around, smiling warmly in return. "I'm Preston. I'm from Before."

"Me too," one of them said, and Starky smiled at them all.

"This here is Jake and the other is Connor. They just got Here," Starky explained. "I was showing them around, you want to come?"

"Sure," Preston replied.

"Come on, I want to show them the tree house," Starky called, running, not flying, toward the trunk as first the two new boys and then Preston dashed after him.

LONDON. eNGLaND 1901

A message came to the house as Mrs. Darling waited for her children to return from the park. The message had come late as far as Mrs. Darling was concerned, and she had been pacing back and forth inside her darkened foyer with its Turkish carpets and red cloth lampshades, when a little boy handed her a note written in a messy, rushed script asking her to "Come to Saint Thomas' Hospital—child injured."

Mrs. Darling hired a coach to take her to the hospital, grabbing her bag and rushing right out into the street. She hadn't considered her husband, figuring that whoever had left that message must also have had the wherewithal to find him. Nevertheless, when she arrived at the hospital it was only Netty and the boys waiting in a tiny entranceway. A secretary who wore a long, linen dress that appeared just a tad too dingy to be worn to work sat behind a large wooden desk, pushing the hair that had fallen out of her loose bun out of her eyes. It didn't look as if her husband had been there and it was only Netty—Netty ringing her hands, Netty pacing back and forth, Netty shaking her head at herself as if she couldn't believe she'd gotten herself into this predicament.

"What's wrong with you?" Mrs. Darling asked once she arrived as John and Michael (she'd never truly consented to calling her youngest son Paul, the name did not seem to suit him) ran up to her. It took her a moment, but only a moment, to realize that Winifred wasn't with them.

"It's Winifred, Mrs. Darling, the two of them were playing on the bridge and I told them to stop, really I did, but they just wouldn't listen and she fell right into the water. Hit her head, she hit her head," Netty cried.

"What's wrong with my daughter, where is she, why can't I see her?" Mrs. Darling demanded of the secretary, ignoring Netty. As a woman who lived in Bloomsbury with an estate that averaged £1200 a year she acted as if this secretary, like her servants, should naturally drop everything for her. She strode toward the calm woman, who sat at her desk, eyes downcast as if she couldn't see her.

"She's in with the doctor, he'll come out and speak to you when he's ready," the woman replied with a professional distance.

"Where is my husband? Netty, didn't you have a message sent to his office?"

"I thought about it, Mrs. Darling, really I did," the bumbling woman cried, twisting a stained white handkerchief between her red, blotchy hands. "But I forgot where he worked and I thought if you came here, you could find him."

"Oh, you. . . ." Mrs. Darling steamed, annoyance masking her worry. She strode back to the secretary's desk and snatched a piece of stationary. She then grabbed a fountain pen that had been lying near the edge of the table and wrote furiously. When she finished she handed the folded paper to Netty. "There you go, it will be the last thing you do for this family. Send word to my husband at the office, the address is there and if he doesn't come within the hour, Netty, I'll have the police sent after you."

"Yes, Ma'am," Netty responded, hustling out the front door as if she hadn't noticed at all that she'd been fired.

Mrs. Darling waited nearly the entire hour for her husband to come, but finally he strode in through the front doors, his broad chest out, coattails following behind him. The boys were playing on the floor, using a cushion as a sea-faring vessel as they "en-garde"-ed at each other, more to keep themselves occupied, more to keep their minds away from the worry in the room, than for play.

"What's the meaning of this?" he asked and Mrs. Darling nearly sighed. He was always, whenever things were imperfect, what's-the-meaning-of-this-ing as if it got him anywhere; it was the same as John and Michael with their en gardeing everywhere. "I got off of work and. . ."

"Winifred is in the hospital. I've been here an hour and the doctor hasn't come out. Netty was here an hour before that and I don't know what could be wrong with her," Mrs. Darling explained, looking over at the secretary, who kept her head down, going through papers, though it was plain as day that she wasn't really working on them. "What is wrong with this place?" she cried out, getting up. She started pacing as her husband looked out the window and John and Michael continued playing.

"I'm Redhanded Jack," John cried, standing on a short wooden bench. "And you're a yellow-livered codfish."

"I am not," Michael called, running at the bench and nearly falling on top of it as he struggled to climb up. "I'll get you."

"No, you won't," John called, and Mrs. Darling sighed.

"Will you two stop this instant," she scolded. "What is wrong with you? What do you think you're doing carrying on like that while your sister is in the hospital? And your father and I, we don't know a thing."

"We were just playing," John explained, embarrassed.

"Is Winifred going to be okay?" Michael asked innocently, shuffling toward his mother and pulling on her long brown skirt.

"I don't know, Michael, I just told you that, I don't know, none of us know, don't you listen?" Mrs. Darling cried, marching away from her children as Michael tumbled over. She paced back toward the large bay window opposite the one her husband was staring out of. She saw all of London there, or enough of it anyway. This wasn't a bad part of the city, this wasn't a poorhouse hospital or anything of the sort, at least Netty had had the good sense to have Winifred taken here, if getting her here had been Netty's doing at all. And she knew they never should have hired that nurse. She had hardly any references and the ones she provided never bothered to answer their letters of inquiry. She was a high-strung old girl, who couldn't control the children, and Mrs. Darling had told her husband on a number of occasions that they should get rid of her. They should be hiring John more tutors and some for Michael and Winifred should be with girls her age, she should be meeting young men soon, she was nearly sixteen.

"Oh, come now, Mary, it's not that bad. She's in a hospital, she's not lost," Mr. Darling tried to comfort her and Mrs. Darling looked up at him. He was a big man with his chest always puffed out as if he were about to blow everyone away. He talked a lot, especially in and about the office, and the children had never been fond of paying much attention to him. "And they've been making such wonderful progress in the field of medicine, they really have been. Just the other day the firm was talking about the son of one of our clients, he's a bright young doctor who has been studying the brain, I believe what he does is called Psychiatry. . . or it could be Neurology. You see, this young doctor had the good sense to realize that the brain and the body are two separate organisms and that the brain needs its own science. Now what do you think of that Mary, what do you think of that?"

"I think your daughter is injured, George," Mrs. Darling cried, pulling away from her husband as he rested a fleshy hand on her arm. "I think you should hope these medical miracles apply to our only daughter." She turned away before she could catch a glimpse of her husband's face. She watched the boys, who were playing quietly, whispering and lightly scuffling, but at least making an effort to behave. And she had thought better of allowing Netty to take the children out when all they wanted was to stay in the yard with Nana that day, but George was always saying that the children needed to get out and why had she not listened to that little voice in her head? Why had she succumbed to the societal pressure that said a child who plays at the park is a happy child?

A door opened on the other side of the room. It was a large, rather open room with dark wooden trim and furniture. The cushions on the seats looked like elaborately woven tapestries and the dark green curtains kept much of the sunlight out, though it was waning now and would soon be night.

The doctor walked toward them. He had a mustache and a balding head. His thin glasses made him seem intelligent, though he bumbled when he walked, nearly dropping a piece of paper crinkled between his hands as he made his way to Mr. and Mrs. Darling, who walked together into the center of the room.

"Mr. and Mrs. Darling?" the doctor asked, looking first Mrs. Darling, and then her husband, in the eye. He was old, his hands shook when he stood still and his voice wobbled when he spoke, which did not inspire confidence.

"Yes," Mr. Darling stated. "We're here about our daughter, what happened to her? How is she?"

"Yes, Winifred Darling, the nurse told my assistant all about it. She fell off a bridge; hit her head on a rock. A young man was there, a medical student and it's a good thing he was, he helped her with her breathing, kept her neck straight," the doctor went on as Mrs. Darling stood before him shaking as if this prognosis had the power to either continue or end her life.

"How is Winifred?" she asked impatiently, feeling the disapproving eyes of her husband on her for getting so worked up.

"Winifred, yes, she hit her head and so we don't know," the doctor responded, looking out at the room and beyond the couple as his hands still fumbled. "That is to say that her body is fine, I checked her out. She's a little bruised, but that's common with this kind of tumble. I'm just a physician; I must confess I haven't studied the brain extensively. She is unconscious, I can tell you that. Her heart is beating, she is breathing, but she is not awake and has not been since we brought her in. Could she have Locked-in Syndrome? I doubt it since there is some movement in her eyes and when a patient is locked-in they are completely paralyzed. Could this be a coma? We're not sure yet, it will take more time to see. I've seen comas before and while she appears to be in one, since her body is working, but she is not responding, there are times when her eyelids flutter, which is out of the ordinary in this kind of case. There does not appear to be any internal damage and we don't know quite what to do with her here. There is a specialist in town, a brain doctor of some kind, and I'm going to have him in to look at her."

"A brain doctor, yes," Mr. Darling repeated, growing excited. "My firm is thinking of working with him. He's the son of one of our best clients. Yes, a Dr. Gladstone, yes, that's a good idea. He's making waves in his specialty, this new neuro-cognitive science." Mrs. Darling watched her husband, noting how proud he looked saying such big words.

"But how is Winifred?" Mrs. Darling asked, looking pleadingly at the doctor.

"We don't know ma'am. I wish I could tell you more, we just don't know. I've seen comas before and sometimes the patient wakes up, but only if the coma lasts a few weeks. Other times they don't, but I've never seen this in a child so young and the eye fluttering is abnormal. We're going to keep her for a couple of days, to see if something goes wrong with her physically and we'll have the specialist in, but if nothing is wrong, and she remains unconscious, then you can take her back home if you like and see what happens there."

"'See what happens there?'" Mrs. Darling repeated at the old man, nearly falling over herself. She felt her knees buckle, and her husband grasped her arm, holding her up as she started crying.

After having held his wife up for a few uncomfortable seconds, Mr. Darling set her down, kneeling on the floor, before he awkwardly shook hands with the doctor. "Thank you, doctor, I'm sure you've done the best you could. I appreciate all the help you've given this family."

"Yes, yes, well, we haven't been very helpful, now have we," the doctor said, looking down at the tearful Mrs. Darling as the tremor in his hands worsened. "If you'd like to go in and see her, she's in the room down back, a private one, you'll see it. Go back whenever you feel like it."

"Thank you, sir," Mr. Darling replied as the doctor turned away, shuffling back to the door and slipping through it.

"Mother, mother," John and Michael called, rushing to Mrs. Darling as she sat on her knees in the middle of the room, the long skirts of her dress surrounding her. "Mother, what's wrong?" they asked in unison, standing directly over her crying, crumpled body. She had never cried in front of them before; in fact they'd never seen this kind of emotion from a grownup before.

"Why are you crying, mother?" Michael asked, his thumb in his mouth. Mrs. Darling looked up at him and tried to smile, her face cracking as she reached out, taking both her boys and holding them close, so close she could sense their breath on her neck, smell the sweat that came with all the little boy games they'd been playing.

"I'm going to see her," Mrs. Darling announced after the boys moved away. She stood up, pulling stray hairs back behind her ears as she looked first at her husband and then around the room. "It's just down the hall, correct? I'd like to see her alone."

"Yes, Mary, but. . . ." Mr. Darling fumbled as his wife pushed past him. He stood scratching his head, wondering if it would be all right to leave the boys with the secretary for a little while should he see a need to go after her. He was rarely alone with the children and always felt out of place amongst their playing. They stood staring at him, an eerie silence between father and sons until the boys started whispering again.

Mrs. Darling walked down a long windowless hall. The lamps lighting her way were dim and somber, like on the staircases at home. There were paintings on the wall, some of men in suits of armor or women wearing fashions that had gone out of style a hundred years ago. Mrs. Darling could hear the clicking of her shoes on the bare wooden floor, she felt a draft sift through the corridor as she first knocked on and then opened the only door she saw.

She was met first with the sour stench of something. She couldn't quite place what it was; being a woman such as herself she only smelled the scents coming from the kitchen, tea in the afternoon, flowers in the gardens. There were other smells of course, her husband at night after drinking at the club, the smell of smoke on his breath, garbage outside the kitchen, but nothing smelled like this. It was a clean smell, even if it was sour, like milk gone bad and mixed with chemicals from a world of science and medicine.

A window covered by thick green curtains stood directly opposite the door near two lamps standing beside a small metal bed that appeared as if it was made of thick wire. There were tables scattered in the room, filled with jars of greenish or bluish goop, and metal instruments, some sharp, some curved. There was a shelf where a couple of syringes and a thermometer sat and a few boards were nailed over the walls with wiring hanging on them.

It was the bed that mattered. And there in the wire-metal bed, covered mostly with a thick white blanket, was a little girl. At first Mrs. Darling couldn't recognize her. Even when she went into the nursery early in the morning to check on them, even when they were fast asleep the children were restless, as if they were dreaming of running with horses. John always had the covers pushed down to his feet and Michael constantly found his way into a ball squeezed tight. And Winifred would be lying there with a smile on her face, turning one way and then another as if absently dancing with a mystery man—the man of her dreams, Mrs. Darling used to call him as she watched her girl sleep.

Now Winifred didn't move, the blanket covered her still form as if it were hiding something. Her face wasn't the same—it was swollen near her left eye and a bruise grew across her delicate features, as if a monster had breathed on her, making what was once beautiful, ugly. Her eyes were closed, her lips only slightly parted, but when she touched her daughter Mrs. Darling could feel that there was something warm about her.

"Winifred?" she asked and of course there was no answer. Yet there was always an answer; there had never been such peace in her. Sometimes as a mother she'd wanted to see her daughter like this, not hurt of course, but still and quiet like a doll, though it all felt wrong, so incredibly wrong now.

The door opened, Mrs. Darling could hear the creaking, and turned to find her husband standing in the doorway. "Where are the children?" she asked.

"They're with the secretary, they're all right, she said it was fine," Mr. Darling mumbled. He looked over his wife and down at his daughter. He did not see the peace in her, only the bruises, and the fact that this new doctor everyone was so excited about would be coming to look at his child. "How're you feeling? Are you all right?" Mr. Darling asked his wife, hands in front of his stomach as if at any moment he might start fiddling with them.

"She's asleep and I can't wake her," she cried. Rushing to her husband, she began to beat on his chest with her delicate hands. "She's not here, George, she's not here, I can feel it! She's somewhere else, I can feel it!" she cried, still beating on him as Mr. Darling held her back, grasping both her wrists in his thick hands as he looked down at her, terrified.

cLaiRe

After the funeral things returned if not back to normal, then at least back to a sense of normalcy. Claire's mother flew back to Chicago, taking her sister with her, old friends stopped calling every other day, sympathy cards no longer poured in but slowed to a trickle until Claire no longer expected them. Claire went to the grocery store to pick up butter and juice, milk and bread, old staples as if they were skimping to save money, though it was only that she and Matthew hadn't had dinner together since the family had left and Claire barely had an appetite anyway. She'd had to relearn how to live, retraining her eating and shopping habits to those of a childless family. Instead of white bread she bought wheat, instead of peanut butter and jelly she got lean turkey and broccoli sprouts. There were one-time meals, pre-made snacks like soda and chips that did not require any work. She'd been more than happy to slave away making healthy meals for her son, but when it was only herself and sometimes her husband, when there was no one else in the house and no prospect of that changing, when she was hungry all she wanted was a slice of toasted bread, or a bag of chips she could open quickly and throw away.

As things started to calm down, at least on the nuts and bolts of everyday living, the police started to zero in on a suspect. They called Claire periodically to ask questions, Detective Jameson stopped by the house every few days, but it was a few weeks after the funeral that they got word of Gregory Hawthorne's arrest. It had happened quietly, like snow falling soundlessly at night until you wake up in the morning and find ten inches on the ground. No police cars roared down the streets, sirens blaring, no one ran out of their house, the telephone did not incessantly ring, it didn't even show up on the news. Matthew simply came home one afternoon and told his wife there had been an arrest.

When he walked in the door Claire could see something was up before he told her. Matthew had been staying later and later at work, "catching up on some papers," though he always smelled of whiskey and cigarettes when he walked in the door. "Did you hear?" he'd said, coming home early for the first time in weeks. "It was on the radio. They arrested him, our neighbor, Gregory, the one who came to the house. I knew it, I knew he did it." Matthew made a fist and looked as if he were about to punch a hole through the wall, but Claire just stood staring, her eyes wide and vacant.

"What happened?" was all she was able to get out. It was just like when she'd first heard, when she'd looked down at her little boy's body at the morgue, it was as if she were floating above herself, barely able to hear what was being said, as if her mind were trying to protect her from something by blotting it out.

"They checked some storage facility in his name. He said he hadn't been to it in almost a year, but when they looked there was the poison and a bunch of syringes." Matthew shook his head and Claire might have gone to him, she might have cried into his chest if he had not looked like he was about to hit someone.

"So what do we do?" Claire asked, fidgeting now, pacing back and forth in the kitchen just as she had that night, recalling those horrible, horrible first few hours. Is this what justice is? Claire thought, being dragged back through it, having to feel it, to see it, to live it all again? If it was justice she wasn't sure she was up for it.

"There's an arraignment for bail next week. We should go to it. We should show up for everything, it'll make the jury feel more sympathetically toward us, toward Preston's side of the case, that's what Jim said."

"Are you sure we have to go to everything? I don't know. . . I don't think. . ."

"Just for a little while, we should make our presence known, that's what Jim suggested. For justice," Matthew said, looking Claire in the eye, and she wondered if she could actually refuse an idea as weighty as justice.

At the end of it all, she could not refuse. The stakes were too high and this was too important to Matthew to blow off. On the day of the first arraignment Claire drove to the courthouse herself, taking the silver Audi she and Matthew had purchased three years ago because there was more legroom for Preston in back. She got out of the car and shut her eyes against the summer glare coming off the sidewalk. Claire glanced back at the car as she walked away from it, wondering if it would ever be the same, if that car would ever smell like children, if she'd turn around to see if a child was sleeping for the sixth time in an hour long trip. She could still see the stain on the floor where Preston had thrown up on it, the scratches where he'd tried to color on the upholstery; she could smell him, like new car smell and when that went away, what would be left?

Matthew was meeting her at the courthouse and part of Claire was afraid to go in by herself. They lived in a fairly small town twenty-five miles north of Boston, a nice town where children did not get poisoned and left to die in the woods, and now three television crews were outside, ready to cover the enormity of what had happened. Claire shuddered, hoping the cameras weren't for her. Maybe there was another child murderer she hadn't heard of, perhaps a serial killer had been caught or the world had ended, anything as long as they did not approach her for an interview.

Claire ascended the steps to the courthouse entrance, which was busy, though she could eventually walk in, placing her purse on the conveyor belt so it could be scanned as she walked past security. A heavy-set security guard waved her through the metal detector as she grabbed her bag, which had also been cleared, and walked down the hall.

It was quiet in the first hall, but hectic in the second. The first hall felt like a back alley, it had dingy white tiles and very few decorations, but the second hall, which led to the courtrooms, sported red carpeting and pictures of judges, mostly men, but a few women, in black robes staring out somberly as if their pose would compel generations to greater civic interest.

Wood paneling went halfway up the walls and whitish gold wallpaper went up the rest of the way. There were desks near corners, with vases filled with carnations and doors with brass numbers on them. Claire passed a couple of large signs, one of which had a layout of the courthouse on it. She walked up to it, noting that Gregory Hawthorne's arraignment, the very first in this process of justice, was to take place in room 2B-4, which was down the hall at the end, on the right.

The halls were still crowded, though no one was being let into Mr. Hawthorne's courtroom, when Matthew arrived. Claire could see his blond hair bobbing with the crowd. He didn't see Claire, even when she raised her hand to wave him over, but he appeared to know where he was going.

Matthew had the same look he'd had since all this started, a look that said that though he was a modern man who adhered to societal conventions, though he knew better than to take matters into his own hands, still all he really wanted to do was punch someone. "Matthew, hi," Claire called, standing on tiptoes and waving at her husband. She felt her body extend, as if her feet were lifting off the floor and she half-closed her eyes, almost tumbling as Matthew waved back, walking toward her.

"I'm glad you found the room," he said. "I was worried it would be hard to find, that they wouldn't want to advertise where the arraignment was."

"I don't know if they can do that," Claire guessed, though her legal knowledge on any matters, and especially these matters, was extremely limited. "So how was work?" Claire asked Matthew, who only nodded at the question and looked around. It was a silly question, words spoken to fill space. How can you ask a man about work when he's about to enter the arraignment of the man accused of killing his son? Claire replayed the words again and again in her mind; she tried to swallow them whole, to take them back from where they'd come, but instead she knotted her fingers together, she rocked back and forth on the balls of her feet and stared at the floor.

They waited several moments before a buzz sounded down the hall. A few people marched by as Claire and Matthew and a few others waited by room 2B-4, some of them carrying cameras while others held microphones and asked frantic questions that could not have been understood. "Ms. Gumm, Ms. Gumm," a woman in a black and white business suit called, following a woman with a drawn face and tousled blond hair, who was walking handcuffed down the hall accompanied by two officers and three men in suits, all of whom were subjected to the frenzy.

Claire had heard a lot about Francine Gumm since Preston's funeral. She'd been arrested several years ago, arrested and convicted of murdering her own children. Apparently she'd done it in cold blood, leaving them in their car, strapped into their car seats as she let the engine run all night. Evidently the car was out of gas when they found the children in the morning asphyxiated, half out of their car seats, their nails having bled from trying to claw their way out of the car. Francine Gumm had confessed to the murders, she hadn't even cited insanity then, she hadn't really put up much of a defense, there had been so much proof against her. She'd been complaining to people at the bars she frequented that she was considering killing her children, though no one had taken her seriously until it was too late; she'd looked up carbon monoxide poisoning on the internet several times and she had a history of child abuse, though nothing, the state swore, that justified removing the children. And apparently now, nearly five years after her conviction, she was citing insanity, demanding another trial because, she declared, the first had been a farce.

"No woman who kills her children is sane," she'd proclaimed in an interview in the local paper. No one who had any real legal knowledge thought she had a chance, but until the courts denied her plea, Francine Gumm would be in the spotlight, Claire would see her on the local news and in the papers, this woman, this monster who had strapped her children into their car seats and left them to die.

"Ms. Gumm, did you really mean to say you were insane at the time of the incident?" one of the reporters asked and one of the suit-wearing men surrounding her replied, "Ms. Gumm is not authorized to speak about her trial at this time."

The hullabaloo moved on, but Claire watched the prisoner. The drawn woman glanced back, their eyes met, and it appeared that Francine knew exactly who Claire Tumber was and what she was doing at the courthouse. The media left as Francine was led away, not even bothering with Gregory Hawthorne's trial, to Claire's relief. Matthew didn't even seem to notice as Francine moved on, though he shook his head when they were gone. Claire expected her husband to say something, to say anything, but he merely stood staring.

"You know," he finally said once the chaos had dwindled and then disappeared from the hall. "You know I hope this thing starts on time. I'm really not up for waiting around and all that—"

"I know," Claire interjected quickly, wanting to keep up the conversation, though her mind returned to the scrapbook she'd started the week before, using pictures of Preston from when he was a little boy. She'd even called her mother and had her send a few shots over. She'd put the scrapbook in a nice neat album using memorabilia and little cloth cutouts from the craft store. It was a scrapbook for a boy, so there were striped pieces of cloth instead of lace, but still the book had looked very nice, as if a professional had done it. Yet when it was finished Claire had felt as if she hadn't done it right, as if the entire thing, a testament to her son, had been a waste of time and so she'd taken all the pictures out, placed them carefully in piles and started again. She'd done this twice with two other scrapbooks but she still couldn't get them right, as if no matter what she did, her son did not live in them and so she undid what she'd done day after day, night after night, like Penelope at her loom undoing the death shroud.

The doors to the courtroom opened from the inside and the people milling around started to file in. Everyone had been so polite, so quiet, since she'd arrived and she wondered why the lack of small talk, the way everyone just stood around, some sipping water from a cooler down the hall, others checking their date-books as they generally stared into space.

It looked like a courtroom inside. Claire had been expecting a mess, or a madhouse, or something so holy, so sacred that it could not be touched. But the courtroom was neither. It was just a room, not even a particularly spacious room, though it had high ceilings and a long aisle that led past a pair of small swinging doors to a high bench where a judge sat, near a smaller and slightly lower witness box. This was a fairly new courtroom in a fairly new town hall, but there was an antique feel to the place, a little piece of old New England charm. The wood was dark and heavily lacquered, so much so that Claire wondered briefly how easy it would be for the place to catch fire. The carpet was a deep dark red, and instead of benches in the back of the room there were rows of gray plush chairs.

Claire and Matthew waited with the rest of the group that had filed in. Those who would occupy the two tables facing the bench, one for the prosecution and one for the defense, had yet to come out, as had the judge. The people were quieter in the courtroom than they had been while waiting in the hall, but a few of them whispered as they scribbled notes on tiny pads or flipped through pocket-sized notebooks. Claire cringed at that, wondering if this story would be in the town paper, or worse yet the *Boston Globe*. She kept her head down, hoping no one was drawing a picture of her, the grieving mother, with her disheveled hair and swollen, haggard, waterlogged eyes.

The place was filling up. The case was a big deal, and very disturbing, and it appeared as if the same strangers who had come to the funeral to pay their respects to a boy they'd never met, had also come to the trial of the man accused of killing him.

Claire rested her head on Matthew's shoulder. It was only when she touched him that she remembered why she loved him. He was thick and strong with a linebacker's body. She felt warm and safe the second her cheek graced the doughy part of his arm. She closed her eyes and wanted to sleep. Her counselor had been wrong, she did not need to deal, to come to terms with this, all she needed was sleep, to hibernate forever in blissful nothingness.

Just then a side door opened and a well-dressed man came out followed by a heavy-set woman and a young man who resembled a teenage boy in his ill-fitting suit and tie, his hair slicked back as if he were about to break into a song and dance number on Broadway. This group sat at the prosecution's table, they rustled papers, looked around, rustled more papers and whispered to each other as another group entered the room.

First a man in a nice blue suit and another in a suit that looked as if it would have been green in the right light came out. Claire was still trying to decipher the exact color of the suit when the prisoner, the accused, the man they said had poisoned her little boy and made it so that she was living this stark and empty life, instead of the one where she made dinner every night and drove Preston to soccer practice, entered. Gregory Hawthorne was brought out handcuffed and shuffling as he hobbled to the defense table with his feet chained together.

He looked like a broken man, one that has been tied up and captured, humbled and injured so as to subdue him. Claire could only look at him for a second, like the flash of an image in a horror movie, though at least now, because of beatings and bruises he'd apparently sustained in jail, at least he looked like an adult and not an overgrown child. He shuffled with his shoulders hunched, his face bruised near his eye and under his chin, and

Claire could tell that only a few days before his features had been even more puffy. Apparently Gregory had not fared well in jail. First of all he was a slight man, a bit effeminate with soft, gentle features. Secondly child killers did not rank high on the prison food chain. Even the most hardened criminal, even a man who might have murdered another man in cold blood could not stand a child killer, and he'd been beaten up twice, from what Claire had learned. Once during dinner he'd been hurt so badly that they'd had to send him to the hospital for three days and when he came back they'd sequestered him.

Gregory Hawthorne could barely open his eyes— he squinted at the light like a rat that has never been outside the walls, his mouth gaping as if his IQ had dropped fifty points. Claire stared at the man, knowing she couldn't just look away. She saw his shoulders slacken, revealing the way they'd shaved the back of his neck, nicking the sides of it and leaving a heavy, red rash.

A man in an officer's uniform entered holding a thick blue Bible, which he held out for Gregory Hawthorne to place his right hand on as the man swore him in with a deep, commanding voice. "All rise," the bailiff then announced and everyone in the galley got to their feet at once, the scuff-scuff sound of shoes and limbs and heads moving at the same time scattering into the air. "The honorable Craig T. Tanner is now presiding. This is case number 2210 on the docket. All come to order. Let's proceed."

With that, the judge, a large man in his black robe, entered from a side door. He took a seat and looked out at the audience before glancing at the prosecution. The judge then looked straight at the defendant and the formalities began.

"This is case number 2210, The People versus Gregory Hawthorne. Mr. Hawthorne, you stand accused of knowingly administering poison to a young male child with the intent to kill him. That boy subsequently died after having been seen last at your home. How do you plead?" the judge asked, words uttered slowly, cautiously, but professionally. How do you plead? As if there was a choice? How do you plead? As if they were inquiring after a traffic ticket. Claire wanted to stand up and say no, no, this is all wrong. This is not how it's supposed to happen. Where were the screaming matches, the fistfights, the surprise witnesses? Why were they letting this pass into a professional, bureaucratic oblivion?

"Not guilty," the defense said.

The trial went on quietly, the prosecution made accusations that opposing counsel then objected to. Protests were made, but not many, and everything went on in a quiet, civilized manner. Bail was set at three hundred thousand dollars and Claire felt as if she should gasp, she felt as if a ripple of emotion should have surged through the gallery, but they just sat there facing forward as such a large sum was named. A couple of people took notes, an older woman wearing a beige suit dabbed the sides of her eyes, but otherwise did not let on that she was particularly upset by what was going on. Even Matthew stayed stoic, eyes on the judge as he pronounced that the trial would resume in two weeks.

That was it? Three hundred thousand dollars and he could walk free? And it wasn't even three hundred thousand; Claire knew that, it was only ten percent, something like thirty thousand. She'd seen Gregory Hawthorne's home, his car, he lived alone, he had no dependants that she was aware of. She was sure he could sell something and come up with the money to secure his freedom. And then what? Then he could do what he liked until the end of the trial. He could fight to clear his name; he could run away to Mexico and get a new identity so no one ever found him.

The Judge left after the bailiff announced his departure and everyone stood up. Unlike before, the entire gallery remained standing. When the door shut, the quiet room began to murmur, stifled sounds, whispers and gossip coming from the walls, "I didn't think it would be that much," one woman standing behind Claire said. "I thought it would be more," another countered and

Claire wondered who they were. They hadn't been to Preston's funeral, nor were they carrying notepads.

"Well that's it," Matthew whispered to his wife as the attorneys on both sides gathered papers, opening and shutting briefcases as two officers walked toward Gregory Hawthorne, about to take him away.

"No!" he cried as the officers moved in. "No, no, no, you can't take me back there. I didn't do anything, I didn't do anything! You can't take me back," he cried as one of the officers reached to grab him, though he was chained and couldn't go anywhere. "Please, please, you have to believe me," he cried out like a child in the midst of a desperate tantrum, hands held together as he dropped to his knees. "I didn't do it!"

One of the officers lifted him up, not bothering to acknowledge the man's hysteria. "You don't understand, they'll kill me in there, they'll find a way," he cried as both officers grabbed his arms, pushing him to his feet and walking him back toward the door he'd come from.

Gregory Hawthorne turned at the last second, twisting his head nearly all the way around, he looked at Claire. He didn't seem to see anyone else, he didn't want to, it was only Claire and she could feel his eyes on her, that cold awful watery blue. She could sense the man shaking as they pulled him back toward the side door that led to the inner chambers of the courthouse. "You have to believe me," he said directly at Claire before one of the officers thrust him forward and he was forced to turn around. They led him through the door and Claire watched him. By the time he was gone the courtroom was buzzing, like on television, on fire with the drama of the case that had seemed so ordinary, so normal only a few minutes ago, despite the heinous crime that had been committed.

"At least that part's over," Matthew said, draping an arm around Claire as he looked down at her. "Let's just go home. I was going to go back to the office, but I don't think I'm up for it."

"Okay," Claire replied, barely paying attention. The media was outside now; she could see a TV crew at the doors of the courtroom near a few people poised with tape recorders to interview her. Claire sat back down, unable to walk. She didn't want to think about returning to her car. She couldn't see herself unlocking the doors, getting inside and turning the key, her hands were unsteady, her eyes weren't focused. She saw Mr. Hawthorne in her mind, his face ingrained there. She wanted to talk to Matthew, she wanted to walk out, but just then all she could do was stare at the floor as if Mr. Hawthorne were somehow there.

This feeling of detachment continued for several weeks. Every morning after the arraignment Claire looked around Preston's room, savoring it as it was and wondering when it would change. When would they tear down these pictures of sports stars and put the baseballs and teddy bears, the plastic toys and adventure chapter books away? They couldn't leave it as it was forever, but neither could she consider changing it. The arraignment had ended only a few weeks ago, she'd heard that Gregory Hawthorne was still working on getting his bail money together, and Claire was not looking forward to the next stage of the trial, or the next one; someone had said these things could take years and she wasn't sure she had years of this in her.

Claire had been staying in the house. She'd been sleeping until noon since the funeral, not that sleeping until noon meant anything without a job to go to or a child to wake up for. Before that she couldn't sleep at all, not without the pills, but now that Matthew had taken away the pills, giving her only a couple of valium a week to "wean her off" the stuff, she was sleeping as she hadn't slept since college. She'd been a little worried that she'd have trouble sleeping after Matthew outlawed the pills. She wasn't concerned so much with the trouble she might have getting to bed or with how tired she'd be, but with the fact that if she stayed awake, she'd be forced to live in this world, to hear that continuous voice that rung inside her head crying that her child was dead at night as well as during the day. But instead, after the funeral, now that the leftovers from the wake were finished and the Tupperware returned, now Claire slept. She slept and slept and slept.

And what was more she'd been sleeping in Preston's room. Since the funeral, after the family left, she'd gone into Preston's light blue room, she'd run her hands over his baseball mitt and the photos of him in his Little League uniform. Matthew had been such a great baseball dad, getting off work early to come to games and offering to coach next year.

She'd sat on Preston's bed and felt so tired. That first night she'd lay down just to rest her eyes, only for a second, and soon it was the middle of the night and Matthew had come in, asking her to come to their room. She'd shaken her head then, she'd looked the other way and turned over in Preston's little bed, which was so small her feet hung over the edge. She'd fallen off it one night and another night she'd awakened at four-thirty and thought that Preston was with her, he felt so close. She'd considered briefly returning to her own room, but the thought of that large cold bed, even next to her husband, was too much for her.

Besides, she'd seen it again today, just like she'd seen it a couple of days before, something had moved in Preston's room, his baseball wasn't on the shelf where Claire distinctly remembered putting it two nights ago, and his monkey doll that she'd left on his bed was now lying on the floor next to it. She'd gone downstairs and questioned Matthew about it, but he'd said he hadn't been in Preston's room in days. She'd shaken her head, she'd been about to walk out, to assume that she was once again acting like an irrational grieving mother, but instead she'd turned around and declared, "Someone has been in his room." Matthew looked at her with pity in his eyes and she'd wanted to hit him.

"Honey, you're just seeing things," he'd said.

"No, I'm not, I swear it's like he's been there, like he's coming back and—" Claire stopped herself; it sounded so silly, so hopeful, unreal and ridiculous.

Matthew shook his head; he approached Claire, draping an arm around her. "I'm sure you're just misremembering," he said as if she were some kind of unruly client. She'd wanted to fall into his arms, to feel the warmth, the strength of him, but after everything and what he'd just said, she shrugged him away, turning around and marching back up the stairs.

Since the fight, even after Matthew left for work, Claire had stayed in her room. Preston's room was where she slept, but she worked in her own bedroom. The spaces needed to remain separate. She was almost finished pulling the pictures from the folds of the scrapbook she was working on. It was imperative that she always be working on one, even if she didn't keep any of them. It was the process that mattered, the working with her hands. And what would she do, how would she fill her days, her thoughts, if she were not working on another scrapbook? And only one scrapbook could exist at a time, it would be silly, perhaps a little bit insane, to start a collection of Preston scrapbooks twenty yards deep. Besides, there wasn't enough material for that.

Claire looked up from her pictures, she'd been staring at them without really seeing them for some time, her thin, delicate hands that still smelled of juniper lotion ran over the edges so much so that she saw her unmanicured nails more than the images on photo paper. But she didn't need to see the pictures, pictures of Preston standing next to his first red "big boy" bike, Preston playing with his friend Tom's golden retriever, Preston slurping spaghetti as if through a straw, sticky red tomato sauce all over his face.

The television had been on since Claire started the project. She clicked the TV on whenever she began working in the morning, if only for the shimmer of light it created, reflecting off the walls and tangling with the sun coming in from the windows. She also liked the pictures, ever changing, moving and evolving;

it was something to focus on when her mind drifted and her eyes wandered. The sound was turned very low. She didn't like to mute the TV, then the subtitles came on and she hated that, they forced her to read them, diverting her attention. Claire could hear tiny fragments of what the television was saying, it was muffled and garbled, more a mass of sound bites than actual speech, but as the news came on, and a picture of a woman wearing an orange jumpsuit appeared, Claire gripped the remote and turned the TV up.

"Francine Gumm will be going on trial this week after the murder of her two children. She has contested her previous trial and demanded that her appeal be heard. She is now pleading insanity." Claire watched the TV as a woman led by two large officers stared down at the ground as she tried to push her puffy blond hair into her face with the movement of her head to keep the cameras from seeing her eyes.

There was more Claire knew about Francine Gumm, partly because she was in her shoes. They may not be the exact same shoes, but they were similar, perhaps a different color or an older style. Claire had been doing her research. Just like she couldn't stop making and un-making these scrapbooks, Claire had gotten it into her head that she had to know everything there was to know about Francine Gumm. She'd done an Internet search and come up with a lot. Apparently there was a following of mothers, none of whom, as far as Claire could see, had actually lost a child, who were rallying for her release on the grounds that any woman who had to take care of her children on her own without help from the lousy good-for-nothing father would of course go insane. She'd learned that Francine Gumm had grown up in Florida with middle class parents. That she'd met her husband there and they'd moved to Boston after declaring bankruptcy. They divorced a few years after their two children were born because the husband had cheated on Francine. He'd then moved back to Florida with the woman he'd been cheating with and

Francine had been left alone with her kids. Francine, who had no college education, worked at grocery stores and chain restaurants to get by, but she was still on the verge of losing her house when her children were found dead in her car.

Claire looked out at her room as the news report came on and she was once again sucked into that world. No matter how heinous, how terrifying that world was, it was another world. Claire had always been the kind of girl who appreciated make-believe. As a child she'd insisted that her dolls go in car seats when her mother took her out, she spent a great deal of her elementary school years with her nose in a book, and she believed until she was ten, well after all her friends had stopped, that Santa Claus and the Easter Bunny were real creatures who came to her house at night to eat cookies and carrots and leave gifts. It wasn't so much that she believed in those things so late in life as much as that she wanted to believe. After it was over and Claire had finally consented to agree that there was no Santa Claus, there was nothing left, and who really cared that her parents left gifts under a tree, that they hid five dollar bills in plastic eggs they scattered around the house? After the belief was gone a holiday was just another day off from school, a family party where she got a few blouses or a pair of socks.

The broadcast ended and the doorbell rang. This was not the kind of neighborhood where people just rang doorbells. Doorbells were rude; they were loud and shrill, and meant only for strangers. Claire was sure that whoever was at the door had knocked, they'd knocked and knocked before giving up and resorting to that cold trick of wires.

When Claire reached the door in her blue spandex and BU sweatshirt, she realized her hair was a mess and hastily pulled it back with the elastic that had been perpetually around her wrist since the day after the funeral. She was sure there were still stray hairs near her face, that her eyes sagged and her shoulders slumped. It didn't matter how much she slept, she looked constantly exhausted.

"Hello," Claire said, squinting at the sunlight as it shone off the even green grass of the yards, shimmering within the bright white sidewalks as if it were a mirage. "Cara, hi, what can I do for you?"

"Hi Claire," Cara List greeted her, casting a demure smile. Cara was wearing a sweat suit not unlike Claire's and her curly brown hair hung just past her cheeks, her tiny eyes squinting, though Cara had always been a woman who seemed to squint. "I was just on your block and thought I'd pop in to say hello. How's the trial going? I meant to ask before."

"It's a trial, not that I know what one's supposed to look like," Claire replied.

"Jim said it looks like the defense might have probable cause, something about there being evidence the storage unit was broken into," Cara retorted. As the wife of a lawyer she always seemed to have information on her husband's cases, and the cases of Jim's friends, not that any of them were supposed to be sharing what they learned in court, but everyone talks about their job and Claire guessed that if it wasn't too egregious it was okay.

"I didn't know that," she replied. "Would you like to come in?" Claire asked automatically. She wasn't so out of it, she wasn't so steeped in depression that she couldn't take a hint, that she didn't know just what she should do when a neighbor rang her bell and said she was just on the block.

"Thank you," Cara replied, stepping in. "I just wanted to see how you were. How're things going, Claire?" Cara asked and Claire could tell that her neighbor did not know what she was doing. She wasn't well versed in playing the caretaker to a woman who had just lost her child, but Cara was going to try her damnedest to get this right.

"I'm fine Cara, thank you for coming by," Claire informed her, thinking this might be enough to get her to go. But it wasn't and Cara came in, she sat down on a white whicker chair in the sitting room, in front of the fireplace that had been rendered defunct until winter.

"I just wanted to see how you were," Cara said again, looking up at Claire, who was still standing. "It's just that...you know with the trial Peyton has been asking a lot of questions about Preston. I don't know what to say to him. I'm thinking of taking him to Father Sherman—he might be able to explain better."

"It depends on what you want your son to know," Claire replied, still standing. "I mean if you want a white-washed description of Heaven, then a priest is the way to go, if you want existentialist philosophy then maybe you should call on a college professor, but if you want something more heartfelt, even if it's not the exact right answer, I think the question should be fielded by you and Jim. Even if you don't know what to say, he'll understand and appreciate it."

"Sometimes I think you should have majored in Child Psychology," Cara responded.

"Thank you," was all Claire could think to say. She turned to look outside, kids were skateboarding by her house, older kids who might not have gone into a stranger's house and eaten the cookies he offered them. Mr. Foster, an old man who usually sat outside with an ancient transistor radio from the nineteen eighties, was outside watering his lawn with an old fashioned metal watering can, "I'm sorry. I'm distracted," Claire said, shaking her head as if she were snapping herself out of a trance. "Can I get you anything, an iced tea? Some juice or water?"

"No, no," Cara replied. "I really just wanted to see how you were holding up."

"I'm fine," Claire said and she knew Cara could tell it was a lie. "How's Peyton doing? What's he up to?" These conversations felt like a weight around her neck, but Claire knew if she didn't start having them she'd never be able to live, she wouldn't even be able to fake it.

"He and Eva have been playing a lot. They've both been quiet. I talked to Eva's mother, I mean, when she's around, and she said she told Eva outright what had happened. I don't know what that means, but however outright she was, I'm glad she hasn't shared that information with my son."

"Eva always did seem wiser than her years."

"It's because she's a girl, girls always seem older than boys, especially at this age."

"True," Claire replied.

"Hey," Cara started as if she were interrupting a room full of people. "Why don't we go for a quick walk before lunch?" she suggested, clapping once like a camp counselor attempting to cheer a bunk full of bored campers.

"I don't know if I'm up for that," Claire hedged and Cara cracked a smile.

"Oh, you look fine, you look better than I do, just throw on a pair of sneakers and let's go," Cara coaxed and Claire shrugged. She knew her neighbor well enough to know she wouldn't take no for an answer and if she did it would require too many no's, more no's than Claire had in her.

Claire did as Cara told her, slipping into an old pair of pink and white sneakers she and Matthew had bought together, getting matching shoes (though his were blue) because they'd decided to take up running when Preston started school. The worn laces slid past her naked foot and Claire bent to tie them, feeling the sweaty soles and knowing full well that she should have found socks. It was just that she was too tired, too lonely and too feeble to go rummaging through her closet.

"Ready to go?" Cara inquired with a can-do smile. Claire knew there would be people smiling at her for the rest of her life and she'd have to learn to deal with it, she'd have to learn someday to smile back. But she couldn't think about that now and the rest of her life—the rest of her life, oh God that was right; she had to live the rest of her life.

As she and Cara walked the sunny sidewalked streets, through the neighborhood with its brightly painted yellow and white, salmon pink and sky blue houses, Claire was reminded of why she lived here. She felt the newish black asphalt absorb the sun, which had gotten hotter as the summer extended, moving from the soft rays of June to the blistering waves of July. "So do you have any plans for the summer?" Claire asked because she knew this was a question one should ask when taking a walk with a neighbor.

"There's always our annual trip to the Cape," Cara started. "I mean it's all set up, but I understand if you don't want to go now. I can call the property and cancel."

"Don't do that yet," Claire replied. She didn't want to spend a week with the Lists on Cape Cod, a summer vacation both families had partaken in for the past four years, but neither did she want to end the tradition at that very moment.

"It's really okay. Jim can't be away from work, he can't take off much now."

"I know," Claire replied. "Matthew's work insisted he come back, though at least they're letting him take half days until the end of August."

"Well that's something. I guess there are no laws to protect those who are grieving, like maternity leave for pregnant women. But there should be, maybe we should get on that," Cara suggested and Claire wondered if she actually meant for her to go campaigning now.

"Perhaps," Claire said, looking out at the neighborhood. The neighbors all looked at her oddly, they all felt guilty, the couple down the street, the woman at the checkout counter who'd heard her story on the news and recognized her from her picture when she went to pick up coffee and cranberry juice, but there was nothing they could do—that's why they all felt so bad. Pain was not a shared emotion, there was no way to let someone else truly feel it. They could give you a sad look, they could express and even feel sympathy, but they couldn't know. Just like the time Claire had a pounding headache at one of Preston's baseball games. Sure the other mothers could say 'Sorry Claire, that stinks.' They could offer her aspirin or hush their children around her, but they couldn't really know her pain, they couldn't feel it in that instance, even if they knew what a pounding headache felt like. And yes, there were people, like Matthew, who were suffering just as badly as she was, but there was no way to hand an ounce of her pain over to Cara so that she could know just what she was dealing with, just as she couldn't have given a piece of her headache to one of the other baseball mothers, and so she was marooned on an island of her own pain, even where Matthew was concerned.

Cara and Claire walked in silence for a while, until they heard a car idling behind them, the cracking of small rocks under tires, the slight squeak of breaks. The car murmured behind the two women for a few seconds before Cara and then Claire turned to find Matthew's silver Audi there, still running. He was turned toward the side of the road, resting at the curb, parking two blocks from the house. The car door opened and her husband appeared in a blue collared shirt, his jacket hanging in the backseat. He pushed the door closed, squinting against the sun as he approached.

"Hi there," he called in a friendly, normal tone, as if he hadn't just stopped his car two streets from his house and gotten out. "What's going on?"

"We're going for a walk. Just around the neighborhood," Cara explained.

"Good, it's a nice day for a walk," Matthew replied. "Mind if I join you?" he asked. Cara shook her head no, and Claire was sure she could sense relief wash over her friend at having the extra, perhaps less silent, company.

They'd been going out again, Claire and Matthew, trying to reconnect. They hadn't slept in the same bed, or had dinner together in weeks, and ever since Matthew had returned to work it had been a constant stream of in at the office early, check out at noon, come home and work from there, locked away in his home office until the middle of the night. But still, the other day, a Saturday when their next-door neighbors were outside playing catch with their preteen sons and the couple across the street were sitting out on their lawn well into the evening as if a little boy had not just been murdered on this block, Claire and Matthew had decided to go for a walk, holding hands. The forced companionship felt rock hard as all their fingers clenched around their palms, but they soldiered on; even as the neighbors stopped to watch them, perhaps wondering why they were out after such a tragedy.

They'd walked to Brookside Park, a large recreation facility close to the house, across from the official confines of the neighborhood by a state route that was usually empty despite its four lanes. They'd wandered through the park's walkways; past kids playing baseball and women out on beach blankets sunning themselves. It had been such a typical Saturday, and Claire cringed, she'd nearly cried, though she'd stopped herself, as she thought of what she and Preston might have done that day. Ice cream first, then a walk into town to look at the specialty shops, maybe a trip to the baseball field with Peyton in tow.

They'd wandered around the park for a while until they hit the children's play area. Claire had thought it might be too much for her, but she liked watching the little kids, the toddlers bouncing around the tire swings as others slid down slides, the older kids making up elaborate games involving a bad guy who chased them with a sword. It was good to see that those games hadn't changed. "On Guard!" one of the children cried as a horde of other kids ran every which way.

Matthew headed toward the basketball court a few feet away. A couple of his friends were engaged in a pickup game and they asked him to join. He did, reluctantly, afraid to let his broken wife go, until she'd insisted. They hadn't been talking much anyway and Claire wanted to see her husband enjoy himself. He didn't look happy on the court, his mind seemed to wander, Claire could see the creases in his forehead, the way he shook his head when he looked up at the sky, careful of the sun. The other guys seemed understanding, or they appeared not to notice, but Matthew did finally get into the game.

It was such a childish game, a pickup game of basketball on a Saturday afternoon, but still it looked like fun. Even in his grief, and his guilt, Matthew appeared to be having fun and it was nice that he could do that, just let himself go.

Claire wandered over by the swings. They were sectioned off from the rest of the playground equipment, since one unintentional whack of a child's legs could send another to the emergency room. A few girls were swinging on the other end and Claire watched them for a while. The swings had always been her favorite playground activity in school. She'd wait in a line sometimes five kids deep for a chance on them, missing most of recess for those few glorious moments when she'd fly through the air on her own power. That's what it had been to her, so freeing, so powerful, and as a child it is very important to be both free and powerful, because you have so little of either in the grand scheme of things, not with Mom and Dad telling you when to eat and sleep, what to wear and how to act. But on those swings. . . .

And so after a while Claire got on. She'd felt silly at first, but if Matthew could play basketball just for the hell of it, why couldn't she swing? They were sized for her; her feet touched the ground, but barely. The girls at the other end, who could have been thirteen, looked at her funny, but soon got back to their game. Claire started pumping, higher and higher. It was strange how her body instinctively knew how to swing, even though she hadn't practiced this skill in years, as if being a child were inherently in her.

She'd wanted to like the swings, to enjoy the thrill of it, the way Mathew appeared able to enjoy scoring a basket. It had been fun for a few minutes, flying high. She closed her eyes and let the wind pick up on her bare cheeks as she tried to remember; she tried so hard to remember. But all she could see in her mind, the only story she could tell, was that her little boy was gone. She saw herself pushing Preston on the swings when he was three years old, she felt the way his back arched as she pushed higher, higher, higher, and then the tears came. Soft and slow, but she swung on. She swung on and on until the act became, not just sad, not simply memory inducing, but tedious. There was nothing to do but swing back and forth, back and forth. Her back hurt and her knees ached from pumping. The swings were not what they used to be. She'd grown up. Even without the memories, she'd grown up.

And so she'd gone back to Matthew, who was finishing up his game. They'd left together, Matthew none the wiser to Claire's revelation on the swings. In college she'd been able to do crazy things like that, maybe not swing, but she'd run around in the dark and gone skinny dipping in her friend's pool. She'd even done things like that after she'd married Matthew and gotten a decent job at a Boston marketing firm, but now, it was gone and it had been gone for years. Now it was just Claire and Matthew, walks in the park and amateur basketball games. There had been someone else, someone to let the fun in again, but he was gone.

Claire watched her husband as she and Cara continued walking. Matthew stayed with them up the block, past Pinetree and Parker Street and toward Belington Court. He did not brighten up the walk as his casual posture seemed to indicate he might, as he walked with his head down, hands in his pockets. He kicked at the road just a bit too much, sending rocks scattering.

"So how was work?" Claire asked at one point and Matthew grunted.

"I'm not doing much, only the Justman account," he replied. "But it's good to be back in the office, it's good to be doing something." Matthew looked down, wondering, Claire was sure, whether he should have said that. Soon, Claire began to worry, her husband was going to start insisting that she do something with her days, perhaps she should go back to work, take up a hobby, or have another child.

They kept walking up Belington—Claire didn't know where they were headed, this neighborhood ran deep, each street leading to another exactly like it. The neighborhood was filled with houses, filled with signs pointing the ways to houses, a couple of parks varied the landscape and the trees, all those trees before all those houses as if they were their own private worlds. Cara didn't appear to know where they were going either, though she was the natural leader of this expedition. Claire was starting to feel like a child again, a girl on the lookout for pirates or Indians as they trudged up the road, three grown adults just walking.

Claire was about to suggest they turn around when she saw lights flashing. At first she wasn't sure what they were. "What's going on?" Matthew asked and Claire shrugged.

Matthew quickened his face, reaching the lights first and leaving the women behind. In another world, at another time, Claire might have begun gossiping with Cara, wondering what was going on, speculating as to which house had been robbed, which couple was involved in what kind of a domestic disturbance. But this wasn't another world, this was the only world she'd be in for the rest of her life and so she remained silent, wrapping her arms around her chest as she marched diligently in the direction of her husband and the lights.

When she got close enough she saw that two police cars were parked outside Gregory Hawthorne's house. The Huxburries were standing by their door, their two boys pointing at the officers who were milling around the front yard and driveway as the dogs next door barked incessantly. Claire wished she could cover her ears, with all that noise, she wanted to fall to her knees and make it stop.

"What's going on?" Claire asked Matthew, who'd just finished speaking with an officer. There were four officers and two squad cars. Two of the officers were walking toward the house, heading to the front door, which had been covered with yellow evidence tape for weeks like the empty entrance to a haunted house. The other two officers were standing out by their car, one talking into a radio.

"Hello," Claire said to them. The man with the radio continued talking as the other nodded at her. "I'm Claire Tumber. The man who lived in this house is accused of killing my little boy," she explained. Never had she said the words so outright, they sounded cold, almost cruel and she could feel them, a sharp metallic taste in her mouth. "Did something happen?"

"Look," the officer said, shaking his head as if he were considering. She could see the thought process going through the officer's mind; he definitely did not have a poker face. Part of him wanted to share this information with the mother of the child who'd been killed, but another part understood protocol and would rather simply state that she call the detective in charge of her case.

Matthew, who'd been pacing back and forth angrily, stopped, staring at the officer, while Cara and the officer on the radio watched as well. "Look, I'm not supposed to tell you this, so don't go spreading it around the neighborhood," the officer said, glancing at the Huxburries house, where all four members of the family were outside staring at the scene. "We're checking out the house, seeing if there's any evidence in it we missed. I don't know, but the man, Gregory Hawthorne, was killed in prison last night."

"He was what?" Claire asked, her mouth gaping open. She was too stunned to notice Cara's or even her husband's reaction.

"It wasn't a good day for the prison. They'd already had a couple fights. And they'd just let Mr. Hawthorne out of solitary. They'd put him in there because there had been some incidents before. Child killers don't do well in prison; even the really bad guys want to get at them. But he'd been okay for a few days, when a fight broke out at the prison, Mr. Hawthorne wasn't even a part of it, he was just standing off to the side, but with the guards occupied, a guy, I can't give his name, he was in for murder though, looked like he was going to go away for a long time, he took out a knife, and who knows how he got a knife in there, and stabbed Mr. Hawthorne twice in the chest. He was dead before they could get him to the infirmary."

"But there hadn't been a trial yet," Claire heard herself saying, feeling suddenly very worried. She hadn't put Gregory Hawthorne in jail, she hadn't even been the one most crusading for his arrest and conviction, but still she felt responsible. "No one convicted him. You can't just condemn a man without due process." She didn't know where these words were coming from, words like "convict" and "due process," a vocabulary that had been living dormant in Claire since her Introduction to Criminal Justice class her sophomore year of college. "I mean, it's just that. . . . and no one was going to kill him, the worst he would have gotten was life in prison and I just don't think. . . ." Matthew shot her a look of annoyance, as if she were volunteering too much information.

"I know," Cara said, seeming confused as to what emotion to display, or feel. She draped an arm around Claire as they both stared at the officer. "I know, it's not fair, even if he was responsible. . . . I mean, you'd have every right to be happy about this, considering what he did to your—"

"If he had done it I'd be glad to see him rot in jail. . . . but what if it wasn't him?" Claire watched Cara, who nodded at her. Claire had never before considered that maybe it wasn't Gregory Hawthorne, the evidence had been very damning and the police never offered another suspect. Someone had to be blamed, someone had to be hated for this and he was right there, they'd shoved him in Claire's face and what else could she do? But what if it wasn't him? What if that housekeeper he'd been screaming about had been real, what if all his stories had been true? She remembered that childlike face. She saw the man she'd known before all this, her neighbor no one really liked, the man no one paid attention to except to stare at his antics on his fake basketball court. She remembered the look in his eyes, and, hoping it was only hindsight now, only some misguided form of guilt, she wondered if he'd looked even a little innocent to her. He'd begged her for forgiveness, she'd seen the look in his pathetic eyes and it was possible. In the realm of the universe anything was possible.

"It's just not fair," Claire said, looking out at Gregory Hawthorne's yard and glancing back at the bellflowers. They seemed to have wilted and she wondered, as she saw their drooping faces, who was going to take care of them now.

"I'm sorry," the officer said as two more men in uniform came out of the house, seemingly empty handed.

"Thank you officers," Matthew said. "We'll call down to the station for details."

"No problem," the officer who'd been so forthcoming replied.

Claire tried to think of a response but couldn't. She tried to feel anything, anger, relief, happiness even, but no emotions were right. Her son was gone, he was dead, that was all that mattered and even if Gregory Hawthorne had killed him, even then this killing did not make up for it. This killing did not make her feel better.

They turned around, silently heading to the Tumber home. No one said a word, though Cara coughed a few times to break the silence and Matthew tried once to drape an arm around Claire, who barely felt the gesture, though she shrugged it away. It was as if she were walking on air, as if she'd disappeared into the very molecules of breath and thought and memory that Preston had. All she could do was stare forward as she returned home.

LONDON, ENGLAND 1901

The days following Winifred's accident were filled with doctors and specialists. Mrs. Darling was happy to see that her husband had gotten that man, that neuroscientist or psychiatrist (both words had been thrown around an awful lot since her accident), Dr. Gladstone, to come have a look at her little girl, even if she wasn't sure she believed in this science of the brain they were all talking about. The doctor had looked at her, he'd peered into her eyes like those old witch doctors "seeing" into the soul and after a while, a week to be exact, Dr. Gladstone, along with the other doctors, had unceremoniously decided there was nothing they could do for Winifred. They were stumped and the hospital needed the room, and so the Darlings were offered the choice of either taking their daughter home or putting her into a permanent institution. Mr. Darling had hedged, but Mrs. Darling declared straight away that her little girl would be coming home with her.

They had put her in the small room at first, not the one reserved for guests or the one looking out to the street that would be John's in a couple of years when he came home from Eton, but the small room, the one Netty had slept in before moving to a more suitable servant's quarters upstairs. This room had one tiny window with bars on it. The bars had been there since before the Darlings bought the house, the previous owners had put them in, though no one had ever explained why. Mrs. Darling had always believed that a member of that previous family must have been a lunatic. It was just that no one had bothered to go so far as to put bars on any of the other windows.

After a couple of days, George consented to move Winifred to a nicer room. Mrs. Darling hadn't had anything to do with it. She'd suggested moving Winifred to the guestroom when she was first brought home from the hospital, but no one, namely her husband, had listened to her. She'd gone to see her daughter in that cold, drafty, cell of a room for weeks, knitting in the corner or going over the pages of a novel or the paper her husband left discarded from breakfast. She brought her friends there to see her daughter, propriety be damned, and then one day George decided, as if out of nowhere, as if the idea had just flown into his skull, that it would be best to move Winifred to the guest bedroom. And so a man had been hired to move a larger, more fitting bed into the room, and George had carried his little girl there himself. That had been hard to watch, but watch Mrs. Darling had, as her husband placed his giant, fleshy hands under her daughter's blankets, as he lifted her up and her head slumped back, arms falling from her sides as she lay virtually lifeless, as if George had pulled her out of the sea drowned. He'd carried her down a flight of stairs to the third floor, to the nice white bed that had already been made up with white sheets and the gold-colored comforter that Winifred had been tucked into since she'd been brought home.

Nothing had changed in the following two weeks except the rooms, Mrs. Darling noted as she sat in a chair in the corner, her hands in her lap, glancing back and forth nervously as Dr. Gladstone once again looked over her daughter. He was a young doctor, a bright young man of the new science of the brain, which her husband had been raving about, mostly because his firm had been so taken with it. Dr. Gladstone glanced over at Mrs. Darling a few times as he held a light to Winifred's eyes, as he looked at her long, slender arms and legs, resting his hands on her lifeless body as if she weren't alive, as if her body did not have a breath in it. One time, when he moved to look under her shirt, Mrs. Darling had stood up, nearly reprimanding him, but her husband had calmed her down, laughing both to himself and with Dr. Gladstone as he tried to explain that his wife, a product of a more prudent era, required more modesty. He then looked condescendingly at his wife and said; "Now dear, you have to understand that this doctor must do what this doctor must do. . . ." Societal conventions and all that, the lecture had gone on, and Mrs. Darling had left the room to check on John and Michael, who were playing quietly in the study.

It still made no sense, Mrs. Darling decided as she watched Dr. Gladstone place an instrument in Winifred's ear, listening for some time before he stood up. He didn't seem to be doing anything but watching and she could have done that on her own. Dr. Gladstone was, however, a bit of a renegade, the kind of doctor who liked to do experimental treatments and he had apparently already saved her life. The problem with Winifred's being unconscious (other than the fact that she was unconscious) was that she could not eat or drink and there wasn't much they could do for that. Dr. Gladstone had put a needle into her arm, one that administered fluids to her body so that Winifred did not dehydrate. It was an experimental treatment, something they did out on the battlefields for cholera victims, it wasn't a treatment for an unconscious little girl, but it was giving Winifred fluids, which bought them more time to wake her up.

"Well I'm not sure, she could be in a coma, should could be locked-in, she could simply be unconscious but not entirely in a coma," Dr. Gladstone proclaimed after several seconds, scratching his blond head with long, thin fingers. Mrs. Darling stood up expectantly. Even though he hadn't been very helpful before, each new time he examined her daughter, each new time anything, anything at all happened, she shot up full of hope as if this time. . . .just this time it would be all right. "This happens sometimes, even to little girls, when the brain has sustained a trauma. The brain still works, it's still supplying blood and oxygen, it's still keeping all her organs functioning and yet the neural impulses aren't firing in such a way that is conducive to consciousness." The doctor fixed his stethoscope around his neck as Mr. Darling moved to shake hands with him.

"Thank you, Dr. Gladstone, you've been most kind. I know it hasn't been easy, and to come all the way from Edinburg."

"It's fine," Dr. Gladstone stated. "I wanted to get a look at this sleeping girl, The Sleeping Beauty, as they've been calling her. And I wish I had more to tell you, like if or when she would wake up, but there's no way of knowing and some people remain like this for years, while others pass on and still others wake up. The mind is a peculiar organ and we still don't know what goes on in it, even with all the medical advancements."

"With all the medical advancements," Mrs. Darling repeated, nearly laughing as she walked closer to the two men who'd been standing there talking over her daughter as if this were an old boys club. "Medical advancements, what medical advancements? You just said you didn't know anything. How is that a medical advancement?"

"Ah, my dear," Mr. Darling said, turning toward his wife he put his hands on her shoulders and looked down at her. He smiled condescendingly, he even chuckled, but she could tell she'd embarrassed him. "You shouldn't be acting emotional, not with the doctor. He's only doing his job." Her husband turned then, smiling good-naturedly at the man. "She's just upset."

"It's natural," the young doctor replied and Mrs. Darling, who wanted desperately to stay and fight those two men, instead turned and walked out of the room. She could tell the conversation continued. Her husband would most likely shake the doctor's hand, he'd ask the good doctor to come back, maybe mention the office as he saw him out.

Mrs. Darling walked down the hall; past the brown and white wallpaper they'd put up three years ago. There were pictures on the walls, paintings of flower gardens and still life's of fruit bowls and pillows on couches; there were a few professional photographs, one of herself and Mr. Darling on their wedding day, he in a dapper black tuxedo with a tall black hat while she wore a dress that seemed to flow as if on butterfly wings, her long dark hair hidden behind her lace veil. She walked past the sideboards and end tables, past the door to the closet and into the nursery.

Mrs. Darling opened the door quietly; though it wouldn't have mattered, the boys were making such a ruckus. "On guard!" one of them called just as she entered and saw that it was little Michael.

"You can't say that," John contradicted, pushing his glasses up on his nose. "It's en garde, it's French, you have to pronounce it right, Michael."

"What're you talking about, it's French? I'm Captain O'Hara of the English fleet," Michael proclaimed.

"And I'm Redhanded Jack," John countered. "I'll get you. . . .you codfish, just like the rest of them." John was standing on his bed while Michael slipped unsteadily on a rocking chair, struggling to hold on as if the rocky seas really were underneath him.

The room was a mess; there were blocks, pieces of puzzles and dolls strewn about the dark wooden floor. Netty had never come back, it seemed she understood what it meant to be fired and Mrs. Darling was going to have a hard time sending her last week's wages to her. But at least the boys had been getting on all right. John and Michael had asked her some hard questions about Winifred, wondering if she would be okay, if there was anything they could do, why she, their mother, was so sad all the time. Mrs. Darling had tried to be honest with them, not that there was much to be honest about since she knew nothing.

"I got you!" Michael called as he stuck a wooden sword between John's arm and side as John flopped onto the bed.

"You haven't seen the last of me," he said as he stifled his own breath, making a gasping sound as he lay on the bed, where his little brother continued to poke him.

"And how are you, Mother?" John asked, getting up.

"I'm fine, just fine," Mrs. Darling replied to her boys. "I just wanted to see how you were."

"Fine, we're just fine as well," John stated and it was as if for a brief second he was a grown man making conversation. "And Winifred?"

"The same," Mrs. Darling said dutifully.

"I'm sorry," Michael offered. "We liked it better when she played with us."

"So did I," Mrs. Darling said. And she had liked it better then, even if her daughter was growing up, even if it was getting frightfully silly, Winifred and her pirate and princess games. Still she'd liked it better, so much better when her daughter had played. "Now I want you to get ready for bed, I'll be by in a few minutes to tuck you in."

"Yes mother," little Michael said, turning toward his dresser.

"Yes mother," John repeated without protest. This was the only change in them, the boys still played like high-spirited children, but they were at least doing what they were told the first time they were asked.

As Mrs. Darling turned she heard a high, sharp yapping sound and when she looked down she saw that she'd stepped on Nana's tail. "Oh, you, I thought my husband put you out," Mrs. Darling said to the large Newfoundland dog.

"Don't put Nana out, we like her here," John protested, and the dog, her paws and belly seeming to sag, lumbered toward the children's beds as if to illustrate their affection for her.

"All right, all right. Nana can stay with you, as long as the nursery doesn't start to smell like a dog," Mrs. Darling relented. "I'll be back to tuck you in in a little while," she informed her boys, turning to leave.

The hallway was just as empty, it felt just as dark as before as she made her way back to Winifred's room. It felt funny thinking of that lonely place as Winifred's, but her little girl had taken possession of it, even if there wasn't much of her there. When she reached Winifred's room there was no one but Winifred in it. Her husband and the doctor must have left. Mrs. Darling could hear her husband's blustery voice downstairs and she could only image their continued conversation about "medicine" and "the mind" and "the office."

The room was darker now. The lamp hanging from the ceiling had been turned off and it was only the one near her bed, the light Mrs. Darling insisted stay on at all times, regardless of the threat of fire. What if their daughter woke up and no one was there, what if it was dark and Winifred got scared? What if there was life behind her eyes, what if she were off in her own little world, but she needed light, she needed something to see it by. How could she tell them about the other side if she couldn't see it?

Winifred looked like herself. Her face wasn't swollen anymore and the bruise had gone away. It was her face, just her face, as she lay there, eyes closed, lungs working, heart beating, a chilly lifeless being with just enough in her to lie there. Mrs. Darling watched her daughter, wondering what she could see. She pictured her little girl in a fairy kingdom where a young, handsome prince might find her and bring her back to his castle. She'd play with unicorns during the day and dance into the night. It was a wonderful world her daughter was in, it had to be. But maybe, maybe once she'd had time to miss her family, at least her mother, she'd return.

The door shut on creaking hinges downstairs and Mrs. Darling was sure her husband had gone to see Dr. Gladstone out. He was probably walking him down the street, just to make sure he got into a hansom cab all right. She heaved a sigh, she felt her entire body weaken, it slumped as she looked at her daughter. She ran a hand across her pale, smooth face, moving her light brown hair from her eyes. "Oh Winifred," she said to her. "Oh Winifred, if only we could know. Where are you?" Mrs. Darling sat staring at her daughter, in the quiet of the room they'd given her, a room of her very own. Finally, their little girl was out of that childish nursery.

After a while Mrs. Darling noticed movement in the house, the sounds of doors opening and footsteps. At first she ignored it, with two boys who were always making noise it was easy enough to do, but as the sound moved up the hall she could tell the noise was coming up the stairs. She heard footsteps first and then voices, hearty, talkative men's voices, voices that were saying important things in important ways and she hoped Doctor Gladstone wasn't coming back to check on something.

"And you see, it's just like this, the way they have the structure set up at the firm," Mr. Darling went on, opening the door to Winifred's room as if a little girl were not sleeping there. "Mary, hello," Mr. Darling said when he saw his wife standing over the bed. "Hello, you remember Mr. Barrie. . . .I met him in the street as I was walking the doctor out and he decided to come up and visit."

"Hello Mr. Barrie," Mrs. Darling welcomed their guest. Mr. Barrie had been a fairly near neighbor of the Darling family's for many years. He was a dignified man with a pretty wife and an illustrious career in letters. He'd written a few plays, published essays and stories that were of some import. Mr. Barrie was a sweet man, from what Mrs. Darling could see. He was small, very small actually, and looked like a miniature version of his own self, as if there were a life-sized, grown-man version of Mr. Barrie wandering around London somewhere looking for his miniature. He had short blackish brown hair cropped close to his head and large eyes that stood out in his rather round face. There was something both very adult and also very childish about him as if the man could not make up his mind about growing up.

Mr. Barrie smiled politely and Mrs. Darling nodded graciously as her husband moved toward the bed. He placed an arm on his wife's shoulder and looked over at her for a second before glancing down at Winifred. "Still the same I take it," he said in a gruff voice and Mrs. Darling merely nodded. "I'll tell you. . . .those doctors. Even Doctor Gladstone, the one I thought was sure to fix everything, even he doesn't seem to know what's wrong with her. She's just sleeping, sleeping forever."

"It's as if she's frozen in time," Mr. Barrie commented, looking down at Winifred.

"Yes, yes, frozen in time, how very poetic of you. Leave it to a writer to come up with that. Soon you'll be telling fairy stories and what not Mr. Barrie. But really, any explanation right now, any explanation. . . ." Mr. Darling went on and on and on talking at his guest.

Mrs. Darling paid little mind to her husband. It didn't seem that she was the one who was supposed to be paying much mind anyway, and she was exhausted after the doctor's visit. She watched Mr. Barrie instead—Mr. Barrie, who was also paying very little attention to what George Darling had to say, which was very little, though he used a great many words to say it. Instead he studied Winifred, his big dark eyes seeming to sense something, seeming to know more than they were letting on. Mr. Barrie reached out, nearly touching Winifred's cheek, though propriety made him bring that hand back, placing it in his pocket as he looked down once more.

"I'm very sorry," Mr. Barrie said, looking over his neighbor George and meeting Mrs. Darling's eyes. "I truly am. This must be hard on the family."

"Yes it is," she replied gratefully, "Thank you."

"Of course, of course, and I couldn't imagine. When my wife and I heard, she sent a note right away, but I couldn't bear to think of it. But I am sorry, so sorry."

"Yes, your note, thank you for that, tell Mary we appreciate her thoughts."

"I will," the little man replied, patting his pockets as if he were fumbling for something, as he looked around distractedly. "I'm sorry to rush out, but I really should be going now, I have work to do, but perhaps I could return to see her?" Mr. Barrie asked.

"Yes, my good man, of course, come any time you like," Mr. Darling replied, roughly patting their neighbor on the back and maneuvering him around the bed, toward the door like a bully pushing on a smaller schoolmate. "Thank you very much for your sympathy," he said, going on and on about something, though Mrs. Darling couldn't tell exactly what, as they walked out the door and down the hall.

George appeared a few minutes later, having let Mr. Barrie out. He looked so very proud of himself. Mrs. Darling couldn't tell why, but all of a sudden that smug look on his face got to her. "Why did you bring him here? To gawk at our daughter? All the time to gawk at our daughter as if her condition should award you some prize."

"Mary, what are you talking about?" Mr. Darling asked, completely taken aback, but straining to maintain his decorum.

"All the time with the doctors the firm sends, and going to parties, even while your daughter is asleep, even as she may never wake up. Work, George, all you do is work, even now at a time like this, I can't have you alone for five minutes, you bring the office with you everywhere."

"I bring the office with me everywhere?" George asked, and Mrs. Darling had forgotten that when he wanted to, her husband could have quite a temper. His face grew red, his eyes huge as he stepped closer to his wife and she shuffled back. "Do you think I like going into the office, talking to those stuffed shirts all day? Do you think those stuffed shirts don't know they're stuffed shirts, do you think they like it any more than you do? Don't you think I'd rather play than work? I'd rather sit in front of a card game all day, maybe go down to the club and drink until it closes? But no, I have to work, adults have to work, they do not sit in mourning all day. And our children, they should learn that too."

"George, they're only boys," Mrs. Darling countered, wondering what he meant, he barely paid any mind to John and Michael.

"All the time with their 'en garde' and their 'I'll get you, you little's' as if they were in constant battle. Well, I'll tell you who's in constant battle, I'm in constant battle, constant battle with the world. My wife is cold to me, I have to fight every day for my position at the office so that I might put food on the table and now pay our daughter's medical bills. And the little boys, they have their part to play in this great big world and they should learn life is not a game Mary, it's not all a silly little pirate game." Mr. Darling stopped; he drew closer to his wife, who stepped back, suddenly afraid. He looked like he was about to reach out and grab her, but he moved back instead.

"That's no way to talk about our children," was all Mrs. Darling could say as her husband shook his head and walked away.

PRESTON

"What's going on?" Preston asked amidst the chatter. It had felt like a guessing game when he'd flown down to the forest floor, not bothering with the elaborate system of ladders and pulleys the Lost Boys had erected, to see a mass of boys gathered at the bottom of the tree.

"Look," Starky said, moving out of the way so Preston could see the raving mad Boxwood running in a circle. He was blue, his entire face, his arms, his hands, his feet. At first Preston wondered if this was the blue people got when they died. He'd heard about it in science class, how the body, without proper blood and air, turned blue at the point of death. He wondered if his own body had done that, if his mother had looked down at him and seen a pale blue boy. But this blue was different, it was much brighter, it came sliding down Boxwood's face and arms in sticky splats and it only took Preston a moment to realize it was paint.

"They painted Boxwood!" Starky declared. "This is not okay, are we going to let them get away with this?" The paint was silly, but not the biggest problem, and Preston wondered if the rest of the Lost Boys could see that Boxwood had a large iron nail sticking out of his chest, in the upper left corner, near his heart. The nail held a crumpled piece of parchment paper marked with writing Preston couldn't make out. Preston couldn't tell if Boxwood was in any pain from the injury. He didn't appear to be touching it as he ran around in circles, screaming and crying as the boys gawked at him. He seemed somehow safer this way, as if he were too wrapped up in himself to attack and so the Lost Boys watched, getting closer to Boxwood than they had in decades.

"Why would they do that? Did you see that nail sticking out of his chest?" Preston asked amidst the horde of boys. "Who would do that?"

"Yeah, they stabbed him. They stabbed him!" Starky cried as if he were not so worried about his fallen comrade as he was about the indignity of someone coming to one of them in the night and painting him blue. And though he was a problem, though he'd gone rotten, Boxwood was still one of them, still a Lost Boy no matter how bad he'd gone.

"The Indians did it," Preston heard one of the Lost Boys cry.

"They're cops now," Starky proclaimed. "I saw it yesterday, they turned into cops and the cowboys turned into firemen when they were having a war."

"Why would they change into cops and firemen?" Preston asked. "And why not cops and robbers?"

"Because robbers are bad," Starky explained, draping an arm around Preston as he walked him away from the raving Boxwood and through the thicket of Lost Boys. "And the cowboys, the Indians, the whatevers, neither of them were really bad, and so neither of them are bad now. They just change sometimes into different games. It helps spice up the war. If it were always cowboys and Indians it would get boring."

"But why are they always fighting?" Preston asked and Starky shrugged.

"It's fun I guess, having a war. No one ever gets hurt. Only when the pirates come." Starky whispered the last part and Dilweed, who'd just come up, smacked his arm.

"But we're going to get those cops for this!" Starky cried loudly so most of the Lost Boys heard him and called out their "hear, hear"s, their "yeah, yeah"s and "uh-huh"s as they stood around.

The boys cried out once more and many of them flew from the ground, hovering overhead as Starky remained near the outer perimeter of the group. "We have to make a plan," he instructed, motioning the boys to fly closer to him. Preston, seeing the swarm of flying boys, stayed on the ground and moved to the side as Starky was engulfed in a horde of hovering children.

Preston looked out at the group. They all left to playfully "avenge" one of their own, unable to understand that a human being, no matter how animalistic, was in pain, as they rushed to go incite a riot at the Indian camp. Preston watched Boxwood, careful not to get too close. "Are you okay?" he asked the weeping, bloody, and bright blue child.

Before Preston could rejoin the boys in flight, Peter flew down. Preston couldn't tell where he'd come from. Since he'd been in Neverland, Peter had disappeared for long stretches. Even when Preston tried to find him, it seemed as if he was gone forever, only to return as if time had stopped and he had no clue how long he'd been away. This time there was a boy with Peter, a small boy with large black eyes. His smooth black hair was long-ish and hung past his cheeks, but he was dressed very nicely, like he'd been to a dinner party, in a stiff white dress shirt and black pants.

"Hi Preston," Peter said as he touched down and stood star-ing at Boxwood, who was still running about and raving. He moved in, flying closer until he'd grabbed the note attached to Boxwood. Once the paper was in Peter's hands Preston could see the large red blood stain on the Lost Boy's shirt. Peter let out a loud scream for the purpose of shooing Boxwood away, the birds scattered, the boy with Peter covered his ears, as did Preston, and Boxwood ran into the woods.

"Hi," Peter said again, this time more happily as if he hadn't noticed what was going on. "This is Nosey, I just found him."

"Did he come out of the woods like me?" Preston asked, wondering how Peter could forget the crazed child who'd just run away.

"No, I got Nosey from the fairies. He was there for a little while, but he's better now. They made it so he can speak."

"You can speak?" Preston asked at the boy, who stared at him with wide eyes.

"Hi," the boy said. His voice was hoarse, but he had one. "I'm Nosey."

"That's a funny name," Preston said. He knew not to say things like that. His mother would have corrected such a blatant display of rudeness, but his mother wasn't here, and this place did not seem to care much about rudeness.

"The fairies gave it to me," the boy said. "I used to talk like this," he went on, mocking a very light whisper. "But now I talk like this," he yelled happily.

"He can't remember his other name," Peter whispered very obviously at Preston so as to make sure Nosey could overhear. "He can't remember Before at all. That's what the fairies do, they make it so they forget."

"Does that help them? I thought you didn't come to forget?" Preston asked, looking over at Nosey. There was something about his body, the way he moved, how his face looked as if he was one of those holograms where the picture changed when you turned it one way and another. When Preston looked at him from one direction he had fine-straight hair and a nice, clear face-but when he turned his head slightly there were the shadows of bruises, his hair was disheveled, blood caked his lips and his eyes were sunken as if there were parts of him missing. Nosey smiled at Preston and all he could feel was pure unrelieved pity for this child who couldn't even remember his mother.

"For some children the only option is forgetting, the adult world; grownups do that to them," Peter explained. "It's not for Neverland to fix everything. That's what the After does. Here, we play. I sure do have to explain an awful lot to you, none of the other Lost Boys ask these questions," Bouncing into the air, Peter started to fly again, doing cartwheels as he went. Nosey shadowed him; rolling in the air in somersaults, he followed Peter into the heart of the Lost Boys, who were gathered close by, concocting a revenge plan for the cops. Nosey remained with them, joining their game as Peter returned to Preston, who was still on the ground. "The cops didn't do this," he said seriously, holding the note that had been nailed to Boxwood in his hand. "I don't know how he got out or why he did it."

"Who?" Preston asked, worried by the uncharacteristically unhappy look on Peter's face.

"Captain Hook. He's not supposed to leave Pirate Cove. He said the Island asked him not to and he doesn't believe in showing bad form. Why would he come here?"

"How do you know it's him?" Preston asked, looking at the note to see that he too could not understand it—and he'd always read at a grade higher than his own.

"No one writes like this. Some boys can write Here, a few have written whole long stories, but they don't write like that, look at how he curves his letters. And the mark on the tree over there, that's a hook slash if it's anything."

"Maybe we should hide," Preston suggested, getting more and more frightened.

"Hiding won't help. And I don't think the Lost Boys can defend against him, only I can fight him, but if he starts taking Lost Boys I don't know. I don't know why he's back. Unless it's because you came out of the forest like she did—nothing else is different."

"You think this is my fault?" Preston asked, worried.

"I don't think you did anything. I don't blame you, no, I just think. . . .but it doesn't matter, you're a Lost Boy and I'm sure this is just a fluke, he won't come back again."

"If it's my fault then maybe I should leave," Preston offered, hoping Peter wouldn't take him up on it.

"No, you're one of us, you're not going back."

"Maybe we should tell the Lost Boys."

"No," Peter said, shaking his head. "No, that'll just scare them. They think it's the cops and let them think that. Let them start another war and when the cops deny it they'll fight all the harder."

"Are you sure, Peter?" Preston asked and the leader nodded.

"Let's go join the war," he suggested, flying away to join the Lost Boys.

"You coming?" Dilweed called as he appeared, flying back over Preston.

"Are we going to fight the firemen?" Preston asked, and Dilweed shook his head.

"No, not at all!" he explained. "Come on, we're going on an Explore. Nosey and Starky are leading." With that Dilweed flew off. Preston glanced back and deciding he had all the time in the world, he flew with his friend, joining up with the throng of Lost Boys as they headed over the trees.

Before he could get to the war, when he was almost to the clearing in the trees at the Indian Territory, Peter reappeared, flying up behind Preston, who jumped at the sight of him as they both descended to the ground. He was carrying something in one hand, slipping it behind his back every few seconds as if he wanted to hide it.

"What's that?" Preston asked, glancing around the leader's body to see that it was a book.

"Nothing," Peter said defensively.

"Is that a book, what book is it, does it say something about Captain Hook? Can I see it?" Preston moved to grab the book, and Peter held it back, the pages flapping open. Preston could tell that the writing was very faded, as if very old and the writing wasn't legible, no one could read that book, but Peter didn't seem to know that.

"It's mine, it's my book, no, you can't see it," Peter said more defensively, as if Preston had just caught him naked in the shower. "I'm reading it now."

"I used to love to read," Preston went on, and Peter tossed the book away.

"There, you see, are you happy? Now none of us can read it," Peter cried, annoyed. Preston stepped back, a little startled by the leader's show of emotion, but Peter calmed down after a second. "I'm sorry, it's just that I was thinking about what Hook just did and I don't think. . . ." he went on, letting his mind wander as they started walking.

As they moved on they found Boxwood sitting by the side of a tree not far from the Ferris wheel. It wasn't like before—instead of foaming at the mouth or running around in pain, he was staring into space, just staring, as if he were made of hollowed out wood. Preston gasped at such a doll-like boy, but Peter went up to him, unafraid.

"Well I guess this is what happens when you stay too long and then get attacked by Hook," Peter guessed as if he were trying to figure this all out too.

He grabbed Boxwood's hand and let it drop; it made a hollow sound, a kind of tinkling and a kind of dong at the same time. Peter pulled his flute out of his pocket and started playing. It made a sweet, melodic sound, music like Preston had never heard, and Preston closed his eyes and listened, though it did nothing for Boxwood. "Someone must be living a very long time," Peter explained, shaking his head. "You know it's not supposed to be this way, people are supposed to let go. When they don't let go they're at least not supposed to live so long. Something else must be going on and it's making him mean, and you don't understand, I wish I could tell them all, I wish they had been here, Boxwood was the nicest, the sweetest boy."

"Are pirates frozen and hard like this?"

"Sometimes, they rot in Neverland, until they're nothing but rot, then they go away. I don't know much about pirates, I never took the time to learn, but they're all that's wrong with grownups, all that is bad about adulthood and for some reason Boxwood is turning into this. He's been Here too long, that's all, too long."

"How old is he?" Preston asked.

"I don't know, must be over a hundred by now. He came here in oh. . . .what was the year. . . .I'm always forgetting the time. It was a long time ago, well before Starky."

"That's a long time," Preston agreed, recalling the story Starky had told and that he'd heard something about a certain war where there had been trains and lines and showers and. . . .but he couldn't remember the time either.

"Someone has to be living a great long while. I thought people forgot when they got old. That's what they always say, that you turn back into a little boy or girl once you get to be a certain age."

"Is that so?" Preston asked. "No one ever told me that."

"It's what grownups say when they're trying to sound wise. I never much cared for grownups. . . ." Peter explained, looking off into the distance, at the plains of Neverland. "Anyway, how did Boxwood come here? How did Boxwood come here? Let me see. . . .it wasn't that he was very sick. It was that he was in a kind of ice skating accident. It was awful, just awful I'm sure. But now he's Here and for some reason they or he or she or it, will not let him go."

"Could there be some kind of mistake?" Preston asked, trying, in his mind at least, to turn the they or he or she or it into one concrete being, maybe a very tall man with a very gray beard, or a very pretty lady with long flowing hair.

"I guess anything is possible, but mistakes are very rarely made. I think maybe we should move him into the tree. He's safe now," Peter offered, crouching down, placing his hand under Boxwood's chin and trying to give him some water out of his canteen. The water spilled clumsily down Boxwood's blue, rotting chin, wetting his clothes. Peter looked at the child, worried, though Preston thought it was a little funny, water dribbling down his chin like that. He then wondered if this was the difference between Peter and the rest of them, the Lost Boys would have laughed, but Peter just stoically stood there. Peter knew what to do and did it, he took care of them, he had fun, he was always smiling; but there was something else—Peter knew things, he understood things deeply the way others did not.

Just then a whoosh came through the trees, as if all the leaves were moving at the exact same time and then a light grew brighter and brighter as a few of the Lost Boys, their hair and clothes soaking wet, flew up, preceded and followed by a group of fairies.

"Peter, Peter," the Lost Boys cried in unison. Here it seemed much easier for boys to cry out in unison than it had in the Before, as if they'd practiced getting the timing just right.

"Peter," Oregano said, his voice breaking away from that of the group, "there's a fireman war. The firemen are fighting the cops. They turned the hoses on the cops and we got caught in the crossfire."

"Well, we can't stand for that!" Peter proclaimed. "To the firemen!" he cried, one fist high in the air as if it were a call to arms.

The Lost Boys laughed, throwing their arms up and spraying the water that had soaked into their clothing all over, getting Peter and Preston and Boxwood wet. "Are you coming?" Peter called from a few feet up in the air as the Lost Boys flew back over the trees. The fairies hovered around Peter, casting shadows over his face so he looked like a smiling, mischievous jack-o-lantern.

"No, I think I'll go back to the tree," Preston said.

"All right, I'll see you later tonight," Peter replied, winking once and giving a long, boisterous crow as he zoomed into the air and flew over the trees, forgetting Boxwood as he caught up with the Lost Boys. Preston took one last look at Boxwood. There didn't seem to be much he could do for him. He considered picking him up, now that he appeared hollow inside maybe he could carry the boy, but he didn't want to risk dropping and perhaps breaking him. What would happen then? Instead, Preston patted the boy's head; smiled down at him, and walked back to the tree house.

The Ferris wheel was still turning and more boys, mostly the new boys, were riding it. The lights of the tree house were still on though the sun was out, and there were a few fairies buzzing about. Preston tried to remember the first time he'd come Here. He'd been too confused to see it with the kind of wonder and amazement that was necessary and he wished he'd come to Neverland the normal way. He now had friends Here. Starky had started coming over to his room to play video games, and he and Oregano had gone on long walks together, but the boys who had come as a group seemed to remain as one, playing with each other, belonging much more than he did. He remembered Peyton and how they ran around the schoolyard chasing Kyle Fargus, and Eva, who was a girl and so she did not play with them at school, where girls had their own games, but who was always with them when they got off the bus.

Preston walked along the tree house, feeling the thick scratchy trunk as he dragged his hand along it. He grabbed at a piece of bark but it would not come off; he pulled harder and harder, stopping in his tracks as the boys on the other side of the tree got a little closer. When they were gone Preston continued pulling. He'd taken bark off the tree before, all the boys did, though it always seemed to come back a few minutes later, but this bark would not budge. Preston looked up at the tree and noted that a knob had appeared. He touched it and a sign emerged "Peter's Room— Do Not Enter Under Penalty of Death." Preston laughed at that, since he knew what penalty of death meant in Neverland and it was never anything more than a couple of scratches, sometimes a few minutes held underwater by the mermaids. He pulled harder at the bark until a white light came flashing at him.

The white light gave off a certain tinkling sound, the sound of very soft, very sad bells. Peter had already explained that this was the fairy language and that only he could understand them. The fairy belled and buzzed at him, twinkling off and on for a couple of seconds until another fairy approached.

"I'm just trying to get in," Preston explained, looking toward the flashing light and wondering if he could reason with it. "I know it's Peter's room, but Peter doesn't have any secrets. How can he have secrets, he's our leader?" The lights twinkled as they flew about Preston's head. "I know that I'm being curious, but still, you must understand what it's like to be curious. Aren't you curious sometimes?" The fairies continued flying the same way and so Preston decided to try another tactic. "You must not be curious, of course you're not curious, being so powerful and all. I really do envy you fairies. You're the real leaders, aren't you? Peter is just for show, but I see how you take care of everything, that it's your dust that helps us fly. You're the ones who are really in charge." The fairies stopped twinkling quickly and one of them rested ever so softly on his shoulder. "It's just that I was wondering what was inside, you must understand that, being so influential, don't you understand wonder?" Preston asked the great ball of light.

Just then the light jumped from his shoulder and moved toward the other light, a twinkling rush at the door as a great buzzing noise could be heard from the less compliant fairy. The door in the tree opened to reveal the great blinding light of the fairy who'd let him in. The other fairy began buzzing back and forth, flying all about the room, knocking into picture frames and turning over a glass vase, though she didn't break anything. The fairy's great bell-voice went off, as did the other fairy's as if they were in an argument. Preston watched it, too amazed by the fairies to even notice the room he was in. After a second the angry fairy, whose light had gone red, flew off while the other remained a great bright light pulsating, as Preston looked about the room.

It was a rustic bedroom, part tree and part house. The walls were made of knotted wood and Preston could see the nicks in the trunk and bark coming through the other side. The floor was made of dirt, covered with a red carpet, which helped make the place look more pleasant. In one corner stood a sturdy chair made of sticks and a wooden bed with a carved headboard and a mattress that, when Preston sat upon it, sounded as if it was filled with crunchy leaves. The room was just any old room inside a tree trunk, but it was what was in the room that caught his eye.

There were, across from the bed, two pictures framed by sticks. They weren't the kinds of pictures Preston's mother used to take, the ones that came up on the computer; they were black and white and a little fuzzy. Black lines ran down the sides as if the film had been damaged, but Preston could clearly see the face of a girl—only it wasn't really a girl, but a woman who looked a little like his mother. She was very pretty, even if her mouth frowned at the edges. She had a small mouth like a bow and a tiny, ever so slightly pointed nose. The woman's long light brown hair hung down around her face in curls, there was a ribbon in her hair, and she wore a dress with grayish-white lace at the neck. The other picture was nearly identical, only the woman's eyes, which were bright and smiling just like her mouth in the first photo, were downcast here, her lips quivering as if she were about to cry.

Against the wall, kitty-corner to the bed, stood a desk without a chair— a sturdy wooden slab that did not look as if it came from the time Preston had. It was large and imposing and looked as if it should have very important papers or incredibly rare objects resting on it. The desk had been kept in good repair, but there were stains on its top and a few scratches at its sides. On the desk sat many drawings done in what looked like charcoal. The drawings were of that same woman, only she wasn't a woman, but a girl about Peter's age. She wasn't wearing a frilly dress, but something more like a long nightgown and her hair was straighter and a little messier as it fell alongside her face. Her eyes were the same as the first picture; only they were smiling, really smiling and her lips looked as if they were about to give a great, gigantic kiss. The most startling thing was that she was not alone in the drawings—Peter was with her. Someone had drawn him there and in one of the drawings she was asleep in his arms, both lying in a bed of leaves, but Peter was awake, looking down at the sleeping girl. In the other drawing, they were sitting by a stream, her head on his shoulder as they both pointed down at a jumping fish. There was laughter in that picture, laughter and life, and Preston half expected them to start dancing on the paper, they had so much energy in them.

Besides the pictures on the desk there were things that made Preston step back and gasp when he noticed them. The first were two jars filled with a kind of bluish-gray liquid. As he looked closer, peering into them, he noticed that they each contained a hand, two large hands with big, hairy knuckles and rotting fingernails. Though they weren't aging or decomposing, they appeared limp and dead. Preston did not go near the desk again, though he noted the greenish-brown hide spread across part of the top. It looked rubbery and bumpy and he might have touched it if he hadn't have first seen those hands.

It appeared the room housed many secrets, none of which Preston could discern on his own, and he stood back, remembering that there was a fairy with him. Her light was still on and was the only reason he could see anything. Preston turned around and another light came through the door, a bright and glaring light that nearly blinded him. Preston cried out, stumbling back as he saw Peter in the doorway, lips pursed, frowning. Preston had never seen him angry, really angry, but with the light on his face and the glare in his eyes, it was as if Peter were on fire, ready to toss rocks and brimstone at him.

"What are you doing here?" Peter asked in a loud, booming voice that was, despite its anger, surprisingly forced and boyish. "You're not supposed to be in here," he cried, upset now, sad. His face melted as he walked into the room, the door closing behind him. He sat on the bed, sinking into it, his head in his hands. "What are you doing here and how did you get in? No one is supposed to get in," he demanded, a single tear sliding down his cheek. "This isn't right. This isn't right and there are things and this…what're you doing here?" Peter asked again as if he couldn't believe that someone would be so cruel as to violate his privacy.

"I'm sorry, I didn't mean to hurt you, it's okay. One of the fairies let me in, but don't blame her, it wasn't her fault, I tricked her," Preston explained, sitting next to Peter.

Peter turned toward the fairy still sitting in the room. She had gone dimmer, but still flickered. "Fairies are supposed to be smarter than that," Peter said in its direction. "They aren't supposed to allow themselves to be tricked."

"I'm sorry I did it, it's my fault and I'll forget everything I saw. Everything."

"You will not," Peter huffed.

"What is it?" Preston asked in spite of himself.

"You lasted five seconds, five seconds. This is why I locked it all up. It's mine and it was supposed to stay mine. Boxwood was the only one who saw it and you see how he is now. I thought it was safe. And now you're here and you're asking questions." Peter stopped, his face brightened for a moment and he looked long and hard at Preston. "I knew you weren't like the others. You came the same way she did. You came like she did so maybe you can bring her back."

"Who?" Preston asked. "The girl in the pictures?"

"Yes, the girl in the pictures," Peter explained, smiling as if he couldn't help himself whenever she was mentioned. "The girl in the pictures, I never put it together, but here it is, here you are and you came just like she did. Only I found her then. The girl in the pictures—don't you see, I'm a married man."

"A married man?" Preston asked, looking at the impish boy standing before him. Yes, he was older than Preston, but he had such a boyish face, such small features. He was nothing like his father or Mr. List or Eva's dad, who he knew were all married men.

"I wasn't always this young," Peter explained. "I used to be older, because children used to stay innocent longer than they do now. I was seventeen at one time and then sixteen. I was seventeen when I met her and I'm fourteen now, maybe thirteen, and if children keep growing up at the rate they do, I'll be a newborn baby before you know it."

"Why are these things so important to you?" Preston asked.

"Because they are. They're my things, things the Lost Boys can't touch, things I did on my own and so no one else can see them. I'm Here to take care of them, you see, and they don't need to know certain things."

"Whose hands are those?" Preston asked, pointing at the murky jars on the desk.

"They're a pirate's hands," Peter explained. "I cut off his first hand a very long time ago and threw it to a crocodile, who chased him for a long time before I killed the crocodile and took its skin," he went on, pointing at the hide on the desk. "I had to kill it, it was making a nuisance of itself, threatening the boys because it had eaten a part of a pirate and nearly became one. It almost got Starky when he was new Here, and so I did what had to be done."

"You killed it," Preston repeated, remembering the times Peter had skinned lions and tigers in the Neverforest around the tree house.

"I killed it," Peter said ominously. "Me and the pirates, only we can kill things. Only I don't kill things like they do, the way he does."

"Is that his hand?" Preston inquired, wide eyed.

"His hand?" Peter asked, scratching his head and looking as confused as a little boy naturally should when talk of cut-off hands is going on. "His hand, yes, the pirate's hand—Hook, Captain Hook, that's his hand. And the other one is as well."

"But from Before," Preston started, thinking out loud.

"Yes, I know, I know, before I had only cut off one hand and he only had one hook. But then later I cut off the other hand and they never had time to get that into the story, because no one has come back since then and so no one knows what has gone on since her."

"Really? You cut off both his hands, he has two hooks?" Preston asked, growing excited, though he had a sinking feeling that any excited feelings about pirates were strictly forbidden.

"Yes," Peter replied simply. "And it was for the best. The things he did with his hands, no wonder I had to cut them off. He's the worst of them you know, the absolute worst and he'll never leave. He stays Here just like I do, but I was Here first and then there were the fairies and then there was Hook."

"And who is she?" Preston asked, pointing once more at the girl in the picture.

"That is Wendy Moira Angela Darling," Peter explained, standing very straight and acting very professional, much more professional than a boy in ripped shorts should act. "She is the only girl to ever come to Neverland and the only living breathing creature to ever return from it. She appeared in the forest just like you did. She was our mother and our sister, our playmate and my wife," Peter explained, and sitting back on the bed, he began playing with his fingernails, cleaning them out as if he were absentmindedly lounging. Preston didn't want to leave—whenever he was with Peter he always wanted to remain with him, but since Peter was always flying off, always disappearing or running away, the boy was harder to catch than a fairy. But now here he was, just sitting there and Preston did not want to leave. Not that he could have left, since the door had been shut when Peter walked in and there was no knob. Preston had no clue how to open it and anyway, he had so many questions to ask Peter, who looked calm enough now to entertain them.

Peter (some one hundred years before)
(But Peter can never remember the time)
He (and sometimes they called him The Boy and other times they called him Pan, though the Lost Boys had come up with some hundred other such names for him over the years) was chasing his shadow. It was always mucking about. Only a few short weeks

ago The Boy hadn't known the thing existed. It had been there, a black and flittering form following him around, but he'd never given it a second thought until Tink started hanging around him more often. She'd been hanging around him for a very long time, not as far back as he could remember, since he could remember everything and there was a time when there had been no fairies, when there had been no land to run on or water to swim in or trees to climb or even air to fly through and there had only been him, him and the Before and the After and he knew he had been put here by something.

Then the land had come with its trees and its waters and its animals, the fairies had arrived and it made this place a little less lonely. The Boy taught the fairies to speak, only he didn't know words then—he didn't learn those until the little boys, the Lost Boys, started coming to the Island—and so he spoke in bells and chimes and the fairies learned that language and never forgot it, refusing to change with the times and use words like everyone else. The fairies were not ones for progress. But then the pirates had come, the pirates first, before the cowboys and Indians, which were not always cowboys and Indians, but kings and noblemen or warriors with skulls painted on them and warriors in armor. But the pirates came first and The Boy learned very quickly, especially when he had the Lost Boys to protect, to stay away from their part of the Island.

By this time there had been many boys coming in and out of the Island. He'd taken them in, they'd built a tree house connected to the house underground and every few years or so the boys brought something new, something grand with them, like the motorcar that they drove around the giant tree in a great circle. Sometimes these things stayed, but most of the time they decayed and the fairies carried them out to sea to make room for the new grand things the latest Lost Boys brought. They had yet to bring a shadow-catcher however, which was really what The Boy needed at that moment. "Come on Tink and let me catch my shadow. Stop scaring it away," The Boy cried and Tink just shone brighter and brighter and The Boy closed his eyes against the enormous light.

Hi shadow kept gliding through the trees, getting caught in the leaves, only the shadow was thin and fluid and The Boy, being something called a Betwixt-and-Between, had a body that was heavier and stronger and so he got caught in the branches while the shadow whizzed about. It seemed as if his shadow thought it was better than him and The Boy did not like that one bit.

"Come on, Tink," he cried as the fairy who had proclaimed herself his fairy and would not leave him alone— not that The Boy minded most of the time—whirled about him, blinking in and out and sending the poor shadow into a tailspin. "Leave my shadow alone, let me catch the silly old thing," The Boy cried and the fairy belled and chimed around him. "You can't be all that fussy," The Boy fumed at the fairy, trying to catch her, but she was much too fast for him. Fairies were too fast for everything and were only caught when they wanted to be. "Come on Tink, I want to catch my shadow. Make it stay in one place." The fairy chimed once more. "I know you know how to stop it, Tink, quit kidding," he cried, annoyed that the silly shadow wouldn't play by his rules.

Upset, he sank to the forest floor, onto a bed of leaves with his head in his hands, a pout on his face. "I just wanted to play with my shadow, not with you," he cried at the fairy, who blinked a few times and dashed away. When the shadow didn't appear, even when Tink was gone, The Boy put his head in his hands and sighed, a single sob escaping from his throat.

"Boy," someone said and it was as if it had come out of nowhere. It was a fairy voice, a fairy voice, except it was speaking in words, and The Boy wondered for a brief moment if the fairies had evolved and consented to speak in words instead of bells. "Boy, why are you crying?" the fairy voice asked and when The Boy turned he saw something sitting by a tree. It looked like a fairy, at least it looked like what The Boy had always imagined a fairy to look like, only he'd never seen them because they were too bright even for him. It looked like him, in any case it was as big as him, well, almost as big as him, it had a face and hands, but it was different too, and not like the other boys either. It had long hair, hair down to its shoulders, but the long hair wasn't messy or raggedy, it was kind of pretty. It wasn't wearing pants or shorts or leaves, but a long kind of blue cloth that hugged its figure and it seemed delicate, just like a boy only nicer.

"What are you?" The Boy asked, intrigued, but so embarrassed by his interest that he sounded mean. "What're you doing Here? I've never seen you before."

"My name is Winifred," it said. "I'm a girl."

"A girl?" The Boy asked. "What's a girl?"

"A girl is like a boy except. . . .only nicer and prettier and usually a great deal smarter, only most grownups I know don't normally think that and. . . ."

Bells chimed and The Boy looked up at Tinkerbelle. "No, it's a girl, it said, a girl."

"She," the girl corrected and The Boy wondered why something so strange wasn't more worried about finding itself in such a foreign place. "You do not call a girl an it, you call a girl a she, just as you call a boy a he."

"And how come I haven't seen anything like you before?" The Boy demanded.

"I don't know," she replied, looking around. "I've never been here before. Is it near London? At Kensington Gardens perhaps?"

"It is not," The Boy said moving closer. "We're somewhere else I take it, on the Island. Second star to the right and straight on 'til morning. But it's not that simple, not at all, and the Island has to be looking for you in order for you to find it. And why was the Island looking for you?"

"I don't know," she said. "I was in the park and we were playing on the bridge and one of my brothers bumped me and I fell and hit my head and now I'm here." She touched her head as if it hurt, though The Boy knew that it couldn't, nothing hurt Here unless you were with a pirate.

"I'm very sorry to hear that," The Boy said, and he had never been sorry to hear of the how or why of any of the boys who came to him. Even the boys the fairies had to take away, he knew they were Here for a reason, that there was a plan at work, but with this girl it was different and he felt bad that she had hit her head and he was overcome with an enormous urge to make it better. "Can I get you some ice? Maybe a wet rag for your head?"

"It doesn't hurt now, silly boy," she said, giggling. "Who are you?"

The Boy stepped closer to her. Tinkerbelle got close as well and The Boy shooed her away, whacking at her with his hand. "Stop that Tink, she is not," The Boy said to the fairy, giving her one last shove before she flew away.

"What was that? What did it say?" the girl asked, her big brown eyes looking so deeply into him that The Boy had to close his own eyes; he could not look at her.

"That is a fairy."

"A fairy, how lovely! Is she beautiful? What did she say?" the girl asked, clapping her hands and bouncing up and down.

"This one. . . .I'm not sure, we don't see them, they're too bright and move too quickly. As to what she said, she said nothing," The Boy lied, wondering why he felt the need to protect her from Tink's scathing words.

"And if there are fairies Here then perhaps I should be asking what you are?" the girl asked looking at him funny.

"The birds call me a Betwixt-and-Between and the Island seems to think that I. . . ." but The Boy thought better of saying that he'd come out of the ether. "I mean I have to be at least a little human to do what I do, but to say that I am all the way human. . . .no, I don't think that either."

"You're a funny boy," the girl said, giggling. "And what is your name?"

"Pan," The Boy replied since that was the last name the Lost Boys had given him. They'd been naming him for quite a while, calling him after their Gods and sometimes he was Ra and sometimes he was Jupiter, but just now a little boy named Carsly had taken to calling him Pan. The Boy never asked what these names meant, he only took them, wore them for a while and tossed them away with the next round of boys.

"Pan?" she asked, not impressed. "That's an awfully short name. Do you have another?"

"Who needs more than one name?"

"I don't know. . . .many people," the girl said. "Let me see, I think that I shall call you Peter. Peter Pan, yes. A neighbor of ours, a Mr. Barrie, he was over just the other day talking about a boy named Peter that he'd met at Kensington Gardens and how he wanted to write a story and yes. . . .I'll call you Peter Pan."

"Peter Pan," The Boy said and by the look on the girl's face he decided he liked it. "All right, I can be Peter Pan."

"Peter Pan, what a lovely name. And a very short one," the girl proclaimed, clapping and smiling as Peter wondered why he was so glad to have made her happy. He made the Lost Boys happy all the time, he never meant to, he just did, making them happy came naturally, but he had never felt particularly good about it.

"And what is your name again?" Peter asked.

"Winifred Moira Angela Darling," she said very importantly and Peter felt as if this were only a jumble of letters that got stuck on the tongue jamming it up so that it couldn't work properly. "But people sometimes call me Winnie," she elaborated.

"Winnie?" Peter asked, scratching behind his ear like the dogs that hung around the tree. "Winnie...like Windy, like the wind that flies over the trees that the Lost Boys sometimes catch and glide on. . . .Windy. . . .no, but that won't do because Windy is already a name for what the air does when it acts up. . . .but let me see. . . ." Peter thought long and hard. "Wendy!" he cried, a single finger in the air as if he'd realized something very important. "Wendy, that's it, your name is Wendy."

"Wendy," the girl repeated the name, rolling it around on her tongue and tasting it. "Wendy, I like it, Peter, I like it."

"I knew you would," Peter replied and holding out his hand, he moved to help the girl up. "You can come with me now. I'll take you to where I live."

"Where you live?" Wendy asked. "Is it far? Is it in England?"

"It is not in England. You're not in England, Wendy, you're on the Island, some of the boys call it Neverland. I'll take you to my tree house."

"The boys?" she asked, stopping in her tracks, she seemed a little scared. There was a look on her face, one that said she did not want to go on, that made Peter want to do anything, absolutely anything, to make it go away. "Where am I?"

"You're in Neverland," Peter answered, since this had always been sufficient information when the Lost Boys came. "It's Neverland and there are cowboys and Indians and fairies and mermaids."

"Mermaids!" she cried, brightening up. "But I'll miss my mother," she went on and Peter wondered what this Mother was and why it was so special. He'd heard the Lost Boys talk about mothers, apparently they washed faces and sent children to bed, but he'd never had one and didn't find the prospect particularly appealing.

"But there are mermaids," Peter said again to tempt her. "Come, I'll take you to my tree house and you can live with me and the Lost Boys."

"The Lost Boys?" she asked, confused as she reached out, grasping Peter's hand. He noticed then how dainty her grasp was, her hands so thin and delicate.

"Come on, we'll fly there," Peter said and with that they were in the sky. Wendy grasped tighter to his hand the higher he flew, and so he flew higher than was safe or necessary so that she might hold even tighter. Peter closed his eyes as he flew; he had every bit of the air around Neverland memorized and could move back and forth across the Island blindfolded. At one point Wendy slipped, and though, Peter had been paying close attention, even though his eyes were closed, his grasp loosened and she went tumbling. Usually the boys could fly on their own pretty quickly, but this Wendy was a girl and so Peter decided she most likely needed more instruction. Wendy cried out, trying to grasp at the air, though Peter knew the air had never been particularly helpful where grabbing was concerned. Peter dove for her quickly, holding her entire body as she wrapped her arms tightly around his neck. The higher he went, once again, the tighter she held on and Peter felt himself never wanting to stop, to remain in the air, holding Wendy, until Neverland disappeared and there was nothing left.

After a while they touched down. Wendy let go of Peter's neck and tried to straighten out her dress, which had gotten blown about in the flight. She glanced around the tree house. It looked different from the last time he'd been there. It always looked different with the car parked near the side of the tree and the sticks used as lanterns forming a controlled fire blazing around the outer edges. Six boys were playing in the dirt in front of the entrance, tossing a ball around, laughing and pointing, though they turned quickly when they saw Peter.

"Hello, hello," Peter announced, waving. Usually he flew to them, but with Wendy he thought it would be more gentlemanly to walk.

Toodles turned around first, followed by Slightly and Nibs, then Curly and the twins, who always did everything together, so much so that Peter was more often than not annoyed by it. He'd had twins before, he'd had three and four identicals and one time he'd had five all at the same time, but these twins were too much alike, so much so that he sometimes did not trust them. Boxwood was there as well. He'd come to Neverland a few batches ago but still acted very much like a newcomer, sweet and innocent and always helping people. Once, when a boy was carried off by a mermaid and didn't return for a long time, Boxwood conducted a prayer service, getting to his knees and reciting something called "The Our Father" thirty-seven times before the boy was brought back.

"Everyone," Peter announced as the boys watched him. "This is Wendy." He smiled, feeling as if he should bow at having brought them such a prize, but the Lost Boys, for the first time, looked past Peter and at the girl.

"I've seen a Wendy before," Slightly stated. "I remember one of them was my mother and when I fell out of my window and came Here, she was quite upset. I remember after I fell out, before it all went dark, there was crying and screaming."

"I remember my mother too," Boxwood said innocently nostalgic. "I was her favorite. There was little Alex and little James and me, but I was her favorite and I remember thinking about her when I fell into the ice."

"I remember my mother...." Nibs went on and Peter stopped listening.

"Yes, yes, Wendy is Here now, but she's not your mother, she's...." Peter looked at her; the girl's eyes were big and bright. "She's my mother."

"Your mother," the Lost Boys said, believing it at once. Toodles stood up and walked toward Wendy, holding out his hand.

"It's nice to meet you. I've always wanted to meet the woman who gave birth to Pan."

"Gave birth?" Wendy gasped, horrified.

"No, no, no, none of that and it's just...." Peter interrupted, feeling stuck. "She's all of our mother, of course, she is all of our mother. Wendy," Peter turned to her. "Do you know how to be a mother? Would you like to be our mother?"

"Your mother?" Wendy asked and Peter tried to read her face, which was scrunched up so that her lips looked like they were tied in a little bow and he wanted desperately to touch them.

"Yes, yes, yes," all the boys cried together. "Be our mother, be our mother."

"All right then," Wendy said, seeming to be getting the hang of the situation. "I'll be your mother and Peter can be your father."

"Peter?" Nibs and Toodles asked together, scratching their shaggy heads since they had never heard him called Peter before.

"I'm Peter," he informed the boys. "Peter Pan, Wendy said so."

"I did say so, and Peter can be your father," Wendy reiterated much too politely.

"Father?" Peter asked. He knew what these were, these mothers and these fathers. They were boys and girls, only they weren't boys and girls, they were men and women who ran the children's lives in the Before. They were supposed to take care of them, just like Peter was supposed to take care of them Here, but they sometimes did a very bad job. Even the ones whose children did not end up with the fairies, even the ones whose children missed them, still they wanted to send the children to school and make them get jobs, they wanted this and that and this and that and Peter never quite understood. He thought the Before would be a lot better without mothers and fathers. "I don't want to be a father," Peter said at Wendy, a bit annoyed, though he felt bad about it a second later.

"Oh please Peter," she said, grasping his hand and holding tight to it. "Please Peter," she said again and he could not say no, he found himself paralyzed when she looked at him.

"Oh, all right," Peter huffed. "But it's only just pretend?"

"Yes," Wendy said, twirling around and around as the Lost Boys crowded about her as she twirled and Peter stood back, watching. He wanted desperately to get close to her, to grasp her hand and twirl around and around with her, but he couldn't get to her with the Lost Boys dancing about.

"Tell us a story, Wendy," Toodles cried.

"Yes, a story," Boxwood echoed. "My little brother James was always good at telling stories."

"A story, all right," Wendy said, sitting in the dirt next to the tree. "Crowd around and I shall tell you the story of Cinderella, a girl who was once a maid, before she goes to a ball and meets a prince and. . . ."

"And then what?" the Lost Boys cried in unison and Peter stood against a tree, watching. Wendy seemed to have gotten comfortable, she was no longer confused as she talked on and on, using words like "witch" and "princess," "fairy godmother," and "happily ever after."

"And they lived happily ever after," Wendy proclaimed as the story drew to a close and the Lost Boys stood, cheering. They hugged Wendy and she held them close, they danced around her and tugged at her dress. "One at a time, boys, one at a time," Wendy announced. "I am your mother and shall hug each and every one of you, but one at a time, please," she instructed and Peter wondered if he should step in, though she seemed to be enjoying herself.

From that moment and for what felt like a long time (though it also felt like no time, since Peter was always forgetting the time) Wendy was their mother and Peter their father. She put the Lost Boys to bed that night, after having met them all. There were so many, always so many—Peter had never noticed it until he watched Wendy with them. It seemed that he didn't ever need to keep track of all the boys he had in his charge. There might have been a hundred, and he knew them all, knew them by story and name and face, but it didn't seem to matter quite so much. With him they played big games. He took them hunting for bears and tigers; he took them to play with the Indians and to gaze at the mermaids. He watched them play on their own, but he was only watching and even when he was doing things with them, he was simply doing, but with Wendy it was different. She tucked each boy into bed, she told them stories, sometimes together and other times one by one. She talked to the boys and made them breakfast and dinner using the food that the boys had caught or the food that they pretended to have, it never mattered Here. But Wendy made the food, though Peter never knew exactly how, since he was always out playing with the boys. She cleaned the tree house, picking up socks and fixing hanging buttons, she sewed pockets into the boys' clothing and made sure they all looked neat and tidy, giving them baths in the stream in the woods using thick lathery soap that stuck to their skin until she rinsed it off. It seemed that her work was harder and yet at the end of the night Wendy always came to Peter. She sat on the big chair he'd made out of sticks, resting her head on his shoulder. Sometimes she'd run her fingers across his arm as she fell asleep. Wendy was always tired at night, and sometimes night did not come to Neverland for five or six days, since time was so confused Here.

Peter showed Wendy everything. He was good at that, giving the grand tour. He showed her the mermaids, who were not very fond of her. One of them grabbed onto her pretty blue dress, ripping it as she tried to pull Wendy into the water. Peter had had to swoop in to rescue Wendy, flying nearly into her and grasping her around the waist, Wendy's arms locked tightly around his neck so that he wanted to hover over Mermaid Lagoon forever, but Wendy tugged on his arm and instructed him to go. After that, they met the cowboys and Indians, who had been dukes and lords until only a few weeks before. The Indians had fascinated Wendy. She'd gone to the Chief, a large man with short red hair and freckles, and asked if she could live with them. The Chief had been flattered, promising to make her an Indian Princess, and she had been so excited by the idea that Peter almost let her do it, but then he remembered that he wanted Wendy with him and so he told their Chief, "She's a mother, she belongs with the Lost Boys." At being reminded of her domestic duties Wendy changed her mind and decided to stay with Peter and the Lost Boys. After a few minutes with the Indians, as one of them was showing her his drum, the cowboys burst in, guns blazing, blasts of noise firing every which way and raising so much smoke that she cried out and covering her ears ran into the forest as Peter followed.

"I don't like them," Wendy cried, pointing at the cowboys, who had just started another war. "I don't like them at all, keep them away from me."

"All right Wendy," Peter said, running a hand through his blond hair. "As long as I'm around, and I'm going to be around forever, I'll keep the cowboys away."

"Oh yes, Peter, please do," Wendy replied, clapping now as the guns kept going off in the background. "And if you are going to be around forever, does that mean I'll be Here forever too?"

"Of course it does," Peter answered, not bothering to consider this any further.

Things went on in Neverland. Wendy was the mother, cleaning the tree house and telling stories while Peter was the father, doing what he had always done, playing games with the children, making sure they were in bed and taken care of, finding the fairies and having them deal with the more complicated issues.

One day Peter saw Wendy sitting by a tree with something in her lap. When he sat next to her she showed him a drawing she'd done of a plant growing out of the side of a tree. The Lost Boys had brought paper and pencils, paints and charcoal, but he'd never seen them make images the way she did.

"You just draw a line like this," Wendy said after handing Peter the paper and charcoal. She grasped his hand and showed him how to draw a line, pulling his hand across the paper. "Then you draw another line like this, and then another and another until you have a picture," but Peter's hand started shaking. He couldn't tell if he was doing it right, all he could feel was her hand on his, her skin pressing against his own. He looked at her, she glanced away and started giggling. "You silly boy, you have to try and make the lines make sense." Peter glanced at his drawing to see a mish-mash, not a picture. "But I do think it's pretty," she went on. After that Peter vowed to spend an hour a day (whatever that was) learning to draw. Sometimes he worked with Wendy and sometimes he tried by himself, but he got in an hour a day, trying to draw Wendy as well as she'd drawn that plant.

One day Wendy disappeared and Peter grew worried that she'd gone back from wherever she'd come from. Since she hadn't come to him the normal way, and because she was so very strange, he didn't know if she could simply disappear just as she'd appeared. Boys did not disappear from him in Neverland. Sometimes they vanished from each other, but Peter always knew where they went because it was he who took them there, toward the After. But he never took them all the way, because Peter was never allowed to go there. But Wendy had not gone to the After because he would have had to have taken her, and anyway, he would have known because there were certain things Peter knew, things Peter could feel that the Lost Boys and the Indians, the cowboys and even the fairies and Pirates didn't understand.

But Wendy was not in the After and she wasn't with the Lost Boys and so Peter set off looking for her. He considered asking the fairies for help, but Tinkerbelle, who was still upset with him, saying that she was no longer his fairy, had already told the fairies not to help Peter where Wendy was concerned. And the Lost Boys were just that, lost. Peter was their leader and it was his job to take care of them, not the other way around. When it came to Wendy, Peter knew he was on his own.

And so he did what a boy naturally does when he cannot find what he's looking for. He called out for her, he rummaged under his bed in the trunk of the tree, he asked the Lost Boys very casually if they knew where she was. He huffed and complained and moaned about it. Peter then decided to go for a walk, making his way to the Indian camp, where he saw that they were having a party, the cowboys being away just then on their own expedition.

Peter knew better than to be intrigued by these parties. He could remember when the Indians were Lords and the cowboys, Dukes and they'd all dress up really fancy and sit at a nice table making polite and very boring conversation with one another while the Lost Boys watched. The Indians were an improvement to say the least, but still it was funny, watching them pow-wow around in front of a fire, half-naked with war paint slathered all over their sweaty bodies. Peter watched the festivities, deciding that maybe if he had a party like this Wendy would come back.

That's when he saw her, a girl dancing amongst the Indians. She had flowing black hair and wore red war paint under her eyes. She was dressed like a girl, but not like Wendy at all. She didn't wear a dress, but a tight skirt and a shirt opened to show half of her stomach. Fringe hanging down from her shirt shook when she moved, her hips gliding fluidly as she raised her arms and cried out "awah ah aww," with the Indians.

Peter strode into the party. He was Peter Pan, the leader, and could do as he wished, and if he wanted to interrupt an Indian party, they never really liked it, but there was nothing they could do. "Who goes there?" the Indian chief asked, standing in front of the new Indian girl.

"Peter Pan," he announced, hand raised to his face in friendship. "I was wondering who your new Indian was," Peter explained and the Chief gave a "humph" before turning around. The girl was standing behind him and as the Chief walked away Peter saw her more clearly. Yes, her hair was shiny black, but it didn't fit right on her head and must have been a wig of some kind, her face was really very pale and as he got closer he noticed her slim, delicate hands and saw the resemblance.

"I'm Tiger Lily," the new Indian girl said, holding her hand out for him to shake.

"You are not," Peter proclaimed. "You're Wendy, Wendy the Lost Boys' mother. I've been looking all over for you."

"I am not Wendy," Tiger Lily cried impatiently and Peter could tell now by her voice that it was. "Wendy's job is hard. Wendy is the mother, she has to clean up after everyone and feed them and make sure they aren't scared at night and that they are entertained during the day, and she has to make sure the father doesn't play too long with the children and that they have had their lessons. Wendy has to grow up and I do not want to be her anymore, I want to be a little girl like Tiger Lily. No, Wendy's job is hard and from now on I'm Tiger Lily."

"But I liked Wendy," Peter argued. "Can't you go back to being Wendy?"

"I cannot Peter Pan. You shall have Tiger Lily or no one at all," she said, and turning away from him, she joined a group of Indians dancing around a fire. The moon was out and full overhead and the fire crackled before them as they "awed" and "ooohed" and howled at the sky. Peter watched Wendy, the way her hips twisted, the shimmer of her dress and he wanted desperately to take her home. He did not like that she was with the Indians, that she had found some new friends and that the Indians did not seem to understand that she was his, just his.

The party went on. Sometimes Peter joined the Indians in their pow-wows, or he got the Lost Boys and let them have a little fun. The Indians were more their friends than anyone else on the Island and yet he couldn't bring himself to do anything but watch Wendy at a distance. She danced with one of the Indians, twirling around and around him and flopping into his arms. Peter considered swooping in and carrying her away, but he felt funny doing that, he felt funny doing anything just then and he was happy, in fact downright grateful when the cowboys showed up.

They came guns blazing, pow-powing with their pistols and rifles and sending the Indians running for cover as they struggled to find their bows and arrows. Wendy cried out once and ran for cover behind a large drum, but one of the cowboys shot at it and she ran screaming into the woods in that short, tight dress. Peter, who would have watched the war under normal circumstances, ran after her.

"Where're you going, Wendy?" he asked as he finally caught up to her. She was easy to catch, since she never flew without him.

"I hate the cowboys," she cried. "And I'm not Wendy anymore, I'm Tiger Lily. I'm an Indian Princess."

"Does that mean you're going to live with the Indians?" Peter asked, scratching the back of his head, really very confused. "Because the Lost Boys think you're their mother and I don't know what I'm going to tell them."

"I'm done being their mother, it's a thankless job. I'd much rather be a free Indian Princess. Indian Princesses do not have to have children and when they do have them, they certainly do not have to clean up after them and cook for them and make sure they each have a story before bedtime."

"I thought you liked telling stories," Peter argued, and it had seemed that when she was telling them stories her eyes lit up and she laughed an awful lot.

"I do like telling stories, but I'm Tiger Lily now, Peter. I'm Tiger Lily."

"And can Tiger Lily still be my mother?" Peter asked and Wendy came closer. She came so close it was like it was when he was carrying her, she seemed to melt into his chest; she draped her arms around his neck and looked at him. She looked so far and so deeply into him that he couldn't look away.

"Oh you sweet tragic boy, I think that I shall give you a kiss," Tiger Lily-Wendy said as she drew closer. Peter, knowing by some power that was greater than himself, exactly what this kiss was without having to be told, brought his face in as well and their lips met in the middle, and the bow of Wendy's mouth moved with the arrow that was Peter's and he held her there with him until he felt as if they were flying. And they were flying as he kissed her, the Tiger Lily-Wendy, and when he noticed that they were in the air he made it so that they came down, ever so slowly, ever so gently, but come down they did until they were lying flat on the grass. He was at least a little human; he knew that, even as a Betwixt-and-Between, even after having come out of the ether, having been born from this place, for this place, he was still human. And that human side stood apart now, it told him to kiss this Wendy, this Tiger Lily, to take her in his arms and so he did until it felt as if his entire body might blow up like the engine of that old car the Lost Boys had brought as he kissed her and kissed her and kissed her until kissing her was not enough, but he knew that too and so did Wendy.

Afterward, Tiger Lily-Wendy consented to take off her wig and return to the Indian camp to retrieve her plain blue dress and be the Lost Boys' mother again. Peter took her by the hand and led her back toward the lights. But something was different, something was terribly changed and Peter didn't know what it was. He knew he could only play this new game with Wendy and he knew Wendy could only play it with him, it was somehow very odd and very strange and not like anything either of them had known before.

Peter took Wendy back to the Lost Boys, after having retrieved her dress from the Indians, who had been using it as a coat for the chief's assistant. Peter flew Wendy back to the tree house where Toodles and Slightly were sitting around cutting pieces of Wendy's drawing pad and stringing up little paper dolls.

"Hello Wendy, hello," Toodles called, smiling wide and waving. "I was feeling foolish today and decided to make some paper dolls and then Slightly remembered how you said you liked dolls and we thought we'd surprise you with a great bunch of them."

"What a lovely idea," Wendy said, smiling as she held Peter's hand. "Your father and I were just out for a stroll, but I'm back now and it's time I tuck you into bed."

"Boxwood helped for a while, actually he helped a lot, he wanted to make sure you were happy," Toodles went on humbly. "But he decided to go play with the car. I didn't want you to think he didn't help."

"Boxwood is very helpful," Wendy stated. "Now, why don't you get your brothers and I'll tell you a story before bed?"

Peter found himself strangely antsy as Wendy gathered the Lost Boys. There were so many of them and yet there were sometimes very few who actually paid attention to this particular game. Wendy gathered them around her on the floor and told them a story about a princess and a pea, it ended with a "happily ever after" and by the time she had all the boys in bed all Peter wanted to do was take Wendy in his arms as he had done in the woods. He moved toward her once the boys were in bed, but as she turned the light out on the boys she pushed Peter away.

"Not now, silly boy," she said. "I'm Wendy here," she went on. "And we'll have to be married in a proper ceremony first."

"Married?" Peter asked, scratching his head. "What's that?"

"It's when two people decide to be a mother and father for real."

"For real? I thought this was just pretend."

"It doesn't appear to be anymore," Wendy said looking at him very seriously. "I'm going to go to bed now. Wake me in the morning so I can start to work on Curly's socks."

"OK," Peter said. If she wanted him to stay away he would stay away, though he didn't know what to think or do or feel.

Peter went to bed that night wondering what it meant, this wedding, this proper ceremony, this "married." Was it something that grownups wrote down on paper? He knew very little about grownups, but he knew that they were always writing things down on paper and acting as if those papers were so very important. Perhaps it had something to do with Religion or Art, or that thing called Politics that some of the boys talked about.

Wendy slept in her bed near the Lost Boys, since she was their mother and might have to get up in the night to fetch them water or scare away monsters, and Peter slept in his old hammock, swinging back and forth as he looked up at the walls of the tree. It was better sleeping in this common room, he could be closer to everyone and Tinkerbelle didn't bother him, that silly fairy always knocking on doors when he closeted himself away.

When Peter woke up the next morning he felt that something was wrong. He picked up a book one of the Lost Boys had left out only to see tiny, incomprehensible scratches. He stared at the words, longing to see what Wendy and the Lost Boys saw, but he saw nothing, until the words went black, he was temporarily blinded as he realized he could not read. He had not known this before, but suddenly he knew it had always been true, since he'd come out of the ether it had been true.

But that wasn't the only abnormality of the night: a few seconds after Peter awoke, the Lost Boys started crying. It had seemed like a fine night to them; nothing out of the ordinary until they all woke up and noticed that Wendy was gone. This sent them into a tailspin and Peter had to forget the problem of being unable to read as he tried to deal with their issue. But it wasn't like before; Peter could tell right away that she hadn't merely wandered back to the Indians. Nor had she disappeared, he could still feel her in Neverland. At first it was the smell. The Lost Boys, especially Toodles, could smell it as soon as they woke up, pinching their noses and doing dances on the floor against the foul odor. The Lost Boys, who had only been in Neverland five, possibly ten years, (and that was assuming Peter's count on what constituted a year was entirely correct), did not know the smell as well as Peter did, in fact they did not know it at all and so they couldn't say where it came from.

"What is that?" Twin One asked, coming down the stairs from his room, the one he shared with his brother. "It smells like fish and dead feet."

"It smells like stale pigs and cockroach tongue," Twin Two elaborated, coming down after his brother.

"That's descriptive," Boxwood called, waking up and turning toward Wendy's bed. "Where's our mother?"

"Where is our mother?" Toodles cried, fat tears falling down his face.

Peter watched them, knowing she really wasn't there. He looked with sharp eyes around the tree house, wondering where he could have come in from, how he had tiptoed so quickly down the steps and into the room, why no one had smelled that awful odor before now. And how had he gotten to the tree house? What had let him in? Peter did not say a word to the Lost Boys; he didn't even bother with a few phrases of comfort as he walked calmly out the door. He stopped and looked at the trees and the bushes and plants around it, all were fine, not a scratch on them. He then turned to the car. It was the car that he'd got, perhaps because it was as fine a vehicle as his Jolly Roger. Right down the side by the steering wheel he'd left a mark—a long, scraped silver line, a gash where his hook had nearly gone through the metal.

Peter knew then what had happened, he knew who had Wendy and where to go for her. The pirates did not leave their port, at least the ship hardly ever left it, and the pirates very rarely ventured outside the boundaries Peter had set up during the Giant War, when he and the Lost Boys, the Lords and the Dukes (as they were then) had all fought the pirates. And the pirates had lost and would have been driven into the sea, except the Island, in the form of a little voice in Peter's head, had said that there must be pirates, it was not for him to decide to get rid of pirates, and so Peter had cut off Hook's hand (he was the Pirate James before that) and tossed it to a crocodile, who fell so in love with the taste of him that he continued to chase Hook around the little cove that Peter set up for the pirates, the only place they could go. But it wasn't meant for the crocodile to have the hand and he spit it up and gave it back to Peter, who kept it in a jar in his own special room. Peter, who had the power to decree things, declared that if the pirates left their space, they should be killed. But Hook—and it could only have been Hook, none of the others would have left—had come in the night and taken her. Something had to have called to him; something had to have let him out.

Peter might have taken Slightly with him if he'd have taken any of them. Perhaps Boxwood, who was strong and tall, though afraid of a great many things, would have been helpful as a lookout, but he knew he couldn't bring either of them. He was their leader, the Island had told him that in the form of a feeling inside his being that trembled and ached whenever one of them did not feel happy, when they missed Wendy or stubbed their toes, and Peter sometimes wondered why the Island let them stub their toes at all. But the welfare of the Lost Boys was on him and he knew that it was not his place to drag them into this. Peter knew that the reason Hook had come, whatever had started this, it was his fault and he would need to go to the Jolly Roger, he'd have to cross the pirate lines and get Wendy back alone.

This was what boys were supposed to do. In any event, this was what he did, never actually rescuing damsels in distress, since there had never been any damsels in Neverland to be in distress before. But boys took swords and knives and ran after their enemies, they flew off balconies (when they could fly) and cried out "*en garde!*" He'd done this with the Indians and the cowboys, though with them it had always been a game, but he'd also done this with pirates. The pirates used real cannonballs, real bullets and though he'd never been hit by one of them, and there was no evidence that he could die, he'd seen the pirates slaughter an Indian once, right in front of him. The pirate took his sword and pushed it through the Indian's stomach. The pirate then took a tiny knife, held the Indian's head and sliced his throat open. Peter wasn't sure how the After worked when it came to Indians, who, like the cowboys and mermaids, simply disappeared; he only knew about the After of children, but to die Here must be a truly horrible thing. The Indian did not wake up, he did not come back, and the pirate who'd killed him took his body away and burned it.

Peter considered getting Tinkerbelle or any of the other fairies to come with him, but that was a very selfish thing to want. The fairies couldn't risk being caught by Hook and his pirates; they were too needed in Neverland. Nor could he bring the cowboys or Indians. This wasn't their fight either and they had never been particularly good at actual combat, anyway. They could wield a play bow and arrow, they could shoot a gun without bullets but Peter had never seen them with real weapons. . . . and the way that Indian had fallen that day, he couldn't watch that again.

And so Peter, sword at his side, a knife hidden in each of his tight leather shoes, flew across Neverland, above the trees and past Mermaid Lagoon. Once he neared the shores past the mermaids, after clearing their underwater castles, Peter landed a few feet from the docks, avoiding flying over Pirate City. He wouldn't fly to the pirates. He could have, though none of the others could; he was Peter Pan and could do anything, but then the pirates would have seen him and given Hook warning.

It was cold on this side of the Island, but never winter. It was as if winter had come without bringing Christmas and snow, ice and the pleasure of coming in from the cold. The cold was stagnant, so flat and stale that Peter was sure it would ice up any fairy's wings. It was black in Pirate Cove and always night, but there were no stars and the Island was positioned so that the pirates could never see the moon. It was dirty as well. Peter was sure the pirates never cleaned it, and scraps of paper and tattered clothes, bottles of gin and whiskey and bugs crawling littered the streets. There were streets here, which was the strangest thing, since everywhere else there were dirt paths or indents in the grass, but there were paved roads in Pirate Cove as well as concrete buildings along with the wooden ones that were falling over so much that Peter could see the black rot coming through. It smelled worse here than it had at the tree house, like dead fish and spoiled meat, sour and murky and Peter could smell things and sense things that he only smelled and sensed here. Very bad and very mean images entered his thoughts, sneaking in through a side door in his mind, so he had to stop to clear his head and think happy thoughts, only happy thoughts—the only way to make it through here, Peter knew, was to keep Pirate Cove out of his head.

The pirates did not bother him on his way to the Jolly Roger. Some of them were hanging around the saloon (and this saloon, unlike the cowboys' saloon, had real alcohol in it), some of them falling over drunk. He passed a house with a red light on its porch. The house was nearly empty, but he could see the shadows of pirates moving about the windows. Peter almost stepped in what looked like animal dung, though it couldn't have belonged to an animal since none of the animals, except that crocodile, came here. He thought for sure, as he reached the harbor and the ship, that one of the pirates would at least call out, but they were the opposite of the Lost Boys, who were not allowed to be lazy, and didn't even bother to look up at him, though they knew who he was. They knew in the pits of their pirate stomachs that he was Peter Pan, protector of the Lost Boys, and still they paid no mind to him, their great archenemy. Perhaps it was that they were too lazy, too sucked dry of all feeling, to bother having an archenemy.

Peter walked through the filthy paved streets, up the gang-plank to the Jolly Roger, which was nothing like Pirate Cove, nothing like the pirates, and sometimes Peter wanted to rescue that poor ship and take it for the Lost Boys. The ship was grand, painted bright red with gold trim; it had beautiful pure white sails and the hull seemed to be in perfect working order, no rot-ting wood or greasy hinges, no dirty crevices. Peter could feel its newness the moment he stepped on board, first looking up to see if anyone was near the masts before making his way to the Captain's Quarters.

The ship was deserted. Peter ascended the gangplank careful-ly, tapping the wooden planks with his foot to see if they would squeak. He went swiftly down to the Captain's quarters below deck, the only place Hook would be if he was on the ship, since he rarely took the helm.

Peter, being a wise leader, who knew how to orchestrate a surprise attack, even if he barely ever engaged in a real fight, first looked through the foggy windows at the spacious and nicely, though somewhat ostentatiously decorated, chamber. Hook's quarters comprised one large room looking out to sea, the walls were painted blood red with gold trimming along the sides, just like the ship. There were pictures of far off places, places from Before that Peter had never seen, large cities with bright lights and beaches spread with white sand and palm trees, there were also various old weapons in glass cases lying on desks and sitting on shelves. A bed with a red- and gold-fringed canopy sat in the midst of a few red and black couches. Peter had never fully understood the word "luxury" that Hook, when he spoke to Peter, was always talking about, but he could see it in Hook's chambers.

He eyed the pirate first. He was hard to miss, standing at six foot, three inches. Hook turned to face the window and Peter ducked, but not before he saw the pirate place that shiny, sharp hook over his wrist. The thing went on mechanically, clicking in place as a smile spread across the old man's face. Only he wasn't an old man. As far as Peter could tell Hook had been in Neverland since before the Lost Boys. He hadn't aged a day since he'd come, hadn't turned to wood or glass and was, as far as Peter could see, 29, perhaps 30 years old. He wore a long wig of pitch black curls that hung below his shoulders, and he was dressed in a cloak that mirrored the red and gold colors of the Jolly Roger. Hook shone in the light of the chandelier hanging overhead. He smiled broadly as he turned to face a chair and in that chair, Peter saw, was Wendy.

Only she wasn't Wendy anymore, Hook had dressed her up. He'd put her back in those Tiger Lily clothes, so her light brown hair was covered by the straight black wig, he had put war paint on her face, though he'd done a poor job (or she had been struggling) and the markings were lopsided. But it was her clothes that Peter noticed most. Hook seemed to have cut her skirt much shorter and her legs glistened in the light as she kicked and struggled, though every time she kicked her skirt rode up higher. Her hands were tied behind the chair and her mouth was gagged with a white handkerchief. Hook walked closer to her and Peter watched. It wasn't that he was unsure of what to do, he knew that when attempting a rescue you burst right in brandishing your sword, but he couldn't move as Hook bent down close to the girl, slowly, gently kissing her cheek.

Peter barged in before Hook could stand up straight, but the old man did not look surprised and laughed as Peter threw open the door. "I didn't think you'd wait so long, Peter," he said with a voice that was not rough like the other pirates, but incredibly polite and professional.

"Let her go!" Peter demanded. "The Island will not stand for this!"

"The Island?" Hook asked slowly, shaking his head and nearly laughing. He then began to pace back and forth as if he were thinking about something. "You think your precious Island has any idea what it's doing right now? Can you believe what it has done; can you believe it, letting a girl in here? Your Island, your perfect, infallible Island has made a very grave, a very bad mistake, my dear boy. These creatures, these women, these foul temptresses are never allowed Here, and there is a reason Peter, there is a reason."

"It's the way it is and little boys and little girls are separated," Peter described, citing all he knew. No one had ever explained anything to him outright, the Island spoke to him in the form of feelings and he could only sense, he could only know so much and there were never any drawn out explanations, any concrete details; he didn't need them, or at least he hadn't until now.

Hook laughed and looked down at the girl. "That, my dear boy, is the fall of man. Ever hear the story of Adam and Eve? All was well in the Garden of Eden until Eve came along and was tempted by the devil. Do you think a man would let himself get tempted by a snake? And she ate the forbidden fruit and made Adam eat it too and poof. . . .we have pirates and Cowboys and little children who die and must come Here."

"It's not her fault," Peter cried, only half understanding the story Hook told. "Let her go. She's our mother, mothers aren't bad."

"Mothers aren't bad?" Hook asked. "Just ask a few of the boys with the fairies if mothers aren't bad." Hook paced calmly again. "Oh, fathers are bad as well, fathers account for the vast majority of the children who end up with the fairies, but mothers, mothers can be just as evil. Mothers drown their children in broad daylight, mothers hit them with wooden spoons and poison their soup."

"You stop that Hook, let her go," Peter demanded, because there was nothing else for him to do, at least not where conversation was concerned. Once the physical fight began, they both knew Peter would win. Peter always won the fights, the sword was his friend and he was, even though he was so young, the strongest, even above the pirates. But conversation, that's where Hook could beat him and he knew it, conversation got all muddled in The Boy's head, words stopped making sense to him the way Hook used them. They both knew this and Peter had to survive the conversation. And Hook, for his part, wanted to keep talking as long as possible.

"And did you know little boy, did you know what you were doing last night? That new little game you were playing?" Hook turned to Peter, looking him in the eye. "Tell me, did you inform the Lost Boys of your new game? Do you think they might like to play it with her as well?"

"Quiet Hook," Peter cried, tight tears forming at the sides of his eyes because he knew, he knew something had changed.

"That's how I knew she was Here. I could smell it in the air and once that had happened, well. . . .it let me out." Peter looked at Hook, suddenly ashamed. "You're not a little boy anymore," Hook went on, sadly shaking his head. "All that boyish innocence, all of it, gone. And here you are, King of Little Children, the boy who would never grow up and all it took was a woman." Hook stopped and pointed at Wendy, who was now too busy watching them to struggle. "And you don't even know what she did to you. Oh Peter, how you've grown up."

Right then Peter knew, just as he knew he had never been born, that he would never die. And something else, something more complex like multiplication tables stammering in the back of his head told him that this was a very sad thing. And he couldn't read, not a single word on the Jolly Roger, not a single syllable of the writing carved on the ship above Hook's head. He could not tell time, he did not understand the formal rules of Logic (with a capital L). He never had known these things and now he knew he never would. He could try for decades, for centuries, to learn them but he knew it was too late. He never would have learned, but now he knew. Now he knew.

"You have no idea, don't you see, I'm here to stop her. Give her to me, let me have her, she belongs with the pirates, she's one of us."

"She is not," Peter cried, not because Hook wasn't making sense, not because he didn't believe Hook. In fairness if Peter had been listening he might have given her up, but he couldn't see past his own heartbeat to understand what Hook was saying. He only knew that he wanted her back and no one else could have her. "She's our mother and she belongs with me."

"Ah, she belongs with you, little boy," Hook said, shaking his head. "But not because she is your mother. No, this woman here is not your mother, and don't you know what fathers and mothers do?"

"Stop it!" Peter cried clenching his fists.

"And it's done Peter, it's done and I can come back to the main Neverland whenever I want, nothing is stopping me and it's all because of you."

"You can't do that," Peter said sternly.

"I can," Hook said calmly. "But I won't. I won't because that would be bad form, because I once said that I would never return and so I won't, unless something else calls. I am a gentleman Peter, I am a grownup and I, unlike you, follow rules."

"I don't believe," Peter replied and Hook shook his head.

"Everything will go on as it has before," Hook said sadly. "Everything will be as it was and you'll have your little Lost Boys, you'll have your cowboy and Indian friends, you can play with your little fairies and tiny Tinkerbelle will come back to you. You just have to pretend, to pretend you are the same uncontaminated creature you were yesterday. You're good at playing pretend, aren't you Peter? Isn't that what the Island wants? Aren't you the ferryman for lost child souls, the Davy Jones of little boys? And you have a job to do, Peter Pan, you might not notice it's a job because you have so much fun doing it, but you have a job to do and you go to work every single day just like a man, and right now your job is telling you, it is demanding, that you sacrifice. You can't have her Peter, she's not yours and you can't have her. But mark my words, you have changed and now you know, now you see what you are, what you've lost, and from now on, little boy, it will only be pretend. So you better get good at it, young man, playing pretend."

Peter was listening. He knew he was listening and his gut told him to pay attention. The Island was telling him and in all these years it had never made a mistake, it had never taken who was not supposed to come, but how could someone so strange, so foreign wash up on these shores? Hook made a great deal of sense. . . . "*En garde!*" Peter cried, flinging such thoughts from his mind, forcing Hook back with the flick of his sword. He held the sword and Hook fumbled for a moment before grabbing his own.

"Oh Peter," the pirate said as if he felt sorry for him. "Proud and insolent youth," he went on and Peter remembered that he'd said these words before, "prepare to meet thy doom."

"Dark and sinister man," Peter replied and he felt as if he'd said these words a hundred times, that he would say them again and again and again until the end of everything, "Have at thee." And with that Peter thrust his sword and it clanged against Hook's.

It was in some sense a fruitless battle. Now that Peter had raised his sword, it was over and they both knew it. Yet Hook was a formidable opponent, the only one who had ever been worth fighting, not only because it was real, but also because he was a skilled swordsman. He had what the pirates called "good form," he did not cheat, he acted always the gentleman and yet there was nothing he would not do (except have bad form) to win. Hook brandished a sword nearly as well as Peter, almost slicing him across the neck as he attempted to strike a blow. Wendy was still struggling, Peter could see her trying to speak through the handkerchief tied across her mouth, but he knew he had to win and winning required attention. Watching the hook as it nearly sliced across his face, Peter ducked out of the way, slicing the pirate's arm, though it only cut through that fancy jacket of his, not seeming to draw blood.

Peter dashed about the room. He might have flown if he'd seen a need for it, but Hook wasn't quite that fast and so Peter ran around him. He saw Wendy struggling and the look in her eyes almost made him stop still. "*En garde*," he called again, looking right at Wendy and he felt a sting, a pinch and when he looked down Hook had sliced through his arm. It stung, the blood flowed down his arm and onto the polished pirate deck. Hook gave a mighty laugh and Peter turned on him; dashing at the old man, he had him up against the wall. Hook brought his sword out and Peter grabbed it, tossing it away as he held him to the wall with one arm. He looked at the man, his sword in his hand, ready to plunge it into his heart. He could see the old man's eyes closing, watching the look of shock and terror on his face. All it would take was one gash, just run the sword through his heart and. . . .But the Island told him not to do it. It was not his place to get rid of the pirates, and with the demise of Hook the pirates would go. Hook seemed to know this and he shut his eyes, relishing the moment as Peter took a knife from his shoe and stabbed it through Hook's shirt at the shoulder. He took the other knife from his other shoe, not knowing his left from his right, and stuck that one through the other side so the old man stayed pinned to the wall. He would rip his shirt eventually; he would pull the knives out, but for a great long while (and Peter was always forgetting the time), Hook would not be able to move from the wall of the Jolly Roger.

"Good bye, old man," Peter cried, turning to Wendy. He flew to her, undoing the complicated knots the pirate had done. He pulled the handkerchief from her mouth and she cried "Oh Peter," as he freed the rest of her. She pulled her skirt down and straightened her wig before Peter picked her up and carried her out of the Captain's Quarters.

"This isn't right, Peter, this isn't the way and you know it Boy," Hook cried, still pinned to the wall. Peter shut the door, venturing out to the deck of the Jolly Roger. He took one last look at the boat with its gleaming helm as he lifted off the deck and flew with Wendy, out of Pirate's Cove and over the forest.

Wendy was crying as she held tight to Peter's neck, and he looked down at her, wondering if there was something he should say. Instead he kept flying, tumbling through the clouds until he felt as if they had gone over the sky; they went around and around, past Neverland and over the great ocean beyond. There was nothing there, they flew for miles, they flew for days and still it was empty. In his mind Peter saw crocodiles and clocks as he gazed down at Wendy. He felt the soil of Neverland course through his blood and the pull of the Island until he and Wendy were once again on dry land. They were standing in the forest, Wendy facing him, still in that Tiger Lily outfit, the wig lopsided across her face.

Peter pushed the wig back into place and she looked at him. "Are you okay, Wendy?" he asked innocently. "Hook didn't hurt you, did he?"

"No, Hook didn't touch me. . . .except to tie me up," she said. "He really is a dreadful old man."

"He really is," Peter concurred and Wendy came closer. She threw her arms around his neck and said "oh Peter, oh Peter," into his ear until he felt he couldn't take it anymore. "You're not Wendy now, you're Tiger Lily," he said before kissing her. She held tight to his neck, pulling him down with her and it was not as it was when he was fighting Hook and yet they were the same emotions, the same pictures flashed through his mind and he pulled away from her.

"I see your dress over there," Peter said, pointing at the blue frock she'd worn to Neverland. It had gotten dirty and a little torn, but it was still lying there, flapping in a bush. Wendy turned to it, seeming to know what to do, she grabbed it from the prickles and stood behind a tree. Peter turned around, he felt as if he should fly away as she changed, and he might have if he weren't so afraid that Hook would return.

When she emerged from the bushes Tiger Lily was gone, the war paint had been wiped from her face and her long, flowing hair had returned. "Are you sure you're okay, Wendy?" Peter asked and she nodded "yes." Peter flew toward her, draped an arm around her and moved to kiss her again, but she placed a hand in front of his face.

"No, no, no, Peter," she said. "You mustn't do that unless we're married. Married in a proper ceremony."

"Married?" Peter asked, remembering their conversation from the night before. "Married. All right, then let's get married," he suggested. "What's a proper ceremony and how is it done? We'll do it tonight at the tree house with the Lost Boys."

"I know exactly how a proper ceremony should go. I was old enough last year to attend my aunt's wedding. There is to be a white gown and rows of chairs and a great big book that someone is to read out of."

"A book?" Peter asked, wondering if any of the Lost Boys knew how to read. "And a white dress. . . .I don't know if we'll be able to get that stuff."

"Oh, leave it to me, Peter, leave it to me. We'll have such a lovely wedding," Wendy said, dancing around him, a joyous smile on her face. It was as if she'd forgotten everything, as if Hook had not kidnapped her at all.

Peter watched her dance for a minute or two before insisting they get back. Wendy flew with him on her own, gliding back down into the tree house. The Lost Boys, who had gotten very worried, ran up to her, asking for stories and snacks and for socks to be mended. Wendy spoke kindly to them for a minute and then announced that there would be a wedding that night. She directed Toodles and Slightly to find a book to read out of and if they couldn't find a suitable book they were to make one out of leaves and sticks. Boxwood and Nibs were to build something called a podium. At first the two boys didn't know what one was or how to make it, but Wendy drew a picture in the dirt and suggested that they use larger sticks and blocks of wood. Curly was to set up the ceremony, gathering a carpet and chairs and putting it all in place. The twins were in charge of getting Peter ready, combing his hair, making sure he took a bath and wore something more becoming than his tattered green shorts. "The rest of you," she said to some dozen or so other Lost Boys, "are in charge of the guests. Remember to invite all the Indians and all the mermaids formally and then you may ask the cowboys, but since I don't care much for them, they can stand in back." The Lost Boys nodded at their directions and went off every which-way, some tumbling into each other and bumping heads as they got ready for the wedding.

"The wedding," Wendy announced, looking as much at Peter, who was standing off to the side wondering just what he'd gotten himself into, "will be held just as the moon comes out, when it starts to get dark," she instructed, one finger in the air as if she were well versed in such matters.

The rest of the day moved very quickly, much too quickly for Peter, who was beginning to think that it was a very bad idea, this wedding. First of all it was creating so much stir, all the Lost Boys running around, Tootles trying to figure out how to make a book out of leaves while the twins, those silly twins, were making him take a bath and insisting on brushing his hair.

Peter didn't do much to prepare for this wedding. He sat in the tree house with a piece of black chalk and started doodling a picture of Wendy; he went to examine the car where Hook had slashed it, to see that no structural damage had been done. He was then forced to sit in his room and stare at the walls after the twins had gotten him ready, making him wear a black suit that they'd found in a pile of leftover clothes from previous Lost Boys. The clothes were formfitting, with shiny brass buttons glittering, and when Peter glanced down at the stream to look at himself, he thought for a moment that he resembled a pirate. "You mustn't get dirty before your wedding," the twins instructed, and Peter wondered how they knew so much about a ceremony that none of them had ever been to, one he had never even heard of before Wendy. In the back of his mind and in his stomach something gnawed at him and he wondered if maybe Hook had been right, maybe Wendy did not belong Here.

It got dark that night before he knew it and Peter was summoned to the front of the tree house. The entire space had been transformed. The trees were lit up, glowing with lights that twinkled so delicately that it took Peter a moment to realize it was the fairies. Tinkerbelle wasn't with them, this Peter knew right away and he wondered how Wendy or the Lost Boys had gotten the rest of the fairies to attend, though a wedding, Peter surmised, was a grand event and the fairies loved anything grand. There was a wooden podium near the front of the trees; it looked lopsided, as if it were about to fall over, and on it stood a book made of large leaves and seaweed, most likely from the mermaids. Slightly was standing near the podium, pretending to examine the book, though he couldn't read a word. There were rows of Lost Boys sitting in the chairs made of sticks, and then rows of Indians and rows of cowboys standing on two sides of a long red carpet that had once been in Peter's room.

"You're supposed to stand up front by Slightly," Toodles informed Peter, nudging him. Peter shook his head, a little amazed and a little perturbed as he marched closer to Slightly. "And keep your hands in front of you, nicely, like that," Toodles instructed him, and Peter wondered when everyone had become so interested in doing everything "nicely."

Peter marched up to Slightly, who smiled happily. "You just gotta stand next to me," he informed him. "Just look at me, like that." Peter did what he was told. He'd never followed a Lost Boy's instructions before, namely because they'd never had any instructions for him. "With your hands at your sides Peter, watch for Wendy," he said, smiling all the more.

Peter waited there with Slightly, watching the crowd of Neverland dwellers as they stared at him. After a moment it grew darker, the moon came out, white and full and someone started to honk the horn on the car. They honked it in a kind of rhythm, a sloppy rhythm, but a rhythm nonetheless and after a few seconds Wendy appeared from behind the tree. Peter could see her in the moonlight as a couple of fairies followed her up the path made through the chairs. Her hair was tied up on top of her head and she was carrying a bouquet of wild flowers. Her dress was white. It was her same dress, Peter could tell by the torn lace at the collar, but it had been painted bright white, and he could see the delicate imprints of seaweed on it, so he knew the mermaids, who were absent because there was no water in the woods, had done it.

Wendy walked toward Peter with a grave face. He wondered if he liked the face at all, it was very grown up, a womanly face, and there was something not right about it, something not real. It was a pirate's face as much as it was a little girl's and Peter wanted nothing more than to make her laugh as she approached him.

"Hello," he said to Wendy when she reached him, but Wendy put her finger to her lips very sternly and shook her head. She was too much of a grown up here and Peter began to mourn for the little girl he'd known only hours before.

"We are gathered here today," Slightly started, his voice ringing out very importantly. His head was in that book, and Peter wanted to grab it to see if he could read it, and if he couldn't then he wanted to tear it up and throw it away. But he knew he couldn't do any of those things, though it was in his nature to do them, because this was a wedding and there was a certain way you were supposed to act, especially when it was your own wedding, regardless of your nature. And he now understood them—grownups: society, emotions, intellect, what he had done with Wendy in the woods, cruelty—it was all laid bare before him as he waited for this ceremony to end so that he could be a married man.

"We are here to join together in Holy mat-i-money, Mr. Peter Pan and Miss Winifred Moira Angela Darling." Peter looked at Wendy; it had been the first time since their meeting that he'd heard her full name and he wasn't sure he liked it. "Marriage is a sacred commitment, a right and a duty of men. . . ." Slightly went on importantly and Peter wanted to laugh at him, he was really trying very hard, too hard, to sound so very dignified, but the scowl on Wendy's face told him to keep quiet.

"Now Wendy," Slightly said after a bit of a long winded speech. "Do you take Peter Pan, to have and to hold, in sickness and in health, as long as you both shall live?"

"I do," Wendy said, her eyes meeting Peter's and the scowl did not go from her face. Peter could see, though, out of the corner of his eye, as if a mischievous little fairy had put it there, there was a smile, a secret smile, a playful grin, she giggled once and Peter decided she was still Wendy and he wanted to kiss her.

"And Peter," Slightly went on. "Do you take Winifred Moira Angela Darling to have and to hold in sickness and in health, for as long as you both shall live?"

That seemed a very long time, as long as he lived, since as long as he lived didn't seem to have an end. "I do," Peter replied because Wendy had said it and it seemed as if she knew what to do.

"So now, with the power vested in me I pronounce you husband and wife," Slightly announced. "You may kiss the bride."

Peter looked expectantly at Wendy as she held her face up, her lips out to him and he knew he was supposed to kiss her. He knew that he had wanted to kiss her, even with all these people about, but when he moved toward her, closing his eyes as she did, he found that there was nothing there. Slightly cried out, there was a general murmur among the audience and when Peter opened his eyes Wendy was gone.

Not a piece of her was left, not her dress or her flowers, not the bow in her hair, those lips or those eyes. She had left nothing for him. And it wasn't as if Hook had taken her again, he would have left that smell at the very least, and it wasn't as if she'd wandered off or run away. He could feel it, because the breath of the universe ran under his skin, she wasn't Here anymore. He or she or it or they had taken her back. The Island had made a mistake and she had returned from whence she'd come. The Lost Boys would look for her, some of them would blame the pirates, the Indians would blame the cowboys and the cowboys the Indians, and all of them for a brief while would decide that the mermaids had done it, but Peter knew where she was. He couldn't explain it to any of them, none but the fairies would understand and as he turned around he saw Tinkerbelle floating above him. She wasn't beaming, she couldn't have been happy, not with Peter so sad, but she was back. Peter looked up at her light and then down at the ground, and for the first time since Wendy had come he saw his shadow.

London, England 1901

Mrs. Darling had been walking in Kensington Gardens when she saw Mr. Barrie. They'd never been particularly close friends, though her husband had always insisted on going to the openings of his plays and speaking to him after the performances. But it was more for show than anything else. Mr. Barrie, while not the most successful playwright in London, did enjoy a bit of stature and he was a very kind man and a very polite neighbor, if not a little odd, and it just seemed the right thing to do, as far as Mr. Darling was concerned, that they make themselves known to him.

But Mr. Barrie had been coming around the house with some frequency recently. Once he'd even come when George wasn't home, asking if he might go up and visit Winifred. Mrs. Darling had been fine with that, ushering him into her little girl's room and taking a seat on the couch near the door as he sat whispering to her. He never stayed long; he'd merely stare down at the girl, whispering little things in her ear and reading from a book about birds. He seemed to squint when he spoke to Winifred and clear his throat an awful lot, as if he didn't know what to say, especially to this lifeless girl.

It was his coming around so much that made it imperative that Mrs. Darling stop and speak to him when she met Mr. Barrie by accident while walking through Kensington Gardens, getting a bit of air since she hadn't left her daughter's side in two days. This had not been the park where Winifred had fallen—Mrs. Darling had made a note to never set foot in that place again. Kensington Gardens was a very large park in the middle of London with long rows of colorful flowers and stacks of benches standing in lines as if they were waiting for some event. There were bronze statues of men on horseback, famous men that Mrs. Darling was sure her husband could name. There were ponds that rippled with tiny, fluttering waves where children were always playing with toy boats or engaging in a game of hide and seek in the narrow rows of bushes as their nurses called after them.

Mrs. Darling had been walking through the park when she'd met up with Mr. Barrie. He'd been sitting alone on a bench, his nose in a notebook he seemed to be writing in. Mrs. Darling saw him and considered saying "Hello," but she knew he was a writer and since he appeared to be writing she didn't want to disturb him. But when she passed by Mr. Barrie looked up and said, "Hello, won't you sit down?" And so Mrs. Darling had taken a seat next to him and they'd started talking.

"And how is your husband?" Mr. Barrie asked first, getting the requisite small talk, out of the way.

"He's fine, thank you, still at the office five days a week."

"I see, I remember talking to him, he loves his work."

"That he does," Mrs. Darling sighed, hoping she did not sound too sorry for herself. "But it makes him happy."

"And a man who can do something that makes him happy is the luckiest in the world," Mr. Barrie added whimsically. "And how is the family, John, Michael?" He was asking about the boys first, only waiting to get to Winifred.

"Oh they're fine, as well as can be expected. John will start school in the fall, but I can't tell if he's excited or terrified, and Michael is his same playful self."

"It's important for children to play. People look at me sometimes—especially when I'm with the Llewellyn Davies boys—and they must think 'what a playful man he is?' because I bother to indulge in the children's fantasies, but even then, even I can feel I'm a bit too grown up for it, as if they know the secret to play and I am only pretending. It poisons us all, growing up, and I wish I had never grown up, not at all, not an inch some days."

"You wish you'd never grown up?" Mrs. Darling asked and her neighbor nodded. "But you're so successful, you have a lovely wife and you must be doing what you love, since no one writes plays unless they love them."

"True, true, adult life has been good to me. But there are still moments when I wish I could simply roll around on the floor."

Mrs. Darling chuckled. "I see, I think we all have moments like that."

"Even women. . .? I always assumed that women rather preferred growing up, much more than boys did."

"Not all the time," Mrs. Darling admitted.

"And Winifred?" he finally asked. "How's she doing? Is there any change?"

"No change. The fluids are still keeping her alive, although they don't know how long that can last, it's been three weeks. She lies there, not really living, but not at all gone either, the doctors keep saying that they don't know what's wrong with her. She might very well live out the rest of her days this way. . . ." Mrs. Darling shuddered to think about it, she closed her eyes, stood up and started walking, wanting to expel that ugly thought from her mind.

"I know, I know," Mr. Barrie said, hastily gathering his papers and moving to follow her. Mrs. Darling didn't know where she was going. It was about time she return to the house and so she walked slowly down a path that would eventually lead her home, in a round about way.

"I'm sorry to have disturbed you," Mr. Barrie offered, walking at a quicker pace to try and catch up with her. "I didn't mean to offend you."

"Oh, you didn't offend me," Mrs. Darling replied. "I just wish I knew what was happening. It's not fair for a mother not to know. . . ."

"That it is. You know I had a little brother named David who died in an ice skating accident. He was the nicest, the sweetest boy. My mother never got over it. He was her favorite and after his death she stayed in her room and cried and cried, forever it seemed. I used to dress up in David's clothing and pretend to be him. You'd think it would have upset my mother, but she seemed to like it and so I did it more and more often, until one day I finally stopped." Mr. Barrie grew quiet as they walked and Mrs. Darling couldn't help but watch the short little man move fluidly through the park. A group of boys were running up and down the paths, one of them tripping the other two as they screeched and hollered, looking a lot like John and Michael. Mr. Barrie stopped to watch them, a soft, sad look in his eyes. "And I think my brother's death, it might have very well affected my whole life, made me what I am. I owe all of my work to him, as if his memory will live on forever in it, and as long as people are seeing my plays there'll be a piece of my brother in the universe."

"I can understand that," Mrs. Darling replied. "I'm sorry for your loss."

"Oh, it's all right. Part of me believes it helped me have such a vivid imagination, because I always wondered where my brother went to after he passed. I try to concoct my own little boy world, a place where children are joyful and innocent and never grow up."

"They never grow up?" Mrs. Darling asked. It was a fine fantasy, but to her the entire point of having children was so that they might one day grow up and join the ranks of society, no matter what playfulness, what kindness and innocence they had to give up to get there. It was all a part of life and certain things must be sacrificed to society and its conventions.

"My mother used to say that also, that her little boy, her little David, we used to call him Boxwood, you know, would never grow up and leave her now that he was gone."

Mrs. Darling wanted to say something akin to "well that's one way to look at it," but instead she merely gazed forward as they reached the gates of the park, which would eventually take them outside, to the heart of London, and into Bloomsbury. Mrs.

Darling stepped cautiously through the gates of Kensington Gardens, unsure if Mr. Barrie would follow, but grateful when he did. "I'm sure it must be very hard," she finally said to her neighbor. "And I'm sure Winifred loves it when you visit her. What do you tell her?"

"I tell her stories," Mr. Barrie explained. "About little boys who run around city parks at night banging drums and talking to birds."

"How lovely," Mrs. Darling exclaimed as they walked the streets, wishing someone had told her such stories when she was a child. "I hope she hears them."

"I hope so, too," Mr. Barrie concurred as they reached her house. They stopped in front of it, both awkwardly nodding as if now that they were in the presence of the house there were certain rules of propriety to follow. Finally Mr. Barrie glanced down the street and pointed in the direction of his own home. "It's been nice speaking with you. Hopefully I'll see you out again. I think it's good for the spirit."

"Yes, of course," Mrs. Darling agreed as she glanced up at the grayish stone front house with the iron bars on its door and the stained glass in half the windows because George could only afford to have stained glass put in the more adult centered rooms. "Thank you for the walk Mr. Barrie," Mrs. Darling offered her neighbor and he nodded, not asking to come up to say hello to Winifred. It seemed wise that he should go, since her husband wasn't home and for all she knew Liza, the new maid, was out with the children.

Mrs. Darling walked cautiously into her foyer. She had been stepping delicately around the house since coming back from the hospital with Winifred. It was as if the house were constantly whispering, keeping its own secrets and holding its own court and she was only a small piece of it, not privy to the real goings on. Her footsteps creaked on the dark wooden staircase. Mrs. Darling nearly held her breath as she walked slowly, expectantly, up the stairway. She glanced out the window, at the outside where the sky was blue and the lawn wide and green and she longed to be once more at Kensington Gardens.

"Mother, mother," John called, running to her, his cheeks flushed. "Mother, come quick, come quick," he cried, jumping up and down. Mrs. Darling could see the excitement in his face, as if he'd been running through the house like this all morning because something, something could not contain him. "Mother come quick, come quick, it's Winifred, it's Winifred," he cried, rushing her up the stairs and down the hall. "It's Winifred," John cried again and Michael came racing out of her room.

"Mama, Mama," Michael called, rushing out. "She's waking up, she's waking up. Come see, come see, it's Winifred, she's waking up!"

"She's what?" Mrs. Darling asked, hand over her mouth in disbelief as she went running down the hall.

Liza nearly fell on her mistress, her feet just about giving way when Mrs. Darling reached the couch at the edge of Winifred's room. "Mrs. Darling, oh Mrs. Darling, I didn't know what to do," the maid exclaimed, eyes large and misty. "She's been stirring for the past half hour. I thought of calling Mr. Darling, but I wasn't sure exactly where, and I didn't know how to find you in the park."

"But you stayed with her?" Mrs. Darling asked. "You saw that she's been stirring, she's been stirring?" she cried, hopeful. "Find Mr. Darling at the office, the address is in the pantry, run and get him if you have to and have him contact the doctor. Get her doctor here right this minute," Mrs. Darling ordered the maid, who stared at her dumbfounded until she shouted, "Go!" at her. The little woman stumbled out of the room, and Mrs. Darling could hear the clopping of her shoes down the stairs as she rushed from the house, slamming the door behind her.

John and Michael were both at Winifred's bed gazing down at her when Mrs. Darling finally had a chance to see her. Her boys had been so full of energy before, but they simply stared at her as Mrs. Darling approached the bed. John, seeming to understand the gravity of what was about to happen, moved out of the way, but Michael wouldn't budge from the side of the bed until John pulled him by his shirtsleeve.

"She's stirring," Mrs. Darling repeated as she looked down at Winifred. And where there had been no movement for so long, where there had been nothing behind those eyes, she could see it all returning. Winifred was moving, her arms contorting, her feet making tiny kicks under the blanket, so much so that Mrs. Darling pulled it back, revealing the long bluish-white nightgown Liza had just put her in. Her eyes were twitching, fighting either to open or to remain closed, she couldn't tell which. Somewhere within her daughter there was a struggle going on. She was murmuring, her lips parting ever so slightly, tiny noises, muffled and strangled inaudible mumblings could be heard coming from her lips, and Mrs. Darling wasn't sure what to make of them. Winifred seemed as if she were being pulled back and forth, and it was as if she were struggling, with her fists clenched and her feet braced against the bed, fighting to stay wherever she was.

It took hours for Winifred to come fully awake. The Darlings rushed the doctor to her; George telegraphed all the specialists he'd collected addresses for over the past few weeks and Doctor Gladstone, who was in London for a conference, had come as soon as he could, catching a hansom cab the moment word got to him.

A few days after her daughter had awakened Mrs. Darling watched the boys play in Winifred's room. It was cautious play, play to keep their minds off the seriousness of what had just happened, but play nonetheless and though it was annoying George and the doctors, Mrs. Darling was grateful for it. It was as if in this short time she'd been awake her daughter was getting used to being a part of this world again, she'd been away so long, she hadn't really moved in nearly three weeks, she was hungry and weak and sick and she was still regaining her muscle and bone strength, or so the doctors said. Even though the doctors had been talking with and at (mostly at) Mrs. Darling since Winifred had fallen into unconsciousness, it wasn't until things started to happen, as Mrs. Darling watched the awed look on the faces of Doctor Gladstone and the others who had taken such an interest in this case, that she knew that they had no idea what they were dealing with and were only hoping to run into a little bit of luck.

". . .and I don't know what to do about those stories," she heard Doctor Gladstone say. "Her body is working, she's awake, but still it's her mind I'm worried about."

"What are you talking about?" Mrs. Darling interrupted the two men, who had been talking in the corner of Winifred's room since the mayhem of a few days ago when Dr. Gladstone had first rushed in, having just gotten word of Winifred's awakening by way of an urgent message Mr. Darling had sent out. Mrs. Darling had been standing with them listening closely, but she'd been careful not to interrupt until she heard something she flat out disagreed with. "She's been the same girl she was before."

"That may be true physically. Her muscles will get used to movement again, she will start eating solid foods soon," the doctor acknowledged, "but I've never seen someone talk so vividly about what they saw while they were unconscious. All the patients I've seen, when they say that they remember anything at all, they describe short flashes, garbled sounds or colors, they don't tell a whole story. And they certainly don't return from a coma claiming to have gotten married." These doctors, Mrs. Darling thought, they had such a lack of imagination. They only understood what they read in books and if something had never happened before then it could definitely never happen now. Her boys would never have felt this way if they were told such a story, no matter how fantastic; they always ate Winifred's tales right up.

Mr. Darling nodded complacently at the doctor. "That's right. It is very strange the way Winifred has been carrying on. I remember the first words out of her mouth—she looked first at me and then at her mother, she had this sad pout on her lips as she said the word 'Peter.' Then she said it again, 'Peter, Peter, but where is Peter?' She asked and asked for him, but we don't know any Peters."

It had been true and Mrs. Darling could not get the look on her daughter's face when she first awoke out of her mind. She'd thought that Winifred would be happy to see her, that once she'd opened her eyes and realized that her mother was there, that her mother had been sitting near her bed nearly the entire time she was sleeping, she'd throw her arms around her mother, she'd cry out, "Mother, mother, how I've missed you, I'm so glad you're here." But instead she'd looked out at the room and closed her eyes again. She'd shaken her head as if she knew that it had been too good to be true, whatever had been going on in her head, wherever she had been when she was in that coma, it must have been magical, because she was so sad, she frowned so hard when she opened her eyes and saw nothing but the room in her house in London.

"I do have to say Doctor Gladstone, it doesn't seem right that a little girl should go around calling herself married, that she has changed her name. And where did she get that name, Wendy? It sounds like something a child would call her doll, the name for a dog," Mr. Darling huffed as he watched his daughter, who was now sitting in her bed listening to Michael explain about pirates as if her six-year-old brother's revelations were much more interesting than those of this doctor.

"It is strange," Doctor Gladstone agreed, nodding as he glanced at the girl. John and Michael were crowded around her as she told them a story. She'd been telling such big, such grand stories since waking up. John and Michael, not bothering to give their sister space, or to let her rest (since she had been essentially resting for the past three weeks) had sat around Winifred and watched as she went on about an Indian Princess named Tiger

Lily who hunted scary cowboys. She talked about a pirate named Captain Hook who'd kidnapped her and of fairies and mermaids and a world where she and all other children could fly. And then she talked about Peter. She went on and on about Peter, and while Mrs. Darling could believe that the other tales she told were just stories, things inside her head that she may have picked up from Mr. Barrie's stories while she was sleeping, Peter was different. The look on her face when she spoke of him—it was as if she were speaking of her first love.

Mrs. Darling remembered having that same look when she went for a long walk about Kew Gardens with a Mr. Conner Bakersfield when she was Winifred's age. He had sneaked around a tree and when she'd turned he'd kissed her right on the lips, holding her tight for a moment before letting her go. Of course, Mr. Conner Bakersfield had long since become a memory, but Mrs. Darling could recall the look on her own face, the way she'd combed out her hair and smiled at the very thought of him when she was still a girl. That was the look Winifred wore when she spoke about Peter, and no dream, no fantasy, no story could cause something as real as that.

"Where were you little girl?" Mrs. Darling asked herself as she stood off to the side watching her daughter tell stories. "What were you doing and where have you been?"

"You know, there are things we can do if the stories persist," Doctor Gladstone commented and Mr. Darling nodded knowingly. Her husband could not stop being encouraged at each "intellectual" thing the good doctor said. "There are places she might go, at least for a little while to get her sanity back."

"Her sanity back?" Mrs. Darling asked, aghast. "Just because a little girl tells stories. . . ."

"It's not that she's telling stories, it's that she believes those stories. There is a difference. No one threw a man in a sanitarium for telling stories about a little white rabbit that went down a hole and took a little girl with him, but if that man had believed he'd actually seen that rabbit, that the world the white rabbit came from was more than a mere story, well then it might have been best for that man, for all who knew him, for society as a whole, if he went away for a little while."

"What're you talking about, Winifred is not going away," Mrs. Darling argued, looking to her husband.

"I agree with my wife here," he stated. "There's no need to get carried away. We can watch her, we can see if she starts acting funny, hearing voices and what not, but we're not sending her away. My firm works with some psychological institutions, and, while some of them are perfectly pleasant, they are no place for a little girl."

"I understand, I just think, if things get worse. . . ." Doctor Gladstone said politely, nodding as he prepared to leave. "But if you want me to come back, if things get more dire, well then it might be for the best. . .." The doctor shook his head, as if he were thinking. "In any event I'm leaving for Scotland in a couple of days, but if you should ever need to contact me, you have my address."

"I do," Mr. Darling said, shifting to shake the doctor's hand. "Thank you for coming again. And thank you for taking such an interest in our daughter."

"Yes," Mrs. Darling added, willing to be more polite, to be the gracious hostess, now that her husband had taken a stand against the doctor. "Thank you for your help and if you're in London for whatever reason, please do call on us."

"Yes, yes, of course," Doctor Gladstone courteously replied, nodding at Mrs. Darling as he took one last look at Winfried before turning to go.

"I'll walk you out, doctor, I'll walk you out," Mr. Darling offered, following the doctor into the hall and down the stairs.

Mrs. Darling wasn't sure if the doctor had bothered to say good-bye to Winifred, who had been his patient for the past three weeks, or to the boys, who had seen him coming in and out of their house on a regular basis. She was glad to have him gone, and Winifred certainly didn't need the man who told her that her stories were nothing more than hallucinations coming to talk to her again.

"Is the doctor gone?" Winifred asked, sitting up wide-eyed in bed while the boys played around her. Michael had a long stick that he fancied a sword, which he was thrusting at John, who kept him back with a pillow he swore was a shield.

"I'm Captain Hook and I'm taking you prisoner, Lost Boy," Michael took a flying leap at John, who bounced backward, nearly stumbling over his own feet as he ran around the couch, hiding.

"The doctor is gone," Mrs. Darling called to her little girl.

"Good, I hope he never comes back," she said and Mrs. Darling walked closer to the bed. "He looked a bit like that Captain Hook." Winifred shook her head, shuddering as she turned to John and Michael.

Mrs. Darling took a seat on the bed near her daughter. Winifred looked just about the same as she had before she'd hit her head. Her long light brown hair fell in waves down her face, past her shoulders to the middle of her back; she was thinner, but her pale features and delicate blue eyes were becoming on her slim, almost womanly frame, and her white nightdress she'd changed into, made her look almost as if she were a bride on her wedding day. Though she had just been telling such magical, such silly stories, Winifred did look in some ways exactly like a married woman.

PRESTON

To celebrate the new batch of reinforcements they'd just received, the cowboys had challenged the Indians to a war. There had been no official announcement of it, whispers of the war had been buzzing over the treetops since that morning and Preston had heard of it from Dilweed, who'd been waiting on the branch outside his room when he'd gotten up that morning. They weren't sure whose side they were on just yet, it depended on how many Lost Boys were participating. Sometimes wars could get very crowded and Preston didn't like to fight in them unless he had plenty of space to run.

Peter was wandering near the trunk, looking about expectantly. Preston hadn't seen him in a long time, not since the last group of Lost Boys had fallen from the sky, and he wasn't sure what to make of it—Peter had never been away that long before. A few fairies crowded around him; he was speaking to them in bells and chimes, some of the fairies brightening and dimming as the conversation went on.

It had been several days, at least Preston thought it was several days, since Peter's confession about the girl Wendy in his secret room and though nothing seemed to have changed between them, in fact Peter was as friendly and as carefree with Preston as ever, Preston saw him in a different light. Since coming Here he'd been thinking about the stories he'd heard Before, the movies his mother had shown him, the cutout picture of a blond fairy in a coloring book at school, but it wasn't until he'd heard the story from Peter that he truly began to wonder about the truth of what he'd heard as a child.

"All right, you two, all right, I've finished my shower, we can join the war," Starky called, having come through a waterfall. Most of the Lost Boys shirked bathing, it was one of the luxuries of being Here, but Starky, maybe because he'd died in a shower, was very interested in cleanliness and constantly complained if he felt in the least bit dirty. Not that he minded getting dirty in a cowboy and Indian war, or when he was off hunting tigers with Peter, but after the fun was over, he needed to be showered and changed as if he still had little mothers on his shoulders whispering to him.

"Let's go," Dilweed called, and all three boys flew over the trees to the Indian camp.

They met other kids watching the war. There were Cliffy and Potchy, who'd come with the last batch, and Gumby and Lumby, who'd come many batches ago and had to stay with the fairies at first. "And it wasn't all our mother's fault," they'd once told Preston. "When she left us in the car, she was just really, really sad all the time and our father was never around and she didn't have any money." There was something about the boys that had been familiar to Preston, as if he'd known them, or at least had heard about them in the Before. Gumby and Lumby brought the boys into the fold as they waited for the war to get into full swing, while Starky and Dilweed pointed at the cowboys and Preston watched it all, wondering if he should bother entering the battle.

All wars were held at the Indian camp since the cowboys were always the aggressors, and so it was today. It was a war like any other war and a few of the Indians' fires had gone out, while some cowboys were shooting off guns, "bang-bang"-ing at the Indians, who in turn shot silent arrows at them. It seemed more dignified to have a quiet weapon, though it appeared that today far more Indians were falling than cowboys. A fresh batch of cowboys had come in; at the very least there appeared to be more of them than Preston could remember from the day before, though the number of Indians hadn't changed. There were Tomahawk and Brave Brave and High Skies and Silver Stream along with a great many other Indians Preston couldn't name because he hadn't really spoken to them at the peace rallies that took place after each war.

But the cowboy contingent had altered. There was Rider Joe and Big Man Jim and Timothy the Hotheaded and Carl, but there were others as well. A man with short-cropped blond hair was standing near the Indian tepees loading his gun and all of a sudden Preston could see that blond man in a bathing suit playing around on a boat. The man then started dancing, whacking his arms out and sending a child into the water. The child began flailing for help and finally the man in the bathing suit dove into the water, he started flailing himself as the water rushed over his head and he was Here.

Silly cowboys, Preston thought, as he heard a rustling behind him. "Are we ready for the war?" Peter asked, crouching, hands on his knees. "Are we fighting today? What side're we on?"

"I don't know if we're fighting," Starky explained. "It looks like an ordinary war. It wouldn't be fair to take one side over the other when they're so evenly matched."

"We could take no side and bother them both," Dilweed suggested.

"You always want to play spoiler," Peter teased.

"I do," Dilweed replied proudly, and Preston looked out at the cowboys.

He saw one that he knew, though not from Neverland. It was one of the new cowboys, standing with his hands on his hips, feet apart as he looked around. Preston could recognize that face, those eyes, the way his hands moved as he shot his rifle, but he did not know him from Here. He knew this cowboy from somewhere else, and a face appeared in his mind, not a cowboy face, but a regular face. He couldn't think of a name, but he knew who it was. Preston stepped back and started shaking, glancing every which way, at the trees, the sky, the ground, but Peter and the Lost Boys were too busy watching the war to notice.

"Whatcha doing back there?" Peter finally asked, turning around. He had his hands on his hips, feet set apart just like the cowboy. "You look scared, what's the matter?" he asked, concerned as he walked toward Preston.

"I think I know that cowboy," Preston replied. "I think I know him from Before. He was the one. . .the one I thought, I mean, I remember him from right before I. . . . He gave me some cookies and I got a stomach ache and laid down and fell asleep and then I was Here and he. . . .but I thought he. . ." Tears welled in Preston's eyes from having to remember, really remember. He had been in Neverland for some time, he knew what had happened to him, that his mother was back in the Before feeling very scared and sad, he knew that he was gone from that and he was going somewhere called the After and yet he had never really cried for it, he'd never truly let it sink in. "And there he is," Preston said, wiping tears as more came.

"It's strange when this happens, but it has happened," Peter explained. "This happened with Starky I remember. The guard who was shot trying to keep Starky out of the showers came back as a cowboy. He would have come back as an Indian since he tried to save a child, but he'd watched hundreds of children go into the showers before Starky and that would have made him a pirate. But because he tried to save Starky, that balanced it out a little and he came Here a cowboy, which is so much better than a pirate," Peter explained, shuddering at the mention of pirates.

"It's not just that. . . it's. . . . " Preston couldn't get the words out.

"It's okay, it's okay. Whoever that is, he's a cowboy and cowboys aren't bad, they're just misguided. Whoever your friend is, he's going to be okay."

"But that's not it," Preston said, wondering how Peter could be so stupid. "I thought it was him. . .that he was the one who killed me. . .but if he's a cowboy then he couldn't have been it and if he couldn't have been it then the one who did it, I don't know who it was. And if they're still out there they could do it again. I mean, I just thought the police would find him, since I'd been at his house, I thought it would be obvious, but if it's not obvious. . ."

"That is a predicament," Peter said, as if it were really no big deal. "But you're Here now, you don't need to worry about that."

"But what about other kids?"

"I don't know," Peter said. "It's my job to take care of the kids Here."

"Could there be a mistake? Maybe he's meant to be a pirate."

Peter shook his head as Starky and Dilweed ran out of the trees to join the war. They joined on neither side; Starky sling-shotting Indians, while Dilweed threw rocks at cowboys. "There was a man in your neighborhood who was very lonely," Peter explained. "And he didn't have any friends even though he had a good job and a nice house. And everyone in the neighborhood thought he was a little weird and he didn't let on, but he knew it, he knew he was strange and everyone was nice to him, but they weren't his friends. And then one day a little boy came by his house and he was so happy to have company, any company, that he invited him inside to have cookies thinking finally someone will like me. And he gave him milk and cookies and tried to make him his friend. That's all. . .that's all," Peter went on. "And he didn't know what was in the cookies, he just didn't know and if he had known he never would have served them."

"You know all that?" Preston asked, though it made perfect sense, of course their leader would know. "Why is he a cowboy?"

"He didn't do anything on purpose, he didn't know there was poison in the cookies, but he still gave you the cookies—that makes him a cowboy," Peter explained. "He's completely tied up in you now, in your fate, that's why he's Here."

Preston watched the cowboy with his big wide eyes and pale face. He turned in their direction and fired at an Indian, who fell at once. Preston could see his blue eyes, his rough chin and slender hands. Then he saw a man, the cowboy, wearing an orange jumpsuit in a concrete room. He saw another man come up to him during a scuffle. He watched the man start punching the cowboy and the cowboy closing his eyes, thinking he deserved it, he didn't do anything, but he deserved it. He saw a knife pulled from the attacker's pants and stabbed into the cowboy's chest until he fell to the ground, his hand to his heart as he tried to breathe.

"Hawthorne," Preston said, suddenly remembering. "His name is Hawthorne."

Peter called after him, but only watched as Preston ran to the cowboy, who was wearing cow-skin pants and a large white hat. He'd stopped to reload his imaginary gun and was surveying the war scene when Preston approached. The Hawthorne-cowboy looked down, but didn't recognize Preston. He just smiled as if this were all a game. Preston threw his arms around the cowboy's waist, holding him for a moment, the cowboy almost tumbling at the sudden force. When Preston let go he looked up at the cowboy, who knelt next to him.

"Why thank you, son," the cowboy said with the drawl of a man in an old western movie. "But you know, we're in a war right now and if you don't let me go I'm going to have to shoot you." He said this last part 'I'm going to have to shoot you,' with a friendly voice, as if the game were just that to him, though he took it very seriously. Preston nodded at the cowboy, looking up once more before running back to the woods. He watched his cowboy from the trees for a few minutes while Starky and Dilweed finished playing spoiler. Other cowboys talked to his cowboy; one of them placed a hand on his shoulder and smiled at him. The Hawthorne-cowboy laughed, he looked happy, he wasn't lonely and people seemed to like him Here.

Peter was standing next to Preston, but it wasn't as if he were watching, it was as if Peter didn't notice anything, until Starky and Dilweed, who had finished playing spoiler, met Oregano and Clover at the edge of the war and called out to him. "Peter!"

Oregano cried, out of breath though he had just been flying, "Peter, they're coming. They're Here," he shouted.

"Already? They're here?" Peter asked, scratching his head as if something deeply confused him. "Really? That's great, let's go get 'em," he shouted, lifting off the ground, though he hovered for a moment, asking Preston, who was still standing on the forest floor, "Are you coming? The new kids are here."

"New kids? Sure, I'm coming," Preston replied, taking one last look at the cowboy, who seemed to be doing just fine—he'd taken two Indians prisoner during the war and had survived an arrow wound by pulling it from his arm before it could do any damage. Peter started up and away and Preston followed. New kids had come only twice since he'd arrived but it had been such a happy time that he forgot what it meant when new kids came, that somewhere else, in the Before, people were incredibly sad.

The Lost Boys had all run off when Preston touched down by the tree house, noticing that most of the new boys had already come. The Ferris wheel was especially crowded, as was the merry-go-round and groups of kids were huddled together talking with each other. Peter hovered in the air, showing a group of new boys how to fly. "You just have to think happy thoughts, but since you kids naturally have happy thoughts that should not be a problem. See, watch me," and with that Peter closed his eyes and started floating above the new boys. They laughed and clapped at him and a couple of boys managed to get their feet off the ground. The other boys, once they'd seen that their fellow newcomers could do it, tried all the harder, and since in Neverland trying and believing were most of the work, more boys lifted themselves off the forest floor and Peter dove up through the trees, cascading over the clouds and doing a cartwheel in the air as other boys attempted to follow him. They weren't expert flyers yet, but some of them managed to hover above the trees a great long while before getting scared and having to come down. "You'll get the hang of it," Peter said and they all cheered. Peter held his arms out wide, relishing their excitement as they clapped and hollered at him. Peter did another cartwheel in the air before gently gliding down to the boys, who crowded around him as he shook their hands, said hello, and introduced old Lost Boys to the new ones.

Preston wandered through the groups of new boys. Starky was showing a few of them how to fly onto the Ferris wheel while it was still moving. Some of the new boys, though they'd forgotten the Before and would not remember it for a few days, as was the rule of Neverland, could still inherently remember the fears they might have had in the Before—fears of heights, fears of the dark, fears of monsters—and so they were a little hesitant. Oregano was playing jacks with a few of them, while Dilweed had taken still more boys up inside the tree house to the inside games.

Preston walked along the trunk, watching as boys stood in groups talking. He liked to watch them before joining in—since he hadn't come with a group he always had trouble breaking into one, even though all the new boys were nice and welcoming. Preston marched along the new boys until he saw a boy standing near the toy pile. The boy was digging his hands deep inside his pockets as Crispy showed him how to pick the exact right toy in the pile. The boy, like the cowboy, looked familiar, and though Preston could not recall the cowboy's name, he knew this new Lost Boy right away.

"Peyton?" he asked, worried that the boy would turn around. The boy did not turn right away and Preston was relieved, thinking he must have been mistaken. But when he said his name again, just for good measure, the boy turned and smiled. It was then, when Preston saw his face, that he knew it was his friend. "Peyton!" he cried, running to him. "Peyton! Peyton! It's you, it's you. What're you doing here?" When he asked the question he realized that it was not such a good thing that Peyton was in Neverland. It was not such a good thing that he himself was Here and someone had been robbed, a great many someone's had been robbed, of a great many years and a great bunch of happiness because they were Here. "What happened to you?" Preston asked and he saw it, he shouldn't have been able to see it, but he did. He saw Peyton grabbing a cookie at a great big party. He saw him crouch under a table, his stomach throbbing. He saw Peyton fall asleep under the table, a big white tablecloth covering him. Peyton closed his eyes and then he was Here. "What happened to you!?" Preston cried, shaking Peyton, who looked at him wide-eyed. He knew because this had happened to him that Peyton would not remember right away. Still he cried, "Don't you remember me? Don't you know who I am?"

"No, who are you?" Peyton asked, and Preston wanted to shake him again, though Lost Boys did not shake one another and he didn't want to scare his friend. "Hi," he then said, calming down and holding out his hand. The new Lost Boys seemed always to get the hang of the ethic of this place right away, even if they didn't know the exact rules.

"Hi," Preston said, taking Peyton's hand and shaking it. "When you remember the Before I want to talk to you. I want to be your friend Here like I was your friend Before."

"Before?" Peyton asked, and Preston knew he had to wait.

Peter came flying up. He had a smile on his face, that impish grin that never quite cracked, except once in his secret room. His face faltered, however, when he saw the look in Preston's eyes. "What's the matter?" he asked, glancing at Crispy, who shrugged as if such matters were beyond him. "What happened?" he asked, looking at Peyton. "Did the fairies miss one? Can he talk?"

"He can talk," Preston started, not knowing how he would explain this, though Peter always appeared to have seen everything before and never thought any of it was a particularly big deal. "It's just that I know him, I know him. He was my best friend in the Before and now he's Here."

"He's Here, your best friend," Peter said with a smile as he patted Preston's back and gave a big, hearty laugh. "That's wonderful—good for you. Very few Lost Boys ever get their best friend from Before with them. I've seen some brothers come in together, but rarely any friends. You're lucky. And don't worry, he'll remember in a couple days and then you two can talk like old times."

"But that's not it," Preston said looking sadly at Peter. "If he's Here and the man who I thought put me Here is also Here, as a cowboy, then that means whoever really put us Here is still out there. Whoever killed us is going to do it again, since they've already done it twice."

"Oh, you're right," Peter replied thoughtfully. "That is bad. That is very bad for the Before. But we don't live in the Before. Don't worry, whoever it was will become a pirate and the pirates cannot hurt us, not unless we go to them and even then there are certain laws. . . ."

"I know, but that's not the point Peter, that's not the point," Preston pressed. "Peyton is my best friend and our mothers are friends and I couldn't bear to have another mother. . . have another child harmed."

"You care about mothers?" Peter asked, making a disgusted face. It was then that Preston saw it, Peter wasn't like them, he wasn't like him. He wasn't human, he was a Betwixt and Between and it appeared he could not see beyond the confines of this place. "You shouldn't care so much about mothers, all they do is leave you anyway, or kick you off into the great big world to get a job and wear a suit."

"And what about Eva?" Preston said to Peyton, who shrugged as if he didn't know what an Eva was or why he should be worried about it. "There was me and Peyton and Eva and I just don't believe. . . Peter don't you think there's a way we can stop this from happening again?"

"Stop this?" Peter asked, confused. "No, we don't do that in Neverland. We are Here, we live Here, we can't go to the Before and it's not as if there's a way to know anything anyway. How're we going to warn anyone if we don't know who did it?"

"We could try and find out who did it, there must be someone, maybe the fairies, who could help." Preston looked at Peter, the boy with an impish face; he saw him as he had been a hundred years ago, a little bit older and hopelessly in love. There was sadness in him and a sense of sacrifice. "You could have gone after her," Preston said because he knew, he just knew.

"The Island asked me not to," Peter quietly replied. "And I listen to the Island."

"But you could have and I have to. . .I have to Peter and if there is any way, any way at all, I won't bring the Lost Boys into it, I won't even bring Peyton, I'll leave him alone, I'll let everyone be. I won't even ask you to help me if you just tell me how."

Peter watched Preston for a long time. Peyton started to squirm; though he didn't really know what was going on, he knew he was a part of it. "You came from the forest," Peter thought out loud. "And so the Island must want something more from you."

"Okay, Peter, okay," Preston pushed the boy's thoughts along.

"There is someone who can help us," Peter finally admitted, though it was a very slow process. "There is someone who can help us, but I don't know if he will, and if he does we'll have to pay a price. A heavy, heavy price."

"Fine, I'll pay anything," Preston replied, wondering what he had to give up.

"I don't know if you have the right kind of payment. But maybe I do," Peter went on. "We need to go see him. If you need help with something like this, it's a pirate matter and we are going to have to go see Captain Hook."

claire

Claire had been there when they found Peyton, a week and three days after Gregory Hawthorne's death, over a month since his imprisonment. She had probably been not fifteen feet from the little boy when he'd died. Like Preston, just like Preston, it had been a quiet death, one that did not beg for help or cry for mercy. Part of Claire was grateful for that, that no one had to watch either child suffer, though maybe, Claire couldn't help wondering, if the children had been in pain, if they'd been able to run home and shriek that their tummies hurt, maybe the adults could have done something.

It happened at a community picnic. The town had a festival every summer called Bay State Days and though Claire had been on the committee to help set up the picnic in Bridgewater Park the year before, the committee members had not expected anything of her this year. They'd politely invited her help, so as not to offend the grieving mother, but they did not press her when she told Millie Thompson that she was not up for committee membership this year.

Still Claire had gone to the picnic. She'd been staying in the house, except for her daily walk or her trips into town for the more essential errands, and she thought it might be nice, in any event it might be helpful, to go out into the world. She and Matthew had driven to the park together, holding hands across the gearshift. Neither of them had felt like holding hands, it was a last ditch effort, a sudden need for contact after weeks of nothing.

It had been a perfect day for a picnic, sunny, bright, the grass a pristine green, the pond near the park a crystal sphere, sun reflecting off of it like a hundred tiny mirrors. Claire and Matthew had eaten grilled chicken and hot dogs; they'd sipped lemonade and iced tea, made conversation with their neighbors, with the woman who volunteered to lead the library book club and the man who always rang the bell for the Salvation Army at the hardware store at Christmas. None of them wanted to look Claire in the eye, condolences concerning Preston, all those "I'm sorry's," were on the tips of their tongues, but they seemed to know too much time had passed and so asked nothing more than "How are you holding up?"

Cara and Jim had been there as well. Jim and Matthew briefly participated in a game of basketball while Cara had taken Claire aside and asked her how she was. "You know, it really is too bad about Gregory Hawthorne," she'd said at one point, grasping Claire's hand. "At the very least it robs you of justice." Claire had just nodded at that, deciding she did not want to talk about Gregory Hawthorne, especially since she had taken to pulling a wagon full of buckets of water to his house every three days to feed his white bellflowers.

Cara left Claire after a while and did not see her again until she frantically ran up to her, asking if she'd seen Peyton. Claire had not seen Peyton at all during her time at the picnic, but she volunteered to look around. Claire had searched the bathrooms, both boys and girls, she'd asked the kids playing tag on the playground if they'd seen him. When Claire found Eva playing with a couple of girls near the trees at the back of the park, she'd asked her where Peyton was and the little girl just shrugged.

"He said he wanted to play with the boys," she'd said innocently and Claire thanked her and left.

Claire hadn't found Peyton; it was one of the fathers who'd been sent to search for him who had. Claire wasn't there when they discovered the body under a picnic table shaded by a large white tablecloth. The father had gotten to his knees, doing mouth to mouth on little Peyton, who wasn't breathing. He'd cried out for someone to call the paramedics, and by the time Cara got to her boy she was already in tears. Claire stayed off to the side, she didn't look, she hadn't seen Preston until it was time to go to the morgue and she didn't want to think about what he could have looked like just after it happened.

Cara started screaming, clutching her son's shirt while he lay there, as a few onlookers pulled her off of him. The paramedics came quickly, driving right into the park and carrying Peyton to the truck on a stretcher. Jim went with him to the hospital while Cindy and David Carver took Cara in their car, all the while trying to calm her down. Peyton had been pronounced dead at the hospital, and it was there, the next day, that they did an autopsy to find that he had the same poison in his system as had been in Preston's. They searched the grounds to find the culprit and while no one turned up and no one had noticed anything, they did find a plate of cookies lying under a bush and when they tested them they found that they were full of poison. What they were not full of were any fingerprints or DNA evidence. All the parents were notified, all the children who'd been at the picnic were tested, but no one else had been harmed. Peyton had been the only one to eat the cookies, which made it all the more strange.

Since finding out about Peyton, Claire had been over to the List's twice. She didn't want to make a nuisance of herself, she knew better than anyone how much of a nuisance any well wisher, no matter how well intentioned, could be at this time, but she wanted to do something. She could picture Cara locked in her room, pacing the floors. She could see Jim crying himself to sleep at night and though before the funeral the house was packed with family, mothers and fathers, sisters and cousins, still no one answered the door when she tried once in the morning and again in the afternoon each day to visit.

The List's house, which had always felt "lived in," the kind of house where dishes stayed for days in the sink unwashed and clothes were strewn about the bedrooms, was stagnant on the day of Peyton's funeral as everyone who had come to mourn gathered at it. It was hard to say who had planned this get-together, it might have been Jim's parents, who'd flown in from Ohio, or Cara's sister Nancy, who'd been staying with the family since the autopsy, but whoever had planned it had done a nice job, the flowers were white and innocent and understated, the hors dourves and salads simple and plentiful. Claire knew how Cara felt, having all the family around; she, too, had needed an army of help with everyday tasks after the death of her son. She'd barely had the wherewithal to pick up coffee at the grocery store.

It felt like déjà vu being at another child's funeral only a month and a half after Preston's. She'd barely had time to heal, she couldn't go a single minute without seeing her boy's face or feeling his presence in his room. When she'd found out about Peyton she'd wanted to run to Cara and hold her up as she wished someone had done for her, but another part of her couldn't get the thought of Preston out of her head. Her little boy was gone and now her friend had lost her son. Was she now the grieving mother or the helpful confidante? Who had done this and when would it end?

It had been a lovely funeral service, with little figures of baseball players lining the area around the casket. Father O'Sherman had delivered a beautiful sermon and Peyton's grandmother spoke for the family. The burial, which Claire had reluctantly attended after seeing how stricken Cara looked during the service, had been very small and reserved, though everyone who attended was asked to throw dirt over the casket at the end, before they moved back to the List's for a solemn get-together of coffee and lemonade, cheese and crackers and salad, the same kind of "party" they'd thrown after Preston's funeral.

The gathering had been tastefully set up before everyone arrived, and when Claire and Matthew drove to the List's from the cemetery, parking their Audi a few doors down from the house, a great many people, neighbors and old friends, people from town

and Jim's office, were already there. Mary Martingale was tossing an avocado into a salad as she kept up a conversation Claire
couldn't make out with a woman standing behind her.

Claire waded through the people standing around holding
plastic cups of water, iced tea or lemonade, feeling as if she were
moving through four feet of water as she sought out her friend.
People moved aside for her, some of them even stopped to give
her a tight-lipped smile. She'd never been an outsider in the
neighborhood, but being at the funeral of yet another child, they
simply did not know what to say to her.

Matthew, it appeared, did not have it any easier. He'd been
over by the List's bay window, sitting on its edge with an iced tea
in his hand talking with Carl and John from down the block. None
of the conversation was very involved and most of it consisted of
"I just can't believe this," "it's too much, just too much," and "in
our neighborhood, that this could happen in our neighborhood."
There were a lot of heads being shaken and stares directed at the
ground, but no one wanted to leave the List's home, even though
the parents of the fallen child were nowhere to be seen.

"So how're you holding up?" a voice asked, and when Claire
turned around there was Matthew, standing behind her, slouch-
ing with his hands in his pockets. "You know if you want to go. . .I
mean, no one would blame you, especially not Cara, if we just left."

"Thank you," Claire replied as her husband draped an arm
around her. "But I'd like to see if I can talk to Cara before we go.
I wonder where she is."

"She's probably upstairs with her family. Remember how you
wanted to run and hide. . .I still feel like taking off for the bath-
room every time someone comes up and tries to talk to me about
it."

"It's still too soon to leave," Claire said to her husband and
he nodded "yes" in agreement. He was the one, the only one, who
could really understand exactly what she was going through, yet
still they shared so little.

"I know. I wonder if the police are going to come ask us more questions now that it seems they had the wrong man." Matthew shook his head as if he were annoyed by the prospect of this.

"Yes," Claire said, not wanting to think about it. "They had the wrong man."

"Hey," Matthew said, trying to perk Claire up. "Maybe he did do it. You never know, maybe this is a copycat crime, or he had a partner. I mean, I know that it's upsetting after what happened to Gregory, but it's not on us to beat ourselves up. It's not our fault. We didn't kill him, we didn't even have him arrested, all we did was lose our son and it's not fair that we have to feel guilty about it."

"I know," Claire replied. "I don't feel guilty, I feel bad. After all this," Claire looked up at her husband. "It's just that all I can do is feel bad."

"I know," Matthew replied. "I feel bad too. Do you want to go home? I think we've shown our respects and maybe it would be best for you to find Cara and talk to her later."

"I agree," Claire said. "We should go soon, but not just yet. I'd like to see if I can find her first."

"Okay. I'm ready to go when you are," Matthew concurred, putting his hands back in his pockets, always the dutiful husband. "Do you want me to come with you; or maybe I can talk to Jim? I don't know, how does this work?" Matthew gave a sad, confused smile and Claire almost giggled at her husband's sheepishness.

"I don't know how this works either," Claire replied before she walked away to find Cara. Matthew hung back, returning to the bay window and the couple of guys he'd been talking to as Claire walked once again through the house, by women in black skirts and blouses talking over small plates of salad, fixing cheese and crackers and looking each other in the eyes as they sadly shook their heads.

Claire passed the kitchen, the boiler room of the house, where most of the movement and all the preparations were taking place.

She'd never met Cara's mother or sisters, but she guessed that the three women huddled in the corner of the kitchen, unashamedly weeping, were, at least, closer to the deceased than most of the people here.

There weren't many children at the funeral. Some of the parents from school had taken their children to the service, but they hadn't wanted to subject them to the burial, to actually watching their school friend being lowered into the ground; and none of the parents thought that it would be wise to take them to this very adult get-together. Claire wondered briefly if, considering her closeness to the family, she might have brought Preston if he were still alive.

Claire bumped into something soft and firm and when she looked down she saw that Eva was standing right in her path. "Hello," she said gently, and the little girl just looked up. She was very pretty, with blond hair that came to just below her chin and wide blue eyes that seemed to sparkle in the light. "How are you?" Claire asked at the little girl, not knowing what to say. Eva had played at the house all the time, but now that Preston was gone, now that Peyton had followed him, it was as if they were strangers. And when did I start acting like a childless woman, someone who doesn't know at all what to say to a little kid? Claire wondered. "How're you doing?" she asked again awkwardly and Eva smiled at her.

"I'm sorry, Mrs. Tumber," the girl replied. "And my mom and dad are sorry too and I really love Preston and Peyton," she said as if she'd rehearsed what to say.

"I know you do, honey, I know you do," Claire said to the little girl. "Thank you."

"You're welcome," she replied.

"I know," was all Claire could say back, as she looked up to find Eva's parents. They were chatting with Mr. and Mrs. Carlson, small plastic cups in hand. Eva's mother looked over at Claire, smiling sweetly at her before she beckoned Eva closer and made a move as if she were about to break away from her conversation to speak with Claire. At this Claire looked away—she didn't know what to say to Eva's mother. Claire turned around, noting that Eva's mother held back. She felt bad snubbing her like that, but she could not take another "I'm sorry" now.

Claire then made her way back through the living room, which was nearly deserted, except for a few neighbors talking together on a white leather couch. "And I just don't know what to think about that man. If another child has been murdered it seems like he didn't do it," one woman said, looking up and then back down again when she saw Claire. "Do you know anything about that man?" the woman asked and Claire shook her head. She might have told her that she'd been to his trial, that she'd looked him in the eye and he'd seemed so sad, so childlike, so desperate, but no one had listened to him, no one had believed him, and now he was gone and no one could either ask him more questions or beg his forgiveness.

"I don't know what to think," was all Claire could say, and it appeared to be all they were expecting. She might have said more if Cara had been one of the women sitting around the living room. It wasn't as if these women had done anything wrong, they were just doing what they normally did, what she might have done under different circumstances, they were merely talking, wondering, guessing.

As Claire walked back around to the dining room, where Matthew was waiting for her, the door from the garage opened and Cara stepped into the house followed by Jim. Jim moved slowly into the party, shaking hands with one of the men from his office, while Cara dashed up the stairs, not bothering to even look around. Jim, seeing Claire, nodded once at her, walking in her direction. "I'm sorry for your loss, Jim," Claire said, realizing how many times people had said these exact words to her only a month and a half ago, and how worthless, how silly those words had sounded. But, now that she was on the other side, they were all there was to say. She couldn't bring Peyton back, she couldn't offer any words or phrases or deeds that would actually help. It was useless, all of it was useless, and perhaps the old saying was true, that the only balm that could attempt to heal this wound was good, old-fashioned time. Not that wounds such as this were meant to be healed—there would always be a mark, a scar, a wall that could never be scaled.

"How's she doing?" Claire asked, though she knew Jim couldn't answer that.

"I don't know," he replied. "I don't think she can believe it. The doctor offered her some sleeping pills, but she hasn't taken them yet. All she does is stay up all night looking at pictures of Peyton. I try to stay with her, but she pushes me away." Jim looked like he was about to cry, he swallowed hard and Claire almost put an arm around that solid, gray-haired man. Up until a little over a month ago they had all been good friends, neighbors who saw each other at cookouts and Little League games, but now it was gone and they were two sets of grieving parents, not as one, but each on their own, two islands of grief in a vast and incredibly deep ocean.

Claire wanted to say something else. She wanted to offer anything other than the obvious. It was as if because she had just been through this she should have learned what to do in this situation, she should have had the words readily available, but there was nothing. Claire merely placed a hand on Jim's shoulder and said, "I'm sorry." Jim nodded, glancing at the floor and heading into the kitchen.

Claire walked past the women still sitting on the couch again. They looked up at her, but Claire didn't notice; it was as if they weren't there. She wondered whether she should climb the stairs and look for Cara or return to Matthew and her own house, her own thoughts, her own tears and her mounds of materials for scrapbooks that attempted again and again to tell the story of Preston's life.

Matthew was still talking to a few guys from the neighborhood and though he didn't appear to be having a good time, he didn't seem uncomfortable. She'd done it many times before, climbing the List's stairs, which were not that different from the stairs in her own home. She'd run up them after Cara when the boys had been extra noisy in Peyton's room; she'd walked hurriedly past Cara once after a particular shopping spree when she really needed to use the washroom. These stairs were as comfortable to her as her own, yet it felt strange to be climbing them now, to feel the light in the hall grow dim and see the pictures hung near the railing, the ones with Peyton in them that now seemed like they were from another time, perhaps even another generation. There was one of Peyton last year, his school photo, when he'd been the only boy to wear a vest and tie, his light brown hair spiked up as he smiled, the gap from his missing front tooth showing. There was the obligatory wedding photo of Cara and Jim. Cara's hair had been blow-dried to look extra large and Jim had had a goatee that he'd shaved a few months later when he got his first job at the law firm. She'd seen these pictures many times before; they were a part of the backdrop, and she couldn't reconcile these photos with the woman who'd run up the stairs, unable to greet her neighbors.

Claire walked down the hall, passing the first door, which was shut. That was Peyton's room and she knew what a crime it would have been to go in there. She moved on, stopping at the third door down the hall, a light door, stained a cheerful color to match the rest of the terra cotta finish, the yellow and pastel orange theme of the house. Claire knocked once but no one answered. She knocked again before grasping the knob and opening the door. It might have been locked, but it wasn't and when Claire entered Cara was sitting on her large canopy bed surrounded by mounds of disheveled white comforter, a small brown pill bottle in her hand.

"Cara?" Claire asked and her friend looked up, wiping tears and mascara from her face. "Cara, it's Claire, are you all right?"

It was as if she were looking at her friend through a mirror, it was the same face, but something was skewed, perhaps by the tears drenching her skin, the squint of her puffy eyes or her uncombed hair. "Hi Claire," Cara said, wiping tears away as she tried to compose herself. "I'm sorry, I just can't go downstairs right now."

"I know, I know," Claire said, remembering how Cara had been there for her after Preston's funeral and how much she hadn't wanted it, though looking back, if no one had come to talk to her, if they had all kept their distance, it would have been worse. "I know what it's like, and I also know that it's probably completely different."

"I know," Cara responded. "But it's just so much. . ." she said, bursting into tears again as she grasped the pill bottle tightly. "And they gave me these to sleep, but I think they might have given me too many. They should know better than to give a whole bottle of sleeping pills to a desperate woman."

"What do you mean, Cara? Are you okay? What do you mean?" Claire worriedly demanded, a bit more forcefully than she meant to.

"Nothing, Claire, I don't mean anything," Cara said, annoyed as Claire took the bottle from her hands, shaking it to see that a great many of the pills were still there. "It's just that it's so much and I don't understand what there is anymore, how there could possibly be anything left, anything at all. . . ."

"I know, I know," Claire replied.

"Does it get better? Do you feel any more okay than you did last month, last week, yesterday?"

"No," Claire said, shaking her head. "No, I feel as if I've been punched in the stomach every day. And all the time I wake up and think that it must be a dream, he's really here, nothing happened to him. And I wake up in his room, yes, I've been sleeping in his room since the funeral, and I wake up there and I realize he's not with me, that there is no more Preston. I will never have him again and I cry every morning and every afternoon and every night."

"Then why even bother? Why go on?"

"I don't know," Claire replied. In that moment she honestly did not know, she'd never known the answer to that question, but now it seemed so pertinent, so necessary. "But I have to think. . . I have to know, I mean there must be. . .not a reason, but a way to go on." Claire, who had been trying not to cry, broke down, tears falling onto her hands. Cara inched closer so that both women were sitting nearly on top of each other. Neither looked at the other and it was as if each was alone, wrapped in a blanket of the other and still very much alone.

"And I don't know," Cara finally said, still in Claire's arms, sniffling. "I think if I had paid better attention. If I had not been such a loosey-goosey mom. I should have known better. I never should have let them play out on their own, I should have watched them like a hawk. I should have told Peyton to never eat anything, even at a community picnic, if he didn't know where it came from and even then to be careful. The old wives tales, the things my mother used to say about never talking to strangers, never taking something that wasn't wrapped, even in a familiar environment, they're true. And we try so hard, we parents, we try so hard, but it's such a difficult job, always watching, always worrying, there's nothing like it, not a job, not a vocation like it. And I remember being 23, before Peyton, and thinking babysitting was hard, thinking making dinner and cleaning the house was a sometimes difficult task, but then there was motherhood. And sometimes it's too much and so you slack off. You need five minutes' rest, you just want to sit, forget about watching TV or reading a magazine, you just want to sit on your butt for five seconds, five measly seconds. So you let your son go play at the park even though it's a little far; you forget to tell him not to eat the cookies. And sometimes you get away with it, most of the time you get away with it. But that one time. . .that one time. . . And I should have protected him better."

"I know Cara, I know," Claire said, holding tighter to her friend.

London, England 1901

It had been three weeks since Wendy had awakened and still there was no Peter. She'd begged her mother to call her Wendy, explaining that if she could convince a boy to take the name Peter Pan then the least her mother could do was call her by the name he'd given her. And the name so felt like the wind in her hair, like rushing along the Nevertrees at dusk, the way she'd gripped her arms around his neck....And he had been so safe, so careful, that sweet, wild and tragic boy. It was no wonder they'd called him Pan. But it had been three weeks and still there was no Peter. She'd been expecting him. If she could simply appear in Neverland, why could he not just as easily come to London? How was London any less magical? Yes, children couldn't fly in London and it didn't appear as if the city had any fairies, but still it had busses and horses and lights out on the street at night and sometimes it snowed and there were bridges over rivers. London was a lovely place and Wendy was sure Peter would like it if only he'd come.

A thought raced across Wendy's mind, lodging somewhere in the back and she realized something. Maybe Peter could not come here; perhaps Peter was not a part of this world at all. She tried to remember if he'd said anything about being able to come to London, but it might have been that Peter had dodged those questions intentionally and maybe he had known. . .maybe he'd always thought she'd stay with him in Neverland and now they were separated, but separated by what? By oceans? By countries? By time? What space must she cross to get to him and how would he find her?

"Wendy, Wendy!" John and Michael called, running in from the nursery. It was early in the morning, just eight o'clock, but the boys had been up and dressed since Liza had gotten them ready at seven. Wendy had been told to stay in bed again today, all day, something about her muscles and bones needing to get used to movement again after such a long time in bed, and so she was still in her nightgown. "Wendy, Wendy," the boys shouted as they rushed in. They had taken to calling her Wendy, unlike the adults in the house, who insisted on calling her by her proper name.

"We left our window open last night so he might come in," John announced importantly. "Just like you said, though Mother complained that we could catch cold."

"Yes, thank you," Wendy replied. "I kept my window open as well. Mother closed it last night and so I got a box, climbed up and opened it after I heard her leave."

"It got cold," Michael informed her, dangling from the bed-clothes so that he pulled the covers down. Wendy laughed as they fell to the floor, politely covering her mouth as her brothers hustled to put the comforter back over their sister.

"Do you think he'll come tonight?" John asked, wide eyed.

"Do you think he'll bring that mean old Captain Hook? Maybe I can fight him; I've gotten pretty good," Michael proclaimed, making punching and kicking motions as he bounced away from the bed.

"I'm sure he'll come eventually," Wendy said and though he hadn't yet come, she still believed he'd be here soon.

"And he'll kill those pirates when he does," Michael announced, running around Winifred's bed and crying "pow-pow." John, for his part, stood close by, upright and gentlemanly, though he stifled a giggle at his little brother.

The door to her room opened and Wendy's mother came in. She moved with the grace of a woman who was more than just a woman, but also a mother, a grownup, a presence. Her long, grayish skirt wrapped about her as she stood in the doorway, her beautiful brown hair done up in an elaborate bun. Her mother had been a dear since Wendy woke up. She'd been kind and loving, making sure she did not want for a cup of tea or a sugar candy. She read her the newspaper, offered her little presents, and had been oh so very good about Peter. She did not go so far as to believe that her nearly sixteen-year-old daughter was a married woman, but she did not deny it. She merely shook her head, smiling demurely when Wendy began to speak of Peter, who always made her blush. "Winifred darling," her mother said, using "darling" as a pet, and not proper, name. "You have a visitor," she went on, smiling sadly at Wendy as she sat up in bed in her white nightgown, her long brown hair falling in a braid down her back as her brothers ran around the room trying to catch one another.

"They may come in," Wendy announced, pulling the covers back over herself.

"It's okay, he won't stay long," Mrs. Darling informed her, looking at the boys, who had stopped running and were now only staring, Michael with one whole hand in his mouth. "Go ahead, you may go in," Mrs. Darling instructed someone out in the hall, and Winifred smiled and fixed her nightdress, thinking for a second, only one brief second, that it was Peter coming to see her.

And of course it wasn't. Peter wouldn't have come in by the front door, he would not even have used the back door. Wendy knew Peter, and he'd have come in through the window. He would not have bothered with her mother; he was not fond of mothers and said that mothers were only good when Wendy herself had been the Lost Boys' mother. And though a very small part of her was let down by the fact that it was not Peter who walked through the door, she was sufficiently delighted to see that their neighbor, Mr. Barrie, had come to see her.

He usually came to visit her parents. Before her accident she could only recall seeing Mr. Barrie at the house a couple of times, and Wendy knew very little about him, only that he was a playwright who had written a few plays that her father respected and admired, though personally did not care for. Since her accident, Mr. Barrie had been coming around more often, Wendy had seen him walking up and down the hall with her father in the middle of the day, and once he'd come to dinner and tried to talk to Wendy about the stories she'd been telling, the ones the doctors were so worried about. Then the dinner party had taken over and Mr. Barrie's wife began to speak to her mother, and her father started to lecture about something or other that had happened at the office, and so she'd never gotten the chance to tell Mr. Barrie anything.

"Hello, Winifred," Mr. Barrie said, sounding a bit shy and looking at the floor. John and Michael, who'd been watching him silently, giggled to themselves as they slunk out of the room, going with their mother, most likely downstairs to start their lessons. "It's good to see you're feeling better."

"Oh, I've been feeling better for a long time," Wendy explained, making sure the blankets were about her. She was nearly sixteen years old and a married woman and so it was a little unbecoming taking a visitor of the opposite sex in her bedroom. Her mother, though she had been very good about the whole thing, still thought of her as a child who could be in bed and take visitors without it mattering. But she knew it; she had grown up, that thing with Peter, not just the wedding, but that other thing in the woods. . . that was why she was not in the nursery anymore. "But for some reason they feel the need to keep me in bed," Wendy informed her visitor.

"I'm sure your doctors are just worried about you," Mr. Barrie said in a friendly, youthful voice. He took one of the wooden chairs in the room (her mother always kept a supply of them there so someone could comfortably sit with her) and pulled it near the bed. "Now," Mr. Barrie said, having gotten comfortable, "I wanted to talk to you about those stories you've been telling." He said this with such seriousness that Wendy had to giggle.

"The doctors are very afraid that I've lost my head," Wendy replied. "They say that a little girl shouldn't go around announcing she's a married woman. They say that if I keep this up they'll have to recommend me to a loony bin."

Mr. Barrie laughed out loud at that. "Doctors are always trying to medicate what they don't understand. Everything they don't already know they are always prescribing medication for." He shook his head, as if it were really very sad. "Well, I don't think your stories are a sign of insanity, not at all. In fact I would say that storytelling is the sign of a normal, healthy, albeit interesting child."

"I think Mother feels that way. She's always asking me questions about my stories and trying to see if there's anything else I know. Father isn't that interested, but every time a doctor insinuates that there's something wrong with me, he gets upset and tells them to leave."

"Your parents are fine people," Mr. Barrie commented, and Wendy realized as she was speaking to this man that he was much more like a child, much more like a Lost Boy than he was a grown man. It was as if he had never grown up and yet he was made to live in this adult world, like a fish flapping at the edge of a boat trying desperately to get back into the sea. "So tell me then, what stories do you have? Where were you and what did you see?"

"I was in a place called Neverland," Wendy related very seriously. "It was supposed to be the place little boys went when they died. But it wasn't bad or sad at all, it was magical. I don't know where it was, and Peter, he was the leader of Neverland, he said that the Island has to be looking for you, you can't just find it. It's an island full of boys and I was the only girl on it, except for the mermaids, but they don't count, Peter said, because they're half fish, and the fairies, who don't count either because they're also not human. But in Neverland there are all these things for boys to play with. There are cowboys and Indians, who one time changed completely and became dukes and lords battling with long swords. But the Indians were really quite interesting, I loved being with them. The cowboys were frightening, though, they had guns and were always talking about going to a place called a 'Saloon.' And there were fairies, which I never really saw, I could only make out shiny, white lights. And there were pirates. Only I didn't really see much of the pirates. One of the pirates kidnapped me, but he was the only one I saw. He came in the night and placed his hand over my mouth. I tried to struggle, but he was too strong. He grabbed my Indian costume and made me change into it once we got outside the tree house, all the while threatening that he would kill Peter if I screamed. He took me back to his ship and held me prisoner until Peter rescued me."

"That sounds magical," Mr. Barrie commented, wide eyed. "And who is this Peter? Your mother seems to think you believe you're married to him."

"Oh, I am," Wendy replied, pulling her braid down around one shoulder in a long rope. "I am married to him. I mean, I suppose I am, I came back during the ceremony, I was pulled away right before the kiss. But Slightly had just asked me if I should take him as my husband, and I said "yes," and then he asked Peter if he should take me as his wife and he'd said "yes" as well. And he loves me, I know he loves me and we were close, so close in Neverland and Peter is such a wonderful boy. He takes care of the Lost Boys, he fights the cowboys and Indians, he slays tigers in the night. There is something carefree, something childish about him, but also something sad and unnerving in the way he acts, as if it is all acting and really he is just as old as the pirates." Wendy turned thoughtful for a moment, picturing Peter and the way he'd spoken to her when it was just the two of them. He had seemed so sad, as if he were about to break apart. "But all the mermaids and the fairies are in love with him. And he fought Captain Hook. He fought him so bravely and so valiantly, and it was as if once Peter started to fight the old man there was no way of him losing. It was as if the Island did not want him to lose."

"How lovely. It's just how I've imagined it," Mr. Barrie said. "And so he is a boy, a boy who never grows up?"

"Yes, he's a boy who never grows up," Wendy said, though that didn't seem quite right. At first she was very proud of that statement, but then she realized the conundrum. If Peter did not grow up, how would he make a good husband? In any event, he could not be her husband here in London. Perhaps he would make a good Neverland husband, but in London people did not take kindly to married men, married boys, who did not grow up. "But I suppose if we are married then he should have to."

"Don't look so sad Winifred," Mr. Barrie said and his kindness was so great that Wendy nearly threw her arms around his neck, but she knew that was not proper, not for a married woman who is sitting in her bed in her nightgown. "I think that your Peter, well. . . your Peter will always be whatever you want, whatever you need him to be."

"I hope so," Wendy replied, though that sounded very general. 'Whatever she needed him to be?' As if he could sprout wings and fly. . . but then again he could.

"You know, I had a feeling there was a Neverland," Mr. Barrie went on. "And since I've been meeting with some children and their mother in the park, I've had visions, if you will, of this magical child-like place."

"It's very good that you have visions of it, it must mean that you are a particularly child-like man," Wendy retorted, watching him and wondering if she could see him as an Indian.

"You know I had a brother, David, who died very young," Mr. Barrie explained, getting just a touch more serious. "He fell through the ice while he was skating. It broke my mother apart when she got the news. David was her favorite of us all. She had many children, and she couldn't always shower us all with attention, but little David, it seemed, she loved just a little bit more. After he passed my mother grew so sad, I think her sadness infected the entire family. She took to her room and I used to try to cheer her up by putting on David's clothes. One time when I came in wearing his good Sunday suit her eyes perked up and she nearly fell to her knees, she thought her little David had returned. But of course it was just me, and nothing can describe the disappointment on her face."

"Was she angry at you?" Wendy asked, feeling very bad for Mr. Barrie.

"No, she wasn't angry. She understood and she even tried to make herself laugh at the prank I'd pulled. Though I hadn't been trying to pull a prank, I'd been trying to help. But I think that losing David, it was the end of her and that death reverberated through my family, not only through my family, but through whomever we touched, and I can still feel the loss of David today. I feel it in my life and my work."

"Really?" Wendy asked. "I didn't see any Lost Boys named David," she went on, trying to be helpful.

"That's okay. We used to call him Boxwood and he was a very clever boy, very kind, he was going to go into the church."

Wendy stopped to think, remembering that there had been a Lost Boy with that name, a very kind, very sweet, very innocent one, but she stopped herself at the last second, deciding not to tell Mr. Barrie this. "I'm sorry Mr. Barrie, I'm sure it must have been hard." She wanted to reach out and grasp his hand, but that too was unbecoming of a married woman.

"It's all right," he said, perking up. "It's just that my mother always used to say that he would never grow up, he'd be her little boy forever."

"And to her he will," Wendy replied and Mr. Barrie smiled.

"In any event, I'm working on something now, it's sort of swimming about in my head. I've been playing with these boys and their mother in Kensington Gardens and the story has taken shape, but your stories, your help, Winifred, has been very illuminating and you might have put the finishing touches on it, is that okay?"

"Yes, it's fine Mr. Barrie, you may have my stories. But please, call me Wendy."

"Wendy?" Mr. Barrie asked, his face lightening. "I knew a girl who used to go by something. . .not Wendy, but something like Wendy and yes. . .it's a lovely name, a lovely name. I take it he gave it to you?"

"Yes, he gave it to me, just as I gave him the name Peter. He told me just to call him Pan, but that was such a small name and Peter is so much more distinguished."

"That it is, Wendy. I know a Peter as well. Thank you for your help," Mr. Barrie said, growing just a bit more formal as he stood. "I should be going, but it was lovely seeing you and I do plan on using your stories, thank you for loaning them to me."

"It's my pleasure. I'm happy to tell them to someone who'll listen."

Mr. Barrie shook his head sadly at that. "Yes, that's true, children should be listened to. Well," he went on, gently giving Wendy his hand to shake. "I shall be off, but I'm sure I'll be around to visit you and your family soon."

"Yes, thank you for the visit," Wendy said politely as Mr. Barrie moved to leave.

"Good bye," he called once more when he was at the door as Wendy watched him walk away. She could hear his footsteps down the hall, and then creaking on the stairs. Wendy took note of her mother saying good-bye in the parlor before Liza showed him out. When she was sure he was gone from the house and was walking down the street, she crept to her window to watch him go.

Wendy then rushed to her closet to pick out some more becoming clothes. She could hear John and Michael downstairs and wanted to go to them. Her legs felt fine, as did the rest of her, her bones and muscles had been rehabilitated and her joints were all in working order. Her health had returned and there was a world beyond this stuffy room, adults and their prognoses be damned.

claire

Every two days Claire lugged a wagon full of buckets out of her garage, down her street, and up the hill by the cul-de-sac to Gregory Hawthorne's yard. It had been every three days, but she found the soil got too parched when she neglected it. She took the large red wagon, the one she'd used for her gardening before, though Claire had barely watered her own flowers in almost two months. She didn't take the smaller wagon, the one that had been Preston's. Even though it seemed more and more that Gregory Hawthorne probably had nothing to do with her son's death, she still couldn't bring herself to carry the water for his bellflowers in her son's toy.

She was sure they watched her; the Hoffstras' up the block and the Montgomery's, Eva's family. She was sure they'd been talking, thinking maybe Claire Tumber had had a nervous breakdown. And really, what was so special about those bellflowers, except that they were all white? And they had done nothing wrong; they were pure and innocent like children. Their caretaker, it was now pretty clear, had done nothing wrong as well and now he was gone and those poor flowers were left with no one to take care of them, no one to water and feed them, no one to make sure the sun didn't bake them or the trees over-shade them.

The block was empty at eleven thirty on a Wednesday afternoon. This was a neighborhood where everyone worked. Sure there were a few housewives lingering about, but even those had committee meetings and club gatherings, shopping for parties and trips to the hospital for their four or five hours of volunteer work a week. This was not a neighborhood where people sat idle, despite the bright pastel facades and manicured lawns. This was a neighborhood where most of the gardens were planted by landscapers, but not Gregory Hawthorne's, Claire could tell right away. Sure, he might have hired someone to do the weeding, maybe he'd even had help with the planting, but the design was all his.

Claire closed her eyes as she sprinkled the last of the water from the bucket. She could see Gregory standing before these plants, not that she'd ever watched him, not until he was a sniveling man begging for her forgiveness for something he had not done. And she hadn't given it. That was her crime. No one had convicted the man, and still she could not offer him a kind word. Now the police were saying that they'd found another set of prints in Gregory Hawthorne's house, that they'd found another storage unit with all the chemicals that were used to kill Preston and Peyton in it (though they didn't know whose it was, since they'd apparently used a fake name to get it and it had only been opened because the occupant had stopped paying the rental bill for the unit). None of it was connected to Gregory and though it must have made him very lonely living in the cul-de-sac with no family, not even a mother or father he saw around the holidays, Claire was glad of that now. After all that had happened to him, it was better that no one who loved him had to watch how he'd suffered.

Claire replaced her last bucket and turned to move out. She never lingered at Gregory's very long; she knew better. Sometimes she sat on the stoop and looked out at the property, the old swing set in the Huxburries' yard or the basketball hoop hanging unused across the way. Sometimes she simply listened to the dogs bark, or stooped to smell the flowers.

Today Claire looked at the house for an extra long time, considering the brass doorknob, the little white knocker so few people had used to visit Gregory Hawthorne before all this. She turned to leave, but then she walked toward the house, wondering what would happen if she took the first step and then the second to the stoop. Claire went up the walkway and reached out, grasping the brass doorknob that still shone in the sunlight. She didn't think the handle would work when she turned it, nor did she really want to be opening the door as she pulled the knob toward her and looked inside. The house was still. Gregory Hawthorne's furniture was perfectly in place, though some pieces were surrounded by yellow and black police tape. Nothing had been moved in weeks and Claire could sense the dry unlived-in feel starting to set in, the kind you see in a rental house.

It seemed as if it should be the type of home where everything had its place, even when Gregory wasn't around to live in it. Being on his own without a child to disturb the order, she was sure Gregory did a much better job than herself at keeping things together, since children disturbed so much order and as a mother there is only so much you can do. Claire walked down the hall expecting to find an adult's living room, but instead it was as if a child, or a very immature college student, lived here. A large television dominated one wall and there were video games out, controllers on the floor, things she could remember from when Preston and Peyton spent too much time playing in front of the TV on rainy days. Posters of sports heroes hung on the walls, just taped up like in a dorm room.

Claire turned toward the kitchen. She wasn't here to snoop, and she decided as long as she stayed on the ground floor, as long as she didn't ascend any stairs, she wasn't doing anything crazy. She wasn't searching a dead man's house, the door had been open and she'd merely gone inside, like Alice falling down the rabbit hole, it had all been some kind of elaborate accident. She would disturb no drawers, open no doors, she was just visiting and when she was finished, she would leave.

It felt strange in the kitchen, where it had happened. Even if Gregory Hawthorne had had nothing to do with Preston's death, he'd admitted to giving him the cookies and so there was no denying that this was where it had happened. Claire glanced out at the kitchen with its granite counters, the nicely carved table, the knife lying out in full view. It all felt still and quiet, so unreal there was something holy about it.

Claire wished she'd brought one of her scrapbooks to leave here. Perhaps that's what she should be doing with them, not undoing them, but leaving them in places that had once belonged to Preston: the school, the playground, Gregory Hawthorne's kitchen.

She was about to sit in one of the wooden chairs when she heard the door move. She did not hear a knob turn or a hinge creak, those sounds might have been a bit less subtle than the slight twisting, the minute creaking of what came from the direction of the entrance. Claire didn't even have time to get nervous as the door opened a little more and she could hear and feel a presence enter with soft footsteps, a hand on the wall gently rattling the knick knacks there.

"Hello?" a voice inquired and Claire peeked her head out from the kitchen. "Hello," the voice said again.

"Cara?" Claire asked, walking toward her friend. "Cara, how are you?" She had not seen her since Peyton's funeral. The List family had piled in their car and driven somewhere not ten minutes after the last guests had left their home. Claire wasn't sure if Jim had gone into work during the time they were gone, but they didn't reappear in the neighborhood until a week later and then they shut themselves up again. Claire had tried Cara's house twice since they'd returned, but no one answered.

"Claire?" Cara asked. "What're you doing here? I didn't even know they left this place unlocked."

"I didn't either, not until today," Claire explained. She did not know whether to be happy or nervous that her friend was here, that she and Cara were having a conversation, a real conversation since the last great tragedy that had befallen them. "I was watering the bellflowers and I just thought. . .I don't even know why I thought it, I just thought it might be interesting to try the door. I didn't think they'd actually leave it open, it must have been a mistake, but then it opened. . .and who knows why I went inside."

"Sometimes it's hard to stay out of rooms we're not supposed to go into," Cara remarked. "I was just going for a walk and I saw that the door was open."

"I'm glad you did," Claire replied. She wanted to ask Cara how she was, she wanted to feed her coffee and cake and get it all out, but she knew better. It had only been two weeks since Peyton and Claire could barely gather the strength to think logically about Preston and it had been over two months since. . .

"I don't know what draw this place holds. Apparently he didn't do it," Cara went on. Claire considered leaving the house, there was nothing here and this had to be trespassing, but Cara moved forward, into the kitchen. She walked as if she knew what she was doing, stopping at the table as if it were her own as she fingered the tops of the chairs and glanced at the refrigerator.

"I don't know either. I mean for me, I know that Preston was here. This was one of the last places, one of the last things he saw. . ." Claire stopped, feeling the strength drain from her legs as if the weight of her body was finally too much for her. She grasped the chair and Cara pulled it out for her, helping her into it as Claire felt the heaviness of her body. She had never thought of how Preston must have felt, what Preston must have seen, that there had been a time when Preston was here and then he wasn't, a moment when it all changed. She'd never considered that—she had only focused on her memories of Preston, and trying desperately to imagine what her life would be like without him.

"And it's funny how it's so cathartic," Cara said, stroking the back of Claire's neck as she looked out at the kitchen and wondered if Preston had noticed the knife-set on the counter or that the refrigerator was more yellow than white.

"Don't you ever wonder what he saw? I mean, right before?" Claire asked and Cara shook her head.

"I try not to. I'm his mother and I can't picture him suffering."

"It's just that there must have been something. I wonder sometimes if he thought about his mother, but that is a very selfish thought and—"

"You're allowed to be selfish," Cara replied. "Even now, even after all this, and what poor Gregory must have gone through, even with all that, you're allowed to be selfish."

"Thank you," Claire replied, looking up at Cara, who took a seat next to her. "It's just that. . .and I wonder what my mother must have thought when she was raising children and her mother and her mother. In my family at least they were all girls."

"Really, all girls?" Cara asked.

"Yes," Claire replied. "My mother used to say that I was the first daughter to ever have a boy, the first boy in the family since Victorian times."

"Really?" Cara asked. "That's funny. My mother had six kids and they were all mixed and her mother had six mixed kids, and her mother and her mother, dating back to my great, great, grandmother in Ireland."

"My family is from England," Claire replied. "I mean, my mother's family is. My great-great-great-grandmother grew up in Bloomsbury in London; in fact she knew JM Barrie, the man who wrote Peter Pan."

"Really, wow, you should advertise that, it'll make you famous," Cara replied.

"They weren't really that close, she only knew him as a child," Claire remarked. "And then her daughter Jane was my great-great-grandmother, who moved to America, and her daughter, Margaret, was my great grandmother and her daughter Elizabeth was my grandmother, and she moved to Chicago before she had her daughter Linda, my mother."

"And then you moved to Boston, heading back east, 'eh?" Cara asked, moving in closer, her arms resting casually on the table as if she were indulging in a little girl talk.

"Not that far east," Claire replied. "I never thought about it, the family tree and all the women who have been on it. My mother never noticed it, but my grandmother, before she passed, said it was very strange, my having a boy, considering that all the girls in the family only had girls, which is why the family name is so diluted. It was only my great- great-great- great grandmother Winifred's mother who had two boys."

"Two boys and a girl," Cara said. "That's what I thought Jim and I would have. But it took so long to conceive again after Peyton and when we finally did I miscarried very early. . . ."

"I'm so sorry," Claire replied, reaching out to hold her friend's hand.

"It's okay. It was bad, but nothing like. . . I don't want to compare the two, I don't think it's fair."

"I understand," Claire sympathized. "We thought of having another, but it never happened, the timing was never right."

"Such is life," Cara sighed, glancing out at the room, her eyes upon the refrigerator. "I wonder what's in there."

"Probably nothing, it's probably been cleaned out, or whatever is in it has gone bad." Claire looked back at the fridge, got up and opened it. It felt so natural, as if this were her own house. There wasn't much on the shelves, the bright, narrow light from the back illuminating only a small corner of the kitchen. There was a blue ceramic dish for butter, carefully closed, and a box of expensive-looking baking soda in the back. It seemed someone had cleared the refrigerator of any leftovers, either that or Gregory Hawthorne had not been the kind of man to eat or leave leftovers. There was police tape on the milk, which had probably gone bad, but which could not be thrown out because of the police tape, and two diet sodas. Claire considered reaching in and taking one of the sodas. They couldn't have gone bad and they were such a harmless drink. Then she remembered what had happened to Preston after taking food from this house, and there was the police tape, and did Claire really want her fingerprints on the fridge? At this thought she pulled back, terrified. What if the police did another sweep for prints and found hers?

"I don't like the look of that police tape," Claire said.

"I didn't think about that, of course, better keep out of there," Cara responded, getting up she walked over to the other side of the kitchen, near the television set. It was a small flat screen, maybe the size of a tabloid newspaper, and it was pushed so far back on the counter that it blended with the fixtures, until Cara pressed the power button. After a second the News came on in flashes of color and sound, light sliding across the room.

"I haven't had a TV in my kitchen since Peyton was born," Cara commented, sitting down. Cara looked to Claire, who nodded knowingly. She had done nothing as indulgent as watching television since Preston's passing, though she had been in essence doing nothing at all, but it had been a restless and absorbed nothing.

"We should go to Cape Cod," Claire said out of nowhere. She had not been thinking about the annual vacation she'd had planned with her neighbors for months. They'd been talking about it since October, and Matthew and Jim had booked the accommodations in early November when the prices were still cheap and prime real estate still available. It was just a week in a rented house on the seashore, and she hadn't even thought about it, what with all that was happening, but just then she couldn't think of anything she'd rather do than get away.

"Maybe we should," Cara replied as the Mid-day News suddenly attracted their attention. A woman in an orange jumpsuit came on the screen, led by three police officers and a large man who appeared to be her lawyer.

"Francine Gumm has just returned from her arraignment after a court psychologist has deemed her fit to stand trial," the professional voice of an invisible female anchor announced live from the courthouse.

"And it seems that now Ms. Gumm's attorney is going to be making a statement regarding the outcome of this initial verdict.

He'll be up in a minute to discuss the progress of the case," the reporter said.

Both women watched as the anchor remained silent, waiting for the attorney to speak. Francine had already been sentenced, she had already confessed and what was more she had done something horrific. It wasn't as if a national hero mesmerized them and Claire wondered why she was so spellbound. It was only that Ms. Gumm had done something so unnatural, so unimaginable, that Claire just could not look away, like flashing lights on the side of the road, she simply could not turn her head.

"It's just awful," Cara said, shaking her head before Ms. Gumm's lawyer approached the podium. And why her attorney would speak to the press while his client was in the middle of a legal battle was beyond Claire. It didn't make any sense and though Claire was not well versed in the ways of the legal world, she knew enough about it, both from Jim and Law and Order respectively, to know that this was not done. "I mean, what she did, I can't even imagine. And now she's saying she was hearing voices, that she was seeing things, actually seeing things."

"She didn't say that when she was on trial before. She didn't say much of anything," Claire commented and it was not until she heard herself speak that she wanted to stop talking. She was sure that people had talked that way about Gregory Hawthorne as well; there were so many people who had blamed the man before his trial even began. Near strangers, people Claire had only known casually, came up to her in the supermarket and said things like, "I'm so glad they finally arrested him," and "Hopefully he'll fry for this," as if any of those comments were going to make Claire feel better. What made her feel bad was total strangers coming up to her and acting as if they were on her side. "She did confess," Claire said more to herself than to Cara. "And it wasn't the kind of confession that could have been coerced or made up, I mean. . ."

"I know. That's the messed up part. And now she's trying to get out of jail by playing the crazy card. She was hearing voices.

Really?" Cara said and her voice turned up in such a way that it was like the time they were in the car together and a guy cut her off. "Really?" Cara said and it was as if only for that moment, that one solitary second, none of this had happened; as if they were two women having a conversation at the kitchen table. They might have had lemonade or salads in front of them; they might have been at Claire's house or Cara's, as if for that one second maybe Preston and Peyton were upstairs playing.

"I don't know what they're going to do with Francine Gumm," Claire said, trying to get the moment back, but it was gone as quickly as it came.

"I know," Cara said, shaking her head. "I know and it's too bad. She gives mothers a bad name and what I wouldn't give. . ." Cara stopped. "I think we should go see her, give her a piece of our minds."

"You want to visit Francine Gumm?" Claire repeated. "I don't know about that, that sounds a little difficult and I don't know if she'd see us."

"Oh she'd see us," Cara replied, as if she knew this for a fact. "Two grieving mothers who have lost their children? Do you know what kind of publicity that would be for her? Do you know how good she'll think it would be for her trial?"

"If it'll be good for her trial then I don't think we should do it," Claire hedged.

"It wouldn't actually be good for it. The woman killed her children and confessed to it; she's not getting out. I just think. . .I'd like to give her a piece of my mind and study her, you know? Besides, I'm sure Jim, I mean, one of the guys at his firm, knows her lawyer and I'm sure we could get a message to her. I'm sure she'd agree to see us," Cara planned.

At least it's perking her up, Claire thought.

"I guess we could," Claire hedged, unsure whether the matter had been decided. She could see herself backing out of this plan at the last minute, and since Cara had never been the kind of woman with a lot of follow-through, the entire notion could die at this kitchen table. Cara looked at Claire and got up, turning the television off as it focused on a shot of Francine's lawyer. The television went black and Cara sat down at the table, leaning back as if she had a glass of soda in her hand. It all looked so natural, like something they had done a hundred times before, as if they should be hearing Peyton and Preston yelling at their video games upstairs.

PRESTON

It felt like it had been only a day, maybe two since Peyton arrived in Neverland. Days never seemed to work out right Here since the Lost Boys were always sleeping whenever they felt like it and waking up the same way, as if night only lasted a minute. But it had felt like a whole day, twenty-four entire hours, had passed when Preston heard a knock on his door.

"Hi there," Peter greeted him that impish smile spread across his face. Preston had just gotten up, he was tired and his hair was sticking straight up. He felt as if he couldn't move right, but Peter seemed as if he'd been flying all night. "Someone wants to talk to you," he announced, moving to the side and revealing Peyton, standing sheepishly behind him. Peyton looked the same as Before—whatever had happened to him it hadn't affected his appearance. He was tall and a little chubby; his light brown hair fell into his face and across his eyes since his mother always waited until the last possible second for a haircut. Peyton smiled, revealing the gap where he'd chipped one of his teeth a couple of weeks ago, and laughed when he looked into Preston's room.

"It looks the same as it did Before, except the TV," Peyton observed as Peter backed further to the side, ushering the Lost Boy in. Preston watched his old friend, wondering when he'd started using words like "Before." He'd never realized how strange this all was until he saw someone he knew acting the same way he'd been acting since he arrived.

"Peyton, are you all right?" Preston asked and his old friend smiled.

"I'm Here; of course I'm all right."

"Yes, of course you are," Preston said sadly. Somehow he thought Peyton would know more than the other new boys, but he was just as curious, just as awestruck by this place and just like the others Peyton did not bother to question what had brought him here or what it meant.

"I'm going to head out, there are tigers to slay," Peter announced a bit too dramatically and Preston waved at him as he flew off the branch and into the sky.

"Do you like Peter?" Preston asked, starting with the most obvious question.

"He's nice," Peyton responded. "He taught me how to fly—do you want to see?"

"Maybe later," Preston replied. "I'm glad you remember; when you first came you didn't know who I was. You always forget, it takes a couple days to remember, but I was afraid you wouldn't."

"Of course I would," Peyton replied. "When I first started to remember, when Peter told me about this place, I mean, it didn't make any sense, but then I remembered that you might be Here and when I asked him about you he brought me over."

"So what happened after I left?"

"Nothing," was Peyton's first response and Preston could remember his old friend getting tongue-tied Before. "I remember my parents talking after dinner. My mom was really worried about your mom, and your mom always looked sad. One time me and Eva were walking through your yard and she was back there. She didn't see us, but we watched her stand over your pool, she looked like she was about to jump into it, but instead she started throwing your toys in. I made a plan with Eva to go in and get them when she went inside, but when we got back all the toys were gone."

"My toys are right here," Preston explained, and Peyton took a good look around at the old teddy bear and video game system, at the baseball mitt and hockey stick.

"I know, but they were in the Before too. And then the man

they thought hurt you, he came to your funeral and your dad tried to beat him up."

"He shouldn't have done that," Preston replied. "He's a good guy."

"I know," was all Peyton could say, as if he really didn't know, but felt compelled to answer in the affirmative anyway.

"Do you remember what happened to you?" Preston asked wondering if he should broach the subject.

"I ate some cookies," Peyton replied. "A woman came up to me. I didn't know her, but we were at a picnic and she just came up with a big plate of cookies. She didn't let any of the other kids touch them. Even when Patrick Harris tried to she said they were just for me. She let me have three right away, even after I said my mom wouldn't want me to eat them."

"Do you remember anything else about her? Who she was, what she looked like?" Preston asked. Maybe if Peyton could remember they wouldn't need to go see Captain Hook, who would ask for a price for the information he gave.

"She was very nice," Peyton explained. "And ugly. She had a couple of bumps on her face that looked like warts and stringy hair and small, beady eyes, and if she hadn't been so nice, if she hadn't have given me cookies, I might have thought she was a witch."

"Did you know her?" Preston pushed.

"No, I don't think I knew her. She said she knew me. She said she worked at our school and that she'd seen you and me and Eva being mean to other kids. She said that we shouldn't be mean; we shouldn't make fun of them. That was very, very bad and we had to be punished for that, she said."

"We never made fun of any kids, did we?" Preston asked. "I mean, there was Bobby Frazier and Connie Sanders, but that was just fun. They knew that."

"She said it wasn't fun for them," Peyton replied. "After I ate the cookies I started feeling sick, almost right away, and I crawled under the table to lay down where it was dark and then I was Here."

"You were Here," Preston repeated, wondering if he could remember any ugly, friendly ladies at the school. There was Mrs. Turner, but she was very old and never would have given a kid cookies, and Mrs. Parker, but she wasn't really all that ugly, and she didn't have bumps on her face. "I don't know what happened to us, but I don't think it's over."

"Why don't you think that? How do we find out?" Peyton asked a bit too hopefully. Preston could see that his friend wasn't as concerned about other kids as much as he was interested in adventure. Here all the kids seemed to be more concerned with excitement, once one game ended they were on to the next, as if there were no repercussions, as if there wasn't a real world they'd left behind. Peter thought it was because he'd simply shown up in the forest that he thought differently from everyone else, but Preston couldn't see how the other boys could pay absolutely no mind to things outside themselves. Peter had been right when he'd said it was like a sense was missing from them.

"You said the lady mentioned Eva. I think she's in trouble," Preston explained. "And the worst part is we wouldn't even realize it because girls don't come Here, girls go Somewhere Else and we wouldn't even know if they got her."

"They could get Eva?" Peyton asked. "We have to save her. How do we save her?" he asked playfully valiant.

"I don't know," Preston replied. "I talked to Peter and he said we have to go see the pirates and Captain Hook."

"The pirates," Peyton gasped. "We can't go see the pirates, Preston, you don't understand, the Lost Boys told me they're not like the pirates in the stories, they don't just play games. They are bad, very, very bad, and the children who don't talk, the one's the fairies take, the pirates did that to them in the Before. They are what is bad and evil and wrong with the Before," he explained as if he were repeating something he'd heard. "We cannot go see them."

"I don't want to go either, and Hook is the worst of them, but I have to. You can stay here, but if I can help Eva—"

"How are you going to get to the Before to help Eva anyway? What is there that Hook could possibly say or do; it's not as if there's any way back."

Preston remembered Peter and the fact that he knew there was a way he could have gone to Wendy again if he'd really wanted to. He didn't know the what or the why or the how, but he knew there was a way. "There has to be something, that's part of why I need to see Captain Hook."

"And Eva is a lady," Peyton stated with childish importance as if he were playing cowboys and Indians, about to make a grave sacrifice in a game of make-believe. "She is a lady and we must rescue her."

"Hear, hear," Preston called, getting caught up in the game. "Now I just need to figure out what Hook might want from me. Peter said we'll have to pay a price, a very big price, but I can't seem to find what he could possibly want."

"What if he wants you or me or Eva in return?" Peyton asked.

"I don't know," Preston replied. He had not thought that Hook would ask for something that important, but then he remembered that with Hook there were no games, it was all real and real sacrifices must be made. "We have to find weapons," Preston realized, flying about his room. He flew to the highest points, up by the shelves, hovering like the fairies did as he looked for something, anything that might be worthy of fighting Hook. There was his baseball bat, that might help, and his pocketknife, but that was very dull, which was the only reason his father had let him have it. Preston scurried about his room, throwing toys out of his chest and crawling under his bed. "We could take the bed apart and use that."

Peyton watched Preston scour the four corners of his room.

"I don't think a baseball bat will be enough," he said thoughtfully. "Do you have anything in your room, anything we can fight with?"

"I have a hockey stick," Peyton offered. "Do you think that's enough? We could hit him over the head and. . ." The story Peyton told, hitting Hook over the head and running, seemed like a good one. Preston could picture it in his mind: they'd come in, they'd go right for the evil pirate, Peter would hold him back and they'd start hitting him with bats and hockey sticks until he talked. Then they'd leave, giving Hook a black eye for good measure. That sounded like a good plan, a nice way to kill an afternoon. They'd learn how to save Eva, they'd figure out who'd been hurting children. He'd save other mothers from grief and maybe even make his own mother a little bit happier. Maybe she wouldn't cry anymore or throw his toys into the pool. But at the same time something told him, something in the pit of his stomach, something just a little bit older than Preston's ten years, something said that this was not enough. That in the real world, the pirate world, baseball bats and hockey sticks did not bring down big, bad men. Secrets were not given up unless something real was sacrificed in return.

"We have to go see Peter," Preston announced. Peyton smiled and started jumping up and down, crying "Yay!"

"We have to go see Peter. Where is he?"

"Don't tell anyone else what we're doing, Peter wouldn't like it," Preston warned his friend, opening the door to his room and flying out. "When we get to Peter's room, let me knock, let me talk," Preston explained and Peyton nodded, relieved to be left out of the grunt work for this expedition.

They flew down from the branch Preston's room rested on, past some Lost Boys playing with the toy pile and around the trunk. Preston looked about to make sure none of the other Lost Boys were paying attention before he scurried around the trunk toward Peter's room. The trunk looked like it normally did, and Preston had to stare into the wood for a long time before he noted the faint line of the door that blended in so seamlessly. He knocked once and the note, "Do Not Enter Upon Penalty of Death," emerged.

"We should probably not go in there," Peyton warned, stepping back as Preston kept knocking.

"It's okay," Preston reassured him, looking back at his friend and smiling to placate him. "Peter, it's me," Preston called and after a long moment the door slipped to the side, revealing the room just as it had been when he'd first come.

There were no fairies inside, but Peter lit a lantern that glowed in the middle of the tiny space. The picture of the girl Wendy was still up and Preston wondered for a brief moment how a photograph had gotten Here. Wendy didn't look like a girl in the picture, and nothing like the young creature in Peter's drawings. Preston could sense Peter's eyes on him as he surveyed the scene. He then beckoned Peyton, who was a bit cautious, to enter.

"Hi Peter," Peyton said, waving sheepishly.

"Always nice to see a Lost Boy," Peter greeted him.

"We want to go see Captain Hook," Preston announced, looking to Peter.

"I thought you'd forget about that," he replied. "I don't think it's a good idea."

"But you said you'd take us," Preston pushed him. "You said you would and I know Pan, he would never go back on his word."

"He would not," Peter replied. "But I just don't think, and he'll want something, he'll want something we won't want to part with. And I cannot guarantee your safety there. I've never taken a Lost Boy to see him; I barely go see him myself. We do not play together, we are not in the midst of a never ending war for the fun of it, and I would have killed him long ago if the Island had let me."

"But I need to see him," Preston countered, pleading. "I need to find out who did this. If it wasn't the cowboy then it has to have been someone else and that person is going to get Eva, my friend Eva, and she..."

"Is she like Wendy?" Peter asked, cocking his head like a dog that does not know what's going on.

"She's like Wendy," Preston replied, wondering just what Peter meant, but not wanting to get into it. "She was very important to me and Peyton and if something were to happen to her. . .and we wouldn't even know because she's a girl and. . ."

"I'd know it," replied Peter. "I'd know it, just like I knew nothing ever happened to Wendy or her children, because I would have felt it, I would have felt them Here or Somewhere Else, where the girls are. Nothing ever happened to her and she lived to be an old woman. I thought when she had kids she'd come back as a mermaid, but I didn't even get that and I'd know. . .I know now and Eva is not Somewhere Else yet."

"Peter we need weapons. All we have are a baseball bat and a hockey stick and we can't go up against Hook with—"

"You can't go up against Hook with a baseball bat and hockey stick," Peter interrupted. "You need knives and swords and a cannon if we had one, which we don't. But maybe we can steal one from the pirates."

"Do you have guns and swords?" Preston asked, remembering that the only weapons the Lost Boys really had were slingshots with no ammo. The cowboys had invisible guns, but they didn't fire real bullets and the Indians carried invisible bows with fake arrows. "Do you have any *real* weapons?"

"Of course I do," Peter replied, scratching his head as if they'd just asked a very silly question. "I'm Peter Pan, of course I do. I've been Here since the pirates came and I had to fend them off, to keep them off the bulk of Neverland for years. I don't think anyone understands, there are things I do that go beyond picking fights with harmless Indians or slaying docile tigers. . ." Peter stopped for a second, looking like a sad grownup. "I've been swinging swords, I've been under attack, of course I have weapons. Here," he said, moving toward a darkened corner of his room. He pulled a sheet off a large wooden trunk and opened it wide, rustling through it and nearly falling inside. "Just a second," Peter instructed. "Here they are," he went on, and getting to his knees he pulled out three things, first a very large sword sheathed in metal and then two smaller swords covered in cloth. "These will have to do."

"Are you sure?" Peyton asked and Peter nodded at him.

"Are those for us?" Preston continued, pointing at the smaller swords.

"They are," Peter replied. "The big one is mine, it's been mine since I stole it from the pirates—I've had to steal all my weapons from the pirates since the Lost Boys don't come with weapons and swords like these are too nice to be made in Neverland."

"They look heavy," Peyton complained and Preston knew not to bother responding, his friend had never been the type to enjoy strenuous activity.

Peter turned on another light and Preston noticed that there were crossbows hanging on the walls. He hadn't spotted these the first time he'd come to this room, they were large, professional crossbows with mechanical string devices hooked into them, not the invisible ones the Indians played with. "What's in there?" Preston asked, pointing to another trunk sitting on the high shelf.

"Those are the guns," Peter answered. "And we're not opening them, we're not bringing them. We won't use any of this unless we absolutely have to, if the pirates come after us and find the tree house, then and only then do we use guns. That's the only reason I have most of these weapons."

"I thought they couldn't do that?" Preston asked.

"They can't come to us because they don't know where the tree house is, but if we go there, and then they follow us back. . ."

"We can't take that risk," Preston decided before he could consider the repercussions of that statement. "We can't let them find the Lost Boys."

"We can't," Peter replied, "which is why we'll have to fly around the world. We'll have to fly up and up and up. I'll take you, we'll have to disappear for a whole week in the air, that's just what we'll have to do. Don't worry, it's not hard, no one gets tired when they're flying no matter how fast or for how long, but it's the only way to make sure they don't find us."

"What're we going to use?" Preston asked looking at the crossbows on the walls and the trunks filled with guns. The crossbows looked cool, but in all honesty he was terrified of using them and even when the cowboys went "bang-bang" he got a little shaken.

"This stuff is awesome!" Peyton cried, having ignored Peter's earlier statement. "Which one is mine?" Peyton looked bug-eyed at the crossbows.

"None of them are yours. This should be a fight among gentlemen; we'll only use swords," Peter informed them. "This is mine," he said, holding the larger one so the blade hid half his face. "The sword of Pan. And only I can use it."

"Neat," Peyton ahhed.

"And here are yours," Peter instructed after he'd placed his own sword on top of one of the trunks, pointing to the smaller swords on the ground.

"How does it work?" Peyton asked, fumbling.

Peter held his sword in his hand; he thrust it and began rushing back and forth, his legs perfectly placed, as if he were dancing. Peter rushed at the wall, pricking it; he flew backwards, did a summersault with the sword and came back at the wall, thrusting all the while. He flipped, landing on the very edge of one of the trunks before gliding seamlessly to the ground and sticking the sword on a latch at the side of his belt. "That is how you use a sword," he said to them.

It had looked so easy that Preston was sure he'd get the hang of it, as if something magical would tell him how to use it, as it had been with flying. He lifted his sword and tried to run at the wall, but he nearly missed Peter, who moved out of the way just in time. Preston then dropped the sword before it got anywhere near its target. "It's heavier than it looks," he stated, massaging his wrist as Peter picked up the weapon and handed it to Preston.

"It's a sword, the blade is made of metal, of course it's heavy. Try again," Peter instructed, watching as Preston wobbled, "en guard-ing" at the wall, but losing his balance and slipping. He might have cut himself if Peter had not flown in and grabbed the sword from him.

"How come you're so good at it?" Preston asked and Peter looked at him for a long second as if he didn't know what to say.

"I'm Pan," he replied. "I'm good with a sword, just because I don't ever use one. I mean. . .what else would I be good at?"

"Let me try," Peyton called, fumbling his weapon. He tried to thrust it and it slipped from his wrist before he even moved. This time Peter wasn't fast enough and Peyton cut his arm. "Ouch," he cried. "Ouch, ouch, ouch, it hurts, it hurts."

"Real weapons hurt," Peter informed them as he flew toward a shelf, coming back with a long white bandage. He flew to Peyton and carefully wrapped the wound. "You'll be okay," he said.

"How long do you think we'll need to practice with these weapons?" Preston asked, holding his sword clumsily by the handle. Peter looked at him and shook his head.

"Twenty years," he said. "You can't just go in there brandishing a sword you've never used before, and it's not as if you'll magically learn, I mean, some things about this place are magical, but learning how to use a weapon, pirate things, are not. No, you're not going to be able to bring swords, maybe sling shots, but that's all."

"But we need swords," Preston argued, on the verge of tears. "We need to see Captain Hook and how can we if we don't have weapons."

"I'll bring the sword and it will be enough," Peter told them. "We'll go tomorrow. When Peter Pan picks a fight he wins. But, and I hate to say this, if we're going tomorrow that means you're going to have to go to bed tonight. When it starts getting dark, you go straight to bed and sleep until morning. We'll go to the pirates before any of the other Lost Boys wake up."

"Are you sure Peter?" Preston asked as he watched Peyton pick at his bandage.

"It'll be fine. That's the only way to see the pirates, early in the morning while they're still hung over. It's something grown-ups get after they've been out too late. Pirates always stay up late and so you have to go to bed early to counter that. And time is stopped in the morning in Pirate Cove, the rest of the day time moves forward very slowly and then you start to grow up when you're there, but in the morning time's stopped and that's when we can go."

"That sounds dangerous," Peyton commented, holding his injured arm.

"It is," Peter replied.

"All right, what about the price he'll ask us to pay?" Preston inquired and Peter shook his head.

"I'll bring the price, I have something he wants and I'm sure he'll take it. It might take some haggling, he might ask for your soul first, but he can always be talked down."

"Okay," Preston replied, and Peyton nodded, giving another dangling "Okay." "Is there anything else we can do?" Preston asked, watching Peter move about his darkened room. There seemed to be nothing in it now but the single light and Peter, looking so big, so grown up with that sword at his side.

"No, there's nothing else you can do. All I want you to do today is play. Just go play."

The next day Peter woke them early, the kind of early Preston had hardly ever been up for. It was still dark out, a tiny sliver of pink-ish light peeking over a horizon that seemed flat, even over the trees. Peyton was already up and dressed when Peter knocked on Preston's door. He might not have gotten up he was so tired, but he remembered Captain Hook and helping Eva. After throwing on a pair of jeans and a thick sweater, he joined Peter, who was not clothed in much more than what he always wore, those leafy green shorts and leather shoes, his green shirt that was ripped around the neck and a brown belt where he carried his sword.

"You ready?" he asked and Preston nodded, looking at Peyton, who'd bundled himself up just as Preston had. Peter took off, not bothering to see if the boys followed. He was halfway across the forest when Preston and Peyton glided into the air, having to speed up to keep with Peter as he flew further into the sun, his shadow a long, black wisp behind him. They flew all over Neverland passing the camps of the cowboys and Indians, who had turned the night before and were now robots and spacemen. They flew low over mermaid lagoon, where a couple of mermaids were out sunning themselves on the shiny black rocks; they passed the Neverbird floating on her nest with her eggs that never hatched, soaring across miles upon miles of forest.

It seemed that they should have reached Pirate Cove, they were flying so fast and for so long. Preston wasn't sure of the time; it was very hard to pin time down in this place and he might have been Here a week or he may have only just arrived or else it had been many years and Eva was an old woman. They flew across Neverland, never reaching Pirate Cove, which did not seem logical, considering the fact that Neverland was only so large and they had been flying for so many minutes or hours or seconds at the same speed and velocity per minute (or second). At last Peter slowed down, descending slowly to the forest floor. Preston and Peyton followed, landing in the middle of a small clearing in a thick, dark forest.

This was not like the rest of the Neverforest. It was cold, very cold, and in addition to his sweatshirt, Preston wished he'd brought a winter coat. There had never been a need for a winter coat, not as long as he'd been in Neverland, and he wondered if he even had one Here. It was darker in this forest and Preston wondered if they'd flown into the night, not simply time-wise, but as if here the night were a living entity they were now inside of. Sounds could be heard, though Preston couldn't pick up on them—they were thin, wobbly sounds. He heard what sounded like an owl, but it was louder, shriller than an owl; he heard a frog croak, but the tone was slightly off, and after a while Preston turned around to see that Peter was checking his sword and Peyton was trying to keep warm by jumping up and down. Preston saw a large red bird, a bird the size of a little boy. It had a long, narrow beak and beady, vacant eyes that lolled about and rolled into the back of his head. The bird stared at Peter and their leader shook his head at it. "You be still," he warned the creature, his voice sharper than it had ever been. "Follow me," Peter ordered and it was like he was a different boy. He was not their friend anymore, he wasn't even their leader. It was as if Peter had taken on the manners of a pirate.

"You two can't fly in Pirate Territory, so we have to stay low to the ground," Peter instructed. "We don't want any of the animals warning Hook we're coming. Then he'll have time to think, and we need the element of surprise."

"Okay, Peter," Preston replied, as Peter bent down.

"We have to crawl," Peter instructed, getting on his knees and then his stomach. Preston crouched down flat, feeling the icy dirt underneath him. It smelled like the garbage and the sewers, like dead fish and spoiled meat, and he could feel himself gagging on the fumes as he watched Peyton bravely gather himself on the ground. "It's a little ways, are you sure you're going to be okay?" Peter asked and both boys nodded at him; there didn't seem to be any other choice and so they were going to have to deal with it. "And whatever you do, don't engage him. Do not talk to Captain Hook," Peter warned before crawling forward.

They crawled on their bellies for some time and though the cold did its best to get to them, it was the sounds that were truly frightening. At first it was the cawing of birds and shrieks of animals. Preston heard a beast roaring far off and gasped. Peter shushed him, telling him it was okay—as long as they crawled the Neverbeasts couldn't get them. They moved on and after a while they could hear a ticking sound, the slightest tick followed by the minutest tock, back and forth, tick and tock, tick and tock, growing more intense as they neared what looked like the end of the forest. "Those are clocks," Peter explained in a whisper that was more like a hiss. "They're all around Pirate Cove and they say if you stay here long enough you grow up."

"Do pirates grow up?" Peyton asked as they reached the light.

"No, they're already grown up, they just get old. They keep getting older and older and older until their bones break and their eyes fall out. This place is a punishment for them. Their biggest crime is being the worst kind of grownup they could be and so they are punished by being the worst kind of grownup there is, very old and very sad."

Peter stood up first. Preston and Peyton followed his lead, watching the sword at his side. Their leader put his finger to his lips and walked forward, crouching low as he walked through a curtain of branches, nearly disappearing. Preston hurriedly followed him, as did Peyton.

Outside the forest was a city. It was not the kind of city Preston had seen on TV, nor was it the city his parents sometimes took him to on special occasions. This city was made of concrete, all one color, a dull, lifeless beige. Skyscrapers littered the landscape; tight and sharp rectangles with pointed edges that looked as if they might stab you if you got too close. A thick, gassy fog hung in the air, and when Preston looked closely, he could see bugs marching down the sidewalk that stretched on all sides of them as if the sky itself were made of concrete.

"What is this place?" Peyton asked, and Peter started walking. The city was deserted, so they could move freely, not that there was any place to hide. All the doors were closed and there were no crevices to squeeze into or benches to crouch under.

"It's Pirate City. The last outpost before Pirate Cove. Usually I bypass this, but you two can't fly here."

"Do pirates live here?" Peyton asked.

"Some of them do," Peter replied. "Some of them live on ships, some just on the streets. Most of them have little rooms in those great big buildings where they just sit all day staring at the walls. At least that's what I've heard. I've never been in a pirate room."

"Does Hook come here?" Preston asked.

"It's not all like the stories," Peter informed them as they marched on.

It felt as if they had been walking for a long, long time, though it also felt as if no time had passed at all and Preston wasn't sure what to make of that. "Time is like a slush pile Here," Peter explained. "It moves very slowly, which is why it takes a pirate so long to age, why they stay Here for almost forever. But sometimes because time moves so slowly it doesn't seem to move at all and then sometimes a long time feels like no time. That's when time just stops. It's stopped now; I made sure we came at a moment when time was stopped. So watch out, time can start moving again at any second and then we'll have to run really fast to keep ahead of it."

"To keep ahead of time?" Preston asked. "What would happen if time...?"

"You'd start to grow up," Peter replied.

They did not see anyone in Pirate City, the concrete came back around on itself as if they were on a conveyor belt, and Preston started to smell something in the air. It was a familiar smell; a not altogether bad smell, something tangy and tart and when he looked up he could see a vast line of blue in the distance.

"That's the horizon," Peter explained. "That's Pirate Cove, where the water is. That's where the pirates congregate, where Hook keeps the Jolly Roger."

"Is that his ship?" Peyton asked and Peter nodded, looking forward valiantly as they trudged ahead.

There had been silence in the concrete city, but all of a sudden the sound of drums and horns burst from the air. The noise overtook them, cymbals clanging, wild cries and feet stomping, as they neared the horizon, which did not seem like a shimmer of blue in the distance, but like cold, white nothingness. Preston had always remembered another horizon popping up after the first one had been reached. But not here, here the horizon marked the end of the world.

Preston could hear pirates signing loud, raucous music, "Yo-ho, yo-ho-ing!" from every direction. After a minute they had passed through the concrete city and into a dock-like area. The air smelled heavier to Preston, and he realized there was salt in it. There were lower, more colorful homes made of rotting wood, signs were painted in garbled English and words like "this way" were spelled "theeeese waah." Peter examined the signs as if he could read them, though he looked confused, until he glanced once toward a large ship in the distance. Preston could barely see the docks, there were too many small buildings in the way, but he could make out the mast of a great ship. The sails were bright white and the mast was made of glowing, shiny wood. Peter seemed to consider the ship for a great long while before he nodded and said, "This way," walking through the double doors of a small, squat building marked 'Saloon.'

There had been pirates outside but they had not been paying attention. They'd been staring off into space with bottles in their hands; a couple of men lying with needles in their arms across a barrel set up as a table. The pirates had stringy hair and their teeth were rotting through, as Preston could see when one opened his mouth and said "Arrrh." It was as if a worm might crawl through them. But the pirates inside were even more raucous, arms waving, bodies lolling against poles and stools and wooden beams. A couple of pirates stopped to watch Peter as he marched bravely into the Saloon, glancing once at the man behind the bar before heading toward the back.

They did not make it all the way to the end of the bar; Peter stopped short at a large wooden table. When Preston stepped closer he could see bugs crawling around the wood, into crevices and holes where food had been dropped to the floor. There had been a feast at the table at one time, but Preston wasn't sure how long ago. The table had been picked clean of food, and now all that was left were empty wine bottles and bones, scraps of rotting apples, cherry pits, pig and lamb carcasses and crumbs.

"Ah, Peter," a man said, cocking his head. He'd blended so well before that it was like he'd crawled out from the decaying wood of his chair. Three pirates had been sitting on dilapidated stools, also blending into the table, until one lifted his head and spoke. The pirate changed, he no longer blended with the bar once he straightened his wig and pulled his jacket more tightly across his chest. He had long black hair that ran in curls past his shoulders and his coat, which was red with gold buttons, was much nicer than even the ship Preston had seen from a distance. "Peter, how nice of you to visit me," the man said with a sticky-sweet voice. "And I see you've brought friends." The pirate smiled, lifting his arms from under the table to reveal two large metal hooks. "Did you get my little note? Are you here to ask what it said? I'm a gentleman, I'll tell you. It said 'I'm back.'" He smiled long and patiently at them, as if he were waiting for it to sink in. "I'm back, and something else called me, perhaps it was that little one," Hook declared, pointing at Preston with his cold metal appendage. "Perhaps it was you and I do hope you cross over soon little boy. I do hope your little Mommy gets over you so that Neverland doesn't have to worry about bad old Captain Hook coming to get you. But you needn't worry," he went on. "I'm a gentleman and I gave my word I wouldn't bother you and so I haven't, but the other pirates, if they ever got wind that you were Here, the great- great-great grandson of that little girl who caused us so much trouble, why they'd just be too excited not to come see you and I cannot be responsible for what happens then."

"Hook, you listen to me, don't you ever—" Peter started and Hook held a shiny claw up to halt him. Peyton gasped and stepped back, while Preston stood bravely next to Peter, trying very hard to stare the pirate down, though he could feel himself failing miserably when he got a look at those hooks. "Don't talk to them, Hook," Peter warned, glaring.

"Now, now, Peter, stop that. Always with the 'Hook,' as if to rub it in. You know what a sore winner that makes you. Bad form Peter, bad form. And really, I have a name. I call you by your name, as ridiculous as it is." The pirate looked first at Peyton and then at Preston. "I'm James, Captain James and how I got stuck with that ludicrous, childish nickname, I don't know. But then again that's what you get when your nemesis is. . .how old are you now Peter, thirteen, fourteen, are you still fifteen years old?"

"Don't listen to him," Peter warned, and Preston remembered what had been said about Hook's way with words.

"What on earth do you want Peter? What on earth do you want? Here to once again indulge your obsession with that little girl? I'll spare you Peter, I'll spare you. She's dead." He looked at Peter so meanly when he said the word "dead," that he lost a bit of his gentlemanly form, and Preston was for the first time truly terrified of him.

Peter looked like he might jump at the pirate, but he stayed still, placing one hand on his sword. "I need your help," Peter spat the words at him.

"You need my help, Peter, you need my help," Hook mocked. "Whatever for? Your little lover girl has been dead for over fifty years." Hook looked at him with false surprise before he started laughing. "Peter Pan needs my help. Once again, Peter Pan needs Captain Hook's help." He looked at the other two pirates with him, the ones with old, old faces and scraggily beards. They did not move and stared off in a glassy eyed daze as their captain went on. "No, Peter, I can't help you. You know that is not how this works." He looked at Peter, who was still standing with his hand on his sword. "Oh, what is it, Peter, what is it, what do you want?" Hook gave in as if he were humoring a child. Peter did not budge, and Preston watched his leader, wondering if the pirates had done something to him.

"We want to know who killed us," Preston shouted at the pirate. "We thought we knew, but we were wrong and we want to know who killed us and how to tell our mothers so they might help other kids before they come Here too."

"You want to know who killed you! How quaint!" Hook declared, clapping his hooks, which clanged monstrously, as a smile spread across his face. "Do you know how many children want to know who killed them? Do you know how many Mommies and Daddies wished they could find the men and women who killed their children? Do you want to know how many? Peter how many is it? Is it all of them or just a few? I know, I know, some of them got sick, some of them can see their killer, some of them have accidents. All right, all right, I'll give you that, but really, Peter, why this one? Do you think he hasn't been asked this before?" Hook directed this last question at Preston. "Do you think he doesn't know very well that this is NOT how it is done? You want to know who killed you, get in line!" Hook shouted, his face going from calm to incredibly scary.

"It's important," Preston shouted back at the pirate. "My friend might be next, just like this friend was and I need to know what's going on. Children are dying in my neighborhood and I have to help them."

"Why is he still talking?" Hook asked one of the pirates, who did not respond. "This is not an acceptable question, little boy. This is not why you're Here. Why don't you go and frolic in the woods with the. . .oh what are they now, what are they—frogs and lions, dinosaurs and camels? I don't know. Go swim in the sea with the mermaids for Heaven sakes, but don't go around asking questions." Hook turned to Peyton, who was standing with his hands fiddling in front of himself, gazing sheepishly at the floor. "You don't want to know who killed you, do you? You're a good little boy, you're just along for the ride, you've come because your little friend here wanted to, because you thought it was a good way to get some face time with Peter. Well Peter's not that special let me tell you. Peter is just as fallible as any man, any boy, any pirate."

"Stop that!" Preston cried as Peter stood sternly watching. "Stop right now."

"And why would I help you, little boy? Why would I help you when every child who has ever come Here came asking the same question, 'why me,' 'who did this to me?' Why, why why!"

"I have your hand," Peter announced reaching into his pack and pulling out the soggy appendage in a jar. "I have your hand and I'll give it back if you tell them everything."

Hook faltered, losing the gentlemanly good form he'd had, and stared lustfully at the jar. "One hand, just one hand Peter? That's all you offer me?"

"I know what you've done with this hand and it's a shame to give it back to you. You can't have them both," Peter called out as if Hook were standing a hundred feet away.

"One hand. . .hm. . .You know I do like my hooks very much; they really do come in handy. But I also miss having an opposable thumb and so I do think it would be a good idea to have at least one hand, one hand and one hook." The pirate stared at the jar and Preston wondered what kept him from simply taking it. Even if all the other pirates were asleep and unable to move, Hook was big and strong, he stood a good foot taller than Peter, and there were swords on the walls and guns in the holsters of the sleeping pirates.

"Tell them who did it," Peter demanded.

"Oh, whatever, what do I care," Hook replied airily, lying lazily back in his chair. "The housekeeper in the kitchen with the poison," he said drily.

"What?" Preston asked.

"The housekeeper. Her name is Erma Glands, she lives in Lawrence, Massachusetts. When she was a little girl people used to make fun of her because she was, well, ugly. The poor woman still is very, very ugly. She's a lunch lady at your school and she doesn't like that you and Peyton and Eva were in with the more popular…what shall we call it…click."

"Yes, but we weren't bad. I didn't tease anyone," Preston argued, remembering how he used to ignore, not gang up on, the unpopular kids at school, how once he'd been partnered in gym class with Jenny Winters who picked her nose and smelled like bad cheese and he'd been nothing but nice to her.

"Of course you don't, you were just having fun, you were just being you. Kids are so cruel, aren't they Peter, aren't they just so cruel? All the time they talk about adults, and how sad it is that they're not innocent children anymore, but believe me, I hold my tongue, I know better than to stare, I don't go around making fun of people or ignoring them for not being popular enough. I'm much better than any little brat," Hook called, shaking his head as he looked right at Peter. "They say grownups are cruel and some are, believe me some are, but children, children can be just as cruel and not even know it." Hook stopped; he looked Peter dead in the eye and then said, "Now I have done my duty by you, will you give me my hand Peter Pan—give me my hand." Hook held his arms out, those shiny hooks greedily snapping open and shut as Peter took two steps closer and placed the jar on the metal hooks. The hooks jingled as the glass jar rested on them and after a moment Hook nudged one of the sleeping pirates, who opened his eyes, took the jar from the captain's hooks and rested it on the table. The pirate then undid the hook on his captain's left wrist and opened the jar, he took the hand out and placed it on top of Hook's wrist. The hand took a moment to settle before it appeared to rest in place. The pirate twisted his wrist around, testing each finger and then the thumb with a dainty wiggle. Hook watched his returned appendage, awestruck, though the pirate who had just put it on went back to sleep as if very little had transpired.

"Ah, there," Hook said. "As good as new, as you might say. Thank you Peter, thank you, it's a pleasure doing business with you. I'm sure you know the way out."

"How do we get back?" Preston called. "This information doesn't help at all if we don't know how to get back."

"That's not my problem, I kept my end of the bargain. Ask Peter to get you back, that little scamp knows so much more than he lets on. You'd be surprised, all the things he's done. He's such a grownup, that little boy." Hook had a sugary voice as he made a face of false sadness. Preston watched Peter for what he might do, but their leader just stood there.

"Don't talk bad about Peter," Preston could not help saying, and Peter gave him a terrible, terrified look.

"Don't talk bad about Peter? What's there to talk bad about? Peter is the savior of this godforsaken place, the Davy Jones of little lost boy souls. How could anyone not like Peter? And the fact that you took that name, the name that little girl gave you." Hook looked Peter in the eye before stretching the fingers on his new hand. "But that's the problem you see. Girls. That's why the Island does its damndest to keep women off it, because what is the point in having them? All they do is mess things up. And it's not all the girls' fault, don't think I'm going to give you a lecture about how awful Eve was—Adam was just as bad—but boys and girls do not go together, it grows them up, that's what it does, putting boys and girls together, isn't that right Peter? The only reason children are so innocent is because children do not recognize the other sex, they do not see it as other, they do not want it, they can't feed on it until it wracks their very soul. That is what is wrong with adults and that is why the Island does its damndest to make sure girls and boys are in their proper places, separated."

"Peter, what's he talking about?" Preston asked and Peter shook his head, shutting his lips tight.

"And grownups, grownups are just dead little children. You think that this is the only place for dead children, but your father is a dead little boy, your friend's father as well," Captain Hook stated very assuredly, eyeing Peyton, who was shaking so hard his entire body trembled. "When we're little boys all we want to do is run and frolic and play," Hook said in a singsong voice, swaying his head with an eerie calm, as if soft music had just begun playing. "We are innocent, we are pure. But what happens to that pure innocent little boy if he does grow up. . . well, he grows up. And then he turns into an adult who cheats on his wife and steals from his boss, who goes home every night to a bottle of gin and stares at the television. He turns into a man who fucks and shits, farts and sweats and gets fat. It is far, far better to be you. And so many of us, we become pirates. But how do you think we ended up as pirates? No one ever asks that question; Peter, you certainly never did. Who makes us a pirate, Pan? Why, my father is Here somewhere and my father's father and his father, all our fathers are Here and our mothers Somewhere Else."

"Who are you?" Preston demanded, mesmerized.

"Me?" Hook asked, pointing innocently at himself with his one hooked appendage. "Me? I'm the beginning of time. I'm the root of all evil. I'm the first pirate, the very first one. And what did I do, what did I do to bring me Here, I don't even know anymore, but hey, I was the third one here. Right, Peter? It was you and then it was those fairies and then it was me. And the fairies were what? 'When the first baby laughed for the first time' and so maybe I'm the opposite, when the first child was murdered in cold blood." Hook's eyes grew bright, as if he'd just thought of something. "Maybe I'm Cain," he declared.

"Who?" Preston asked.

"Peter, he doesn't know who Cain is, can you believe that, he doesn't even know who Cain is. And do you know why? Because he's only ten of course he doesn't know who Cain is. But you, you know who Cain is, don't you? You're a smart little man, Pan."

"Stop it," Peter yelled, grasping his sword, holding it in front of himself but not moving to strike.

"Michaels, Arlo," Hook called at the two pirates who'd been sleeping, their mouths gaping open. The pirates got up and slunk toward them. As they moved closer, Peyton took a step back and they went for him, each grasping one of his arms and holding him. "And you see, now I have your friend. Gee, wasn't that easy? Peter, you are losing your touch, young man, you are losing your touch."

Peter thrust his sword and rushed at Hook, who sat calmly in place. "You see I learned something," Hook stated calmly. "I learned something, Pan, that if I simply don't fight you, you can't win. All I have to do is sit here and there's nothing you can do. You can't read, you can't tell time, you can't understand the most basic Logic and now, if I don't fight you, you can't fight. You see," Hook went on, looking at Preston. "I'm sure Peter explained to you what it means to grow up; about intellectual and emotional maturity, adherence to societal conventions, physical relations of a sexual nature and, of course, cruelty. Well, don't think he's off the hook, pun not intended, don't think your precious leader isn't at least some of those things." Preston watched the pirate, only understanding half of what he'd just said.

"Hook, stand up and fight like a man," Peter declared, and Preston could see the corners of his eyes tighten as if he were trying to hold something terrible in.

"Like a man?" Hook asked, sarcastically. "You want me to fight like a man, oh Peter dear, I am fighting like a man. Men don't fight, men use their words, men don't run around with swords or shoot off fake pop guns. It's you who doesn't fight like a man, it's you who are stuck, sinking forever in quicksand because you are not a little boy, you Betwixt-and-Between, and you are not a man, and it's a curse, isn't it young sir, it's a curse."

"Don't call me cursed," Peter cried.

"And you were always so terrible with words, flubbering when you tried to make a speech. He can't read you know," Hook said to Preston.

"Stop it," Peter cried as if listening to this talk were hurting him.

"And you know," Hook went on. "If you'd be willing to give me my other hand I might be willing to call off my dogs, give you your little friend back. Or better yet, I'll keep your friend, you don't really need him anyway, he's not the one you're interested in. You," Hook said, pointing at Preston, "have Pan wrapped around your little finger. Just peak his interest a little, let him think there's the tiniest chance he can get that little girl back and he'll do anything. See, he's just like everybody else, stupid over a woman. But you give me my other hand and I'll give you the Jolly Roger. It's a great ship. It's a good, a kind ship, not a bad bone in its body, and you can have it, you can play phony water wars with your little kids and be a captain, a real captain of a real sea faring vessel, and all I need is my other hand."

"No!" Peter declared, before shutting his mouth tight.

"And you," Hook said, looking at Preston. "Wanting to save your little friend, wanting to help your mother. Don't you know what mothers are, that they are nothing but fickle creatures. Don't you know the story of all mothers, that a certain little boy who ran away from home to live with the birds went to visit his mother, only he found when he returned to her that there were locks on the windows and when he looked inside she was playing with another little boy and had completely forgotten him. That's why you're Here, because of your mother, and when you leave it will be because your mother has forgotten you. And how many boys leave Neverland every year? How many little boys have their mothers forget them?"

"They don't forget," Preston argued, wondering why Peter wasn't speaking.

"Oh he won't talk," Hook said, standing up and hovering so tall he seemed to ascend into the shadowy darkness of the rafters. "Peter won't talk because he's too stupid. All he does is sit around all day playing with toys and pretending and. . .who knows what, but none of it is real and none of it lasts, does it Peter, does it last? Tell them, do you enjoy any of it, do you not go through every moment of every day hoping, praying that something will change, that you'll open your eyes and be a man of thirty, of forty, of eighty-five and on his deathbed?" Hook looked long and hard at Peter, and Preston followed his look, but their leader did not budge, he did not betray an inch of feeling, and it broke Preston's heart to see that he did not want to defend himself.

"My mother won't forget me," Preston argued, looking Hook in the eye as he gradually sat back down.

"Oh, your mother—" Hook started and was stopped when Peter ran his sword across Hook's head, swiping his long black wig off. The mass of hair fell onto the table where it landed with a thud. Hook, completely bald now, gazed calmly at it hiding his surprise.

Preston thought Peter might cry out, he might turn to those holding Peyton, who was struggling valiantly to get away, and swipe his sword at them, but he did not. He moved swiftly, running at Hook once and then twice, nicking his arm and coming back at his neck. He held the sword there, right where he might kill the pirate and Hook simply looked at him, as if to say, 'You got me.'

"It wasn't as if I couldn't try," Hook said to Peter with a sad smile. "And maybe someday I'll talk some sense into you. Perhaps I'll talk some sense into that one as well," Hook said at Preston.

"Come on," Peter called, looking back at Preston as he approached, sword to the pirates holding Peyton. The pirates let the child go without a struggle and Peyton spat on them for good measure before Peter grabbed Preston and then Peyton around their waists, whisking them all away, since he was the only one who could fly in Pirate Cove. Preston knew better than to speak, something about the look on Peter's face called for cold, hard silence. He watched the land. They flew up and up and up, somehow knowing just where to go, as Peter headed for the sun, that brightness guiding the way.

Now that they were flying, Peter carried them out of Pirate Cove, but after a while, he let them go and Preston found he could once again fly on his own. At first he thought they were going to fly into the sun, but after a while even that seemed too far away, and it was as if they were enveloped in the bright white lights of a million fairies. He closed his eyes against it, but when he opened them, and found he was still in the light, it didn't hurt and though he couldn't see anything, it didn't bother him either. He wasn't sure if he was following Peter, but he didn't have time to think, and couldn't check his bearings or gauge his trajectory—it was as if all he could do was fly. At one point he considered touching down, he even tried to, descending as he had descended many times before without thinking about it, just as he never really thought about walking. But he couldn't do it just then. It was as if a sense had been striped from him as he flew up and up into the light.

Despite Peter's earlier explanation about flying around the world, Preston had given up hope that he'd ever see land again. He wondered if the pirates had done something to him, if he was now doomed to wander forever in this bright whiteness, when he felt the ground under his feet. When he opened his eyes there was the forest. It was trees, all those trees, warm and fresh, light streaming through the branches, no animals making scary noises, no child-sized birds lazily standing guard. Preston looked around, getting used to the dimness of the forest after having been in the sun's bright light. It took him a second to adjust and when he did there was Peter standing in the middle of a small clearing, Peyton still in his arms.

"Is he okay?" Preston asked. "I didn't see them get him, did they get him?"

Peter set Peyton down, helping him to stand on his own. Peyton looked dazed but all right as he stumbled to gain his bearings before standing up straight. "What was that?" he asked with that dopey face.

"He's okay, no one got him. I think the flight around the world was just hard for him, but you did fine I take it?" Peter asked. He turned slightly and the sword hanging from his waist was thrust outward.

"What was the matter with you?" Preston yelled at him. "It took you forever to fight Captain Hook. My friend could have been killed."

"That's not the way things work," Peter stated calmly, like a grownup, as if he knew something Preston didn't. "I can't just fight a man who won't fight me, that's bad form."

"So what about bad form, my friend was in danger and if it weren't for my talking to Captain Hook we never would have gotten any information at all. Why didn't you fight for it, why didn't you argue?"

"I don't argue well," Peter said, kicking at the dirt, his head down. "Look, I got you what you wanted, I fought him in the end, everything is okay and it's okay because of me. We got out of there because of me," Peter cried back at him, fists clenched tightly at his sides. Preston noticed for the first time that Peter looked like a little boy, a sad and scared little boy. "You got us into this and I got us out."

"Where were we just now?" Preston demanded. "Did we fly around the world?"

"We did," the leader replied.

"So does that mean we can stop while we're flying around the world, can you take me back to my mother? Can you take me back?" Preston begged. "Was I near my mother?"

"No," Peter replied hastily as if he were trying to keep something from him. "No, that's not how it works, that's not how any of it works and I think you should just forget what Captain Hook told you, he's right, it won't do any good Here."

"What are you talking about?" Preston cried. "I have to save Eva, she's in danger and I have to help her."

"That's not the way it works," Peter said again.

"That's not the way it works, that's not the way it works," Preston mocked. "That's all you say as if you're some sort of all mighty—"

"Because that's not the way it works. And Hook was right, I have to stop coddling you. Just because you came from the forest doesn't mean—" Peter stopped and looked at the ground.

"And what was it he said, I'm the great-great-great-grandson of who? What was he talking about? Why am I special, and if what he means by special is that I can summon Hook to the Lost Boys, then he's got a funny definition of special."

"I don't know," Peter cried, shaking his head. "Go away, I don't know."

"I need to get back to the Before, you said you'd help me, Peter, you said you'd help and you can't turn back now. Knowing who did this is nothing if I can't tell my mom, if I can't let them know—"

"You can't go back," Peter cried. "You wouldn't be able to if you tried."

"But Hook said that you—?"

"Don't listen to what Hook says," Peter replied. "Don't listen to him, I don't even know if I'd believe his answer at all. And here I am, giving him his hand back and I did it for nothing. You can't go back. All it does is hurt and hurt and hurt just a little more every time. Why do you want to be there? Why do you want to hurt and be sad? That doesn't exist Here. At least it's not supposed to and why are you making yourself sad when all you have to do is be happy? Just be happy Preston, why won't you let yourself be happy?" Peter looked at them desperately as if he simply did not understand.

"Are you okay Peter?" Peyton asked innocently, inching closer to the leader.

"When Hook said you weren't happy, when he said you'd rather grow up and yet—" Preston moved toward the leader, reaching to place a hand on his arm, but Peter turned around.

"Go away," he cried, spinning from both boys, keeping his head down and his back arched. "Go away!" he cried again and Preston rushed past him, something in the shrillness of Peter's voice told him not to linger. He grabbed Peyton's hand and flew through the forest, leaving Peter behind. He didn't know what direction they were going or what they'd get to first, but he kept moving, sure that soon they'd find something. When they landed, Peyton kicked extra hard on the ground, lifting leaves and twigs and unsettling dust.

When they reached the tree house, neither Preston nor his friend really knew where they were going. The lights around the tree house were so bright they closed their eyes for a second. Starky ran from the Ferris wheel to greet them, his hands in the air and a smile on his face. "Boys, boys, where were you?" he asked as Dilweed came up behind him.

"We were just around," Preston replied, wondering what Peter would want him to say. But Peter wasn't with them, Peter had turned them away and so he had to figure out how to explain on his own.

"Were you with Peter?" Starky asked, hands in the pockets of his tattered clothes. "We haven't seen Peter in a while and we thought he was with you."

"We left Peter in the forest," Peyton replied.

"Oh, yeah. Then he must be out hunting tigers," Starky surmised.

"Or he could be causing trouble with those Indians. I think we should check the Indian tents again. They're Indians again, cowboys and Indians, and I think they're gonna have a war soon," Dilweed went on. "There's nothing like a good cowboy and Indian war, you know? Nothing like it, it's so much better than those robots and spacemen."

"I bet," Preston replied and part of him, even after all this, had a hankering for a good cowboy and Indian war.

"Yeah, let's go check it out, I bet Peter's already there. I bet

Peter knew this was gonna happen and he's waiting for us to figure it out," Starky called lifting off and flying across the forest.

Preston watched Peyton, who had his fingers in his mouth and was looking about as if he didn't know what to do. Honestly, Preston wasn't sure either. He hadn't considered it before, but what they'd done had gone against the rules of this place, and this place had rules. The Lost Boys could do what they wanted, they could run and jump and play and spit, but they could not break the rules; mostly because they didn't realize there were rules to begin with. It was only Peter who knew the rules at all, at least enough to break them. And then Preston had come and maybe because he'd appeared in the forest he was different and he was willing to break the rules like no one else had ever considered. Even Peyton, who, though he was genuinely worried about Eva, had never thought to go looking for their killer, to talk to Captain Hook of all people. But Peter had, and Preston wanted to run to him, their leader, and tell him that it was all okay, he'd forget what Captain Hook had said to him, he'd forget about going to the Before and he'd run and jump and play with the rest of the boys.

"Are we going with Starky and Dilweed?" Peyton finally asked. "Are we going?" He looked at Preston expectantly and Preston shook his head yes, hovering over the ground for a second before they took off.

By the time they reached the Indian camp the war was in full swing. Starky and Dilweed were sitting off to the side, hidden behind a bush watching. Preston walked slowly up to them as quietly as possible and Starky put his finger to his lips, shushing them. "They're pretty evenly matched," Starky explained. "I don't wanna disturb them."

"Okay," Preston replied, watching.

The Indians moved wildly about, their shiny, sweaty bodies brandishing tomahawks and clubs as the cowboys pushed popguns in their faces and went "pow-pow!" Preston watched silently. It took a while to make out the Hawthorne-cowboy holding a long rifle as he pointed it at an Indian. The Indian held his arms up in surrender and the Hawthorne-cowboy laughed as he ordered him over to the Prisoner's Tent, a section marked off by white rocks where the Indians who were "out" were sent. The Hawthorne-cowboy then ran back into the fighting, brandishing his rifle with such skill that Preston was shocked when an Indian hit him with a club and he fell into the dirt, grasping his arm and crying "I've been shot, I've been shot!" as he started laughing.

After a while the war died down. Dilweed had considered joining it, especially when it looked like the Indians had the cowboys outnumbered, he always liked to help out the underdog. But instead Starky decided it was time to head out and they walked back through the forest. "We should look for Peter," Starky announced. "I don't like it when he's gone, then I'm in charge. They all look to me because I've been Here the longest, except for Boxwood, but he doesn't count." Starky made a face and Preston wondered if Starky could put two and two together: that Boxwood was like he was because he'd been Here too long, and Starky, Peter had once said, was dangerously close to having been Here too long as well. But Starky didn't seem to notice that as he led them. They walked for a while in the woods before they reached the spot where Boxwood usually stayed, since he'd basically turned to glass and stopped being able to move. It was just outside the tree house, in a thicket a safe distance away from the house, but close enough so he wasn't left out. It never rained in the thicket because the trees formed a roof overhead, and the boys and Peter had decided that Boxwood wouldn't want to be inside since he'd been so wild before.

When they reached Boxwood's spot he wasn't there. Starky scratched his head and shrugged. "I thought he was here, am I wrong?" Dilweed looked around, investigating under the bushes, he went a few paces one way and a few the other, but he didn't seem to see him either.

"I don't know where he went. Maybe he went away, maybe he's in the After. Peter must be happy about that," Starky ventured a guess. "If not, I bet Peter took him somewhere else."

Preston, having realized that Starky and Dilweed were on the wrong trail, pushed the bushes surrounding Boxwood's spot apart and walked further into the forest. After a while light fell less brightly through the thick trees, but Preston could sense the other Lost Boys behind him. He stepped on a twig at one point and it snapped, a crack that made the boys jump. "What was that?" Starky asked, getting more and more nervous. "You didn't see a pirate, did you?"

"Shut up," Dilweed called, hitting Starky on the shoulder. "You're not supposed to talk about pirates." Starky giggled and they kept walking.

After a while Preston stopped. He wanted the other Lost Boys to stay behind, he wished he had not taken them this far. They should not see what was in front of them. And maybe it was that what was in front of them wasn't meant for anyone's eyes, it wasn't meant for the Island at all, it was a breaking of the rules just like going to Captain Hook, like Preston wanting to know who had killed him. Preston looked at the ground and there was a boy, The Boy, in his tattered green shorts and his leather shoes, messy blond hair in his face. He was sitting in the clearing with his head in his hands, sobbing as his body shook. In his fist he held Boxwood's shirt, he looked at it as if it were a very important prize and shook his head when he saw Preston watching him.

"It was time," Peter said, still crying a little, though he tried to pull himself together when he caught Starky and Dilweed staring at him. "It was time. I tried to take him and it was really very hard, and he woke up, first he started kicking and screaming. It was not at all like it's supposed to go, but finally he went, he changed, he was happy as he went, he was the boy I first met, the boy who lived with us for years and years before he went rotten. He's gone now and I've done my job," Peter said, looking longingly at Preston, as if he wanted, perhaps needed something from him. Preston wanted to tell Peter he was right, that he'd never try to break another rule, but instead he just stared at their leader, he moved to help him up but Peter shrugged him away, standing on his own and giving a fake smile to the other boys, who seemed to easily buy his false disposition.

"What happened?" Preston asked.

"Nothing happened. Boxwood is gone, it was time," Peter replied, trying to shrug the question off.

"But really Peter, why now? Why did you take him now?" Preston pulled on the leader's shirt and he looked at him, annoyed.

"I had to take him, if the Island can get things wrong, if it can be wrong about so much it had to be wrong about Boxwood, and I had to, no matter how I had to do it."

"Okay Peter," Preston replied timidly, giving up and backing away as Peter left.

"Back to the tree," the leader called and the Lost Boys gathered around him, ready to follow. The tears were gone from Peter's eyes and voice, and he stood very straight and very big. "I hear the cowboys and Indians are back, that they're gonna have another war," he cried as he flew up through the trees, the Lost Boys following.

LONDON, ENGLAND 1904

Mrs. Darling sat in Winifred's room. It had been three years since she'd awakened from her coma and still they'd kept her room, turning it from a sick room to a proper young lady's chamber. They'd moved all her things out of the nursery since, George had insisted, it was time their daughter have a room of her own. It had been a bit drab when Winifred first moved in, but George had hired painters and they'd painted the walls a very lovely light pink with white trim. It wasn't at all the style, but Winifred demanded pink walls and Mrs. Darling thought that if you are going to demand pink walls then you might as well have white trim. And so George had ordered it, paying for it with the bonus money he'd made that quarter. And really, for all Mrs. Darling's complaints about George and the office, it did pay for a great deal.

It was a lovely room now, so very fit for a girl who was nearly nineteen. And once the room was hers, it was as if Winifred grew up right away. There was no more talk of Peter, at least not any deliberate talk, though every time someone mentioned him, when John accidentally wondered about the boy who might come in through the window, when Michael started telling stories about the dreaded Captain Hook. Even that one time when they'd been at dinner and Winifred had been talking about a Mr. Mark Carrington, and Mrs. Darling had asked, rather by accident "What about Peter?" George had thrown a glance at his wife, and Mrs. Darling had turned white, but that old nostalgic look blushed red on her daughter's face and she almost breathed his name. "Yes, Peter," she'd said, before taking a small sip of water to disguise the emotion she was feeling.

It had been nearly three years since her accident, nearly three years since she'd awakened from that dreadful coma. Winifred went to parties now, and was welcomed in the homes of other good, upstanding girls. George had been promoted. His dealings with that doctor, the one the firm was so fond of, had been well received at the office and they'd promoted him from Assistant Manager of Something or Other to Executive Manager of Something or Other with talk of someday making Partner. George was very proud of his promotion and even more proud of the promotions he had not yet received but surely would. He was away a lot more, at the office until all hours, going in to work on the weekends, waking up early to be off before his family awoke, but he did seem very happy and he wasn't around to bother his wife as she went about her daily chores.

George was downstairs just then as Mrs. Darling sat in Winifred's room. A Mr. Carl Thompson had come to the house early this morning to talk business and had yet to leave. George had been quoting from a certain economics journal he'd just received and Mr. Thompson was chuckling good naturedly, the kind of chuckle that said something really wasn't all that funny, an adult form of play.

She did not understand why adults and children did not play the same games. But they did not, playing nursery with a band of dolls was substituted for teas and dinner parties, cowboys and Indians were replaced with drinks at the club and discussions of the office, and though Mrs. Darling loved her children, though she wished with all her heart some days that she could go into their room, don a pirate hat, grab a sword and start "en guarding" with her sons, Mrs. Darling knew that after a few minutes tea must be served and guests must be received, not just because of societal conventions, but because of who she was. At the end of the day she did enjoy receiving guests, she did enjoy putting out tea. Ah, is this what it means to grow up? Is this what it means, that one can no longer play? And still there were other things, some consolations she supposed, like walks in Kensington Gardens, talks with Mr. Barrie and looking at the trees and the flowers and seeing something else in them, something the children did not see, that made growing up so grand.

"Unhand me, you yellow-livered son of a cowboy," John cried and Michael, not to be out done, shouted "pow-pow, I'll get you" at his brother. There was movement in the room down the hall and then a crash, perhaps a picture frame had fallen off a wall or a pitcher had rolled from the clapboard to the floor. Whatever it was, it didn't matter. Mrs. Darling hadn't heard anything shatter and so it was likely that nothing was broken. The boys, for their part, didn't even stop to check on what they'd done as they kept shouting at one another. She could picture them, John in the garb of a pirate, a handkerchief tied around his head, and Michael as an Indian, with a feather in his hair. Since Winifred had awakened from her coma she'd done nothing but talk of Indians and how she preferred them to cowboys and ever since then Michael had wanted to be one.

"Pow-pow!" Michael cried and more ruckus ensued. Mrs. Darling was sure that if George were not so engrossed in his conversation downstairs he might come up and see why there was so much yelling or he might demand that Liza mind them better. But Liza, for her part, knew how to allow children to have their play and she only scolded the boys when it seemed they had done something really wrong, and to Liza, playing was not wrong on its face.

Besides, John would be leaving home soon to return to Eton and then it would be only Michael again. It was a week until John left. His bags were packed, the train tickets bought, and he would be at Eton until the Christmas holiday, when he would return for a few weeks before going back to school for the Spring term. This was to go on for years, until it was time for University. It had been only a reprieve having him home for the holiday, but after next week there would be only one child in the house again. She'd never truly gotten John back, not wholly and completely, though at least he still played with his brother when he was home. It was just as she'd never gotten Winifred back after she'd awakened, breathing the name Peter. Her girl still lived in the house, but she wasn't the same—she'd grown up, something had happened while she was in that coma, something dire and profound. At least with Winifred Mrs. Darling had been able to watch the change, but with John she could only watch his growing up in spurts. One day he was a child and the next he was a young man returning for his first school holiday, and then he was an older young man returning for his first summer holiday, and then he would be an even older young man whose voice had dropped and he'd start to wear more fashionable glasses and his clothing would change with the times and the crowds he went with, and it would never be the same. It is a mother's cross to bear, the hardships of raising young children followed by the sadness of realizing they are no longer young.

"I'm not a cowboy, you codfish!" Michael called out, thoroughly offended.

"And you know, Carl," Mrs. Darling could now hear her husband downstairs, as well. He might have a cigar in his hand, perhaps a brandy, though it was early for that. He'd be in his chair, this Carl Something-or-Other sitting opposite him as they conversed. "You know Carl it does seem as if. . . ." Mrs. Darling did not bother to keep listening, even though her husband's words were loud enough to drown out an elephant trumpeting.

"Pow-pow! I'll get you!" Michael cried, and she could just picture two wooden play swords clashing. Michael was the only one left. Only it was different when there was only one and Mrs. Darling knew it. She'd been the youngest, left while her brothers went away to school to have adventures, left when her sisters were old enough to get married. The Darlings were a different family now, a family with barely any young children, a family that would soon not have any. The magic had grown up right along with Winifred and John and soon Michael.

Mrs. Darling listened to her son's playing, "pow-pow" and "now see here, unhand my treasure," and she giggled to herself. But along with that there were the sounds of George and his colleague arguing about the value of the pound and the price of silver as if it were so damned important, when perhaps they should have been plotting to grab a ship and steal themselves some of their own treasure. George couldn't see, he just couldn't see, and yes he had to work, and no, Mrs. Darling did not really wish to play pirates herself, but still, just to watch it, to enjoy it from afar when one has the chance, was that too much to ask?

Children used to live in this house. There used to be pirates and Indians, princesses and castles, but that was soon to be over. John would run down the stairs with a sword or Winifred would sit by the window and tell story after story. They used to run around in the park and no one could control them and sometimes they'd act all Mary-Ann-y, throwing a fit or what have you, but it was all in fun and there had been something unreal, something marvelous in that. But now Winifred would soon be thinking about settling down, of being actually married, not pretend married, and John would have a career and Michael would soon follow and it was all so much to think of. And there used to be children in this house, there used to be magic and oh, how they all grow up and leave you.

Mrs. Darling sat on Winifred's bed, fingering the stitching of her comforter. Her own mother had made it when she was about to marry George, it had been a special treat and of such fine fabric, and she wondered if she had worried her own mother with her growing up.

"Mother?" Winifred asked, coming into her room. She was wearing a long blue dress with a white sash and her hair was done up in curls. She had taken, when she went out at least, to wearing her hair done up in curls as was the fashion. Her shoes clicked on the wooden floor before she reached the carpet and her lips were just a tad too pink, maybe from the air outside. "Mother, how are you? I barely saw you sitting there," Winifred said. "Do you like my dress, my hair? Liza helped me with it. I have Elizabeth's party tonight and what do you think of my shoes?" She twirled around and Mrs. Darling remembered how her daughter used to do that as a little girl, only she'd lift her dress up too far and make her father gasp.

"You look wonderful, Winifred, absolutely ravishing," Mrs. Darling replied, placing her hand to her mouth to hold back tears. But one tear escaped, it fell from her eye and down her cheek, resting just above her lip and she did not have the heart to flick it away.

"Thank you mother, I knew you'd like it, I just knew it. And Camilla Fisher will be there and Mrs. Danbury's son and it will be a lovely party, I only wish I could bring you and father, but it's for younger girls you know."

"I know," Mrs. Darling replied.

"And after the party Mrs. Foster has arranged for her son Trevor to escort me home and for a coach to drive us so you needn't worry, I'll be fine getting back."

"I know you'll be fine," Mrs. Darling replied. "But I'll wait up. I won't be able to sleep a wink. This is your first real party, you know. I mean, the others I was there, or your father and I, that was just practice, but for this you're on your own."

"Oh, I know," Winifred squealed. "I'm nervous, but it'll be wonderful, absolutely wonderful." Winifred looked as if she might swoon and Mrs. Darling laughed.

"And Elizabeth would like us to see Mr. Barrie's play, Peter Pan, perhaps next week, you and I with her and her mother," Winifred announced. Mrs. Darling watched her daughter, noting that she did not get that look in her eye, that secret smile on her face, at the mention of Peter Pan anymore.

"You really do have a very full datebook," Mrs. Darling sighed, fingering the soft stitching of the sleeve of her dress. "It's supposed to be just a marvelous play," Mrs. Darling went on.

"It's a shame we haven't gotten to it already. Of course, yes, that sounds lovely."

"It does, doesn't it?" Winifred replied looking it seemed for the first time at her mother. "What's this?" she asked, reaching for her and wiping the tear from her cheek. "Are you all right mother? Are you sad, what's wrong?" she asked, a look of genuine worry on her face.

"Nothing, Winifred, absolutely nothing. I'm fine; really I'm fine. It's just that I am so proud of my children, so very proud of my children."

cLaiRe

Cara's idea to visit Francine Gumm did not die at Gregory Haw-thorne's table. Cara, displaying a can-do attitude that must have been lying dormant in her for years, made phone calls and pes-tered her husband to call in favors. She looked up visiting pro-cedures and did her own research on Francine. In the end it was an old law school friend of Jim's who came through. One of the lawyer's at his firm, who had represented Ms. Gumm at her first trial, called a friend, who called a friend, who got in touch with Ms. Gumm, setting the whole thing up so that all the two women had to do was show up at the prison. It was, the friend said, under the circumstances, the least he could do.

It was a long drive to the prison. Although the crime had oc-curred near Lawrence, Massachusetts, Francine had been moved to a maximum-security prison out of town. They couldn't have a woman who'd killed her children, who had locked them in a car and left the engine running, who'd been writing letters and dropping hints and looking up websites that dealt with carbon monoxide poisoning, to simply sit in jail. She had to feel the jail, she had to experience the guards and the inmates to their fullest extent, and so Francine Gumm was put in maximum security a few towns away.

The drive had been long, but nothing compared to the move through the prison from sign in, to metal detectors, to pat down, to pat down, to metal detectors, to yet another pat down, and Claire had never felt more violated. No, that wasn't right—when she'd seen Preston, when she'd heard the news, then she'd felt as if someone had taken her heart and ripped it open leaving her exposed and naked. Still it was something awful having to walk into the prison, having her purse and then her body scanned for weapons or communication devices, as if two housewives could plot a prison break. Four uniformed women had searched both Cara and Claire before they'd been escorted to an elevator, taken to yet another room, searched again and then asked to wait. All the while everyone acted as if they were criminals, as if the only reason to be in this place was because you either were a criminal, knew a criminal or were trying to help one.

Once they'd entered the prison they felt like two normally good girls who had been sent to detention for the first time. Every word they uttered, like when Cara commented on the color of the carpet, a guard looked back at them and they shut up. It had taken a while to get to Francine, but after a few minutes in the final waiting room, after their purses had been checked and their bodies searched one last time, a guard led them back to a small, dark room with a row of chairs and a row of what looked like desks in small cubicles. One side of each desk was partitioned by thick glass and there was a phone on each wall. A heavy-set woman with long brown hair was sitting at the desk closest to the door talking to a woman in an orange jumpsuit who had a shaved head and a dragon tattoo on her face. Claire couldn't hear what the inmate was saying, but the heavy-set woman kept crying into the phone that "it isn't fair, it isn't fair."

Claire and Cara were ushered to a partitioned cubical-like space closer to the back of the room. This space had been prepared for them, and though there was one phone, two chairs were placed next to each other, facing another chair on the other side of the glass. The lights were harsher on the other side and two guards stood against the back wall. Claire considered saying something to Cara, like thanking her for having her husband take care of all the details, making their access thus far relatively easy and smooth. Strings had been pulled, favors had been called in—usually a maximum security prisoner was not allowed to see two people at once, but for these grieving mothers an exception had been made.

Once the door to the back opened, a guard walked in, looked around (as if there hadn't been enough guards looking around already) and walked out. A few seconds later a woman was led out. Claire recognized her not as Francine Gumm, but as the woman on TV. She had the same puffy white blond hair that looked dyed though she didn't appear to have dark roots. She was thinner in person, though still a little bit heavy, and her face looked bloated. The Francine Gumm Claire had seen on television, had never looked particularly friendly nor exceptionally mean, and Claire could recall a photo of her being shown, one of her taken before the murders. It was of Francine and her children all sitting together on a porch, the children in too-small bathing suits as they clung to their mother, who smiled down at them as she tried to open a Popsicle wrapper.

This was not the same woman. There was something harsher about her, something more cold and un-motherly, than the prisoner who had tried to hide her face from the TV cameras. Claire watched her sit down and pick up her receiver. Cara took their phone from its cradle, fiddling with it for a second before she figured out the right button to push to get it to work. Cara sat there, as did Claire, looking at this woman. She had seemed so large, so interesting, even though they both hated her there had been something about her. Now, being face to face, Claire didn't know why she was here. What on earth have I done, she thought as she stared forward, fearing that her big eyes gave away her terror.

Cara held the phone to her ear and Claire wondered who should speak first. They had asked for the meeting, they had gone through channels and lawyers and braved the prison to see her; it only made sense that they should initiate conversation. "Hello," Claire said into the phone, holding it between herself and Cara. "Hello."

"Hi," the woman said, her voice scratchy, with a raspiness that suggested years of chain smoking. She didn't say more and Claire knew she'd have to go on.

"We're just here. . .I mean, we just thought, we saw you on the News and we thought we might talk to you," Claire explained, nervously fidgeting with her hands in her lap.

"You're the two women," Francine said, her voice rougher now. "The two women in a single summer who lost their kids."

"Yes," Claire replied, not wanting to elaborate.

"I'm surprised the police aren't looking at you two," Francine commented, her voice so passive it was as if she were making dinner conversation.

"Why would they look at us?" Cara asked defensively.

"They always look at the mother. It's like when a girl gets murdered and they look at the boyfriend first, they always look at the mother when a child dies."

"Why would they look at the mother? Why would the mother. . .?" Cara asked, flabbergasted.

"Who else would kill their kids? I mean really, when have you ever heard of a father killing his children? Sometimes the father kills the mother, sometimes they go crazy and kill their whole family or they're physically abusive and go too far, but that's different, that's not premeditated. Mothers care for the kids, mothers take on most if not all of the responsibility, even when the husband lives in the same house, even when he's home at five on the dot and they both work, who gives the baths, who changes the clothes, who looks at the homework? It's the mothers and so the mothers always end up killing them because they are so damn tired of it all."

"What are you talking about?" Claire asked. She wanted to get up and she might have if she wasn't so afraid of what these guards might do if she moved.

"Sometimes it's a crazy person, like they think it was with you, with that guy. . .what was his name?" Francine cocked her head, squinting as if she were facing the sun.

"Gregory Hawthorne," Claire replied. "And he was apparently innocent."

"Sometimes it's a crazy person, but when it's not, it's the mother, every time, it's always the mother. Motherhood is hard, it's like being a grownup on overdrive. It's responsibility, it's society and what it thinks of you, it's constant worry and constant care and constant complaining and constantly being at fault. It's like having a job, only you never get to go home. NEVER."

"I don't think I can talk to her," Cara said, placing the phone on the ledge and getting up. She stepped a couple paces back and watched the guard, who didn't move.

"What are you talking about, it's always the mother? Just because you did it—"Claire stopped herself, wondering if she was allowed to talk about the case.

"Just because I what? You can say it, just because I gassed my children?"

"How can you. . .I mean. . ."That's what Claire didn't understand, that's what she had to know, how on earth could a woman do such a thing? Yes, being a mother was hard and with no money or support she could only imagine it being harder, but still, so many mothers had it harder and they didn't gas their kids.

"It was horrible," Francine admitted. "And if I had it all to do over, if I could rewind, would I do it again? No, of course not. I'd try to handle my problems differently. But that's where the insanity defense comes in and it's not as if I was hearing voices, it's not as if I thought I was doing them a favor, but I did think I was helping them. I did think that if I had to live in this world, this world that is so hard, that is so cruel, that will do nothing to help you, when you cannot make ends meet, when you cannot get a stray thought in edgewise, when you cannot sit down for five minutes. It's enough to drive any person insane, enough to make you desperate. Sometimes I wished I could run away and be a different woman, maybe a teenager again, the kind who wore short skirts and smoked with her boyfriend. Mothers have it hard; mothers have it very hard. Fathers do not, at least most of them don't. They get home from work and sit on the couch for five minutes. Fathers get five whole minutes to themselves— when was the last time a mother got five minutes while her kids were awake? Fathers coach little league or drive the kids to soccer and then they're out. They don't give the baths; they don't have the kids pawing all over them. No, fathers don't know what it's like and most of them take off. Most of them see their kids on the weekends and then complain that it's too much, they pay a few hundred bucks every few months and think that they're being saints, that they're actually helping out, actually putting food on the table."

"My husband came home from work and gave my son a bath, my husband did the dishes after dinner," Claire said, realizing she was using the past tense. It wasn't just that Preston was gone, it was that she and Matthew didn't make dinner anymore, there were no dishes to wash, no tables to clear.

"Then you're a lucky woman, a lucky woman."

Claire looked back as Cara, who appeared to be finished pacing, took a seat back with them. "It's just that we wanted to talk to you. I don't even know why. I guess it's just that after what happened to us. . . . We just don't understand it. And now with your insanity defense in the public eye. . . ." Claire blurted out.

"My husband doesn't think your insanity defense will stick," Cara said, jerking the phone from Claire and nearly spitting into it.

"I know it doesn't sound like the legal definition of insanity," Francine explained. "I knew what I was doing was wrong. I don't think it'll stick either, but I had to try to tell people how I felt, what my story was, my actual story." Francine looked through the glass and she no longer seemed hard or scary, her eyes had softened and she almost cracked a sad, secret smile.

"What do you mean?" Claire asked, now holding the phone between herself and Cara.

"I mean that a woman has to be crazy, a mother has to be completely insane to harm her children. It's against nature. That doesn't mean she doesn't deserve this, to go to jail, to spend her life here. That doesn't mean she should get off, but it's just that there were circumstances. And motherhood was so hard, so incredibly hard and sometimes I felt like I wanted to run away from it all, that no matter how good it was, no matter how my kids, I called them Gumby and Lumby, loved me, it didn't matter, and I wanted to spend two weeks sitting on the couch watching sitcoms or I wanted to run off to Tahiti, I don't know. There is more to insanity than the legal definition of it."

"But how do you think you were crazy?" Claire prodded.

"I don't know," Francine admitted. "It's just that since being here, I mean, I've had a lot of time, when I haven't been doing jail work or legal stuff, I've had a lot of time to think. I converted to Zen Buddhism; I bet you didn't know that? I meditate. And recently I've been able to hear the voices of my children when I meditate, the voices are soft and faint, but they're my children, I know it. And they tell me that everything is all right, that they're in a better place, a happy place and that they don't hate me. I wish the voices weren't so faint, I wish I could talk back to them." Francine let the phone fall and the hard shell that had started this conversation cracked. Claire almost felt sorry for her as she watched the hefty woman hide her face in her hands, her back arching. The guards did nothing to comfort her, but they didn't bother her either.

"I'm sorry," Claire said into the phone, though Francine couldn't hear.

"Francine, Francine?" Cara asked, pressing buttons on the phone as if there were a button that would jerk Francine upright and make her stop crying.

After a second, Francine lifted her face from her hands, running her fingers briskly though her hair and trying to pat dry her cheeks. She grabbed the phone and looked at Claire and Cara.

"Talk to your children, they know everything," Francine said.

Claire watched Francine Gumm as she carefully placed the phone back in its cradle, wiping her eyes once more. Cara asked "Hello?" into the receiver a couple of times, but Claire could see that the conversation was over. It took Francine a second to stand, but when she did she called for a guard, who came over, escorting her out after handcuffing her, and though the entire ordeal was a bit rough, her exit, with all eyes on her, was almost like that of royalty.

Cara looked over at Claire, who wondered what they were supposed to do now. She was sure there would be as much hoopla leaving the prison as there had been getting into it and she wasn't sure how to begin the procession back to their car. "I don't know what to make of that," Cara said. "She never even told us why."

"I think she did," Claire explained. "I think there is no why."

"Maybe," Cara replied, setting the phone back in its cradle and standing up. As they stood this time and walked toward the door a guard nodded at them, pushing a button and letting them out. Claire took one last look back at the room. It hadn't been cold in there, but just then she shivered.

They left the same way they had come, through halls with bright, intruding lights, past men and women with guns, some of whom patted them down before they were allowed to walk out of one locked room and into another. They went through metal detectors and finally picked up their purses before walking out of the doors of the prison, escorted by a guard until the last possible second, when they were allowed to turn right, walk through a fenced-in gate crowned with barbed wire and make their way to their car.

Outside the gate it seemed a normal parking lot. They passed two women in guard's uniforms talking casually with one another; even nodding at Claire and Cara as they walked past. The trees were above them, large shade trees creating a green canopy for the sunlight to tumble through as they marched down an asphalt path to the lot where Cara was parked.

Claire wasn't sure what she'd gotten from the visit. Francine Gumm had been so much more as an enigma. Ever since she'd lost Preston, ever since that woman had shown up on her TV, she'd been not just a symbol of evil, but a figure to study. And she still could not comprehend how a mother could take her child's life. Yes, she pitied her; yes, she believed this tore Francine apart. But it was like finally consenting not to believe in Santa Claus. Christmas was no longer magical and Francine was no longer anything more than a woman who had locked her children in her car and left it running.

Just as life had been so much less once Preston was gone, once Claire had seen Francine Gumm she lost a little bit more. It wasn't the same, not at all, but it was as if she had one less thing to think about. She didn't have to speculate as to what that woman on TV was thinking or feeling, she didn't have to over-analyze her, wondering if she were anything like herself. Claire now knew all she needed to know about Francine Gumm and now it was only herself, herself and her scrapbooks.

Cara must have felt a sense of loss at the end of the trip as well. She'd piled all her energy into making it happen, fielding phone calls, writing letters to the warden, researching what to expect when visiting a prison, and now that that was over she'd been calling Claire a lot more often and coming over at odd times. She made lunch for them every day, bringing sandwiches to Claire's house in a wicker picnic basket, and that Saturday, a day Claire was hoping to have to herself, Cara had called her and asked if she and Matthew might want to come over for dinner.

"It'll be so much fun," she'd said, as if Claire could ever be in the mood for fun again. "I'll make something Spanish, we'll just sit around, it won't be that much, I promise." Claire had not wanted to go, but she went, donning a nice pair of slacks and a shirt from one of the upscale malls she hadn't put on in months, she pulled a comb through her hair and even put on a little make up, because if she was going to go to a dinner party, she may as well do it right.

It was late, nearly eight o'clock, but still light out when Claire and Matthew rang the bell at Cara and Jim's for dinner. Cara let them in, ushering Claire and Matthew through the front door and into the living room. "Come in, come in," she said as if she were welcoming them to a large festive gathering that had been planned for weeks instead of hours. Cara was wearing an elaborate red dress with a pattern on it that reminded Claire of a Persian rug, and her hair, which was curled and styled just a bit, seemed to flow about her face, which was made up just a tad more than a housewife's face usually would be in her home, even if she was having her first dinner guests since her life had been thrown into disarray.

"Come in, come in," Cara ushered them in and just then Jim came out of the kitchen with a glass of red wine dangling from each hand.

"I'll get more," he said, placing the glasses on the end table and turning around.

"It's special wine from Turkey," Cara explained, taking a seat on the couch and motioning for Claire and Matthew to do the same as she twirled the wine around in its glass.

"I remember when Claire and I were in Greece," Matthew said draping an around his wife and making conversation. "The best wine there was from Turkey. The best wine in the Mediterranean was always Turkish."

"Or Italy," Jim piped in, walking out of the kitchen with two more glasses. "My Tuscan mother would turn over in her grave if she heard that. She swore by her Chianti."

"Here, here," Claire said, taking her wine glass and holding it up as if they were about to give a toast. Everyone raised their glasses, Matthew even touched his with hers, but the toast died before it started, as if no one really had the energy for it.

"Dinner's almost ready. I made paella, something my mother

always cooked," Cara said to fill the silence that grew heavy the moment it started. "I had to buy so much stuff at the store for it. I forgot how little I've been shopping since...." Cara's voice trailed off, and it was as if she were trying to swallow her words back.

"Shopping, errands, yard work...still with everything," Jim elaborated, filling more space. "I think we all need a vacation."

"Peyton and Jim on vacation were always--"Cara stopped, and it wasn't as if she'd forgotten about Peyton. But maybe it was that she had, not for long, maybe for a split second, but when she said his name, it all came back and Cara stopped herself, glancing at the living room.

"You know we never cancelled that trip to Cape Cod," Jim stated, not understanding the moment both Cara and Claire had witnessed. "I mean I didn't cancel my end."

"We didn't cancel either," Matthew replied. "I completely forgot about it. I just figured that vacations were out and we'd deal with it sooner or later."

"I know," Jim sighed. "Now it's both sooner and later...."

"But we booked a whole house on the Cape," Cara broke in. "And by now it's too late to get the deposit back. If you two don't want to go then Claire and I will," Cara offered for her.

"I don't know," Claire hedged when everyone looked to her.

"I think we could use the time away, time to sit by the ocean and think," Cara elaborated.

"And the Cape is beautiful this time of year," Jim added.

"But with Matthew back at work and everything..." Claire hesitated. Matthew looked at her, their eyes met and she could see that he did not particularly want to go, but he could be persuaded. "We'll see," Claire said, taking a small sip of wine. "This wine is really very good. I remember one time in Greece, Matthew and I went to the Temple of Apollo in this tiny mountain town and I wore these horrible sandals for the hike and Matthew had to carry me. But the wine afterward at this little taverna, it was delicious, made up for all the calluses."

"Ah, yes, the honeymoon phase, when all they do is carry you," Cara stated. "I remember on our honeymoon, Jim couldn't keep his hands off me."

"You know, my life was carefree, I was a little boy and things were so uncomplicated and then I discovered girls," Jim pondered aloud. "It was like one day I was playing with my friends and the next I couldn't take my eyes, or my thoughts, off Constance Hall three desks away."

"Ah yes, girls, the downfall of men, the downfall of boys," Matthew commented and Cara laughed.

"Not that boys are any better for girls. I remember when my friends all wanted to play Barbies and then a month later it was all make-up and shoes and who was taking who to the dance and it was ridiculous." Cara laughed again and Claire laughed along with her.

The room stopped and Claire watched it. Cara had a smile on her face, the first genuine one she'd seen her friend crack since the festival at the park. She saw the normalcy in Matthew's eyes; the calm in Jim's laugh, and it didn't make sense.

There had been a time when Claire was a teenager when two brothers, 17 and 14, had died in a car accident together. Their deaths had caused a stir at the church Claire attended and when the funerals were held, Claire, who'd been more active in the Catholic community then, had been asked to work as an usher. That tragedy had been hard on the community, and the funeral of those boys, who Claire had never known, had gotten to her. But it was the mother Claire remembered, the mother who stuck always in her mind. As her two sons' caskets stood next to each other by the altar Claire had watched the mother cry, her hands to her face through the entire eulogy as she half-laid upon the front pew, unable to sit or stand. That mother's wailing during the funeral, wailing no one stopped, stayed with Claire.

But it was a moment six months afterward that superseded the wailing in Claire's mind. Not even a year later she saw this woman again with her older son, the surviving brother in the family. She was walking past Claire near the altar after mass. Claire recognized her right away, her face was too painful a sight to forget, but this time the face was not wailing, this time it was laughing. She was looking back at her son and laughing as he said something. A thought flashed across Claire's mind, "How can you laugh when your children are dead?" she had thought, and that thought had translated into a look on her face. The woman saw Claire, she was sure she could tell her thoughts by her face and she stopped laughing, and remembering that she was still a grieving mother, she stared at the floor and went on her way. Claire felt bad instantly. She didn't know this woman, but she'd almost run after her and apologized; of course it was all right if she laughed, her children would have wanted that. But she'd been a shy girl then and she'd scolded herself, she'd said three Our Fathers and seven Hail Mary's for it and gone on living her life. Until this moment, when she heard herself laugh, when she watched Cara push her hair behind her ear, casual but self-consciously, as if she were on a first date.

"I have to. . . .I think I should," Claire said, desperately looking around the List's living room as if she'd lost a contact or an earring. The wine was very good, and perhaps it was getting to her because when Claire stood up she felt light headed, as if she might faint. "I just don't think. . .Matthew, I think I should go home." Claire stood up straight, getting her bearings as her husband held her arm just as he had after they found out. . . .

"Honey, are you all right?" he asked, concerned.

"I think I have a headache," Claire replied, looking sheepishly at Cara, who gazed back at her with wide black eyes like a child's in a cartoon. "I'm sorry, I really am, I'm sure your dinner is lovely I just can't. . . ." Claire swallowed hard, tasting the salt and snot and tears that had yet to come as Cara nodded at her understandingly.

"Go home and rest," she said, standing with Claire and Matthew and walking them to the door. "I'll bring you leftovers tomorrow. Don't worry about us. It was just nice to see you. . .and have an excuse to dress up and open a bottle of wine."

"Thank you," Claire replied, looking back at her friend.

"Please don't worry about it," she said when she'd reached her door.

"And I promise, in a few weeks, for the Cape. . ." Claire could feel the tears about to come as Matthew put an arm around her and ushered her out.

"Don't worry about that either, we'll figure it out," Cara replied, glancing back at Jim sitting on the couch with his wine glass, one hand in his lap.

"Thanks so much for having us," Matthew reiterated as they stood on the stoop about to walk away. "I'm sorry we have to go so quickly, but next time. . . ."

"Of course," Cara replied, closing the door behind them once they'd taken a few steps down the walkway.

"I'm sorry," Claire said, still holding the tears in as they walked down the block.

Claire and Matthew didn't talk during their trek through the neighborhood. They didn't have to; both of them knew why they'd left. It had been such a nice few minutes and dinner had smelled so good and Claire had sat in her kitchen while Preston was dying. She'd waited until he was nearly an hour late to call the police. There had to be a punishment for that, there had to be. Claire passed the Wilkinson's, Chad was playing basketball with his teenaged sons, they stopped and waved and she barely had the strength to lift her hand to them as Matthew led her back toward their street.

When they got inside the house he didn't say anything, not when Claire slipped her shoes off in the foyer, when she hung her purse on the coat rack or moved to check the phone messages. "I'm sorry," she said when he entered the kitchen, realizing she'd not only run out on a party, but deprived her husband of dinner. "I can make you a salad or something, maybe a frozen pizza?"

"It's okay, Claire, it's okay," Matthew said quietly and Claire knew he never got this quiet unless he was upset.

"I'm sorry, it's just I couldn't do it. I couldn't be there, in that room. I couldn't just let myself go and I don't know if I'll ever—"

"That's fine Claire, that's fine," Matthew nearly whispered. "I just wish you'd talk to me about it. I wish you'd let me in. You sleep in our son's room; you walk into another room when I come home. I stay out late and you don't care, you don't even ask me where I've been. I don't care if you have to leave a party because you're sad, I'm sad too, I'm sad all the time, I just wish you'd talk to me about it."

"I just thought. . .. And you have your work, you can leave this house and do something else and all I have. . .all I had was him."

"You think I want to go to work?" Matthew asked. "If they'd give me the time off I'd do nothing but stay home. But there are bills to pay as the old saying goes. And even before all this, I wish I could have just stayed home with Preston. Do you think I wanted to go into the office every day, do you think when our son was a baby I wanted to sit at a desk when I could have been playing with him? It's what it means to be an adult."

Claire watched her husband. She'd never thought he felt this way, then again she'd never thought her husband had felt a great many things he seemed to be feeling. She could remember a time when Matthew had had a particularly important meeting the next day at work. It was a Sunday afternoon and the family was supposed to go out for a picnic, but instead they'd stayed in so Matthew could get work done. Peyton had come over and the boys had been so loud, banging on the walls and firing fake guns at each other. "On guard!" Peyton had called at one point and Matthew opened the door to his office. Claire had expected him to yell, but instead he'd just given Claire a look and she'd known to take the boys outside. She'd always assumed he liked his work, and maybe a part of him did, but she never considered that while they were missing out on time with Matthew, Matthew had been missing life.

"I'm sorry," Claire said quietly and Matthew nodded sadly, solemnly at her.

"It's okay Claire, it's okay. You don't have to be an adult right now. No one is expecting that of you, you can break down, we all can. I just wish you'd talk to me."

"We talk at therapy," Claire replied.

"That's not what I mean. We say what we need to say in therapy and it's not enough. It's not enough for me. My wife hasn't slept in our bed in months. I cry every night, there, I said it, I cry every night and I think you do too, but we don't even know how the other is feeling not enough to—"

"I know, I know, Matthew. It's just that I don't know what to do with myself and I think that if I'm not strong, if I don't hold myself together, hold it all inside, then I'll fall apart." Matthew approached her, he reached out and she grasped his hand before tumbling into his arms as if she were diving into a deep, blue black sea. She knew what it was to be held by Matthew, to kiss him, to love him, they'd had that before Preston was born. All during her son's life his mother and father had loved each other and now that he was gone, she couldn't lose Matthew as well. Claire looked up at her husband; she saw his face and kissed him hard. The pain did not stop, but it moved to the side, having been pushed away for a little while.

PRESTON

Preston felt as if he had never been to Pirate Cove, he could no longer recall the rancid smell of the docks or the way those pirates had looked, eerily lazy, so vacant and gone as they wasted away. It was as if he'd never gone to see Captain Hook as he played in the woods with Starky. He'd been trying to forget everything the pirate had said, the whole pirate adventure, it had been a waste of time and there was no way back, no way to get to his mother. And what would he do if he could talk to her? It wasn't even a guarantee that he could make her listen. Peter had been right, it was better to just play, just play. . . .

Preston closed his eyes and counted to ten, his hands at his sides as he waited for Starky to hide. He'd already hidden from Starky in the darkness of the thicket, but Starky was a good finder, some said he was the best on the Island, and when they played this game he always won. That's why most of the boys didn't want to play hide and seek with Starky, but Preston didn't mind being beaten, he liked Starky's company and the boy seemed to know things the others didn't. Besides, Starky didn't like keeping secrets, which was why he was always letting things slip.

". . .eight, nine, ten," Preston shouted into the echo of the forest. "Ready or not, here I come," he cried and three fairies came whirling at him. They had been around a lot lately since his return from Pirate Cove. They never wanted anything, not even to play; they just flew at his head or danced around his limbs, sometimes doing a waltz or tango up and down his arm as if he were their special friend. Preston giggled as the fairies came at him, but he remembered that he was supposed to be finding Starky and pushed them away, walking deeper into the forest.

Preston looked under some bushes and inside the hole of a knotted tree. Nothing was there and the tree was very small, but some of the Lost Boys were very good at getting into places they shouldn't go, like inside the holes of trees. This is what made hide and seek so hard in Neverland—the boys were braver, they'd hide anywhere and they could alter their bodies, only slightly, just enough to fit places where a little boy could not naturally fit.

Preston scurried up a tree; he'd never been able to climb like this in the Before, but as he spent more and more time in Neverland he could do all sorts of things, like wrestle tigers and fall off high branches, without getting hurt. He climbed to the treetops to see if Starky was crouched on a higher branch. He was just about to give up and call to Starky that he'd won— Starky always won—when he heard a sneeze. Preston turned northward and another sneeze came, followed by another and another and another. The sneeze was coming from a rosebush in the middle of the forest. It seemed as if someone had planted it there, maybe the fairies, who were very fond of roses and were always leaving them places. "There you are, Starky, there you are!" Preston cried, and Starky came out of the rosebush covered in red petals.

"You got me, Preston, you got me," he said, hands up as he shook his head and sneezed again. "I just seem not to be feeling myself today," he went on. "And I don't know, maybe it's just all those office supplies we got in the other day and those newbie's down on the sixth floor."

"What?" Preston asked. "There are no office supplies in the tree house or newbie's on any sixth floor?"

"Of course there are. And E equals MC Squared and I before E except after C and one and one is two and seven multiplied by nine is seventy-three." Starky stopped and stared at Preston as if he wasn't there. "I would have been a scientist when I grew up," he explained slow and seriously. "I would have worked in a lab and taught at a university and gotten married and had dinner every night before reading a book and going to bed."

"Starky, what are you talking about?" Preston asked, nervous.

"Fire and brimstone and wizards and. . ..and. . .and calculus!" he proclaimed.

"Starky, you sound crazy." Just then Starky looked at Preston with mean, spiteful eyes.

"I am not crazy," he cried, posing to fight Preston with bared teeth, but just as he got close enough, he slipped on what Preston couldn't see—it appeared he'd slipped on nothing. Starky fell to the ground and Preston rushed to help him up, but Starky started to shake, his eyes lolled inside his head and he turned to one side. "Crazy, I'm not crazy," Starky cried, white foam oozing from his lips like a dog about to wildly attack. He then lay in the grass with his mouth open, eyes vacantly fixed on the canopy of trees and Preston thought for a moment that he looked a lot like Boxwood.

"Starky!" Preston cried, shaking his friend. "Starky, Starky! No, Starky!" He held tight to him, trying to shake him awake. And how could they send him Here, whoever the he or she or it or they were, how could they think that Neverland wasn't as bad as the world they were so hard on, if this could happen to Starky? He'd already seen a boy Here who'd gone bad, gone cruel and foamed at the mouth like a dog. He couldn't help Eva, he couldn't forget, but it was no use remembering and why, why was it this way and how did Peter think this was better than Before?

"What's wrong?" someone asked and Preston scurried to his feet to see who was coming. "Are you okay?" someone inquired and it was Peyton. He was walking toward Preston with a chocolate bar in his hand, a brown smudge at the corner of his mouth. It seemed he'd forgotten all about their trip to Captain Hook. After they'd returned he never mentioned it and the one time when Preston brought up Eva's safety later, Peyton had looked at him as if he didn't know what he was talking about.

"It's Starky, something's wrong with Starky," Preston cried, starting to run back toward the tree house. "We have to get Peter, we have to help him."

"Help him?" Peyton asked. "What do we do?"

"Don't you remember, he's going to turn out like Boxwood, but maybe if we get to him sooner. . . . And what about Eva? We couldn't help Eva, but the least we can do is help Starky."

"We couldn't help Eva?" Peyton asked. "I thought we did—" But Preston was already racing away. Peyton didn't seem as if he wanted to move as Preston began to head toward the camp. Peyton followed, though he didn't fly very fast.

Preston saw the trees overhead, sun breaking through them, as he flew to get help. When he turned around in the air, now with Peyton ahead of him, Peter was there, floating as if the air was water and he was doing the backstroke. "Hi," he said brightly. "Whatcha worried about?"

"It's Starky," Preston cried. "It's Starky, he started foaming at the mouth, he tried to bite me like Boxwood, I don't know I think he's in trouble. I think he's. . ."

"Oh," Peter said, a perturbed look on his face that Preston could tell he was trying to hide. "Oh I don't like that at all. Let's go, follow me," Peter instructed, whizzing in the direction Preston pointed. Preston called to Peyton, who had flown on ahead. His friend stopped, scratched his head and turned around, once again following.

Starky jabbing at was the ground, poking it with a stick, when they returned to him. He seemed better now and Preston was starting to wonder if his little outburst, the crazy words, the foaming at the mouth, had ever happened. Dilweed was there with Hopper, a new kid, and Oregano. A group of boys stood by Starky now, though they didn't seem to know what was going on.

"Are you all right, Preston? You seem scared." Starky asked, patting him on the back as if everything were normal.

"I'm okay," Preston said. "Are you okay?" he asked his friend, looking him deep in the eye, though Starky gazed back almost stupidly.

"Yeah, sure, I'm fine. Why wouldn't I be?"

"Nothing," Preston said. "You started foaming at the mouth is all, but maybe it was just a game."

"Foaming, I don't remember foaming. I remember closing my eyes and going to sleep and when I woke up Hopper and Oregano were here and they said they saw you leave all upset about something."

"Oh," Preston replied, not wanting to argue.

"See, we're all okay," Starky said and Oregano agreed. "Come on, let's go see if we can't find us some Indians," Starky cried and they ran off after him into the woods, Peyton struggling to keep up.

"Boy?" someone asked and he looked up to see Peter standing next to him. He had a half-smile on his face. Peter had become okay with him since their falling out. He seemed to have forgotten it completely that same night when Preston had returned to the tree house to find Peter wearing a tiger skin and proclaiming that he was the greatest hunter in the world. He'd smiled at Preston, tipping his tiger head hat, and Preston had nodded politely at the leader as he'd made his way to his room.

"I just wanted to help him," Preston said, wiping a tear from his cold cheek. "Just like I wish I could help her. I wish I could find my mother, just for five minutes and tell her."

"Aw, it's okay Preston, your friend, I'm sure, I mean, someone will find that killer," Peter tried to comfort him.

"I just want to talk to my mom. I want that more than anything. I'll never be able to save Eva. I'll never be able to help and it was a waste, you were right, it was a waste giving up Hook's hand."

"You're not like Starky or Dilweed or even Peyton, do you know that? They remember the past, but they forget something, too. A part of them is already gone when they come Here, like they've lost a sense, a feeling, and it's all play, which is good, it should be all play, but you, you're like her, you remember the world and what it means when something is important, which is why you're sad now about missing your Mom. Everyone misses their Mom, but they're not sad. It's like a little part of you, the emotional part, is grown up."

Peter stopped Preston's pacing; he put his boy hands on his shoulders and looked at him. He saw Peter's eyes, they were a little blue and a little hazel, he saw the way his chin jutted out just a bit, and the contours of his face. Just then he saw not their leader, not even a boy, but a human being with thoughts and emotions, a person who had been in love and had his heart broken. "Don't worry," Peter said, pulling Preston in and hugging him. "Don't worry. You're like me. You're more like me than the rest of them. And I'm going to make sure nothing ever happens to you. I'm going to take care of everything." Peter held him and Preston felt as if he wanted to melt into his arms, to become a part of Peter, as their leader held him up, and the moment he looked down he realized they were flying. "I'm going to take you somewhere," Peter explained after he'd let him go still hovering over the trees. Peter looked out, watching for pirates, before dashing ahead of Preston, who followed.

They flew for a long time, past the cowboy and Indian camps, by Mermaid Lagoon and the Neverbird's nest. The trees grew taller and taller and the light grew brighter and brighter. Peter hovered for a second over a clearing Preston had never seen, which was funny because he thought he'd been everywhere in Neverland. "You can't tell anyone about this place," Peter informed him, placing a finger over his lips to indicate silence. "You have to be quiet and not disturb anything, don't even touch, just look."

"Where are we?" Preston asked, a fluttery nervousness dancing inside his stomach.

"We're at the edge of the Fairy Forest. I can't take you all the way inside, they'd never allow that, but we can sit at the edge, there's a stream there, a stream like a mirror where you can see the Before. The fairies use it sometimes for the children who can't speak, it helps them heal if they see their abusers are in jail or at least very, very sad and pathetic. If I show you I have to know that you won't tell anyone about this."

"I won't, Peter," Preston promised, honored he would trust him so much.

"Anyway, you wouldn't be able to get back if you tried; the Lost Boys always forget the way to the Fairy Forest, I'm the only one who knows," Peter informed him, slowly sinking from high above the trees to lower and lower among them until they were resting on the ground.

The Fairy Forest, even the outskirts, was beautiful. Streams and valleys, whole oceans seemed to exist inside a single, tiny plot of land. It didn't look like a real forest as much as a forest in a piece of art, something priceless hung at a museum. Preston took one step and quickly jerked back worried that his feet would sink into the ground that seemed so delicate, like glass. He waded further out, careful as if the land might swallow him, and after he'd walked a few paces more they reached a little pool of water that was reflecting light.

"Look in there and you'll see your Mom, but only for a minute. Don't try to talk to her and please don't let this make you sad," Peter instructed him, stepping away from the pool.

Preston looked down and saw nothing but water. He thought there might be some magic words Peter had neglected to tell him, but after a second the water started to move frantically as if there were a tiny tidal wave. Preston stepped back and there was his own bedroom. It looked exactly as it looked Here, except for the television and video games, his posters were on the walls, his trophies set up on the shelf near his window. At least they hadn't changed anything, not that Preston believed his parents would forget him. The scene flickered and there was his mother sitting on his bed. Her long brown hair was a little messy, a strand of it hanging in her face as she stared down at a piece of paper she was cutting. There appeared to be little cut outs all around her, as if she were making dolls. "Preston," she said his name and he remembered her voice, the one that used to explain the plot of his television shows to him, the one that talked to his class when she volunteered at his holiday parties. He heard her voice and he missed her. She was pale and thinner than Preston remembered, but she was his Mom and he reached out, nearly touching the water before Peter swooped in, and grasping him around the waist he flew upward until they were above the trees.

"You can't touch it," Peter warned. "Are you okay?"

"I'm fine, I'm fine, thank you," Preston replied, wiping a tear from his cheek. He did not want to cry in front of Peter, he did not want The Boy to think he'd made a mistake by showing him this as they hovered silently over the Fairy Forest.

LONDON, ENGLAND 1921

It had been a whim really. He'd been jousting with Hook, having a lone war, Peter against the pirates because it could get so lonely, so incredibly lonely in Neverland and he thought maybe the pirates would just kill him. He'd stood still and let them thrust their swords through his skin and nothing had happened. The pirates had not killed him and he'd had to go and wrestle with Hook, taking the pirate's other hand in the process. After he'd flown into the sun, after he'd gone around the world, he felt a certain pull and he knew that if he stopped at one moment, a single precise second, he would be in London, the place where Wendy lived. He looked at Tinkerbelle, who hovered in the air with him, she twinkled once, which said she would take him there, since there would be no fairy dust in the Before and he would need to bring his own supply.

And so he'd kept flying, past the Neverforest and the tree house, past the shores of the Island, by cowboy and Indian territory to the edge of the world, and there everything ended, it all stopped and there was a great black space and in that space were shining purple and red and blue orbs and he flew by them so fast, faster than he had ever flown until he was headed for a blue and green ball and there he kept going and going, not knowing where he was or how he was getting there, only that Tink knew the way and she'd help him. Down and down they flew and Peter was so frightened (and he'd never been scared before). They landed in a park, a very lovely park with flowers and trees and a little stream. There were rolling hills and magical rocks and mushrooms everywhere and he thought that this would be a perfect place for the fairies to live. But after a while he shivered, and Peter found, though he'd never have known it in Neverland, that he was not dressed for this place. In fact, he'd never have had a thought like that, imagine, not being dressed for something in Neverland!

It was snowing; only Peter had not known what snow was except as it pertained to pirates. They had snow in Neverland, but it wasn't this cold or this wet and it certainly didn't make him shiver. Peter hugged himself and tried to pull his shorts further over his legs. Nothing helped and so he'd gotten up and flown. That had not helped him get any warmer, but at least he was moving as he flew high in the sky, so as not to be seen by anyone on the ground, and over toward the house where he felt Wendy. He didn't know why he felt her, he wasn't sure how, but she was the reason he was in the Before and so this world, the Before (though it was the Now here), was telling him where to go. Peter looked down on London and Wendy had been right, there really was something magical about it. There were high rooftops that looked like mountains, and spires and clocks standing straight in the air. Colorful washing hung from lines and smoke stacks puffed and creaked as he flew past. He looked down and saw grownups, lots of grownups, like bands of pirates. It was dark out and Peter knew that when it got dark in the Before children went to bed. He saw many groups of adults in suits that clung to them, or dresses with corsets that made the women walk funny. And it was the women, really the women; Peter had never seen so many of them.

And so he'd flown and flown and flown 'til he'd dropped down at Wendy's front door. He knew it by the touch of it, and when he grasped the handle on the knocker he could feel that Wendy at some time or other had touched it. He didn't know what to do once he had the knocker in his hand; he attempted to pull it, but the thick metal thing would not budge; he tried hitting it, but it only hurt his fist and when he turned around a very tall man wearing a black coat and a hat that covered most of his forehead was watching him.

"Are you all right young man?" the grownup asked, standing very tall so that Peter felt incredibly tiny. "Are you supposed to be out this late?"

"I'm fine," Peter answered. He'd never heard himself speak here and his voice seemed to carry differently.

"Are you sure you shouldn't be off? I don't think you should be bothering these nice people at this time of night. Maybe the police should come, are you sure you're not lost?" the man asked and Peter looked innocently at him, having no idea what "the police" were. Another man dressed the same as the first, as if grownups wore some kind of uniform when they went out, came up and they both stood on the sidewalk watching Peter, who was now feeling especially small. If he hadn't liked grownups before, he certainly didn't like them now, the way they stood around, casting judgment, pretending to know best, when Peter knew most of them made mistakes left and right.

"What's this? Is this an orphan?" the new man asked and the other took off his hat and scratched his head.

"I hadn't thought of that, I was worried he was trying to rob the place."

"Rob the place, why he wouldn't go by the front door, even this late in the evening and I think we should call Scotland Yard and see. . ." The other man went on and Peter, not thinking, bolted upright into the air. He hovered far above their heads for a second to make sure the men had not noticed. He'd moved so fast, and they'd been so busily engaged with each other, that it seemed to them as if he'd simply disappeared. Peter flew around the house, heading toward the back of it, into its tiny yard. He almost touched down, but a dog began barking at him and he didn't want to get entangled with an animal. On the Island he could skin a tiger without trying, and the animals were very friendly to him, but he wasn't sure what would happen if a dog were to bite him in the Before. Peter hovered for a while by the side of the house, hoping no one was looking out their window to see a little boy in a pair of green shorts peering into one of the rooms.

Peter hovered at a large window connected to a thin concrete ledge. He held onto the bars and looked into the house. The darkened room looked nothing like the tree house, in fact it reminded him of Captain Hook's chambers. Everything was stuffy and seemed as if it would make him sneeze. The walls were a reddish color, a little lighter than scarlet, and there was dark wood trim around the doors and the floor was a little shiny, though Peter couldn't really see because only one small light was on. There was a bed in one corner with an ornate purple and white blanket hung over it and a carpet on the floor with a pattern that seemed to move in a slow, stilted manner. Peter sat at the window ledge for what felt like a while (though even here Peter was always forgetting the time); he was getting colder and colder and beginning to feel as if it might have been a mistake coming to the Before. Tinkerbelle chimed inside the sack he was carrying her in and he said, "I know, I know, it was silly."

He was about to turn and fly back around the world, straight toward Neverland, when the door to the room opened, revealing a grand yellow light coming from the hall. A girl emerged from the doorway, walking into the room she turned on another light, pushing the gas on a lamp before she sat down on the bed. She put her face in her hands for a second; she shook her head and glanced once more at the door before looking up and out the window.

At first her face went white and Peter was worried he'd frightened her. She turned from him for a moment, but then spun back, her face melting as if she'd recognized something, as she ran to the window. The girl was wearing a long gray dress, her hair was done up in curls piled high on her head and when she moved to unlock the window and let him in he saw that her hands were slender and nimble, the fingers just slightly long. It was those hands that he remembered, those hands that had so gracefully used the charcoal, fiddling nervously with the lock as if they hadn't aged a day.

"Peter!" she exclaimed, ushering him in. Peter flew hesitantly through the window and stood in the middle of the room, looking down at the carpet as if it might swallow him up. He felt his dagger at his side, ready to use it if something should crawl out of these walls. "Peter, it's you, it's really you."

"Hello?" Peter asked, not recognizing who it was anymore. The lady was really much older than she'd first seemed.

"Peter, it's me, it's me, it's Wendy. Wendy Moira Angela Darling —well it's Thomas now, but you needn't concern yourself with that." Peter looked at her, scratching his head as she stood before him, hands in front of herself as if she didn't know what else to say and so she fumbled on. "I mean they call me Winifred these days. And I've been waiting for you, since I came back, I've been waiting for you and oh Peter, where have you been?"

"Me?" Peter asked, scratching his head. "I'm looking for Wendy. I'm looking for my wife," he said, ready to attack this woman, for she must be keeping Wendy prisoner. "Maybe you're her mother? Are you Wendy's mother, if you are then I'm very pleased to meet you," Peter said, holding his hand out politely for this woman to shake. He knew grownups in the Before preferred something called politeness, which consisted of hand shaking and kind word saying.

The woman chuckled, covering her mouth with her hand. "Oh Peter, it is me. It's just that. . .I've grown up and I'm 'ever so much more than twenty' and all that. It really was a beautiful line; Mr. Barrie knew how to write a play. I'm thirty-six years old now. But here you are and I've grown up Peter, that's all, I've grown up. But it's me, it's me."

Peter had never witnessed this before, this growing up. He saw the finished product, he'd known pirates and Indians and cowboys, but he'd never seen a child become a grownup, that's not what Neverland was for and he could not believe. . .and yet there she was and it seemed a very funny state to be in, being grown up.

"I was afraid of cowboys," Wendy offered as proof, standing before him as if she were willing to be tested. "The cowboys never made it into the play, too confusing and all that, but I was afraid of them and I wore red war paint when I was Tiger Lilly and when you came to get me from Captain Hook, he said that girls should not be in Neverland and none of that is in the play Mr. Barrie wrote, so no one else would know that Peter, no one else but me."

"Wendy," Peter said, smiling. "I guess it is you."

"It is me, Peter, it is me," she said and though he knew somewhere that it was her, that logically it all made sense, he had never been good with Logic and Hook was always tripping him up that way. It was one of the things he could not have, one of the things he could not understand, and so he had to just believe her or be forever questioning. "Oh Peter, how I've missed you. And when I first came back all I did was look for you. And where have you been Peter, why did it take you so long? If you'd only come sooner, maybe I would have flown back to Neverland with you and stayed forever."

"I didn't know it had been so long," Peter replied, as he had never been very good with time. "I thought maybe. . .but then there were the cowboy and Indian wars and the pirates and one time all the mermaids had a falling out with the Lost Boys and Tink has been a mighty pain these days and I didn't stop to think that so much time had passed. And then one day I really wanted to see you and so I flew and flew and here I am, but I guess I came too late and that's my fault."

"Oh, Peter it's okay now, it's okay. Only I'm a married woman. I have three children of my own."

"But how could you get married?" Peter asked, scratching his head. "Is that how it works, you get married once and then you do it again?"

"Oh no, Peter, no. It's just that. . .and then. . .when you didn't come back. . . And they told me you weren't real. They said it was all a dream, that I had an overactive imagination. I never believed them, I never did, but still, I mean, you weren't here, you never came back and I was worried that even if you were real you were in another place where I would never be able to find you. And so when I grew older, I got married. I wore a white dress with a pink sash and I was sure that you'd come to the church and try to stop the wedding, but when you didn't, then I knew you weren't coming back. And then there were Jane and Sally and Kathy and I can't, Peter, I just can't. . .." Her eyes started to narrow, her body quiver, and for a moment she looked like she'd seen a cowboy.

"You can't what?" Peter asked. He wanted to run up to her, to fly into her arms and kiss her again, but he couldn't think about kissing her, not with her hair tied up and her lips bigger and thinner and her skin. . .she looked the same, but there was something about her skin. Wendy stood before him and he tried to see the girl he had known. But she was dead, she was gone and only this woman in a gray dress, this woman who tied her hair in knots and lived in a pirate room with stuffy wallpaper and fancy rugs, was all that was left of that playful little girl. "I miss Wendy," he said softly and Wendy shook her head sadly.

"I miss her too some days, Peter, I miss her too, I really do. But you could stay here. You could grow up like me. You would look so nice with a beard and if you stayed. . .well," Wendy put one finger to her lips, thinking. "If you stayed I'd leave here, we'd have to take the children of course, but we could run away, maybe to America and you and I, I mean, I could say you were my nephew at first, but after a while you'd grow up, too, and look like my husband, and we could live on a farm and milk cows and grow corn and I don't know, but it could be lovely."

Peter looked at her. He did not want to do any of that. The prospect of working on a farm confused him. Some of the Lost Boys had brought farms with them to Neverland and though they seemed to enjoy feeding pigs and harvesting corn, he had never been fond of it. And to take children, girl children, and to leave London and to be always with Wendy, who was not Wendy anymore, but Winifred, Winifred Moira Angela Darling—no Thomas. But he would—he decided that he would if it meant he could have Wendy, even a tiny sliver of who she had been. "Then let's run away to America," Peter proclaimed, and Wendy, whose face had lit up as she was talking about leaving, now grew solemn and scared.

"No Peter, I don't think we could really do that. I have a husband and children and responsibilities and you have the Lost Boys." She was trying to say something, there was something more there, something heavy and hard between them, and Peter couldn't see it, try as he might he couldn't see it, but he knew it was there. He knew he was just too much of a child to see it.

"I do have the Lost Boys," Peter whispered.

He thought then that he had better go before he started to grow up. Time did not stop here as it did in Pirate Cove and if he wasn't careful he'd grow that beard Wendy thought he'd look so nice in. "I have to go," Peter announced sadly, looking out the window at the stars. "I'm very sorry Wendy."

"I'm very sorry too, Peter," she said softly as if she were giving something up, but knew she had to.

"I didn't mean to make you sad," Peter said, moving closer to her. "It was a silly idea."

"Oh, but you always were a silly boy, a silly, tragic boy," Wendy cried, coming closer to him. Peter looked at her face. It wasn't the same face at all, but there was something natural, something lovely about it. She looked closely at him and he smiled at her. The grownup Wendy ran her fingers across his face, those hands, hands that were still the same, caressed the sides of his cheeks, her thumbs pressing his temples. He closed his eyes, letting the hands wash over him and he felt safe, comforted and happy with her. When Peter opened his eyes Wendy was still looking at him. She drew closer, kissing him like she had before. Peter could feel it as he'd felt it so many years ago, parting his lips and receiving her. He put an arm around her and she held him closer. Only it was she holding him, since she was not a little girl anymore. But he kissed her, he kissed her and kissed her and kissed her, and when he closed his eyes it was as if he were back in Neverland, he was a boy who had never kissed a girl and she was the fresh faced child she'd been there.

When it was finished Wendy stepped back. She smiled sadly at him and sat on the bed. "A married woman is not supposed to do that, certainly not with another man, her first husband no less." She wiped her upper lip and tried to fix her hair, since some of the curls had come undone.

"What?" Peter asked, scratching his head.

"Oh Peter you were always so. . .so. . .so innocent," she said, shaking her head as if she might cry. "I'm sorry I can't go with you and you can't stay. But I really am a married woman and there's Jane and Sally and Kathy, and the house. My husband bought my family's house after my parents passed, and John and Michael, both with careers in the law, and. . .But it is not so bad, growing up. You get to have your own children, and love them, I did not know love, this kind of love, until I had children, and you get to make decisions and live in the world and see plays and go to parties. Peter, it's not all bad, I promise, it's not all bad growing up."

"What?" Peter asked, not understanding as he looked around the room. It was very large and very decorated and incredibly grotesque. He missed the tree house, the Lost Boys and the Indians and cowboys, the Nevertrees that hung like a great ceiling that let you see the sky, unlike this thick, artificial vertical wall. There were very different, he and Wendy, they lived across a cavern not even the power of flight could cross.

"Oh Peter," Wendy said, seeming to understand completely. "It's only too bad you can't stay and I can't go with you."

"It is," Peter replied, moving closer to the window. He could feel the chilly breeze through it and he did not want to go back out in the cold.

"But I'll always remember you and sometime perhaps you'll return to me?" she asked hopefully.

"Yes, of course, if that's what you want. I know how. I mean,

I always knew how; it was just a question of timing and I am always so bad with the time."

"Thank you, Peter," Wendy said, escorting him to the window. He stopped just at the ledge and she looked at him one more time. She leaned in and kissed him, only this time her lips did not part, this time she merely tweaked his lips and nipped his nose. "You're a good little boy, Peter."

"Thank you," Peter replied, not knowing what else to say. "Thank you," he said again, looking one more time at Wendy. For a split second he could see that little girl, it was in her eyes, the way they twinkled, and as he flew out the window he hovered there wanting to climb back in, to stay with her forever and run away.

He looked out at the room once more. It was like a light then, a light going slowly out, with its reddish walls and darkish wood, intricate carpets and blankets over carved beds. It was all so much. And then there was Wendy and she waved to him, her hair done up, in her long dress. The lights were still on in the room, but he could sense them dimming, he could hear someone moving in the halls of the house and Peter dashed out, going up and up and up as far as he could go.

cLaire

The kitchen was not the same anymore. It was an unfamiliar place, a quiet, a restful and therefore useless place. It had never been just a room, a space where people sat, where they stared at a television or read a magazine. The kitchen was a practical place; things got done here, the cutting of raw vegetables, the preparing of salads or the seasoning of steaks, but very little had been getting done these past two and a half months. Claire cooked on occasion, she and Matthew were even starting to share meals together, but none of it felt useful, it barely felt real. Claire stared at the counter where she used to prepare meat for burgers with Preston. She wiped the last of the coffee cups with a yellow dishrag, reaching the top shelf of the blond wood cabinets and hoisting them back up to be taken down the next morning and the next morning and the next. No matter how hollow the kitchen felt there was still a need for coffee.

She wondered what the mugs would look like at Eva's house. She'd never spent much time at the Murphy's. She'd had lemonade on their back porch last summer while Preston and Eva made a fort with boxes from their new entertainment center; she'd knocked on the door and waited on the stoop as the housekeeper got Preston for her when he was late coming home. She'd had a few conversations with Mrs. Murphy at their kitchen counter, and while all of it was friendly, they'd never been close. Mrs. Murphy was a doctor at one of the children's hospitals in Boston and her husband was a surgeon somewhere close by. They kept odd hours and were gone a lot. When they were home there was a rushed frantic quality to the household, as if they were trying to squeeze twenty-four hours worth of home into three or four.

That's why it had come as such a surprise when Eva's mother called Claire a couple of nights ago and invited her over for coffee. "I just think it's time we got to know each other," she'd said kindly. "I've been meaning to talk to you for a while, I just haven't found the time." She hadn't found the time? Her daughter had just lost both her best friends this summer, the entire neighborhood was in mourning and she couldn't find the time to reach out, not for two and a half months? She hoped she hadn't waited this long to deal with her own daughter's issues.

Claire continued wiping the kitchen counter. She'd made pasta last night for Matthew and they'd eaten it in the kitchen instead of venturing all the way to the dining room. Claire had forgotten to put the placemats out, something she never would have done before, and there were rings from their glasses and stains from the sauce in the blue and white granite that needed to be dealt with—later.

A knock came from the front doorway, a small, quiet, timid knock and Claire wondered at it. Her neighbors might have knocked, but more forcefully. A deliveryman would have rung the doorbell once and left, and the service guys knew to go around back. The knock sounded again and Claire walked toward her front door. There hadn't been a timid knock on that door, an actual "can-I-please-come-in-?" knock in so long, not since children stopped coming to the house.

When she opened the door a boy was standing on the stoop. He had stopped knocking and was fiddling with a worn canvas backpack, trying to keep something down in it. He wrestled with it for a second as Claire looked at him.

"Are you okay? Can I help you?" she asked and the boy looked up at her.

"I'm all right," he said. "It's only a firefly in a jar," he went on, lifting the jar for Claire to see. The firefly was very bright and it didn't move, it just shone until the boy shoved it back into his pack and tied the ends of it. "There we go," he said, smiling. "I'm sorry I didn't come sooner, it's just that I'm always forgetting the time."

The boy, who looked about fourteen, maybe fifteen, had the most mischievous smile, as if his mouth were his whole face. He had shaggy dark blond hair and a small nose with freckles drifting across it and his chin jutted out just a bit, as if it couldn't decide whether it belonged to a grown-up or a child. He was wearing dirty sneakers, sneakers that looked as if they'd gone out of style years before and his green shorts and T-shirt seemed as if they'd come from a church shelter. If an adult had come to her dressed this way she might have tried to get rid of them. But this was obviously a child and children couldn't help it when they dressed like that.

"Hi," the boy said again. "Hi, it's nice to meet you," he went on, giving Claire his hand to shake as if he were here on very official business. "My name is Peter."

"Hello Peter," Claire replied. "Do you want to come in?" she moved from the doorway and he walked inside, diligently kicking his sneakers off before following Claire through the living room and into the kitchen. Claire stood near the counter and Peter climbed onto one of the stools, making himself comfortable as he folded his arms and looked about the room. "So what can I do for you, Peter?" Claire asked.

"I'm sorry to bother you, Mrs. Tumber," the boy started. "It's just that I knew Preston and Peyton. I'm a few grades older than them, but I knew them and I wanted to come see you."

"Oh," Claire said quietly. "Oh, I see, did you come to the funeral?"

"No, I'm sorry, I couldn't make it to that. How was it?"

"It was a lovely service. The priest gave a very respectful sermon and my husband said the eulogy. . ." She stopped, watching the child, unsure of what to say to him. "It was nice," she summed up, not wanting to go on for fear she might bore him.

"Good, I'm glad. I'm sorry I couldn't make it, I was somewhere else."

"I see," Claire replied. "Some of the parents didn't want their children going to a funeral so young. I don't know what they're going to say to you when school starts back up. What has your mother said to you about what's happened?"

"Me?" Peter asked, surprised to be asked such a direct question. "I don't know. I don't have a mother."

"Oh, I see," Claire replied, and all of a sudden the dirty clothes made sense. "I'm sorry, Peter. I didn't realize. Well, your father then, I'm sure your father has explained to you…"

"I know a little bit," Peter broke in. "I've never really known everything, they won't tell me, but I think that's for the best."

"That's very wise of you."

"So do they know anything?" the boy asked, excited, as if he was playing a game of detective. "I mean about who did it. No one will tell me much, but do they think it was the same person?"

"They do. The crimes were too similar and they don't think a copycat would do that. I mean it didn't make much sense to the police. They had a man, but they were wrong about him."

"Mr. Hawthorne?" Peter asked. "No, it wasn't him. He was a nice guy. Just the other day I saw him help a friend of mine up when he was shot in the arm with an arrow."

"What?" Claire asked and Peter gave her a frightened look, as if he'd let something slip.

"I mean, a pretend arrow," he elaborated. "Just the other day my friend was shot with a pretend arrow and—"

"I didn't realize Mr. Hawthorne got out that much. But yes, it's beginning to look more and more like Mr. Hawthorne was just a nice man who kept to himself. I've been watering his bell-flowers. They're lovely flowers and they're going to die soon if I don't take care of them, at least until next year, by then someone else will own the house and I just wanted to make sure they had one more season."

"That's very nice of you. He'd be happy to know that."

"I hope so," Claire replied, looking out the window at the yard. Matthew had yet to take down the play-set. He'd even mentioned that perhaps they'd have another child, but even if they did, she would not want that child playing on Preston's play-set and they'd have to put a new one up.

"So who did it then?" Peter asked innocently as he started to pick at his fingernails, which Claire could see were very dirty.

"I don't know," she replied. "The police are asking around the school and they've searched the bakeries, since both times it was cookies."

"What about people who make cookies and stuff for a living, but don't work in a bakery or even a restaurant? Maybe you should check your neighbor's house."

"I'm sure there are a few people like that, but I don't know if you could just find them," Claire replied. "And my neighbor's house?" she asked, surprised.

"I know, but what if, I mean, what if Mr. Hawthorne knew someone who made him cookies and that person is now baking for someone else around here," Peter explained very seriously and for a moment Claire thought she was talking to an adult.

"I know, but no one could find that woman, the housekeeper he was talking about. They didn't even know her name, Mr. Hawthorne said her name was Mary Clark, but there was no such person, which is why we thought he was making her up. And there was no Mary Clark that we know of at the picnic."

"Then Mary Clark isn't her name," Peter said. "What about Eva? How is she?"

"I don't know. The police thought Eva might be in danger, since they were all three such close friends, but it's been a while since Peyton and they're not sure. They were watching the house until last week, but they don't think. . ."

"Okay. I just think, I mean, someone who does cooking, but isn't working in a bakery. I don't know. . .who else could that be?" The boy was getting so serious.

"Are you sure your father knows you're here?"

"No one knows I'm here," the boy said as if it were a silly question. "I came on my own."

"Are you sure you're allowed to be here? Maybe I should call your father," Claire suggested, remembering how she'd felt when she'd been looking for Preston, that sharp sinking feeling came back to her and she wanted desperately for Peter to leave. "I don't want your father to think something happened to you."

"No one will think that," Peter informed her. "Now let's see, I just think if you consider people who worked at the school as well, people who act as housekeepers in the summer to make ends meet. Have the police looked there?"

"Peter, I think you should go," Claire said. "I have a commitment in a couple of minutes. Thank you for stopping by, thank you for paying your respects, but I have a feeling your father must be looking for you."

"Okay," Peter said simply, only a child could take being cut off like that this well. "Thank you for letting me in," he added, climbing down off the stool.

"You're welcome," Claire replied, walking Peter to the front door. "It was very nice to meet you. I hope I see you around the neighborhood."

"Thank you, Mrs. Tumber," the boy said, looking back at her as he stood in the doorway, that canvas bag slung over his shoulder. It seemed to rustle, to move ever so slightly as he hoisted it higher before slipping on his sneakers and moving to leave. "You're a good mother and Preston loves you very much."

"Thank you, Peter," Claire replied, watching as he walked a few paces down the walkway before closing the door. Something about that boy, not just what he'd said, made Claire feel good about herself, exceedingly happy as she had not been in months. She wanted to open the door and call out to him, to keep him talking, but when she looked out, he wasn't there.

She had to leave for the Murphys' anyway, and so Claire

walked out expecting to catch up with Peter, maybe he was going the same direction, but the boy was gone. Claire looked down her yard, walking a few paces toward the Hoffstras', just to see if he'd taken a short cut, but he wasn't anywhere. Maybe it was like the toys that had been moved in Preston's room. Claire knew better than to wonder if she'd actually seen him, she wasn't so crazy that she'd started making up conversations with little boys, but she made a note to ask around about him.

It was a short walk to the Murphys', such a short walk that Claire wondered why she hadn't done it more often. There were neighbors Claire never spoke to, like Gregory Hawthorne, but for the most part Claire tried to be friendly, especially with a neighbor whose daughter had been a good friend to her son.

Eva had always been a friendly girl. She was very pretty and very smart, she'd been in the gifted class with Preston and Claire had sometimes wondered if, when they got older, something more might have blossomed between the two children. When Claire got to the house she noticed a purple car with splashes of rust on it parked at the edge of the driveway. It didn't seem like something the Murphy's would own, but the way it was parked seemed to suggest some dominion over the house. Eva was at the window, her blond hair had been cut to frame her face and her big eyes looked wide at Claire as she made her way up the walk-way. When she reached it, ringing the Murphys' bell, Eva dashed away from the window, the pattering of little girl's feet sounding through the walls as she met her mother at the door.

"Claire, hello," Mrs. Murphy greeted her. She was a tall woman with short blond hair and plain, though well taken care of, features. "It's so nice to see you, come in," she said, ushering Claire through the foyer and into the sitting room.

"Hello Gloria," Claire said, taking a look around the house. It was done in pinkish colors, though there was a central brown theme and a few white couches and loveseats offset the décor. It was a room that had been professionally decorated, professionally shopped for and cleaned twice a week without fail. It had that unlived in feel, almost like a hotel, that houses run by professionals had. There were no knickknacks on the shelves, no toys scattered around or books lying out on tables. The television wasn't on and the newspaper wasn't out and Claire was almost afraid to sit on the couch, even as Gloria Murphy settled into it.

"Claire, how are you? I'm so sorry it's been so long," Eva's mother started and Claire watched the little girl stand near the couch, her hands behind her back as she eyed both women. "I've been meaning to have you over for so long, but I've been working so much and with all that's gone on, I mean, I'm sorry, I'm so sorry." Eva's mother grasped her hand and Claire squeezed it in return.

"Thank you, Gloria, that means a lot. And I know you've been busy and your work is so important. I mean you're helping sick children."

"Thank you," Gloria Murphy replied. "I watch those sick children and think about Preston and Peyton now. I see those parents and I remember you and Matthew. I was thinking of having Cara over as well, but I thought it might be too much for both of you, and I don't know. . ." she went on. She'd seemed so perfectly poised, but Gloria's voice became more frantic as she looked first at Claire and then at her daughter.

"Honey, why don't you go play with Mrs. Glands, I think she needs your help in the kitchen," Eva's mother offered and the little girl quietly turned on her heels, giving Claire a tiny smile as she left.

"How's Eva doing?" Claire asked, whispering as if this were a secret.

"She's okay. She isn't talking much. I mean, she talks, and I've tried to discuss all that's happened with her. Derrick and I thought it would be best to be honest. We were going to explain death to her in a few years, just so she'd be prepared, but who knew she'd need to be prepared for something like this."

"I know," Claire replied, shaking her head. A month ago she might have broken down at a conversation like this, even now she felt as if she were tearing up, but Claire swallowed hard, she looked at the Murphys' back wall, where sunlight swallowed a painting of a woman in a bathtub.

"I'm sorry, it's just. . . And I meant to see you sooner, but with everything and then Eva. She's not been the same. She holes up in her room. She's just now starting to come out of it more often. In fact, we got this housekeeper, this fabulous woman. She came over here from the Ukraine a few years ago and hardly knows anyone, I wasn't going to hire her, because she didn't have any references, but right away when Eva started talking to her at the interview she started to open up, and Eva was acting like she had before. . . And so I had to snatch her up. In fact if she had been a horrible housekeeper, if I'd had to hire another woman to do the cooking and cleaning so she could just spend time with Eva, I would have. Eva has been so much better with her."

"Has she been opening up to anyone else?" Claire asked.

"She still won't talk to her father. I don't know why she blames Derrick. Maybe because her two good friends were boys and they left her. She'll only let me tuck her into bed. Me or Erma."

"I see," Claire replied, looking back at the kitchen. She could see a sliver of it from where she sat. Light filtered through the windows, dust dancing in it, as the little girl smiled up at a very tall woman. Claire could only make out the shape of the woman; she had long brown hair and wore glasses. Eva laughed at her as she kneaded a slab of dough, her hands rocking back and forth in the honey colored concoction.

"And I'm sure she'll be okay, though you never know. Trauma like this leaves its mark on a person. They've done studies. Did you know that they think JM Barrie, the man who wrote *Peter Pan*, they say now that the reason he was so short and child-like physically was because of the psychological trauma he suffered when his older brother died?"

"I didn't realize that," Claire replied. The most she knew about *Peter Pan* was that Preston had gone through a phase where he'd wanted to watch the Disney version of the story every day for three weeks straight.

"I'm sorry, I don't mean to be citing studies at you. That's not what this is about. I just thought it might be nice—" Mrs. Murphy stopped as the housekeeper entered with a tray of coffee. The porcelain cups rattled and Claire could see the silver pot shaking as she set the tray on the table, picking up the pot and filling two cups while Gloria reached for the cream. "Cream and sugar?" she asked Claire, who nodded "yes" to both.

"Thank you," she said to the housekeeper, who looked down once at Claire. She had small eyes and when she opened her mouth she saw that she had a couple of blackening teeth.

"You know Erma works at the school as well, she's a lunch lady," Gloria said, as if to be a lunch lady was some sort of honor. "But we're talking about taking her on full-time; then she could quit that job and just work here."

"I'd like that," Erma said, smiling at Gloria as Eva entered the room, standing back by the doorway, waiting for Erma. "I'm making fresh bread right now, it's about to go into the oven. It'll be a while, but I baked some this morning and I'll bring that out soon."

"Thank you Erma, always going above and beyond," Mrs. Murphy said more for the housekeeper's benefit than for Claire's. "She's really a nice lady," Eva's mother went on. "And her coffee is always so much better than mine, and we use the same beans, the same beans, I don't get it."

"Funny how that is, some people just have that magic touch," Claire commented. "You know, I got the strangest visit from a boy today," she went on. "He said his name was Peter. I didn't get his last name. He said he didn't have a mother; there must be a single father in the neighborhood. Apparently the boy knew Preston. Have you met him?"

"No," Mrs. Murphy replied, shaking her head. "I don't know him. Maybe Eva does. Then again, they'd started to have different friends. Eva's been playing with more and more girls at school and she said that Preston and Peyton were always off playing soccer or basketball with the boys. Maybe this Peter is one of those."

"Maybe," Claire pondered, trying to picture the children at all of Preston's birthday parties, all the school functions, the other parents she'd met up with, the play dates, the trips to the park. She couldn't picture this boy, not in any of the scenarios that ran through her mind. "He looked a little older than them, maybe even fifteen."

"Eva," Gloria Murphy called to her daughter. "Eva, come here," she said and the little girl appeared from the kitchen. She had a touch of yellowish dough on her nose that reminded Claire distinctly of Preston and how he looked after licking cookie batter, which he had always done after cookies were in the oven, no matter how old he got. "Do you know a boy named Peter?"

"No," the girl said, licking the dough from her finger after she wiped it off her nose. "No, no Peters."

"You can't remember Preston or Peyton talking about knowing anyone named Peter? He might have been a little older," her mother went on, speaking in that half-whisper-half-condescending voice that mothers got when they are around other mothers and want to appear kind, but in control.

"No," the little girl replied. "Should I have?"

"It's okay, honey," Claire said, watching Eva lick the last of the dough from her finger. She wasn't sure what came over her, maybe it was all that talk of Peter, but she grabbed Eva's hand and smelled where the dough had been. She got nothing from her finger, it smelled like a child, like skin and sweat more than anything else and yet she knew, she just knew there was something wrong with it. Claire wiped the girl's fingers with a napkin and Eva watched, perplexed. "Eva, honey, have you been eating a lot of that bread?"

"No," the little girl said, shaking her head.

"How long have you had your housekeeper?" Claire asked, remembering something Peter had said about bakers who did not work in bakeries.

"I don't know, a couple of weeks, why?" Mrs. Murphy replied, perplexed. "Is everything all right?"

"I think you should get that bread checked. You should check everything she's ever baked for you."

"What?" Mrs. Murphy asked, laughing to cover her discomfort. "What are you talking about? Erma's a professional woman. What're you saying?"

"I just think there's a chance. . ." Claire looked at Eva and smiled at her. "Could you go up into your room honey, I need to talk to your mother?"

"Okay," the little girl said, turning around and running up the stairs. Claire listened to her feet tramping up them before she turned to Eva's mother, who was looking at her as if she wasn't sure if she should be angry or concerned for Claire's mental health.

"I just think that. . .I mean, both Preston and Peyton were poisoned and I don't think that. . .I mean, how well do you know this woman?" Claire started and even after all that had happened, it still felt silly talking this way. "Look, if I'm crazy, then I'm crazy, but you should have the bread she's making checked out. You should take a sample of everything she makes, and don't give it to Eva. Or let Erma think you're giving it to Eva, but don't."

"Claire, you sound. . ." Gloria Murphy said, shaking her head. "I mean I understand after such trauma, I really do, that you might feel this way. I think you should be talking to someone, if you haven't already started. But I just think. . .and Erma has been cooking for us for two weeks, nothing has happened."

"I know," Claire replied. "I know how this sounds. But I also know, I know in my gut that something is wrong. I know in my gut that Preston wouldn't want anything to happen to Eva and I just think. . ."

Gloria Murphy cocked her head as she watched Erma walk through the kitchen and into the living room with a plate of bread. She set it down before them, nodding kindly in their direction. "Should I bring butter?"

"Yes," Eva's mother replied, glancing up the stairs. "Thank you."

Claire eyed the bread. The crust looked crisp and the inside soft, it seemed buttery on its own and smelled homemade. Even Claire wanted to reach out and try a slice.

"It looks good," Claire commented and just then Eva ran down the stairs. Both mothers watched her feet cascade down the steps as Erma caught her as she nearly slipped on the slick tile at the end of them. The girl laughed and Erma took a slice of bread from her apron. It seemed so odd, if the bread were poisoned, that she would just give it to the girl right in the open, and maybe Gloria was right, it did seem a little far-fetched, but this entire summer had been far-fetched and still things had happened, horrible things.

Eva ran to the couch with the bread in her hand and Gloria jumped for it, reaching across Claire she grabbed the bread from her, standing over her daughter. "No, Eva, no, no bread now," she said, smiling at her and calming down. "Right now you don't need bread. You'll load up on carbs before lunch and we don't want that," she said, trying to smooth it over as Erma watched.

"Is there something wrong, Ma'am?" the housekeeper asked innocently, grasping her apron and pulling at the strings. "I thought it would be okay if she had a little bread, I don't think it will spoil her lunch."

"It's okay, Mrs. Glands, it's okay. Thank you for the bread, it smells very good. Why don't you take the rest of the day off? I'll pay you for it. I just realized that Eva has an appointment this afternoon and after that we should all rest in the house. Why don't you go home and I'll see you tomorrow?"

"Ma'am, the bread is still in the oven. I can stay while the bread is baking and let myself out."

"Thank you, that's okay. I'd like to spend some alone time with my daughter," Gloria Murphy said a tad more curtly.

"If that's what you want," Erma Glands shrugged, taking off her apron and holding it in her fist. She grabbed her purse from the coat rack by the door and moved to leave. "I'll see you tomorrow."

"Good bye, Erma!" the little girl called, smiling as the housekeeper walked out.

"I don't know. . ." Eva's mother started. "But when I saw her eating that bread, I knew she couldn't. . . it's just that I have to be sure now that you've put this into my head."

"I'm sorry," Claire said. "I'm sorry and I'm sure it's nothing, but maybe if I take this bread to the police, both breads, it'll put our minds at ease."

"Fine," Gloria Murphy replied, looking at Eva, who'd moved to the window to watch her housekeeper go. "If only so I don't have to look at Erma funny every time she walks into my house. I can take it to the police if you don't want to."

"No," Claire replied. "If you give me a couple of samples, I'll take it in. They might be more willing to test it if it comes from me. Even if I sound crazy, they'll be understanding."

"I hope your feeling is wrong," Gloria Murphy stated, watching her daughter as she walked toward the kitchen. "I'll get you your samples. But if they don't find anything I think I might have to give Erma a raise, I'll feel so guilty about this."

"Fair enough," Claire replied. She'd never had a feeling this strong before, not even when Preston was in the woods losing his breath, not even then, and it seemed unfair that she was getting this feeling now and not then. If she didn't get this bread tested she'd never forgive herself, someone was telling her something, they had to be. . .and after what Peter had said, she couldn't get his words out of her head. She hadn't been out on a crusade before, but if she could find the person who did this, it was little consolation in its own right, but if Eva was in danger and she could help, it was her job to butt in. If this feeling wasn't real, Claire wasn't sure what to do with herself.

PRESTON

The Lost Boys gathered around the tree house, where most of them stayed when Peter went missing. He hadn't run off to hunt tigers or visit the fairies, he wasn't there at all and it was cold and hollow in Neverland as it had never been, not since Preston had arrived. Peyton was playing on the Ferris wheel and Dilweed and Clover were distractedly rifling through the mound of toys. The Inside Boys, who always played their video games, were even out watching the woods as if something might jump out of them. It wasn't that the boys were nervous, they weren't even really asking questions, but there was a sense that permeated through everyone that something was askew. The entire Island was off balance, as if the wind had gone away or the sun had not come out, though there was still daylight.

"I remember when it felt like this before," Starky said, whittling a stick with a short, sharp knife. "It got cold and we all thought we were going to freeze to death."

"When was this?" Preston inquired.

"When?" Starky asked as if it were a ridiculous question. "I don't know, before you came."

"Oh. He'll be back," Preston reassured his friend. He didn't know how, but he knew Peter and was sure he would return.

"I know, Peter has to come back, it's what he does, just like we have to be Here until we're not anymore. Look at Peyton," Starky cried, pointing at Preston's friend, who was now waiting for a turn on the merry-go-round. "He's got the right idea, just live it up, live it up that's it."

"I wasn't really worried about Peter," Preston commented.

"It's just that I've been thinking and maybe I should tell you. . .I mean, I don't think you'd really care. . ." Preston started, wondering if he should confess his adventure at Pirate Cove to Starky.

"Look!" Starky called, pushing past Preston. "Look, there he is," he cried and when Preston looked up he saw a boy in the sky. He couldn't make out who it was at first, boys flew around all the time, but this figure was so bright, it seemed to rise like the sun. All the other boys crowded around the Ferris wheel, congregating along the path he was headed in. They were all pointing in the air, the Ferris wheel stopped and the boys got down from it, the merry-go-round emptied and a string of lights, so many more fairies than Preston had ever seen, crowded around.

When Peter landed the Lost Boys shuffled back, giving him space. He stopped and looked at them all and it wasn't as if he were expecting such a grand welcome, but it didn't surprise him either. Preston noticed, as Peter touched down, that the wind picked up on the Island, it hadn't been calm before so much as slow, like thick mud, but now it was a pleasant breeze and everything was growing warmer. Peter smiled at the Lost Boys, laughing at them.

"Come to see your fearless leader!" he cried, bowing three times as they clapped.

"Peter where were you?" one of the boys asked.

"Did you fight Hook? Did you kill him this time?" another called.

Preston stood toward the back of the group as Peyton fought his way toward Peter, who was nearly impossible to get to as more and more boys crowded around. "I found some new stories!" Peter cried and the boys cheered. "Just today I saved a little girl from certain death!"

"Yay!" the boys called. Some of these boys had come from Preston's time. They'd played video games with elaborate storylines, they'd seen the news their parents watched, some were as old as fifteen and still they jumped up and down on hearing Peter's simple story.

"You see what happened was there was this little girl and a mean old monster was stalking her. It had been stalking her for a while and she was in so much danger, except she didn't even know she was in danger until I came. I touched down and went to where her protector lived and I went in and slew that monster. I went right in there with my sword and tore off its head."

The boys clapped and cheered. "You saved her!" one of them called. "Long live Peter the Protector!" they cried together.

The boys kept cheering for Peter as he flew out of their midst and up into the trees. They dispersed quickly after Peter left, not bothering to fly after him, even though he'd be easy enough to find. Once the boys dispersed, Preston marched out of the group and back toward the woods, parting two branches at the entrance. The sound of boys playing could be heard behind him, muffled by the leaves and off key as he walked toward the Indian camp, where it was always quiet unless there was a war or party going on.

Preston thought he could see the leaves on the trees moving as if they could make themselves dance on their own and when he turned around, Peter was there. "Hi," he said, holding something behind his back with one hand. "Did you like my story?"

"I liked it very much if it was true," Preston replied.

"I don't tell lies," Peter said. "That's part of the rules. I mean, I can tell stories, or I can tell the Lost Boys I'm keeping a secret, but I don't lie, I keep my word and I say what I mean, unless I don't say anything at all."

"I know," Preston responded.

"I got something for you," the leader said, still with one hand behind his back. "But it's not really for you, it's for you to give to someone."

"Really? What is it?" Preston asked.

"Here," Peter said, handing Preston a white flower. "It's a bellflower, a white bellflower. There were a bunch of them and I thought you might like to see it. It's for the cowboy, the one you know, the Hawthorne-cowboy."

"They were robots and aliens yesterday," Preston informed Peter.

"They do that sometimes, but they're cowboys again now. Cowboys and Indians are their default states; they always go back to that. I mean, not always, but since there have been cowboys and Indians, they keep returning to that."

"Cowboys and Indians are the best ones," Preston went on, examining the white flower. It looked familiar and though he had most of his memory from Before, he couldn't picture this. He could see grass and sun, his own yard and other yards he'd played in flickering in and out of his mind; he saw the sun coming through the trees and the little knickknacks on his mother's shelves, he smelled banana bread in the kitchen and sensed the way rubber swings felt under his knees when he swung on them. He could see all that, he could even see his mother, but he couldn't see those flowers; though their name was on the tip of his tongue, at the edge of his memory.

"Why did you give this to me?"

"It's your cowboy's," Peter urged, not understanding. "Don't you want to give it to him?"

"I do, I just...where'd you get this? How'd you get this? Peter what did you do, where were you?"

"I was away for a while, that's why it got so cold. I can only bring so much back with me, but there it is. I'm sure he'd want to have it, even if he won't remember what it is."

"You're not going to say anything more are you?" Preston asked, looking closely at the white flower. It seemed almost like glass it was so pristine. He carefully touched a petal and it sprung back at him.

"I am not, except to say that Eva is safe," Peter replied, smiling coyly. "Come on, let's go see the cowboy," he called, flying above the trees and hovering there.

The cowboy camp was deserted. It always looked this way when they weren't planning for a war and Preston knew that they were all hunkered down in the Saloon, a dilapidated wooden building that stood lopsided to the right. Peter was already at the swinging double doors to the Saloon when Preston flew into the camp. He pointed inside and Preston marched toward the doors, pushing them open with the force typical of a cowboy. Even though the Lost Boys were allowed to go anywhere on the Island, except Pirate Cove, the cowboys were used to their privacy inside the Saloon, in fact it was speculated that the reason the cowboys sometimes holed up in there was to stay out of the way of all the other types on the Island so they could strategize. The cowboys had an obsession with strategy that bordered on a fixation.

There were a few cowboys in the main room of the saloon, which, when Preston opened the doors, seemed much larger than the tiny shack it had looked like on the outside. There was a long, wide bar polished a very shiny black, where a few cowboys were sitting going over a book, and ten or twelve tables on a large, dirty floor littered with peanut shells. One of the cowboys tipped his hat to Peter as he walked in after Preston, and another one called a low "Howdy," though the rest of them just sat staring. Music had been coming from a piano in the back, but even that abruptly stopped as Preston walked in, looking for Hawthorne.

He was sitting near the back, at a table with three other cow-boys who were going over a crumpled piece of paper. "And I think if we take our position at the north tree…" one cowboy was suggesting as Preston drew closer. There were glasses on the table that weren't filled with anything, even though one of the cowboys kept sipping from his empty glass as if he couldn't get enough of the air inside it. "Howdy," all four cowboys said, looking up from their strategy notes when Preston approached.

"Howdy," Preston said, feeling a little frightened with all these cowboys around. He looked at Hawthorne, who took his big white cowboy hat off when the boys approached. "I have something for you," he said, pointing at him. Hawthorne pointed back at himself, confused.

"What've you got for me, Lost Boy?" he asked with a voice that might have been off-putting if it hadn't been so playful. The other cowboys got up, sliding their chairs out with a slow creaking and standing before the table.

"Well, we'll leave you two alone, supposing you don't need us around," one of them said, and the others nodded as they walked off toward the bar. The music started up again, the cowboys began talking and Preston felt as if he could finally speak freely.

"I got this for you," he said, holding the white bellflower out to him. "I don't know if you can remember it or not, but it was important to you once, Before—"

"Before?" the cowboy-Hawthorne asked.

"Yeah, Before," Preston said, remembering. "You were nice to me once and it really hurt you. And I just. . .I wanted you to have this, for being nice to me and all."

"Did I save you from the Indians?" the Hawthorne-cowboy asked, trying to figure out what was going on. He seemed to know that something had happened, that there was a thing he was supposed to know but didn't, and it made Preston sad that all the adults forgot in Neverland. "I was nice to you, is that part of the game? I know the cowboys don't hate the Lost Boys like they hate the Indians, but you Lost Boys coming in and playing spoiler all the time, it's enough to drive a man crazy. I don't know, why was I nice to you?"

"You just were," Preston said, tears in his eyes. "You just were, you were really nice to me and it got you in a lot of trouble and I wanted you to have this. It was important to you once." He thrust the flower toward the Hawthorne-cowboy and held his breath. The cowboy gently took the stem between two pinched fingers, examining the white petals. "It's yours and I wanted you to have it back," Preston went on, crying. He could barely hold himself up and the cowboy looked back at him, completely confused.

"Well thank you then, Lost Boy, thank you very much." He set the flower down and got up from his chair, kneeling before

Preston. "I don't know what this is, but it's special," he said, opening his arms and hugging Preston. He could feel the roughness of the cowboy's shirt, and he smelled something on him, like woods and a fire burning inside a steel drum on a misty night.

"Thank you," Preston said to the cowboy, composing himself when he let go.

"And thank you for that," the Hawthorne-cowboy replied, pointing at the flower on the table. "I'll take good care of it."

"You're welcome," Preston retorted, wiping his eyes as he turned around. Peter was standing behind him, a few feet away. He was sure the cowboys had been watching him closely the whole time, waiting for a chance to talk to him. He was the leader and everyone naturally wanted to talk to Peter. Preston turned around and walked out of the Saloon. He looked at Peter as he left and the boy followed, walking back through the swinging double doors, the sound of lively music behind them starting up once more.

"It's okay," Peter said as Preston marched further from the saloon. "It's okay. I mean I knew he wouldn't remember it, but I didn't think it would upset you this much. Most of the Lost Boys never care what's remembered and what's not. I mean, they remember, but then again part of them doesn't, but you remember everything."

"Does that make me strange?" Preston asked.

"Not any stranger than anyone else Here," Peter replied. "You can be whatever you want Here, that's the rule. That's the only rule."

"Seems like a silly rule if you ask me."

"Rules are meant to be silly," Peter replied, flying a few feet above ground and hovering as Preston walked on. When Preston didn't follow him into the air, and usually when Peter started to fly the Lost Boys flew with him, Peter touched down and walked. "Are you okay?"

"I'm fine," Preston replied. "I just. . .where did you get that flower?"

"I already said I can't say," Peter replied. "I think it would be best if you didn't ask questions. I did something I'm not supposed to do. I've done it before and I said I'd never do it again, but there I was and it's best if I don't talk about it."

"How did you get there?" Preston asked. "Why didn't you tell me? Why couldn't you take me?"

"I took Tink, the fairies are the only ones who know how to get there and it's only Tinkerbelle, she's my fairy even if she's very old, she loves me very much, and she's the only one who loves me enough to break that rule. I got there because she helped me, I needed her fairy dust and she knows the way back."

"Why didn't you take me? If you were breaking the rules anyway, why didn't you take me?" Preston accused the leader.

"You can't go back," Peter replied. "It wouldn't work. I could try to take you, but you'd just end up back Here. I'm a Betwixt and Between, I can go back because I'm not from the Before, but you don't belong there anymore." They walked in silence for a while as Preston processed this before Peter went on. "Look, I'm sorry if it bothers you, but Eva is safe. I made sure of it, that's all I can say. I can feel it now. She's okay," Peter announced and Preston nodded at him. Somehow he'd known all along that Peter would make it all right. They'd gone to all the trouble of visiting the pirates, of talking to Captain Hook, just so he could find out, just so he could go and save her and Peter had done it. Peter had done it, just like he said.

"Thank you," Preston whispered.

"You're welcome," Peter replied. "And one more thing. I never tell the Lost Boys this, but you seem to be really close to Starky and so I'll break one more rule."

"What?"

"Tonight you should make sure to say good bye," Peter informed Preston.

"Why?" Preston asked. "He's been Here forever."

"Because he's been Here forever. He can't stay anymore. I've made a decision. Since you've come I've begun to see that maybe I should not so blindly listen to the Island. I have to make my own decisions, the Island entrusts me to take care of the Lost Boys so it can trust me to know what's best. I can't let Starky become like Boxwood. Boxwood's family, wherever they were, they never let him go until long after they were gone, and he rotted and rotted on the Island because of that and finally I decided that it was time to let him be at peace. I was worried something would happen, but do you know what happened when I took him? Boxwood woke up, he became the Lost Boy I met, he was a regular kid again and he went to the After happy. So I can't let Starky start rotting and he will soon–you saw him that day– the Lost Boys didn't know what was happening, but you did and so did I. He's been Here too long and I have to let him go. It's for Starky, it's for his own good." Peter looked to Preston pleadingly and Preston threw his arms around his leader's neck, he held him, feeling the beating of his heart—he had a heart, and the air inside his lung—he had lungs. He was the little boy who would never grow up and yet he was wiser, smarter, stronger than all of them. It seemed somehow wrong, an aberration, a hideous exception that he should have to be this way.

"Thank you, Peter," Preston said letting him go as he pointed back toward the woods. "I'm going to find Starky."

"Have fun," he called, that impish smile returning as he took off above the Island.

Preston kept walking through the woods, the sound of the Neverbird cawing in the distance as he wandered through swimming patches of light, over piles of sticks and by the rock statues some of the boys had made. The air started to feel cooler as he moved through the forest until finally he could hear the sound of boys crying out once again, running around and playing with toys. When the light shone through the trees and Preston could see the tree house outside the forest, he could tell they were having some sort of party. A giant fire burned inside a steel drum at the front of the tree, and a great number of boys, more boys than there had ever been together at one time, were running around it, some of them slinging guns or arrows, a few playing instruments, while others ate candy or drank sodas.

It took Preston a while to find Starky. He spotted his friend near the side of the tree playing jacks with five or six other boys and was overcome by an incredible need to talk to him. "And that's seven, my friend, that's seven," Starky announced getting up as the other boys handed him a wad of playing cards, which had been the official currency in Neverland since gambling games were brought to it many, many years ago. Starky took his cards and started to count them, his head down as he turned and nearly smacked into Preston. "I didn't see you there. Next time I play jacks I'll try and find you."

"So you can take my cards?" Preston teased, trying not to let on what he knew.

"As much as I can get," Starky kidded as they walked through the boys and their party. "So how're you doing? Did you run off with Peter?"

"Yep," Preston replied as they waded through a group crowded around the merry-go-round.

"You're always running around with Peter."

"Not always, he ran away from me just like he ran away from everyone."

"I know, it's just funny, you know, Peter goes away and we all miss him."

"You never thought he might not come back?" Preston asked and Starky looked at him oddly as they headed toward a clearing.

"Why would he not come back? He's Peter, no one can get him. He can't die. Why wouldn't he come back?"

"I don't know. It's just, have you ever thought about where the Lost Boys go when they leave?"

"They go over there," Starky replied indicating nowhere in particular. "They go where they need to go."

"Did you ever think about what it will be like?"

"No," Starky replied. "Peter said it would be better. It's very good Here, I like it Here, but if Peter thinks it's better There then it must be."

Preston looked at Starky. He was a little kid. He had thick, straight brown hair slicked back with gel or grease; he wore tattered pants and a dirty blazer. He was one of those boys with bright eyes and a rascally smile, he wanted to play with cars and toy planes and horseshoes and asked questions all the time. He was a little boy and Preston knew he'd been this way for decades. He tried to picture what Starky might have looked like at twenty or thirty, forty or fifty. He wondered what kind of man he would have been, but he saw nothing, just this little boy, forever and ever this little boy. Preston threw his arms around his friend, glad that Starky had never grown up, glad his friend had not become what Hook called a grownup, someone who cheated on his wife and drank every night. He was glad Starky had not become that scientist he'd seen a brief glimpse of; the white lab coat would not become him. Starky let him hug him for a second, draping an arm around Preston as he said, "There, there, what's wrong?"

"Good bye Starky," Preston said seriously.

"Are you going somewhere?" Starky asked, confused. "I can come with you."

"No, that's okay," Preston replied. "I'm not going anywhere. But maybe if we just walked in the woods a little more."

"Okay," Starky replied, keeping in step with Preston as they moved through the Neverforest. He considered telling Starky outright what was about to happen, but he knew that was Peter's job.

"I'll miss you is all, you know," Preston said and Starky nodded, deciding, it appeared, to simply go with whatever Preston said even if he didn't understand it. They walked further into the woods, toward the Indian camp. They could hear the Indians howling, which meant they were about to start fighting. Starky raced through the forest, toward the light that would part at the Indian's tepees. Preston watched him, hoping his friend got in one last war.

LONDON, ENGLAND 1960

On a certain day of the week of a certain year in a certain part of a certain city, which happened to be called London, a funeral was held. It wasn't particularly crowded as far as funerals went, but many people had shown up, many people with handkerchiefs to their faces, wearing black coats and carrying umbrellas, though it had yet to rain. On that certain day at that certain funeral, the people attending could have seen someone magical, someone quite important if only they had been paying attention. A little boy was in attendance, one who seemed not to have come with anyone. He wasn't dressed for a funeral at all, not with his ragged green pants and torn shirt, and that in and of itself should have been enough to make him stand out, but the boy did not stand out. Mrs. Higgins, whose son Edward, who went by Crispy in the place the little boy came from, could have heard some interesting stories about her son, who would have been twenty-four this year if he had not died of cancer when he was seven.

Peter stood at the back of a group of people gathered around a black box. He'd considered pushing his way to the front, he'd never really seen a casket before, he barely knew what one was, only that it was a box they put you in that you never got out of. He hadn't liked that idea at all, but Peter knew, because of the nature of who and what he was, that there was Something Else, even for people who died when they were very old. Those who did not go to him at all, those who lived their lives into adulthood and died naturally, there was still Something Else and so the box had not upset him that much because he knew in the grand scheme of things that nothing was in it. Whoever was inside it had already gone Somewhere Else.

They were at a large park with acres of flowing green space interrupted every few feet or so by a stone sticking out of the ground. In a few places there were even large box-like structures that looked like little houses. Hey, that's an idea, Peter thought, I'll get the Lost Boys little houses instead of rooms in the tree, maybe I'll build them on the branches. But even as he had that thought, he knew there was something more he was supposed to be watching. The black box with gold trim that stood hanging from two very sturdy ropes above a hole in the ground looked as if it might start swaying as the wind picked up and a few men and a couple of women gasped and held their hats to the tops of their heads.

"And did you hear," one old woman with gray hair piled on top of her head said to another old woman with white hair piled up in just the same way. "This is the second funeral in just as many weeks."

"It's so sad, so sad," the other old lady replied. "Both of them connected to that play. They say that Mr. Barrie wrote the play for him, that Peter Llewellyn Davies, but that he got many of the stories from Winifred, who claimed after she awoke from that ghastly coma, the one that very nearly killed her mother with worry, that she'd gone to a magical island for children. And of course Mr. Barrie had so much of the story already, he had such a vivid imagination, but then she told him her stories and they all blended together and became Peter Pan."

Peter's ears perked up at the sound of his name. He knew about the play. He'd even been to see Wendy once after she'd returned from a special showing of it. He'd stood outside the window and listened to Wendy talk to a little girl and a grown woman about it. She'd said the production had been marvelous and that this Peter, played by a woman who only resembled a boy, had been the most Peter Pan-like she'd ever seen. And that name, that Peter Pan, in London at least, had ceased to be only his name. Here it belonged to so many other people that he'd learned, when he chanced to hear it in a crowd, to simply ignore it, though sometimes it was very hard, since it was in fact his name and had been for nearly 60 years (but he was always forgetting the time).

He'd gone to that play once, gone to see it with Wendy, though she'd had no idea he was there with her. She'd sat in the front with a very dapper looking gray-haired gentleman and Peter had taken an empty seat in the back. It had been a very good play. It took some liberties of course, and the Peter character wasn't quite him, that Peter had been a bit too self-centered, a bit too boastful at times and Peter had never thought of himself as cocky. And of course Wendy hadn't known he'd come. After that first time, when he'd seen how old she'd gotten, not just in her face, but in her voice, in the way she stood and the words she used, he hadn't let Wendy know he was there when he watched her. Still, he'd been there when Jane got married, he'd been there for Sally's baby shower, he was there when Wendy's husband was buried in a plot nearly identical to this one. In all the events of her life, as Wendy grew up, there Peter had been, standing off to the side, away from everyone, a little blond boy dressed nearly in rags, who never aged, who never changed, to whom no one spoke and who spoke to no one.

And London had grown up right along with Wendy. It wasn't the same place he'd first come to, it was getting on in years, its buildings, its streets, all of them crumbling and the ones laid in their places weren't any grander. It was as if nothing, not something as small as a girl or as large as a city could escape the effects of time. Everything, it appeared, grew up.

"And did you hear what he did, that Peter Llewellyn Davies," the gray haired woman went on. "He jumped right out in front of a train is what he did. They said he was stone drunk and really throwing himself in front of a train like that." The old woman shook her head sadly.

"But it isn't any shock after what he went through. Losing his parents so young, and his wife's illness, having that play named after him. And then the war and having to fight in it and everything...and it really isn't any wonder that Peter Pan jumped out in front of a train to end it all. The world can be so hard on some."

"I know, such a shame, such a shame," the white haired woman concurred. "And then Winifred only a week later, a stroke of all things. And this time they couldn't bring her back from it."

"It's for the best, have you ever seen a person who has had a bad stroke? They sit around drooling, staring into space. This is better."

"It's just so sad, so sad that both of them..." The other woman went off. But Peter knew it, though he couldn't read or tell time or understand something called Logic, he knew that it was all a part of growing up to be introspective sometimes.

"But she had such a lovely life and it's good that she lived so long. And buying her parents' house. And John being elected to Parliament and Michael marrying that textile heiress and running off to France."

"Yes, but two of her daughters left for America, which nearly broke her heart. And then her husband Stephen being hit by a car. It was so hard for her, burying her husband."

"Yes, but she had a happy life, telling those stories to the children at the Great Ormond Street Children's Hospital and having all those glorious parties."

"True, true," the white haired woman agreed. "It's all you can say about a person in the end, that they had a lovely life. And she grew up into such a fine woman, her mother would've been proud."

The gray haired woman shook her head and Peter noted the lines on her face. He tried to remember Wendy. He'd seen her many times since last they spoke, he tried to recall if the lines littered her face, if they fell from her mouth and eyes like the creases of a waterfall. And he couldn't quite place what they were talking about. A daughter moving to America, a husband hit by a car, it all seemed like too much and why couldn't a husband, when he was hit by a car, simply stand up, dust off his pants and be on his way? Was that a sign of growing up as well?

An old man dressed all in black, except for a white collar, stood apart from the crowd gathered around the black box. He cleared his throat and everyone who'd been milling around, making low, polite conversation was lulled into a quiet hush. It was gray there on the grass, with the mass of headstones in the background, and Peter thought for a second that he could feel raindrops. It rained very often in London.

"We are gathered here today to mourn the loss of a very dear friend of ours," the old man began. "To mourn the loss of a Mrs. Winifred Moira Angela Thomas, or Wendy, as some people playfully called her."

Peter watched the crowd. The two old ladies were standing stoically nearby, their heads down, white handkerchiefs in their hands, though they had yet to use them. A few others, a couple of younger girls and a man were crying very hard, one of the girls even had to sit down in a folding chair she was so upset. Peter watched it and then, turning around, he walked away.

Everyone gathered around the black box was too busy listening to the old man's sermon to notice the little boy dressed nearly in rags walking in the opposite direction. He had a burlap bag around one shoulder and, if anyone had taken the time to look extra closely, they would have seen an incredible light shining from it. But they were all too busy, too busy crying and remembering and being sad.

But Peter had already decided that Wendy wasn't there, they were crying not at a little girl or a grown woman, but at a box. There was something about the whole of Wendy, the essentialness of her that had been left in Neverland, but not only there—parts of her had returned to London, but had been shed as she grew older. As she forgot who she really was and became instead a part of this world where husbands were hit by cars and daughters moved to America and broke their mother's hearts. The Wendy he'd known had never been through that, the Wendy he'd known had been pure and innocent, uncorrupted by the world (both the pain and joy of it). She had been like a white rose growing slowly and slowly red. And she was gone, she'd been gone for many years, many decades and Peter swore that he would never do this again. He'd had his Wendy and there was no need for any more lessons, no need for any more experiments or marriage ceremonies or Thimbles, as the play called them. He was never coming back. He didn't like it here, the air was too sluggish, it smelled like seaweed and staleness. There was no reason for it, no reason for this kind of travel, not unless he someday found someone he loved as much as he loved Wendy.

cLaiRe

It was seven o'clock on Cape Cod; about the time cars started rumbling over the gravely road by the beach as the neighbors got ready to go out to dinner at fish places by-the-sea and Italian restaurants that sported red pepper flake holders and checkered tablecloths. Claire and Matthew, along with the Lists, had rented a house on the Cape for the week, but the neighbors were close, and Claire had been hearing them coming and going for the past couple of days. It was only seven and the sun wouldn't be setting for another half hour or so, but she could see it fading on the horizon, glittering above the water, the ocean a kind of hazel, a murky light blue just like Preston's eyes. She could sense the ebb and flow of the tide as she closed her eyes and visualized her toes in the wet sand a few hours before, or the time she'd taken Preston when he was just a baby, maybe two years old, and they'd played run-away-from-the-ocean. When he was four, remembering that game, he'd told Claire "If I'm not careful the ocean will eat me." He'd screamed that piercing childish cry and run off, down the beach to meet his father, who'd been flying a Winnie-the-Pooh kite poorly; the thing kept lop-siding and threatening to careen into a neighboring picnic area, though it never touched the ground.

A twig snapped under the second floor balcony and Claire could hear Cara and Jim whispering below her. The balcony was off of Claire and Matthew's bedroom, but she was sure her friends had forgotten that. It didn't matter; the whispering was so soft Claire could barely hear it, though she could sense the texture of the conversation as the words "Erma," "trial" and "countersuit" wafted through the air.

It had only taken a week after that little boy had come, the little boy no one in the neighborhood had ever heard of, to get Erma Glands arrested. Claire had gone to the police that day with the bread Erma had made in a plastic baggie. She'd never been a fan of those CSI shows, but she'd hoped that Eva's and her own fingerprints wouldn't taint the specimen. At first the police had been reluctant to see her. They knew her case, she was a mother who'd just lost her son, and so of course they humored her; but as a mother who'd just lost her son she had very little credibility coming in there announcing that she knew who had done it. Still she'd managed to get Detective Toby, one of the men who'd first come to her that night (that night, that night; and Claire would spend the rest of her life dreading, hating, trying to forget that night), consented to have the bread sent to the lab.

Someone had called the next day to say that while the tests were inconclusive, they were inconclusive in a very strange way, so strange a way that they were wondering if they might get another sample. Claire called Eva's mother and they arranged to send over another bit of Erma's baking. By then Erma had stopped baking so often, but one day Mrs. Murphy showed up at Claire's door with a sample of a chocolate chip cookie.

"It was hard to convince her that Eva couldn't have them yet. I said something about a dentist appointment. I don't want her sensing something is up and running out of town," Mrs. Murphy had said, leaving the baggie for Claire to bring to the police. At first it had taken a bit of convincing to get Mrs. Murphy to keep Erma Glands on, but since the police were now suspicious of the woman they had agreed to watch the house whenever Erma was there, and Mrs. Murphy had hired a second housekeeper, a woman to have around when Erma was at the house. And it went without saying that she never left her daughter alone with Erma.

Still it had taken the second batch of cookies to confirm that they were poisoned. The test had come back positive—large amounts of cyanide and Wisteria, a concentrated dose of the seeds and pods of a poisonous plant, had been found along with trace amounts of windshield wiper fluid and anti-freeze. Once that information was in, the police got a warrant to raid Erma Glands' small apartment in nearby Lawrence, and there they'd found diary entries describing her detailed plan, which was to poison all three children for having snubbed another child once on the playground. That was all they'd done and for that Erma Glands had decided the children should die, Claire couldn't get over that and she wasn't sure she'd ever be able to forgive it.

Apparently Erma Glands was incredibly unstable and after she'd accomplished this task she'd planned to kill herself. It turned out that Erma Glands, while never this homicidal before, had a history of mental illness and was in the process of asking the court to allow her to plead insanity to the charges. She'd said she'd taken the job at the Hawthorne house in order to get close to the children, making poor Gregory a pawn in her scheme. Yet when she'd started working for Gregory Hawthorne she'd changed her name to Mary Clark on her tax forms, which seemed to indicate that she knew what she was doing. She'd even said that when Preston had been poisoned she had been rushed, because she hadn't expected him to just show up at the Hawthorne house; but once she saw him there, she quickly injected the poison into the cookies she'd just finished baking, and then left for the day. And to carry around poison like that, with a syringe of all things, that took planning and cunning with a tinge of instability thrown in.

"And I think this trial. . . ." Claire could hear Cara say, the spray of the ocean covering most of her words. Claire closed her eyes, trying to drown out images of another trial, going to another prison, another courthouse. She knew she had a duty to go and she would go, at least a couple of times, if the prosecution needed her for anything she would be there, but she found both courthouses and prisons unpleasant, and after having gone to see Francine Gumm she never wanted to enter either again. She and Matthew, when they'd just arrived at the Cape the night before, had decided together to stay away from the trial, though knowing their friends, they were certain Cara and Jim would jump right into the throes of the case, which was their right.

Claire could still hear the shuffling of feet over the gravel under the balcony when a knock at the door sounded, and she turned to see Matthew in a white apron with a bright red lobster on it, a dishtowel in hand.

"Jim and I just finished dinner, you hungry?"

"I am," Claire replied, lifting herself out of the chair to take one last look at the ocean before turning to her husband. She kissed him lightly on the cheek, noting the scent of fresh dill and rosemary. "What's for dinner?"

"Fresh bass with a touch of rosemary and lime, new potatoes and asparagus," Matthew replied, one hand on her back as he led her out of their rented bedroom. It was blue and white, like their room at home, only there were photographs of the ocean and sitting on little wooden shelves were sculptures of kittens that looked as if they had been handmade, the painted calico smudged and their mouths too long and lopsided.

"You know I hate asparagus," Claire commented playfully.

"You hate all vegetables, speaking of which, you should have a balanced meal."

"Of course," Claire replied, remembering how she'd always made sure to make a vegetable for Preston, she had choked down beets and green beans, peas and cauliflower for her son's health, and she hadn't had a single green thing, nothing of any color that had come out of the ground until a couple of days ago when she and Matthew had made salmon, rice and broccoli for dinner, eating together in the dining room for the first time in months.

They walked down the hall, past the List's bedroom and by the small room on the right, the one Peyton and Preston would have shared for this vacation. The door was shut, there was no way to lock it, but Claire was sure if there were, it would have been bolted from the world. Still it sat there, a gaping hole in the house like the one Claire felt shaking in her limbs, throbbing through her head, gnawing its way inside her stomach every day—even after so long, still she felt it. The stairs creaked as Claire walked down them and she could hear the sounds of her friends in the kitchen. When Claire entered the room, Cara was standing next to the stove, a glass of white wine extended in her hand as if she were about to make a speech. "I just think if you're going to make fish," she said, noting Claire and Matthew's entrance, "then you should make it with lemon. Who ever thought of making fish with lime; what kind of men are you?"

"I saw it in a *Cook's Illustrated* recipe," Jim replied. "It looked good. Lime is the new black."

"Lime is in," Matthew added, chuckling as he grabbed a glass of wine from the table. "I've tasted it, it's very good, I promise."

"Well, as long as you promise," Cara playfully replied, smiling at Claire, who was standing at the other end of the kitchen watching her good friends, neighbors for the past ten years, discuss dinner and cooking magazines, while the men wore aprons and the tide rose, covering the sand behind them. Claire might have turned around and gone back to her room to rip open the last of her scrapbooks, the one she'd made the other day using the best of the best, the pictures that got to the heart of who her son had been. But she knew she had to stay, she knew she had to let herself laugh, to watch these friends until one day she didn't have to force herself.

"It's almost ready, the table's set," Matthew announced, walking into the dining room carrying a white casserole dish with two lobster claw potholders. "This is hot, let's go," Matthew said and Cara nodded, picking up the bowl of asparagus as Jim took the potatoes and Claire grabbed the bottle of wine.

The dining room looked out to the ocean; in fact the wall facing the water consisted of large French doors that opened out to sea. It was a beautiful design, and Claire and Matthew took the seats facing the water since Cara and Jim didn't seem to mind having their backs to the scenery. Watching the sun sink lower into the horizon, Claire placed her napkin in her lap and watched Matthew serve her portion of fish over a white china plate. "Is that enough?" he asked, meeting Claire's eyes and she smiled at him, nodding "yes."

Claire served herself and Matthew the potatoes before passing them on. She skipped the asparagus, though everyone else seemed to like it, and Matthew gave her a look that said "shame-shame," but she was on vacation.

"So now that you're the Murphy's saving grace, have they invited you over again?" Cara asked, reaching across the table to take more asparagus.

"Gloria asked me to tea next week. I still don't know if I'm going to go. I feel so strange in that house after what happened," Claire replied.

"I'd go. I think the both of us should try to stay close to Eva, I mean, in a way she's all we've got," Cara commented, looking down. Matthew grasped Claire's hand under the table, and she looked at him—really looked at him, at his blue eyes and the way his hair fell slightly into his face, the little wrinkles near his mouth. It was only last week, that she'd finally gone to sleep in her own bed. She'd been walking down the hall, toward Preston's room, when she'd turned around and headed back to her own. Matthew had met her a few minutes later and that night she did not hear him crying as they fell asleep separated by pillows and comforters instead of walls.

"I just think it's odd that the police never thought to check on Erma before," Jim commented. "I mean, I know she used a different name at Gregory's and yet another one at the picnic, but she worked at the school, that's the terrifying part, she worked at the school with a history of mental illness and she might have done more, she might have had it in for all the children, and how someone like that—" Jim stopped and swallowed hard, he took a drink and Cara grasped his knee.

"I don't know how much of the trial we want to attend," Matthew admitted. "I mean if they need us we'll go, but I don't know if watching it every day will help us."

"I know," Cara replied, shaking her head. "Nothing is going to bring them back."

"But they are going to be brought to justice, thanks to Claire," Jim stated, lifting his glass to her. The words were too heavy and none of them raised their glasses with him. It might have been something they toasted if the thought weren't so incredibly sad, if it weren't that they'd be toasting the finding of their little boys' killer. Claire saw that boy Peter again in her mind, his impish face, the dirt on his clothes. She'd mentioned him to Matthew and she'd asked about him offhandedly, but she hadn't told many people the whole story.

"I've decided to attend the trial," Cara stated. "I'll keep you posted if you like."

"Thank you," Claire replied, looking down at her food; it had been very good and she was almost finished. "I think I'll take some asparagus now," she announced, taking the bowl and serving herself a miniscule amount. "I mean it's good for me."

"That it is," Matthew replied, his smile tight as he looked at her.

Dinner wound down and everything was eaten. Cara opened another bottle of wine and once the conversation had waned and there was no more food left to offer, the men decided that they'd do the dishes. "The men have taken up the mantle of dinner tonight," Jim announced as he stood up, picking up Cara and then Claire's empty plates. "Tomorrow will be the women's responsibility."

"Here, here," Matthew called, taking the serving trays from the table as he followed Jim to the kitchen.

"We have good guys, don't we, Claire," Cara commented, looking across the near-empty table at the two men working away in the kitchen.

"We do," Claire replied. "And you know Cara, I really

appreciate. . .I mean, I know that this has been the worst time, but I mean, it's been helpful having you. . . ."

"You too," Cara said knowingly. "I mean, all of it, and I still have trouble sleeping at night, I still think he's asleep in his bed or in the middle of the day he's off playing with Preston and I hope, sometimes I just sit there and hope that the last two months have been a dream and I'll wake up and he'll be with us. It's crazy, I know, but this makes you crazy."

"I know," Claire replied, and reaching across the table she grasped her friend's hand. A brisk sea breeze filled with salt and fish smells, gulls squawking and the hint of blowing sand, whispered through the door and Claire gazed out. "I think I'm going to go outside for a little bit."

"I'll follow if you don't mind," Cara said, getting up as Claire made her way across the dining room and out the open French doors. Claire hadn't bothered to wear shoes in the house, and she didn't trouble herself with them by the water. The incoming tide was almost up to the house, stopping perhaps ten or fifteen feet away, and they could hear its murmur, the soft beating of the waves as it approached. In The Iliad, Homer had called it the "wine black sea," and Claire had never known what he'd meant until she saw the Atlantic at night. She could feel the sand grow wet from the incoming tide and moved back a couple of paces before sitting down on the sand. The lights were on at the wood-framed house, both the ones near the ground floor and the ones on Claire's balcony, but those lights were diminished by the sight of the full moon, that great white rock hovering in the sky above.

"It's funny, all the stars," Cara said, hugging her knees close to her stomach as they settled in the sand. "I remember when I learned that stars were basically suns, some were brighter than others, but they were all basically the same thing, and then I started to wonder if there could be other life out there, and I realized that there had to be. I mean, I know that isn't a particularly deep revelation, most people begin to put two and two together sometime in their lives, but it was still so fascinating."

"I know," Claire said, looking out at the ocean and then up at the stars. "Don't you ever wonder if they're out there?"

"Yes," Cara replied, not even blinking, as if Claire had asked a perfectly reasonable question. "Sometimes I think they must be somewhere else now, but somewhere, that I'll see them someday and it'll be magical."

"I know," Claire sighed, grasping Cara's hand. "I remember when Preston was little and we'd look up at the stars, he would ask me which star was Peter Pan's. Which star was the "second star to the right"? When my cousin John got his pilot's license Preston used to ask him if he'd fly him to Never-Neverland. He used to jump up and down and say 'second star to the right and straight on 'til morning, just go there, go there and you'll find it.'"

"That's so cute," Cara replied. "I remember when that happened, Peyton came home saying they were going to visit Tiger Lilly and the Indians."

"And at least they'll always have that. They'll always be our little boys. They won't ever have to grow up, get jobs, they won't ever lose that childish innocence, the world will always be a magical place to them."

"They'll always be our little boys," Cara repeated, looking up at the stars and then out at the ocean, that great, that deep and vast, that never-ending ocean. And it was just so big, no matter how far you went it was always somewhere, it rolled past Africa and China, reached down to Antarctica and around the Americas, it dipped into pockets of the earth by Egypt, Greece and Italy. It was all there, always, and Claire watched it, wondering where these water molecules had been. Part of her wanted to get up and walk into it at that very second, to strip off her clothes and feel the icy night water holding her up as the tide tried desperately to pull her into the sea.

Though she couldn't swing on the playground anymore, though she couldn't sit in her room and play with dolls as she had as a girl, she had raised Preston, at least until he was ten years old and so she'd been able to understand, to revel in the joy, the innocence of children. But it wasn't only that; there was something to being a grownup as well, even now, even with all this pain. A child, no matter how well behaved, never would have been able to sit still and appreciate, truly wonder at and appreciate, the stars and the ocean, its bigness, its invariable aliveness. She smelled the salt air and her time in Greece and Italy; her summer in Spain and her college semester in Ecuador came back to her. Her love for Matthew and Preston returned to the front of her mind, and she was glad she could be grateful for it all.

Movement rustled behind them and one of the French doors closed gently. Claire and Cara looked back to see Matthew standing there, the lights from the house shining down on his tall, lean frame as he stood with his hands on either side of his waist, watching. He smiled softly and Cara got up, tapping Claire gently on the shoulder before she tiptoed through the sand, back toward the house. Claire looked once at the ocean, closed her eyes and breathed deeply, and in a few seconds Matthew was sitting next to her.

"So how're you doing?" he asked, grasping his knees and looking out.

"I'm doing all right actually. How were the dishes?"

"Not bad at all, this place has a dishwasher. Jim's in there scrubbing the last of the pans."

"We have nice neighbors," Claire replied. "I'm glad they're here, I mean, I'm not glad this happened. . . ."

". . .But if we have to share this with someone. . ." Matthew finished for her. "I mean, I guess all our lives, we're never going to be the same."

"Not at all the same and I don't think. . .I mean, not a day will go by when I won't think about him, I mean, his class will go on to middle school, they'll graduate high school, there will be a day when he would have been eighteen, twenty-one, thirty-five with a wife and kids and those days will tear me apart." Claire swallowed hard, but the tears came. They might have been coming for the past hour, or since the detectives had first knocked on their door. "The what-ifs, Matthew, the what-might-have-beens, that's what really gets to me. . . ."

"I know," he replied, holding Claire close. He rocked her back and forth and she could feel his skin salty and sweaty under his Polo shirt, she could hear his heartbeat with the murmur of the ocean and she wondered which one was louder, which possessed more raw power—one drives the sea, but the other keeps an entire man alive—and which was better, which was more?

The French doors opened once again, although Claire could barely hear them against the sound of the waves. "Matthew?" Jim's voice came timidly from the back. "I'm sorry to interrupt but there's something wrong with the dishwasher, can you take a look?"

"Sure," Matthew replied as he lifted himself from the sand. "I'll be right back," he said to Claire, who smiled at her husband, nodding. Matthew stood up straight, brushing the sand from his pants as he walked back to the house.

Claire could hear the two men murmuring about plumbing and strange "whooshing" noises as the doors shut once more and she watched the black water. She could see it and feel it and it was as if she were alone, completely and utterly alone. It wasn't just that she was so very small compared with all this sky, this barren beach, this ocean; it was that all of it was so very big. And Cara was right, there were whole other worlds, worlds Claire couldn't even imagine and maybe Preston was there, or if not there then somewhere else, sometime before or after, and she'd always have those first ten years.

Somewhere in the wide breadth of the universe it had been decided, she would never be completely all right, this sadness would linger, it was a part of her, and as she realized this she began to accept it, to see the sadness for what it really was, a continuation of her life and the great wide world. "I love you Preston," Claire whispered as she looked out to sea. "Wherever, whatever you are, I'll always love you, little boy. I hope you're okay."

The French doors opened once more, Claire could sense the twisting of the handle as she turned around and saw the light from the house and Matthew standing there waiting for her. Claire looked out at the ocean once more. It reached back and forth, the heavy crashing of the waves, white crests cascading into that empty, that all reaching darkness. It was just so big, so magnificent, so beautiful, she could not look away. One more second, just one more look. . .and then Claire thought, what am I waiting for, for the waves to stop, for the ocean to exert less power? It was never going to end. The waves would not cease to fall one into another, the full-mooned tide ebbing and flowing out to that earth-covering sea. There was no end ever. The ocean would never cease to be this big, this dark, this powerful. She had to make the decision to turn her back and so she looked out once more, took a deep breath and walked away from the waves and back to Matthew.

PRESTON

Peter woke Preston up at the crack of dawn, whenever, whatever, dawn was—Peter had never been particularly good with time. It was still dark, the stars hung heavy in the sky and there was a moon so full, so white, it looked like it might fall to the ground. Preston wasn't sure what to do when he opened the door to the soft knocking and found the leader standing there, his hair a messy mop on his head, a thoughtful smile on his face. "Hi," Peter greeted him.

"Hi, is it morning yet?" Preston asked innocently still in his pajamas.

"Kind of, I guess, I don't know," Peter replied and with that he played a series of notes on the flute he carried around his neck. "I have to take you somewhere," he said simply, letting the flute fall against his chest.

"Really? Where? Is anyone else coming?"

"No," Peter replied. "But we have to go now, I have to take you."

"Can I get dressed?" Preston asked. The question was rhetorical, of course he could get dressed, even Here the boys didn't go out in their bedclothes. This time, however, Peter shook his head "No," and Preston felt a light, fluttery feeling in the back of his stomach that said he should listen to him.

"It's time to go, it won't matter, we'll be there soon."

"Okay," he replied, taking one last look at his room, at the TV and gaming system, the baseball bat and mitt, the blue walls, just like the room his mother had made for him. "Let's go," he said, shrugging as Peter lifted off, flying higher above the tree house before he blazed down through the branches. They passed Clover's room—he was fast asleep; and Dilweed's,—Dilweed hated to sleep and was up playing video games, his body leaning one way and then the other as he twisted his bulky 1990's controller. They passed Starky's old room. Peter told him they never got rid of rooms, the rooms in the tree just sort of disappeared on their own, as if they were alive and knew when they were empty, but since Starky had only been gone a couple of days the room hadn't left yet.

Peter did not stop flying altogether; he just sort of hovered, slowing down considerably when they reached Peyton's room. Preston looked in to find candy wrappers strewn around his friend's bed, his television still on. It looked like he'd fallen asleep playing a video game and the screen had frozen on a superhero's masked face. Clothes were strewn all over the room and Preston giggled to himself, remembering how Mrs. List used to complain that her son never picked up his things. Peter watched Preston as he peeked in on his friend, he had an approving look on his face, a sad, secret smile, as he lifted off once more and they kept flying.

They flew over Mermaid Lagoon. It was dark, but the moon was big, a giant rock in the forever horizon and so the Mermaids were out, soaking in the rays on the slick black rocks. They waved at Peter, but would not look at Preston. Peter waved back, whistling playfully at them as they kept going. They flew over the Indian Camp, which was down for the night, all the Indians sleeping in their stretched leather tepees painted in war colors.

Next they passed the cowboys, who were all up at this hour. Preston had heard of this, though he'd never seen it, the cowboys practicing by the light of the moon. They were always in the Saloon during the day, when they weren't exploring or fighting the Indians, and it was a known fact that cowboys liked to sleep; but just before the sun came up, it was said, when the moon was out and extra white, they all got up and practiced shooting their popguns and aiming their slingshots. There were about twenty of them scattered in a field, protected by trees. Some of them were sitting on stumps cleaning their guns; others aimed at each other, pretending to fire as a few fell to the ground as if they'd been hit.

The Hawthorne-cowboy stood in the back near a group of trees, talking with another cowboy. He had a gun in his hand that he wiped with a white rag as he looked up to watch the boys flying by. Peter waved and he waved back, and Preston watched the man, noting the single white bellflower tucked into the pocket of his flannel shirt. "Don't worry," Peter called as they passed the cowboy camp, "he'll be okay." Preston nodded, following Peter, who shot on ahead of him, up over the trees, skirting past Pirate Cove, though Preston could see the mast of that ship, the Jolly Roger, pointing toward Neverland.

"Where're we going?" Preston asked again as they flew further from things familiar. Preston thought he'd known all of Neverland. He'd explored it so many times—Peter had taken him out and so had Dilweed and Starky, and he'd been one of the only Lost Boys to ever enter Pirate Cove. Still, the trees grew higher and higher and the forest became unfamiliar. The leaves were different colors, like fall in the Before, only the colors were brighter, there were shining purples and deep reds, royal blues and emerald greens like gemstones. There was fruit on these trees, fruit that glistened like it was covered with glitter, sparkling in the waning rays of the moon and Preston could see the sun coming up, as it appeared just over the horizon and hovered there like it was waiting for something.

"This is where the sun comes from," Peter explained, hovering over the trees. "It sits there all night until it's time to get up, which should be soon."

"Where are we going?" Preston asked. "Where is this?"

"This is the Fairy Forest, this is where they come from. They like their privacy, the fairies, and only I know where they live," Peter replied.

"Aren't you worried I'll tell the other Lost Boys?" Preston asked, surprised and honored by Peter's trust in him.

"I'm not," the boy answered simply. "Now come on, we have to go," he went on, rising into the sky, higher and higher, as Preston struggled to keep up.

They flew past the Fairy Forest and toward the sun. It was getting brighter and brighter, almost like the fairies themselves, only the fairies did them the courtesy of blinking off and on, but this unblinking sun hurt his eyes and Preston nearly had to cover them as they kept flying. "Peter, where're we going?" he demanded as the boy flew ahead of him.

"We're almost there," Peter said, still flying, his body stretched toward the sun as they moved through the bright white sky. It felt as if there was nothing underneath them, not land or water, air or even space. After a while Peter stopped, hovering for a moment until they reached the edge of a cliff. "Here," Peter said and Preston touched down on the tan rocky surface.

"What's this?" Preston asked, noting that the cliff seemed to stretch for miles on one end, a tiny sliver of rock at the shore of the world, dropping off into that bright, near-blinding whiteness. "Where are we?"

"This is where you go," Peter started, sounding altogether very knowledgeable, "to the After." Preston looked at him and Peter rested a hand on his shoulder. "But you know that, they all end up knowing."

"Does this mean my Mom and Dad are okay? That they've gotten over me?"

"You know they can't ever get over you completely, you know in some sense they'll never be okay. What this means is that they're on their way to healing, they've decided to try to move forward, to live their lives. It's such a heart-breaking thing, losing a child, and the mothers and fathers need Neverland more than the little boys who come Here. And they love you Preston, you know that. They love you and I don't know what's there, in the After, but Love is there, it moves in and out of the universe, it fluctuates, it changes, but it is always Love and it is always there and it's the only thing you get to keep, it's all you take with you."

Preston looked past the cliff. It wasn't that there was nothing beyond it, there were a great many things, he just couldn't see them, he only had to feel them. It was white, so blinding white, a wall of light that enveloped the entire everything, and Preston wondered why he hadn't seen it all before. "Because you weren't ready to see it, Preston, just like Peyton can't see it yet, and Dilweed and Clover, but they will soon. Starky saw it," Peter explained as if he knew what Preston was thinking.

"I see," Preston replied.

"And you needn't worry about the After. It's good, everything about it is good and I would never take my little boys here if it weren't the most wonderful place, the most fantastic existence. I wouldn't let them go for anything but this. I love them all."

"I know Peter," Preston replied. And of course it was good, of course it was the most wonderful place there was, he knew that now. He also knew that it was not simply a place, or a person, a thing or an idea, it was something else and it was everything. Preston reached out, grasping Peter to him, he felt the little boy arms, the little boy skin and muscles clutching the back of his shirt, the little boy heart beating, but there was something else there, something that was just like this place mixing with something just like him because he was, Preston knew, a Betwixt and Between. "I love you too."

"Thank you, Preston, and it was very nice knowing you. It was very nice getting to see you and help you. It was quite a journey we went on together, quite a journey."

"And thank you for helping Eva," Preston added.

"I'm glad I did it," Peter replied. "Something tells me Eva is a very special girl."

"Something tells me that as well," Preston replied and he wondered how it was that now that he was moving toward it, this whiteness, this light, this nothing and everything all at once, that he suddenly knew so much. He understood it all and he could have explained it, except there weren't any words or need for words anymore. Preston walked off the cliff, he didn't slip, he didn't fly, he just kept walking toward the whiteness. He turned around after a second and looked at Peter, at his messy blond hair and dusty blue eyes, at his tattered clothes and dirty skin, the way he stood, that flute around his neck, the fact that he could not read or tell time and yet he knew so much, he knew everything and nothing and only someone so good, so innocent, so child-like could know that they are one and the same.

"So what do you think is out there?" Preston asked one more time, looking toward it.

"I don't know," Peter replied. "But I promise it will be an awfully great adventure."

acknowledgements

This book is for my children, Addison and Jacqueline. If it weren't for my son there wouldn't be a book. When he was two years old he discovered his shadow and started playing with it. After giving him a thorough explanation of what a shadow is I said, "I know a story about a boy who lost his shadow." I then proceeded to tell him the story of Peter Pan and as I told that story, the concept for this novel, in fact the entire story, appeared in my head. My children, both of them, inspire and encourage me every day.

A special thanks goes to my husband, Adam, who has always encouraged me. And to my parents, David and Gina Stilling. Part of the reason I have had the wherewithal to withstand the hardships of writing and ultimately publishing a novel is by watching their example of hard work. Part of that is also due to the fact that I come from the Midwest. To my brother and sister, Ian and Stephanie, my in-laws, Donald, Karen, Katie and Claudiu, whose graphic design talents have been so useful with the promotion of this book. To my grandmother-in-law, Ruth Savin Greenberg for her unbelievable edits not only to this book, but to so many other things I've written. To Kay and Jim Stilling, Joe Price and Kerri Price. To Hannah Frederick, who takes such good care of my children. To my publishers whose belief in me might just be business as usual to them, but to me, it changed my whole life. Thanks to my former professors, Fred Reynolds, Colette Brooks, Linsey Abrams and Felicia Bonaparte, the smartest, bravest, most wonderful woman I have ever known. I would also like to acknowledge all those who write, whether anyone sees your work or not. I admire you, keep writing, it will sustain you.